Praise for
ON FIRE'S WINGS
by Christie Golden

"Ms. Golden weaves a splendiferous tale of exotic magic
and the courage of the human heart. Her characters
stand out within a tapestry of emotions, where hope is
the loom upon which love and desire, fear and despair and
stubborn perseverance continue to weave. An elemental tale
with an amazing, and unforeseen, climax keeps
the pages turning seemingly by themselves. This is a
definite gem in the world of sci-fi fantasy and a must-read
for those who love to hope and hope to love."
—*The Best Reviews*

"*On Fire's Wings* is a sweeping story peopled by emotionally
complex characters—characters the reader is given time to
get to know, understand, and either love or despise. Yes, there's
a strong romantic subplot involved, but the story is about
Kevla's life—from her meager beginnings to the days in which
she realizes her own inner power and is faced with what that
power brings to her…and ultimately takes from her."
—*Revision 14*

"Truly a gifted author, Christie Golden pens a rare tale
overflowing with emotion. With carefully chosen words, she
draws her readers into the lives of Kevla, Jeshemi and the
Arukan clans, imprinting them on our hearts. *On Fire's Wings*
is a work of art, filled with pictures, sounds and colorful
characters, all combining to form an unforgettable adventure."
—*In the Library Reviews*

In Stone's Clasp

CHRISTIE GOLDEN

LUNA™

www.LUNA-Books.com

LUNA™

First edition September 2005

IN STONE'S CLASP

ISBN 0-373-80229-3

www.LUNA-Books.com

Printed in U.S.A.

This one's for the men—

May it serve to honor the Fisher Kings and wounded heroes
who have survived their own seemingly endless winters
and emerged, whole, into spring.

Cast of Characters

In Arukan

Jashemi-kha-Tahmu: Tahmu's son, Kevla's half-brother and the Flame Dancer's Lorekeeper, deceased

Kevla-sha-Tahmu, formerly Kevla Bai-Sha: the Flame Dancer

Dragon, the: Kevla's Companion animal

Meli-sha-Tahmu: Kevla's half sister

Sahlik: head servant of the Clan of the Four Waters, five-score

Tahmu-kha-Rakyn: Kevla's father, *khashim* of the Clan of the Four Waters

Yeshi Bai-Sha, formerly Yeshi-sha-Rusan: wife of Thamu, mother of Jashemi and Meli

In Lamal

Hanru: *Taaskali* guide

Ice Maiden, the: legendary coldhearted woman

Ivo: headman of Skalka Valley

Lukkari, Altan: Lamali bard, twin brother to stillborn Ilta

Lukkari, Ilta: stillborn twin to Altan

Lukkari, Ritva: Altan's mother

Lukkari, Veli: Altan's father

Ovaak, Larr: Jareth's boyhood friend

Paiva: wise-woman/healer

Ranin: friend to Olar Tulari

Relaanan, Kivi: wife to Orvo, mother to Taya and Vikka

Relaanan, Orvo: headman of Two Lakes, father to Taya and Vikka

Relaanan, Vikka: youngest daughter of Orvo and Kivi

Tulari, Gelsan: head woman of Arrun Woods

Tulari, Mylikki: daughter of Gelsan

Tulari, Olar: son of Gelsan

Vasalen, Annu: Jareth's daughter

Vasalen, Jareth: the Stone Dancer

Vasalen, Parvan: Jareth's son

Vasalen, Taya: Jareth's wife

Other Players

Advisors to the Emperor

Emperor, the: enemy of the Dancers, very powerful

Ki-lyn, the: magical creature imprisoned by the Emperor

Taaskali Range ⚏

Lamal

Two Lakes

Skalka Valley

⚏ Riversong

⚏ Arrun Woods

⚏ Galak-by-
the-Lake

Prologue

"We have failed," the Stone Dancer whispered.

She and her Lorekeeper, her soul, her beloved in this life and others, stood hand in hand on the shore and watched the Shadow come.

"We didn't even have a chance to fight!" Her voice was raw with pain and disbelief. She turned large brown eyes to him, as if he could somehow change what was about to unfold. "We didn't even...."

Her gaze drifted back to the obliteration that was slowly, inexorably approaching. The Lorekeeper folded her into his arms, equally unable to tear his gaze away from the pulsing gray Shadow as it closed in upon them, this island, this world.

Although she was the one with the ability to harness the

power of the earth, of stone and soil and growing things, he had been her guide, her protector, her comforter. He had been blessed with the knowledge of all that had gone before. Older than she by more than a few years, he had known her from birth. He had been the one to train her. Since he remembered what she was capable of in past existences, he comprehended the scope of her powers better than she herself did. And during the years of training, he had fallen in love despite himself with this steady, tender, graceful girl who would one day help save their world.

He tasted bitterness in his throat. *Save their world.* No, not save it. Watch helplessly, unable to do anything, as nothingness marched steadily onward, prepared to engulf and erase them as if they had never been. How futile now seemed the discussions they had had, late at night by the fire. They had worried about how she would leave the island, where they would go, how they would find the other Dancers. What a waste of finite time those conversations had been. He wanted those lost hours back. He would spend them making love to this girl, telling her how precious she was to him.

They both knew what had happened. Somewhere, far away from this tranquil, white sand beach, this calm place of sea and sun, a Dancer had died.

The Lorekeeper found himself wondering with a macabre sense of curiosity which one it had been. Sea? Wind? Soul? Flame? How he—or she—had died. How old that ill-fated Dancer had been.

In the sheltering circle of the Lorekeeper's arms, the Stone Dancer shivered, though the sun was yet warm on their bronze skins.

"It's so unfair!" she cried, and despite himself, the Lorekeeper smiled at her outburst. She had barely known eighteen summers, and while she was possessed of an ancient power, sometimes she seemed to him very young indeed. "I never met the others...we never stood together, as we were born to do...."

She began to sob, and he held her even tighter, feeling tears sting his own eyes as he pressed her head to his breast.

"Things aren't always fair," he whispered, realizing how inane the words sounded even as he uttered them. "There will be another chance."

She nodded and pulled away a little, wiping at her wet face. "Yes," she stammered. "So you have said. One final chance." She looked up at him and the love that washed though him almost tore him apart. He would do anything to spare her further pain; anything.

"We will be together again," she whispered.

He reached and pulled her to him, kissing her urgently. He had loved her in all their incarnations; sometimes chastely, as a friend or parent; sometimes passionately, as he did now. He would love her again, whatever shape or age or form they would take. He would always love her. In the face of uncertainty and approaching destruction, he knew that, at least, would never change.

She returned his kiss and for a long moment, they clung to one another. The Lorekeeper hoped that this was how the Shadow would take them—locked in an embrace, heedless of the obliteration about to descend.

But the Dancer turned again to look out over the sea. The Shadow was beginning to hide the sun, and the ocean was no longer tranquil and blue, but gray, as if a storm was approaching. Gray and still. Whatever it was that created the ceaseless motion of the waves, the Shadow had taken it.

They faced the ocean together, she pressed into him, he clasping her about the waist.

"What will it feel like?"

"I don't know," he admitted. "I cannot remember. The Lorekeepers recall much, but not that; not even what form the Shadow has taken each time."

"Will it hurt?" she said. "To be...erased...or will we feel nothing?"

He, who knew her better than any living person, realized she was terrified. And he could say nothing to reassure her. This woman he adored more than life itself was about to die, perhaps painfully, certainly in the grasp of fear.

He could not permit that.

He pressed a kiss on her shoulder. "It won't hurt," he said, knowing he spoke the truth, at least for her. "You won't feel a thing." For the last time in this life, he whispered with infinite tenderness, "I love you."

And then he placed his powerful hands on either side of her face and snapped her neck.

The Lorekeeper held the Dancer as she fell, taking her down to the sand with him. Cradling her limp body tenderly, he closed the slightly slanted brown eyes, placed her head against his shoulder, and waited for the Shadow to descend.

PART I:

Spring-Bringer

1

"Are you sure it was this tree?" Jareth Vasalen called to his friend.

"Yes, I'm positive," Larr Ovaak called up.

Jareth sighed, blowing a stray strand of yellow hair out of blue eyes. Thirteen-year-old muscles quivering with the effort, he kept climbing.

Larr had spotted the blessing cloth—or, at least, what had certainly *looked* like a blessing cloth; no one had ever actually seen such a thing—dancing in the wind. It had led the two boys a merry chase, away from chores and family and other mundane things, and now Larr was convinced that it had gotten lodged in the topmost branches of this ancient oak tree.

"Think about it, Jareth!" Larr had exclaimed. "I'll let you share it, since we both saw it. Everyone'll be jealous!"

But of course, it was Larr who would keep the cloth, and Jareth who was expected to make the tricky climb on branches bare and slick with ice. Jareth didn't really mind; he loved this old oak. Often he would sit for hours, cradled in its large branches, looking out over the farmland and watching it turn from green to gold to brown and finally, as now, swathed in winter's cold blanket of white. He sometimes felt as if this ancient forest was more his home than the house he shared with his elderly parents, both of whom seemed exasperated by his frequent need to climb to the topmost limbs and look out over the world.

But though he had climbed the tree more times than he could count, Jareth had never ventured quite this high before. Up here, the branches were thinner, and seemed reluctant to bear his weight. Once he slipped, and his breath caught in his throat as he grabbed on to another limb. After a moment he regained his footing and continued to climb. If the prize was what they thought it was, it would be well worth it.

The people of Lamal believed the blessing cloths were woven by the mysterious, seldom-glimpsed people called the *taaskali*. Dark of skin, hair and eye—or so the songs said—the *taaskali* had unusual skills, even perhaps magic, and were believed to have a special connection to the gods who lived on top of the mountains. The *taaskali* were nomads, their entire reason for being to follow and protect the herds of the equally mysterious and seldom-glimpsed animals called *selvas*, whose milk bestowed health and long life.

The songs weren't exactly clear on what the *selvas* looked

like. Jareth imagined them as white deer with golden horns and hooves. Cloaks woven from their thick white wool were believed to turn arrows. All *taaskali* clothing was made from *selva* wool, including, and especially, the blessing cloths. Jareth remembered the *huskaa* of Two Lakes telling the tale beside the fire when he visited not so long ago.

"And each season," he had said to his rapt audience, "the *selva* settle in their grazing fields. That's when *taaskali* take that season's magic and weave it into the cloths. They sing and play as the fabric is woven, infusing it with their hopes, and dreams, and blessings for the *selva*, themselves, and indeed all the people of Lamal. Then they release them, and the blessings fly all over the land."

Jareth was more than half-certain that the cloth tangled in the tree was no more magical than the fabric that comprised his own clothing, but he was almost there now, and he was not about to descend without it.

"Can you see it?"

Jareth turned his head carefully, making sure he had a good grip on the branches. "No, I don't think—wait."

It looked just like any other scrap of cloth, but then his hand closed on it and he gasped. Slim, strong fingers, rough from working in the fields and forest since childhood, had never before touched something this soft. It was...he couldn't think of any words to describe it.

Gently he untangled it with one hand. It came loose easily, and now he saw that it was more than simply white—it seemed to have the soft glow of the moon about it. Slowly, his heart racing, Jareth brought it to his face and inhaled its scent deeply.

Summer. This one had been woven in summer. He

smelled the fragrance of soft breezes, flowers, good clean earth, all manner of fresh and growing things. It was un-believable—this overwhelming scent of summer in the middle of winter.

They were real. The blessing cloths were *real*. That meant that the *selva* were real, and the *taaskali,* and—

"Did you find it?"

Jareth started from his reverie. He stared at the cloth. He couldn't possibly bring this down and give it to Larr, who would shove it in his pouch along with his knife, interesting bits of bone and dried meats and whatever else his friend felt like carrying. He couldn't have this brought out and showed around, an object to elevate himself and Larr in the eyes of their friends. This cloth was more important than that. It had a task—to bring blessings everywhere across Lamal. It was never made to be crumpled into a boy's pouch like a skipping stone.

Jareth made his decision. He shifted his grip slightly for better purchase. When a breeze stirred his long blond hair, Jareth threw the piece of cloth as far up as he could. The zephyr gladly took it, and Jareth could have sworn he heard the cloth...singing. He watched as it danced away and van-ished from sight.

"I'm coming down," he called to his friend, not answering the question. Jareth was not looking forward to the inevitable confrontation but was secure in the knowledge that he had made the right decision. The thought of that beautiful bless-ing cloth crumpled and dirty made him feel slightly sick.

He had made it to the last branch and was about to jump down to the ground when he heard a loud *crack.* The limb broke beneath him and Jareth landed hard.

Larr helped him to his feet, laughing as Jareth gasped for air like a fish out of water. "You'll be all right," Larr chuckled, slapping his friend on the back. "But so much for all your bragging about climbing trees. So, where is it?"

Jareth got to his feet, wincing a little. "I let it go."

"*What?*"

"That's what you're supposed to do," Jareth said firmly.

"You didn't even *show* it to me?"

Jareth hesitated, then said, "You said you wanted to keep it. I took you at your word. And it...Larr, it just wasn't meant for keeping. I can't explain it any better than that. I had to let it go."

While Larr fumed silently, Jareth turned to look at the betraying limb. It was a bit taller than he, slightly thinner than his arm. A thought occurred to him as he picked it up.

"I could make a staff out of this," he told Larr.

Larr frowned. "I want a staff too," he said. Jareth looked at him searchingly. Larr had already begun to forget about the blessing cloth and all that it meant. Now he wanted a staff. Jareth smiled.

"Then let's go find you one," he said.

When Jareth finally returned home, the shadows were lengthening. He winced as he remembered all the chores he was supposed to do. Opening the door of his parents' small house, he stepped inside. His father, recovering from the second illness he'd had this winter, lay on a pallet beside the fire. Jareth knelt beside him.

"I'm sorry," he said, reaching to hold his father's hand. "I was playing with Larr, and the day ran away from us. I'll work twice as hard tomorrow, I promise."

His father looked up at him with red-rimmed eyes and squeezed Jareth's hand. "It's all right, son," he said, and then began to cough. Jareth cast a worried glance at the smoky fire. He couldn't help but think the smoke was aggravating his father's condition, but there was nothing anyone could do. Fire was life here in the winter, and the smoke would have to find its way out as best it could.

His mother called. He hurried to where she was preparing the evening meal of fish and root vegetables.

"With your father so ill, we rely on you more than ever, Jareth," she said quietly.

"I know," he said. "I'm sorry. It won't happen again."

She turned from cutting the vegetables to regard him with pale blue eyes. He noticed for the first time that her once-golden hair was now almost silver.

"Winter is hard," she said. "We can't have you running off when there's so much to be done. You were supposed to bring more wood. Now we barely have enough to get through the night, and your father needs the warmth."

"I'll do it right now." He turned, determined to do something, anything, to remove the disappointed look on his mother's face.

"Jareth, is something the matter?"

He froze. Had he—

"No. Nothing's wrong. Light's fading, I'd best get out there." He almost ran out of the house before his mother could ask any more questions.

Jareth brought piles of wood from the village's small central hut, carrying more in a single load than he had ever before. He was warm even as a light snow began to fall, but he threw himself into the task. Maybe if he exhausted himself, he would not have the dreams tonight.

The taaskal *was the most beautiful woman he had ever seen. Tall, voluptuous, lithe, the scrap of fabric that served her for clothing revealed more than it concealed. Her skin was brown as bark, her hair black as the night sky, and her eyes warm and rich as loam. Were they all this beautiful? They must be, these weavers of the blessing cloths. If so, he wondered why more Lamali did not bring home* taaskali *wives and husbands. She smiled at him and turned away, walking slowly across the snow, seemingly unaffected by the cold.*

Before his eyes, she shifted her shape and became a god. Even more lithe than she was in her human form, the great blue tiger strode boldly across the snow. Jareth felt tears sting his eyes as he saw the snow melt beneath each padded footfall. And when the god-tiger raised her paw, Jareth could see that just as the legends said, flowers bloomed.

"Spring-Bringer!"

The voices were loud and happy as the people of his village emerged from their houses and began to follow the god as she brought the welcome season. Jareth fell in with them, laughing and dancing as they all followed the great blue tiger. He heard other voices, too, and knew that they issued from no human throat. The thought ought to have frightened him, but it only comforted him. Soft hands slipped into his, easing him to the muddy, snowy earth that felt warm and welcoming. He was suddenly unclothed. Breasts trailed across his chest, lips closed on his mouth, hands caressed him between his legs and he surrendered to the pleasure.

Hands were on his face now, strong hands belonging to

someone who was standing behind him. Jareth didn't know who it was, but he felt safe even as great sorrow washed over him. He stared out over a vast expanse of water, felt the hands move on his jaw, and there was an explosion of light—

Jareth bolted upright, his sleeping cloths wet with sweat, his groin covered in sticky fluid. His throat was raw and he knew he had been screaming, and when hands closed around his arms he struggled.

"Jareth, wake up!" His mother's voice penetrated the haze of fear and confusion and his heart began to slow.

His mother held him, much as she had when he was a child, but her arms no longer went around a body that was growing stronger and larger with each day. Still, Jareth surrendered to the embrace and slowly calm descended on him.

"Tomorrow," his mother murmured in his ear, "you will go see Paiva."

After completing his chores, Jareth trudged through the snow down to the lake and the stonesteaming hut. The hut was the heart of every village, and Skalka Valley was no different. It looked like a small version of traditional houses, made of wood with a bark and sod roof. But every hole and crack was tightly sealed—there were no windows—and once inside, it was understood that one was in a different space.

Here babies were born, and the dead prepared for burial. Here wheat was dried, malt was fermented, meats were smoked. Here deep ritual was conducted, and here was where the people of the valley gathered to sit and let the heat and steam penetrate to their bones for restful, healing sleep.

Jareth knew the etiquette for ritual preparation. He

stepped into the little room attached to the stonesteaming hut and stripped, shivering. He reached for a scrap of cloth from the pile that sat on the bench and wrapped it around his loins. It was all he would be permitted to wear; all the wise-woman would be wearing as well. Ritual was the only time men and women stonesteamed together.

He opened the little door. Steam, smoke, and the sweet scent of burning herbs greeted him when he stepped inside, closing the door behind him.

"Jareth Vasalen." Paiva's voice always surprised him. It was musical and strong, better suited to a much younger woman "Come forward. Sit on the bench with me."

His eyes, adapting to the darkness, could make out the glowing stones, heated slowly for hours until they were the right temperature. The faint light illuminated Paiva's slender form, upright and strong despite her years. Her unbound gray hair and slightly sagging breasts swayed as she reached and poured a ladleful of water onto the stones. More steam swirled and Jareth watched it raptly. This was the *hamantu,* the spirit of the stonesteaming. Jareth began to feel moisture on his skin as he obeyed the old woman's command.

Paiva threw more herbs on the hot stones. Jareth breathed deeply of the pungent, sweet aroma. He was starting to feel both relaxed and a little dizzy.

"Your parents say you are having strange dreams," she said. "Tell them to me."

Jareth swallowed. Then, slowly, he began to speak. She listened attentively, then laughed.

"These do not worry me at all. It is natural and healthy for a young man your age to begin to dream of mating. And to have...appropriate physical reactions. Have no fears about these, Jareth. But I find it hard to believe your parents would be concerned about these dreams. They are not unfamiliar with such things. Is there more you wish to tell me?"

In a low voice, he spoke of the other parts of his recurring dream: of the *taaskali* woman, of the gods bringing spring, of the stranger sitting behind him whom he trusted but whom at the end, he always feared.

"And I dream that everything around me—even the rocks, even the grass—has a *voice*," he continued, trying to put the images and sounds and sensations into something as confining as words. "Sometimes, I think the trees are trying to talk to me."

Sweat gathered on his skin, trickled down in slow rivulets. Here in the smoky darkness, the only light provided by the glowing stones, his thoughts didn't seem quite so foolish. "And when I walk with bare feet in summer...it's almost as if I'm walking on something that's—that's *alive*," he finished in a whisper.

"There is something else you haven't told me," Paiva said. Jareth swallowed. Did the woman see into his very thoughts?

"Yesterday—yesterday I found a blessing cloth."

Paiva's eyes widened. "Are you sure?"

He nodded. "There was no mistaking it. It smelled like summer, and it glowed, just like the stories said."

"What did you do with it?"

"I let it go. Larr wanted to keep it, and so did I at first, but—when I touched it, I couldn't. I just...couldn't."

Paiva reached into a pouch and threw marked bones for a while, perusing the symbols in silence. Then she took Jareth's hand in hers and held it for a moment. Her hand was gnarled, the palm sweaty and moist. She closed her eyes and concentrated. At last, she sighed and released him.

"Whatever these dreams are," she said, "I sense nothing evil in them, or in you. You are as sweet as the day I brought you into this world, Jareth."

He blushed, and thought that "sweet" was hardly a compliment for a growing young man like himself.

"That you dream of the gods is a sign that you are protected by them," she said, "and perhaps you are simply more aware of the spirits than the rest of us. The dream of the *taaskali* is clearly associated with the blessing cloth. As for the man standing behind you, he may represent your fear of the dreams. No one likes to be different, child, and these dreams are telling you that you are different in some way. Blessing cloths don't come to just anyone. And it is at this point in the dream that you awaken, wanting to trust the dreams and yet afraid of them."

She pursed her lips, considering. "Prepare something nice for the tree spirits to eat, since you seem so close to the forest, and leave it out at sunrise."

He nodded his understanding. And for the rest of the time, they sat in silence, letting the heat penetrate them and cleanse both skin and spirit.

The next morning Jareth went out at first light to leave the offerings. He had gone to his old friend the oak, who had given him the branch that was going to be a wonderful staff. At the oak's feet, he offered his week's share of honey, dried fruit and milk, pouring it all so it formed a puddle. Then, unable to resist its inviting branches, he climbed the oak.

The wind shifted and Jareth gently swayed in his perch. The breeze stirred up the heady fragrance of the pine trees that were neighbors to this ancient oak, and he closed his eyes and inhaled deeply.

He was tired of winter. It seemed to him as if it had lasted forever, that he had been waking to falling snow and crusted ice in the water basin for years. He had to remind himself that while this winter was harsher than most, it, too, would eventually yield to spring.

He was glad he had gone to see Paiva yesterday. He had slept well last night, and all his dreams had been pleasant. Smiling, he settled back into the crook and let his thoughts drift. He closed his eyes.

The Change must come.

Jareth jerked awake, wondering who had spoken. The words had been very clear and had probably saved his life; it was hardly wise to drift off to sleep in a tree.

"Hello?" he called down. He peered through the oak's skeletal branches, but saw no one.

A chill ran up his spine. Maybe it was the tree talking to him. There were spirits in the woods and waters, everyone knew that. It was just that nobody had really ever seen one. *Just like no one had ever seen a blessing cloth,* he thought.

He waited, his breathing shallow, rising from his reddened lips in soft little puffs. The voice did not come again, but he had heard it: *The Change must come.*

Like one in a dream, Jareth climbed down the tree, landing softly beside the damp spot where he had placed his offering. The liquids had soaked into the ground, and the fruit had been taken—by spirits or squirrels, he didn't know or care.

He felt drawn as he threaded his way through the closely growing trunks to a clear space in the woods. Even here, the light was dim; it was winter still, after all. Slowly, Jareth knelt on the soft blanket of snow, his knees getting wet almost immediately. He unwound the wrappings from both his hands.

The Change must come.

He didn't know what he was doing, or why, only that he must. Jareth leaned forward, stretched out his pale, pink hands, extended his fingers, and plunged them through the snow, past the carpet of fallen leaves and pine needles, into the cold, nearly frozen soil.

And the Change came.

2

Jareth's hand closed around the berries. They were small and warm, kissed by the sun, and slightly dusty. They nestled in his work-roughened palm like small animals. He felt them, their life, their essence; different now from when they had been on the vine, but bearing no pain at the separation. *This is what berries do,* he thought. They began as small white flowers, transitioned to fruit, and fell from the mother plant to begin the cycle again. Whether it was human hands that plucked them or animal teeth, it mattered not to them.

He couldn't resist tossing a handful into his mouth right then, bursting the skins and feeling the sweet yet tangy juice and pulp against his tongue. He took the nourishment into himself with gratitude.

Everything was different since that long-ago winter day, when the earth itself had summoned him.

Everything.

Savoring the berries, Jareth glanced at the other harvesters. Like him, they were barefoot, their feet coated in pale dust. But they didn't *feel* the earth beneath their feet as he did. They grabbed handfuls of berries without a second thought, distracted only by the occasional tasty bite of the luscious fruit, not, as he was, by the marvel that the berries inherently were. The sun beat down on Jareth's golden hair, cut now to shoulder-length as befitted a man.

Twenty summers he had known, and for nearly half of them he had been the *Kevat-aanta*—the Spring-Bringer. Rumors of what he could do had traveled, and he was embarrassed by the adulation he received. More *huskaas* had come to Skalka Valley in the last nine years than in the last fifty before, he had been told; *huskaas* eager to meet the nearly legendary figure and to compose their own songs about his ability.

The seasons had changed before, of course; but now, they changed when Jareth asked it of the earth, the way he asked it. He took nothing for granted anymore—not the stones and grass and soil beneath his feet, not the rustling of the leaves and the heady smell of pine, not the taste of berries in summer.

He loved this land. He belonged here. He was well aware that his ability to connect with the earth and all the wondrous living things that took sustenance from it was a precious gift to be cherished, not a right to be demanded. He'd talked about this with Paiva, who nodded her approval and said that he was quite wise for one so young.

Not for the first time, Jareth had chafed at the "compliment" Paiva bestowed. He wondered if Paiva, who seemed as ancient to him as his beloved oak tree, would ever consider him an adult.

A few rows away, his boyhood friend Larr placed his basket down and straightened. Their eyes met. Larr frowned, stretched and rubbed the small of his back, then continued with his task. Jareth felt a stab of sorrow. The *huskaas* might sing his praises as highly as they did that of the gods, but Jareth knew he was no better a man than Larr or any other. A distance had grown between them since that day that Jareth had been unable to bridge. Jareth was the Spring-Bringer, who could touch the earth and make things grow, but the gift had come with a high price. It had forever set him apart from everyone else.

What Paiva did not know—what no one knew—was how fearful Jareth was that the gift would one day disappear as mysteriously as it had come. Each time Jareth held a handful of seeds, sensing the adult plant dormant within— all that life within one small space—he wondered if it would be the last. Each time he knelt in the snow and asked summer to slip into autumn, or winter to turn to spring, his heart raced with worry that this time, the earth would not listen. He cherished his bond with the earth, and was glad that through it he could take good care of his village, but he wondered sometimes if Larr were happier than he. Jareth's parents had passed a few years ago, and he had no siblings or other kin. The most popular man in the village lived alone.

Jareth picked up his pace and grabbed more handfuls of the little miracles. A high voice calling his name caught his attention. It was six-year-old Altan Lukkari, dust flying from his bare feet, short legs pumping as he ran. Jareth smiled. He had assisted Paiva in bringing this bright little boy into the world. But in Jareth's eyes, Altan would always have a shadow—the stillborn twin sister their mother had named Ilta, who would never get to run barefoot on dirt paths on a warm summer day. Ilta had died in the womb, the birth-cord meant to give life wrapped tightly around her little neck, bestowing death instead. The sight of the tiny, gray-ish-green corpse had horrified Jareth, and he wondered if he would ever be able to look upon Altan without thinking of the tragic Ilta.

"I thought you were supposed to be practicing your *kyn-dela*," Jareth chided halfheartedly. The last *huskaa* who had come to the valley had been impressed by Altan's sweet voice and ability to remember songs and had given the child an old *kyndela*. Altan had taken to it and now spent most of his time teaching himself to play. His parents had promised him that he could be apprenticed to the *huskaa* of Two Lakes when he was thirteen if he continued to show such dedica-tion to the craft.

"I was, but Mama sent me to find you," Altan gasped. "Oooh..." He squatted and reached for a handful of berries, popping them into his mouth. Juice dribbled down his face and he wiped it off with the back of his hand. "Those are good."

"Yes, they are," Jareth agreed, "but I doubt your mother sent you to find me so you could eat berries. What's going on?"

"The headman from Two Lakes is here. He needs your help. His youngest daughter has gone missing."

* * *

By early afternoon, Jareth and Orvo Relaanan, the headman, arrived in Two Lakes. It looked like everyone in the village had turned out to meet them, but two women stood in the forefront of the gathered crowd. One was Kivi, the headman's wife. In the prime of life, she remained a handsome woman, with a full figure and only a few wrinkles around her blue eyes.

And her eldest daughter…

Jareth tried not to stare, but it was difficult. Taya Relaanan, his own age or slightly younger, was the most beautiful girl he had ever seen. She was petite, like her mother, with large eyes the color of the sky in autumn and a soft, pink mouth. It struck him that if he were to hold her, her head would barely reach his heart, and then blushed at the thought. Her breasts nicely filled out the front of her dress, but the sash about her waist accentuated her trimness. Right now, her eyes and mouth were swollen with crying. When she looked up at him, lip quivering and hope in her eyes, Jareth was lost.

He had been determined to find the little girl from the moment he had heard her worried father speak, the man's big, rough hands clasping and unclasping. But now Jareth's resolve was doubled. He couldn't bear to see this lovely young woman cry anymore. He found himself longing to hear what her laughter sounded like.

Jareth jumped from the wagon seat. "Where was Vikka last seen?" he asked, trying to regain his composure.

"Right outside the house," Taya said. Her voice was soft and husky from crying. "I was inside spinning and she was carding the wool for me. When I came out she was gone."

"We've searched the areas where we know the children play," her mother said. "No one has seen her."

Jareth nodded absently, his mind already working. His eyes fell on the stool and the abandoned pile of wool Taya had mentioned, and he knelt on the ground. He had never tried anything like this before and he hoped it would work. If it didn't...

Taking a deep breath, he placed his big hands on the soil, feeling the yellowing blades of grass, the small stones, the earth itself. He had touched it so before, coaxing the seasons to change. But this time was different.

"Tell me," he whispered, his eyes closed. "Tell me about the little girl, who sat on a stool here earlier today."

He heard voices murmuring at him, but he ignored them. He strained to listen for the voice of the earth, praying to the gods who had given him this gift that it would answer.

Earth am I, soil and sand, ever-changing and ever the same. I am the flesh that was once living beings, and the anchor to the roots of the trees and grass and all growing things. Earth am I, and I shall speak.

The child scorned the stool, and pressed herself to me as she worked, singing songs of harvest and coming snow. Passed the hours so, golden sun streaming over and warming us both. Up she leaped, with a shout of joy, and away she ran. The long-eared one surprised her and she gave a merry chase. More, I know not.

Relief and awe commingled swept through him. The earth had deigned to respond to his question.

Jareth opened his eyes. "She ran after a rabbit," he said. He moved farther along the ground, searching with eyes and fingers for tracks. He found them, and again knelt and asked the grass for aid.

Grass am I, green in my youth, dry and yellow as the winter comes. I cover the earth and grasp it safely in my roots, holding it here instead of letting it rush away with the wind and rain and snow. Grass am I, and I shall speak.

The long-eared one was not afraid, for the child could not hope to catch one as fleet as he. Across me they came, both laughing and free. Their path took them to the forest, where the trees and the moss and the stone stand guardians over things more ancient than the season's grass. More, I know not.

Hope surged in Jareth. Despite his initial uncertainty, every time he asked, he received an answer. Once at the forest's edge, Jareth placed his hands on the gnarled roots of a tree and again asked for its wisdom.

Farther he went into the forest, listening to the trees and the stones and the soil tell him of the carefree flight of the little girl. Hushed and reverent, the small crowd followed him. Vikka had been gone only a few hours, but her sense of adventure was great and it took some time before he found her, curled up sleeping in a hollow area beneath an overhanging pine bough. If he had not known where to look, he would have walked right past her.

Thank you, he thought, tears of gratitude stinging his eyes. *Thank you for keeping her safe.*

He moved aside the sheltering bough and she blinked sleepily. She was clad in a white underdress with a red over-tunic, stained now from grass and dirt. Her eyes were large and trusting and her hair was such a pale shade of yellow it was almost white.

"Hello," she said, smiling and unafraid.

Charmed, Jareth smiled back at her. She was the cutest little girl he'd ever seen. *If I am ever a father, I want a daughter just like her.*

"Looks like the warm day lulled you to sleep," he said gently, kneeling and extending his arms. Vikka crawled into them, her smooth brow furrowing as she realized the import of what had happened from the faces of her family and village standing behind Jareth.

"Oh," she said as he picked her up. "They will be angry with me—the rabbit was so funny I had to follow him...."

"Shh, shh, sweetheart," soothed her father, taking the precious burden from Jareth's arms. "We're not angry. We were worried about you, that's all. You're lucky the Spring-Bringer found you or you might have slept away the night in the woods."

Still drowsy, Vikka looked at Jareth. "Thank you, Spring-Bringer," she said, yawned, and slipped her hands around her father's neck.

"Yes," said Taya, her eyes shining. "Thank you, Spring-Bringer."

He knew that everyone thought he had magic, but he could have sworn that it was Taya who was magical. His heart sped up and his tongue cleaved to his throat. Unable to speak, he offered her what to others might seem a paltry gift.

At his feet, blooming in a patch of sunlight, was a single flower. He bent, his fingers closing on the green stem, and whispered softly, "I would give you to this lady, as a token of my feelings for her."

Wildflower am I, petals red as blood, heart blue as sky, I follow the sun on its path from dawn to dusk. Wildflower am I, and I shall speak.

I sense what you feel for this woman, and know this, that I offer myself freely, gladly, as a token of your love.

He winced as he plucked it, hearing the stem break with a snap, feeling it die between his fingers. Almost overcome with the sensation, he turned and handed it to Taya.

"This is for you," he said, his voice trembling. She took it between her own slender fingers and trailed it over her cheek. And at that gesture, Jareth envied the flower.

3

Jareth gazed at the autumn sky reflected in the lake, at the trees who now wore garments of gold and russet and brown instead of green. The breeze, not yet the biting wind of winter, tousled his golden hair. Autumn was a melancholy season, but still sweet and tender; the last haunting note sounded before winter, like the final chord of a *kyndela's* song.

The sun ducked briefly behind one of the puffy white clouds that ambled across the sky and Jareth felt the chill. The harvests were fast approaching: grain, fruit and vegetable, and then the slaughtering of the animals for winter food storage. Jareth found he felt better if he walked among the fields, orchards and stables before the time of reaping came. There was a soft brush of sorrow and then acceptance, from the wheat or the apples or the sheep. They grasped even better than he their roles. He knew, as they knew, that next spring the wheat would sprout again, the orchards would be redolent with the scent of apple blossoms, and lambs would dot the green hills like little white clouds come to earth. But there could not be rebirth without death, and that always made Jareth sorrowful.

He walked through the wheat, his golden hair akin to their golden heads, saying his own farewell, then joined the others in bringing sickle to stalk.

Others talked animatedly, eager for the festival that would be coming in a few days. Truth be told, Jareth was no less eager than they. For the closest villages to Skalka Valley would be coming for the festival, to barter their own harvests and to participate in a lavish feast, followed by dancing and an enormous bonfire.

He had not seen nor heard from the lovely Taya Relaanan since that day several months ago when he had asked the earth and trees to find her little sister Vikka. He was taken with the girl, and had thought the interest was at least somewhat mutual, but perhaps it had been only gratitude that shone in her eyes when she accepted the flower.

The thought of the young woman, whose hair put the glory of the sun to shame and whose face haunted his dreams, made Jareth's loins ache. He shifted position and tried to concentrate on his task. But once she had floated into his mind, Taya had taken up residence. Jareth desperately hoped he would see her at the festival.

And then what? He was no stranger to the delights of the flesh. Tall, handsome, well-formed, he would have drawn women to him like bees to honey even had he not been the Spring-Bringer. More than one village girl—and some from other villages as well—had come to him in the night, climbing quietly into his bed. They had given him great pleasure, and Jareth ensured that they, too, left satisfied. He suspected that some of them had not wanted him for himself, but had coupled with him in hopes of conceiving a child blessed with his so-called "magical" talents. To bear such a child would bring her honor. And more than one girl had desired a more formal union and had offered a gift made by her own hands as a bride price, for in Lamal, women did the asking. Jareth had accepted none of these hopeful young women. No, the *Kevat-aanta* did not have to go without a willing woman in his bed unless he so chose.

Surprising everyone, including himself, he often did so choose. At first, when he was younger, the coupling was exciting. But as time passed, Jareth realized he wanted a deeper connection than attraction and mutual desire. His feelings toward the women who shared his bed were like that of most people toward the forest and earth—pleasant, but nothing very deep. The earth itself had taught him what it was like to have a powerful bond, and he wanted one with a woman—one woman, to share a lifetime with.

Taya was more than just beautiful. He'd seen beauty before and while he was not unmoved by it, he wanted more. Taya carried herself as if she was proud of who she was. He suspected she would push him and challenge him if she were his wife—and she would be a mate who would be a partner and friend, not just a bedfellow.

You've only met her once, Jareth. You're assuming a great

deal. Anyone who chooses you will have to share your burden, and that is no small thing.

Cursing himself, he returned to his task. In thinking of Taya, he had closed down the connection between himself and the grain. Now, he deliberately opened it again, concentrating on accepting the wheat's pain as he brought the scythe down again and again, sending the tall stalks falling gently to the brown soil.

When Taya and her family disembarked from the wagon and her eyes fell on Jareth, he felt himself blush and ducked behind a nearby tree. What kind of hold did this girl have over him? He was behaving like an infatuated boy, and he was a man grown at twenty! He forced himself to step out from the shelter of the tree, but Taya had moved on. Jareth contented himself with greeting her parents, accepting their thanks yet again for his rescue of Vikka, and calmed his nervousness by picking up the giggling child and carrying her around on his shoulders for the next little while.

His anxiety did not diminish as the day slipped past, the golden sunlight waning to twilight as the three villages bartered and haggled over various goods. He noticed that there was a beautiful woolen blanket, in shades of blue and gold and green, that Taya had brought which never left the wagon. Idly he wondered why she had bothered to bring it if she hadn't planned to barter it, then turned his attention to the feast that was being brought out.

With three villages providing food, it was a lavish spread indeed: bread of all varieties, soups, roasted fish, fowl and meats, mustards and jellies and nuts, and bowl and after bowl of raw, roasted, and stewed vegetables every color of the rainbow. Skalka Valley's most famous contribution was also the most popular. The valley was known for the quality and quantity of the honeywine it produced. Jareth was able to calm the bees that made the golden fluid that was the heart of the drink, rendering the honey itself uncommonly delicious and enabling the beekeepers to painlessly extract more combs, though Jareth insisted that the bees must always have plenty for themselves. "It's their food," he maintained. "They share it with us, not the other way around."

At twilight, old Paiva stepped in front of the huge bonfire, a burning branch in her hand. Ivo, the headman, had presided over most of the events thus far, but now they were headed into ritual space, and that was Paiva's realm.

"We have been blessed by the gods," she said in a voice that carried. Not for the first time, Jareth marveled at the strength that still dwelt in the increasingly feeble body. He felt a surge of affection for her. Of all the residents of Skalka Valley, she alone had continued to treat him as she always had.

"We have plenty of food for the winter. We have good friends in nearby villages. And tonight, we have the warmth of the sun contained in the fire. Burn!"

She thrust the brand forward. The bonfire had been well-made and doused liberally with oil, and all gasped and clapped as the yellow licking flames chased away the darkness. Paiva was now a black figure outlined by the crackling glow.

"Come forward and free yourselves from the burdens you have carried this year. Let the fire take and transform your suffering."

This was an old, old tradition, and everyone knew how

to proceed. They formed an orderly line, accepting small bundles of dried wheat stalks from which the precious grain had been extracted, and stepped forward. One by one, some weaving a little thanks to the drink they had imbibed earlier, they whispered what they wished to be free of, and tossed the sheaf onto the flame. When Jareth reached the fire and felt the heat bathe his face, he realized he knew exactly what his longing was. He was honored and envied, but no one knew the pain he suffered.

Speaking aloud, but softly so that this private moment would not be overheard, he said firmly, "I wish to be free of my doubt."

He hurled the sheaf forward, watched as it twisted and blackened in the fire, and took a deep breath. No calm certainty rushed to bathe him yet, but Paiva often reminded those who participated in this ancient rite that sometimes it took a while for the wish to be answered. But the gods always heard their petitioners.

He stepped aside, his heart speeding up when Taya moved toward the fire a few moments later. Jareth couldn't hear what she said, but he noticed that she was smiling when she walked away.

It took time for the ceremony to be completed, but at last everyone had participated and the mood shifted from sacred to celebratory. There was much laughter and passing of honeywine sacks as everyone gathered around the fire. A chill was in the air at night now, and the warmth was welcome.

He looked about for Taya, but didn't see her. Then the crowd parted slightly and she stood alone for a brief moment. Fire bathed her in yellow and orange, and to Jareth, she looked like the sun come to life. Perhaps feeling his gaze,

Taya turned slowly. Their eyes met and her lips curved in a slight smile. Summoning his courage, Jareth stepped forward and—

A small hand curled trustingly around his. He looked down to see little Altan beaming up at him.

"Guess what, Jareth? The *huskaa* of Two Lakes heard me singing and playing this afternoon and he has agreed to take me on as a *huskaa-lal!*"

This was a high honor and at any other time, Jareth would have been thrilled for Altan. But tonight... He glanced up.

Taya was gone. The stab of disappointment was surprising in its keenness.

"Jareth?" Altan tugged on his hand. Jareth forced a smile.

"That's wonderful, Altan. I'm very proud of you. You have a lot of talent and you've worked very hard. You're going to make a fine *huskaa.*" The words were true and he tried to sound like he meant them. He must have succeeded, for Altan's brow unfurrowed and he beamed up at his friend.

"Come and sit!" Altan urged. "He's starting to play. I want to be just like him when I grow up. And just like you, too."

Jareth's heart melted. It was always hard to resist Altan. Somehow, he always felt he owed the Lukkari family a debt for their lost daughter, although Paiva had assured him that his presence at Altan's birth had not been responsible for Ilta Lukkari's death. Indeed, Altan's mother claimed loudly and repeatedly that it was "the Spring-Bringer's presence" that had graced Altan with life and talent.

What did it matter if he sat and listened to songs all evening? Taya was nowhere to be seen. Jareth sighed, found a spot on one of the logs provided as seats, pulled Altan into his lap, and decided to make the best of it.

The *huskaa* was worth listening to. He went through a repertoire of standard songs, some merry, some sad. Jareth thought he had never heard the Ice Maiden song cycle, "Circle of Ice," performed so powerfully. As the evening wore down, Altan did too. He was asleep in Jareth's arms by the time the performer turned to more adult themes. As he listened to one of the singer's original compositions, written specifically for this night, Jareth grew wistful.

The golden turns to purple;
The purple fades to gray.
Come leave the darkling fields behind
To the dying of the day.
Come rest thy weary body
Beside the fire's light,
For the harvest has been gathered in
And we celebrate tonight.

Behold our table laden
With fruit of tree and vine.
Partake of golden wheaten bread
And taste the sweet red wine.
Our larder's filled with winter stores,
A fair and welcome sight,
For the harvest has been gathered in
And we celebrate tonight.

I'll rub thy weary shoulders,
And lie with thee till dawn.
Perhaps tonight we'll sow the seed
For a harvest later on;

A child born in nine month's time
To be raised in love and light—
For the harvest has been gathered in
And we celebrate tonight.

Jareth's thoughts turned to Taya. Others were pairing off, leaving the ring of firelight or sitting holding hands. The harvest was about bounty and family, about facing the coming darkness and deprivation of winter together. And once again, he would be alone.

The winds blow crisp and cold now,
The mighty trees are bare.
Aye, Summer sweet has breathed her last,
But we shall not despair.
Though winter looms before us,
Our love burns ever bright,
For the harvest has been gathered in
And we celebrate tonight.

For the harvest has been gathered in,
And we celebrate tonight.

There was a soft smattering of applause. The *huskaa* nodded his thanks and went into another equally soft, sweet song. Jareth rose, carrying Altan. The little boy shifted and his arms went around Jareth's neck.

Jareth went to Altan's house and lay the boy down on his pallet. Altan woke up briefly. Sleepily he said, "I love you, Jareth."

"I love you too," Jareth said, stroking the child's soft

golden hair and pulling the blanket around him. "Now sleep, little one."

The cool, crisp air tingled through his body when he stepped outside. Jareth gazed up at the stars, tiny dots in the enormous black sky, and when his feet took him down the path toward the recently harvested fields, he was not surprised. If he could not be with Taya, he wanted to be with the land, to sit on the cold soil, and help it prepare for winter. And, he had to admit, to glean what comfort he could from it.

His sure strides faltered. Someone was here before him, sitting quietly on a blanket, a cloak wrapped around her. The moon was bright, and he recognized the face that turned toward him.

"I thought you'd eventually come here tonight," Taya said.

Jareth opened his mouth, but nothing came out. Taya patted the space beside her on the blanket and Jareth sat. He felt the warmth of her body where his knee touched hers. His mind raced, but he couldn't think of anything to say.

"How is Vikka doing?" he finally managed.

"She's fine," Taya replied, chuckling a little. "Brags to all her little friends about how the Spring-Bringer rescued her."

"I'm just glad I could help. The woods can be dangerous after nightfall." He mentally kicked himself. What a foolish thing to say. Everyone knew that.

An awkward silence fell. He wanted to pull her into his arms and kiss her, breathe in her scent of flowers and sunlight, see what her body looked like when it was clad only in the moon's pale glow. But he couldn't move.

Finally, she said, "I had hoped you would have occasion to return to Two Lakes before now."

He turned to look at her, his heart beating even faster. "I had hoped so too," he said. "Or that you might have cause to come to the valley."

She turned toward him. Her face was a white oval in the moonlight. "I'm here now."

Jareth was having trouble breathing. "Taya..."

"Do you like the blanket?"

He blinked. "What?"

"The blanket. I made it myself." She hesitated, then said, "I made it for you. If you will accept it."

She was offering a bride price. He suddenly recalled standing in front of the blazing bonfire a few hours ago, and tossing in his sheaf with the silent prayer of being free from doubt. Like a weight physically lifted from his shoulders, he felt all uncertainty vanish. He knew what he wanted...*who* he wanted.

"It's lovely," he said, with the words accepting her offer of marriage. "You honor me. Thank you."

He reached for her hand and closed his fingers over it. Impulsively, he pressed it gently down into the earth, over the cool soil, the bits and pieces of harvested wheat.

"Do you feel anything?" he asked. He hoped...

She smiled. "Only your hand on mine," she said. Then, intensely, she asked, "Jareth...what do *you* feel when you do this?"

Haltingly, he said, "I feel the earth. The living things it sustains. All of it, all at once. Like some great giant heartbeat." The words sounded foolish in his ears, and yet at the same time they failed to capture even the smallest fragment of the sensations that coursed through him when he permitted himself to open to them.

Her hand was still beneath his, on the ground. Slowly, she lifted it and curled her fingers around his. She raised their entwined hands and placed them between her breasts.

"Now what do you feel?" she whispered.

"A heartbeat," he said, his voice also dropping into a hushed tone. His lips were dry and he spread his fingers, trying to press his palm to her heart, feeling it fluttering in her tiny rib cage like a small bird. As he did so, he suddenly became aware of how dirty his hand was. Ashamed, he tried to pull back.

"I'm sorry, my hands—"

"No," she whispered. "Your hands are beautiful. And mine are dirty, too."

He wanted to look into her amazing eyes again, but the moon's light only seemed to cast shadows on her face.

"I can't feel what you feel," she said, "but I know your ability means more to you than just controlling when the spring and autumn come. More than providing good crops. Do you know what's in this pouch around my neck, Jareth?"

Blood hammered in his ears, raced through his body, made him ache for her. He shook his head.

"The flower you gave me this summer," Taya said. "I saw you wince when you plucked it. I know you felt it die, yet you were willing to do that in order to give it to me. Of course I cherished it."

She knew. She understood. She couldn't share it with him—he now reluctantly realized that no one could—but she understood what this power meant to him.

"I fell in love with you at that moment," she whispered, leaning in to him. Slowly, as if drawn, he bent forward. His hand still on her heart, their lips met.

He kissed her gently, tenderly, exploring, savoring. Her lips were as soft as the petals of the flower that had given up its life for her, as sweet as honey from the comb. He moved his hand from her heart to run his fingers through her hair, trail them along the back of her neck. Wrapping his arms around her, he pulled her into his lap.

"You're so little," he whispered, marveling. "I can hold all of you just like this."

"Keep holding me," Taya whispered, and reached up to touch his face. He pressed a kiss against her questing hand, then tangled his fingers in her long, soft blond hair and pulled her mouth to his. How long they stayed together, locked in that kiss, Jareth neither knew nor cared. When they broke apart, he was trembling and breathing heavily.

He could see her eyes now; they caught and held the moonlight, like twin lakes. She gazed up at him rapturously, one little hand reaching to stroke his cheek, his lips.

"You're so beautiful," Taya said, amazement in her voice.

Jareth chuckled. "I'm supposed to say that."

"Then say it."

Her finger ran across his lower lip. He opened his mouth and caught the finger, biting very gently. She gasped softly. He let it go.

"You *are* beautiful, Taya. Since the day we met, I've done nothing but think about you. Dream about you. I don't want to be without you ever again."

"You don't have to."

He reached for her and she closed her eyes, anticipating another kiss, but instead he removed the little pouch from around her neck. She had spoken truly; the flower, carefully preserved, was contained within. With gentle fingers he withdrew it. As he touched it, the brown, dried leaves uncurled and became green again, the petals swelling with new life.

"What are you—"

"Shhh," he said, easing her down onto the blanket she had woven for him. Gently, he began to stroke her with the blossom, following each delicate brush of petal or leaf with a soft kiss. Taya closed her eyes and whimpered softly.

Taking his time, Jareth stroked and kissed her face, her ears, the hollow of her throat; her hands, the sensitive insides of her wrists and elbows; trailed flower and lips along ankle, calf and thigh, over covered belly and breasts. Gods, how he wanted this woman. Wanted her here, under the moon, on the good earth covered with the last of the wheat's harvest. Wanted her in his bed, wrapped in the blanket she had made, their bodies warm and supple and heedless of the winter's chill. Wanted her in the shadowed, scented forest, in the sunlit meadows.

Wanted her forever.

Abruptly she sat up, shocking him by removing her overtunic, leaving only the soft, translucent underdress between them. He could see the dark circles of her nipples beneath the white fabric as she moved.

Before he could react, Taya surprised him again by leaning forward to tug off his shirt. Delighted by her boldness, Jareth assisted her. The autumnal night air ought to have been chill on his naked torso, but he burned with a heat that banished any cold. He gasped as she explored him. He let her take the lead, though his hands and lips ached to caress her. She put both hands on his chest and pushed lightly.

"Move off the blanket. Lie on the earth," she said, her voice a husky growl. "Feel it. Take it into you, my love."

The request moved him deeply. But before he obeyed, he leaned forward and pulled off Taya's underdress. She sat proudly in front of him, her skin gleaming like a swan in the moonlight. She made no attempt to cover herself and his hands moved as if of their own will to cup her breasts, white and soft as down, the tips hard as pebbles against the palms of his hands. Her head fell back and she moaned, softly, sweetly, the sound inflaming him further.

Slowly, he lay on the cool soil, pulling her with him, crushing her small, perfect breasts to his chest and forcing her mouth open with his tongue. He felt the cold earth, the sharp pricks of dried and broken stalks stabbing into his back, the hardness of small stones, and the discomfort was exquisite pleasure. He let the essence of the earth fill him. His skin tingled and he felt more open, more exposed, more receptive and aroused than he had ever felt before.

Taya undulated against him, her movement delightful torment. Unable to wait any longer, Jareth slid a hand between their bodies and freed himself from the confinement of his breeches. Taya gasped as she felt him press against her and she pulled back for a brief moment. Cool air rushed to fill the space between them.

Jareth gritted his teeth. He had never wanted a woman as badly as he wanted this tiny slip of a girl, never felt as dizzy with desire as he did now, with the deep, endless support of the earth at his back and this woman in his arms. He forced himself to stay still, wanting Taya to make the ever so slight movement that would bring him fully inside her, fighting the urge to thrust upward into her wet warmth. She leaned down and her hair fell in a soft curtain on his chest. Shaking, he brushed it back with hands that seemed huge against her tiny face.

"Don't leave me!" The words were raw, almost physically ripped from him, and he knew he was speaking to both Taya and the earth upon which he lay.

"Never," Taya whispered against his mouth, and the earth echoed: *Never.* And Jareth believed them both.

"Do you feel it?"

Struck dumb again at her insight, he nodded. The power of his profound union with the earth was coursing through him and the sensations were almost overwhelming.

"Good," Taya whispered. "Now," she said, lifting her hips slightly and then slowly, sweetly, taking his hardness into her, "make love to me."

They were married before the first snowfall.

4

Taya held her newborn son to her breast while Annu spun in the corner. The fire crackled, Altan sat beside it strumming his *kyndela* and humming, and Jareth stood looking out the window at the cool blue and white hues of snow. He didn't think he had ever been quite so content.

Twenty springs had passed since he had felt the call that lured him down from his favorite tree to dig his fingers into icy soil and call forth the rebirth of life. And thirteen summers had blossomed and faded since he and his wife had first coupled passionately in the autumn field, the harvest moon shining upon them and the good earth blessing them. She had conceived, either that night or shortly thereafter, and had been with child by the time Paiva had formally wed them. Nine months later, as the song performed by the *hus-kaa* of Two Lakes had suggested might happen, lovely Annu had come into the world.

No father could have doted on a daughter more, and it was entirely due to her own innate good sense that Annu was not thoroughly spoiled. She had her mother's beauty, level head, and sense of humor, and her father's height and love for the natural world. Another blessing had come their way a few weeks ago, when Parvan had been born. Paiva was no longer with them to bring the little boy into the world; she had passed five years ago and now her former apprentice had that solemn yet joyful duty.

When Altan's parents, too, had passed, he had all but become a part of Jareth's family, coming for visits as short as half a day and sometimes as long as two or three days. Jareth already looked upon the *huskaa* as a baby brother. And who would not wish to have a *huskaa* on hand, willing and able to provide music soothing or merry as the occasion demanded? Besides, Annu was a young woman now, having celebrated her first blood moon. Taya thought that the two youngsters would be a natural and wonderful match, and encouraged the eighteen-year-old Altan to spend time with the girl. And most of the time Jareth agreed, although Altan was subject to occasional dark moods that rendered the normally pleasant youth sullen and brooding.

"He's eighteen and he's blessed with talent," Taya said once. "Of course he's moody."

Jareth had burst into startled laughter, and even now the memory of the exchange made him smile. Jareth thought about his good life as the snow continued to fall. *It's almost time.*

"I will tell Ivo that it will be soon," he said, turning to look over his shoulder at his family. "Five, perhaps six days. The land is ready to be awakened from its slumber."

In truth the land was more than ready, but the headman always wanted a few days' notice so he could send messengers to nearby villages. Jareth had long since resigned himself to the fact that when the *Kevat-aanta* brought spring, it was an occasion. Ivo noticed that when people came for the event, they tended to bring items to trade and make a celebration out of it, and who was Jareth to begrudge his fellow villagers some laughter and a chance to trade for baubles or foodstuffs?

He turned his attention back to the snow as it fell, and suddenly, for no reason he could discern, felt a shiver run down his spine. For the first time since the feel of Taya's warm body pressing against his had banished his fear, he tasted the old, bitter tang of worry.

Five days later, dressed in a beautifully embroidered dark green cloak, leather boots and brown and gold breeches and shirt, Jareth stood ready to perform his most well-known seasonal transformation.

Taya's eyes roamed over him approvingly. "The years have blessed you, my husband," she said, stepping close to him and stroking his freshly shaven cheek. She had to reach up quite a bit, for as Jareth had predicted that long-ago summer, Taya's head barely came to the center of his chest. He pressed the little hand to his lips.

"They have indeed, by seeing to it that you have only grown more beautiful."

"I am still swollen from childbirth," she laughed, "from foot to face!"

Jareth bent. "I love what I see," he whispered, and captured her lips with his. He pulled back in time to see Annu rolling her eyes and Altan grinning.

"I don't think there's time for that, you two," Altan said wryly. "Your people await you, Jareth. And I am longing to perform my new song!"

Jareth turned to his daughter. Annu was taller than her mother and her head came to his chin, making it convenient for him to plant a kiss on the top of the golden hair.

"The cloak is beautiful," he said. "My favorite color, too. You have quite a talent for one so young."

Again, Annu rolled her eyes. "I'm *twelve*, Father. I'm not a child anymore."

He sighed, tousled her hair, and then turned toward the door, reaching for the staff he had made when he was thirteen. He opened the door to see the beaming headman, and forced himself to adopt a regal pose, smiling and nodding at the upturned, expectant faces in the crowd.

The parade of onlookers followed Jareth as he strode through the center of the village. Altan had contrived a way to carry his instrument and play it at the same time by attaching it to a sturdy leather strap hung over his shoulder— a first for a *kyndela* player as far as Jareth knew. But that was Altan, always breaking the traditions even as he personified the best the *huskaa* tradition had to offer. Grumpy or charming, sarcastic or pleasant, the boy was brilliant, no question about it, and Jareth was proud to be his friend.

The day had dawned clear, but now snow was starting to fall. That was all right with Jareth; it would turn to rain soon enough. The path he had trod for the past twenty years led through the forests that embraced the village and into a small clearing. The snow continued to fall, becoming heavier. Over the bright sound of Altan's instrument, Jareth heard some concerned mutterings.

He reached and touched his old friend the oak, which had held him so supportively through many summers as a youth and even as an adult. A frown touched his lips. Usually he could feel at least something when he touched this mighty tree, no matter what the season. He forced his apprehension down. It had been a hard winter this year, despite his efforts to gentle the harshness; perhaps the tree was simply slumbering more deeply than usual.

Leaning his staff against the oak's trunk, Jareth stepped into the clearing. He closed his eyes and slowed his breathing.

"I have been blessed by the gods, and I have heard the call," he said, his voice resonant. "I am the protector and guardian of the earth's seasons, summoning them and continuing the cycle of what was, and is, and ever shall be."

He knelt. The snow seeped through his breeches almost immediately, but the woolen cloak on his back blocked most of the wind that now started to pick up. His fair hair was growing wet with the falling flakes. He flexed his fingers, readied himself, and plunged them into the snow.

It was so cold it felt almost hot to him, tingling and biting his unprotected flesh. His fingertips brushed frozen sod. He took another deep breath and forced his fingers down into the earth.

Nothing happened.

The wind increased, toying with his damp locks. Again he reached, trying to sense the earth, rouse it, melt the snow, summon spring. He heard confused voices, wondering what was going on.

He dug deeper, his hands aching with the cold. *Come, spring. It is time. For many months has the winter held sway over these lands, but now it is your turn.*

There was no response. It was as if the earth was as dead to him now as it was to everyone else. Jareth felt sweat gather at his hairline, trickle down his face. The earth *always* heard him before when he tried to reach it. The stones spoke to him, the animals came when he called them, the trees bloomed and grew strong and tall....

He felt a gentle hand on his shoulder. He looked up to see Taya gazing at him with love and concern. Her eyes widened as she read the fear in her husband's face, understanding him as if he had spoken aloud.

His worst fears had materialized. His powers were gone.

The winter had lasted for six months now.

Three months had been natural; harsh, but part of the cycle that Jareth had learned to understand and which had become as much a part of him as breathing.

Three more months had been the unnatural winter, with snow that muffled sounds, blocked trade, and was slowly killing both plant and animal.

Unless the weather was so bad that the storm threatened to sweep in should the door be opened, Jareth had slogged every day through the ever-deepening snow toward the clearing. Sometimes grim-faced, sometimes ranting, he dug down until he reached the earth and tried desperately to waken it.

It was like touching a corpse. It felt familiar, but there was no hint of life within. Where there had once been voices, even songs, now there was only this ominous silence. Stones were cold to him, the trees quiet. From time to time, he wasn't sure why or how, he could still summon animals. This pained him; it was as if the only power he had left was to bring death, even though the death of the beasts meant life for the people of Skalka Valley.

There had been near panic right after his first attempt, but Ivo had managed to calm the crowd. And even then, the assumption was that even if the Spring-Bringer brought spring no longer, the thaw would simply come on its own time, as it had before Jareth had begun to call it. But when that did not happen, and the winter continued, there were some that called for Jareth's exile. Many, Jareth's boyhood friend Larr chief among them, said loudly that the gods were angry with Jareth for usurping their powers, and were punishing Lamal.

A sort of sullen, simmering truce had evolved between the villagers and Jareth Vasalen, one that tormented him more than an outright attack. That, at least, he could defend himself against.

The only one who routinely made the trek from the cluster of houses to Jareth's, set much closer to the forests and the hills, was Altan. Jareth welcomed the youth's arrival, not for himself but for his family. As the wife and children of the *Kevat-aanta,* they were as shunned as he was.

"Jareth?" Taya's voice held a note of fear and worry, as it always did now. "You haven't eaten all day."

"I'm not hungry." He didn't move from the window where he watched the snow continue to fall. He was growing to hate the fat flakes that wafted down to form more drifts, more winter.

A touch on his arm. He jerked away, shame flooding him as he saw Annu cringe as if he might strike her. Jareth had never laid a hand on any member of his family save in a caress, but he sickly admitted to himself that his demeanor over the past few months might make them think he would lash out at any moment.

"I'm sorry, Annu," he said, softening his voice. "I didn't mean to scare you."

She smiled bravely. "You didn't scare me, Father," she lied, blinking away the tears in her eyes. "Come eat. Please, come eat something."

So he permitted her to lead him to the center of the small house. He sat on a stool and spooned thin, tasteless soup into his mouth, and forced a smile for his wife, son, and daughter. And as he had every night for the last hundred nights, ever since his connection to the land had forsaken him, he turned his back to his wife and ignored her soft pleas for lovemaking, or even simply to be held.

He couldn't do it. It was all he could do to be civil to her during the day. At night, to hold her, run his hands over her familiar, beloved hills and valleys—no. He wasn't worthy of that, not anymore. Jareth had been the Spring-Bringer, the *Kevat-aanta,* who took care of his people. He had let them all down, and they were suffering badly now.

"Jareth?"

He did not answer. Perhaps if she thought him asleep...

"I know you're awake." Her hand reached out, ran tentatively along his shoulder and down his side. He shrank from her touch. "It's going to be all right."

He laughed harshly. "My powers have vanished. The gods are angry with me. Winter has lasted twice as long as it ever has before. I don't think it's going to be all right, not unless I can somehow stop this."

Silence. "You know that none of us thinks any less of you—not Annu or Altan or I. We love you, and it doesn't matter to us if you never get these powers back."

He couldn't take it anymore. "You didn't fall in love with Jareth," he spat angrily, trying and failing to keep his voice low so as not to disturb the others. "You fell in love with the *Kevat-aanta*. With the man who found your lost baby sister."

He heard the rustle as she sat up. "You think I fell in love with you for what you could *do?*"

Jareth turned, furious. "Didn't you? What if I hadn't found Vikka? What if she'd died, lost in the forest?"

"Of course I was happy you found her, but—"

"And who rolled me off the blanket so I could feel the earth at my back as you rode me like a—"

He bit back the worst of the words, but it was already too late. He knew he had gone too far. She froze, then slowly sank back down on the bed. His impotent anger bled away as he turned to touch her, and this time it was Taya who refused her mate's caress. Even in the dim light, he could see the sparkle of tears on her face.

"I loved you because you cared, Jareth," Taya said thickly. "Not for what you did. I saw how much you wanted to find Vikka. I saw how you felt the pain of the dying flower. Don't you realize how others would perceive this ability? Other men would set themselves up as all-powerful rulers, withholding spring or harvest to punish those who didn't follow them. That never even entered your thoughts. You loved the earth and stones and flowers, and you felt their joy and their pain. You protected them even as you guided them through the seasons. You asked for them to yield their bounty, you never demanded it. *That's* the man I fell in love with."

She fell silent. Then: "I wonder where that man has gone."

5

After a cloudless night in which the gods danced in the sky, their blue and white coats sending sparks of colors to paint the night in vibrant hues, the dawn that followed was cold and clear. As Jareth fastened his cloak, he stated, "I am going hunting with the men. The sky is clear, for the moment, and we must not waste this opportunity."

His wife and daughter nodded, their eyes downcast. Jareth remembered when he used to love looking into both sets of blue eyes. One woman held love and a deep passion; the other adoration and unconditional devotion. Neither wanted to look at him now, and he supposed he couldn't blame them.

It will be better tonight, he thought. *When the men and I re-*

turn with food for the tables, it will be better. At least I will have been able to provide something for my family.

He thought about speaking the words aloud, but decided against it. He would let his actions speak for him. He rose and went for the door. As he placed his hand on it, he heard Taya say softly, "Be careful."

He nodded, his back to her, unable, unwilling to look at her, to kiss her goodbye. Annu stood beside the door, holding Parvan. She focused her attention on the baby to avoid looking at her father. The infant's soft gurgle melted something inside Jareth, and he reached to stroke the soft curve of his son's cheek. Parvan reached up a tiny hand and clutched Jareth's finger, and the trusting gesture broke Jareth's heart. Tears stung his eyes, and abruptly he tugged open the door.

It will be better tonight.

The men had gathered in the center of the village, carrying bows and arrows, large hunting knives and small axes. The blades were sharp, the arrows straight and well-fletched. During the long, dark days while the storms raged, there was nothing else to do but stay inside and hone weapons. Jareth knew the cycle. Weapons meant a kill, a kill meant food, and food meant life.

The land should have been well into late spring. The beasts of field and forests had already dropped their young. Jareth and the others had often come across small, frozen bodies that ought to have grown strong and sturdy from mother's milk and warm sunshine. And even as he mourned the deaths that should not have been, Jareth assisted the hunters as they gathered up the corpses and brought them home. Food was food.

He wondered how the bees fared. Were they all dead in their hives by now? The trees had not blossomed; there would be no flowers for them now, no fruit for humans later. Soon the villagers' stores would run out, careful as they all were with their dwindling supplies, and they would be forced to eat the seeds they had set aside to plant this year.

Rumors had reached them, from the occasional *huskaa* mad enough to wander into the valley claiming the *Huskaa* Law of hospitality. Rumors of men who had left their villages on rampages, taking others' food and leaving their bodies behind. Such things had never been heard of before. Raids on other villages? Before, Jareth would have dismissed this news as a fantastic tale, but now he could read the truth in the performer's eyes when he spoke of it.

Always in winter, someone would mention the legendary Ice Maiden. It was well and good to sing the familiar, haunting songs by a warm fire, secure in the knowledge—as they always had been before—of spring to come. But now, some were beginning to think the legends real. The seemingly eternal winter was, indeed, nothing natural. Some muttered that perhaps the Ice Maiden was behind it all.

The men were talking among themselves in quiet voices, falling silent as Jareth walked up to them. He stood tall and straight, forcing his expression to remain calm. He would not let these people know how painful their rejection was. He knew that the only reason they permitted him to accompany them was because sometimes, utterly randomly, he was able to help them. Larr gazed at him with barely disguised hatred, and Jareth wondered if he had tried to talk the others into forbidding Jareth from accompanying them entirely.

If only he knew what had happened—why he had fallen so out of favor with the gods! He had tried everything to beseech them to have mercy on his beleaguered people. He had taken to not eating his share of what little his family ate these days, secretly hoarding it to place as an offering at the foot of the oak tree that had once been his friend. Like all the villagers, weight was dropping off his powerful frame. And still, the gods' hearts were not moved.

Every time the men went forth to hunt, the task took longer and was less fruitful. Several days ago, when they had previously had a clear day, they had stumbled upon a fox gnawing the frozen carcass of a fawn. The fox's winter coat of white was long gone, and its orange and red fur was easy to spot on the white drifts. The fawn was all long legs, white spots on its brown coat marking its young age. The hunting party shot the fox, betrayed by his own red coat, and carried the fawn home. Both were eaten that night.

The animals were perhaps even harder hit than the humans by this extended winter, for they were creatures of instinct, totally dependant on the natural rhythms and cycles. Humans could choose to wear warm furs and heavy woolen cloaks, but the fox's coat had changed all on its own, contributing to its death.

This time, hours passed, yet Jareth was able to sense nothing. At last, he felt a brush of something, some faint stirring of life in this frozen realm. Rabbits, holed up in their warren. Reaching further with his mind, he realized he sensed a doe with a litter of kits. To call her would be to doom her offspring, which would mean six fewer adult rabbits in a few months.

He agonized over what to do. He could call forth the

mother and point the party to the warren, and the entire litter would be eaten tonight. He could ignore the presence of the animals, and let them continue to deal with the brutal winter as best they could, which could mean long, slow starvation. Or he could alert his companions to the rabbits and suggest they bring back the mother and her kits and raise them to eat later.

Even as the last option crossed his mind, he knew it would never happen. There was nothing for them to eat. Every scrap of food was necessary to maintain the lives of the villagers. Eleven had already died, a large number in such a small community.

Jareth made his decision. In the end, it was perhaps the most merciful one, both for the long-eared creatures as well as the humans.

Come to me, he thought, keeping his eyes closed. *We will thank you for your sacrifice. Your young will not suffer from cold, nor from terror as the teeth of a predator crunch down upon them. Come to me, and we will honor you.*

Slowly he opened his eyes and pointed to the warren's entrance, well hidden by an overhanging branch. They would never have seen it, had not Jareth known exactly where to look. The rabbit, ribs clearly visible in its mangy brown fur, emerged, trembling in the cold.

Thank you. I'm sorry.

There was the brief whine of an arrow and the rabbit spasmed. It fell over, dead at once, its scarlet lifeblood steaming on the snow.

"There are kits in the warren," Jareth said. His voice sounded harsh and raw in his ears. "We should get them, too."

It made Jareth both angry and sorrowful as the men

leaped into action. Men who would have, in a regular spring, let the doe and her kits be. Men who had children who were now growing painfully thin with each passing day.

Larr brushed past Jareth. "At least you're good for something," he muttered.

The urge to strike his childhood friend was so powerful Jareth actually surged forward a step, fist raised. A hand on his arm stopped him before he leaped upon Larr and vented his own fear, frustration and helplessness upon the other man.

"Larr is frightened," Ivo said, for Jareth's ears only. "It's why he speaks so—to hide it."

Jareth nodded as if he believed the older man. The wind picked up and he shivered, and then the snow started falling again. He looked up at the sky, so blue and clear earlier and now a dull pewter color. His heart sank.

"Storm," he said.

It was becoming alarmingly easy now to recognize the signs. The storms came so frequently they were almost a daily occurrence. The other men, shoving the squealing kits into a sack, paused and looked up. There was no time to try to make it back to the village; they'd have to shelter where they were as best they could.

Jareth looked about. They were in an open area, and the wind whistled as it buffeted him. He pointed to a small cluster of trees and a few large stones, which would provide at least some protection. Working as quickly as increasingly numb fingers would permit, they tied a length of rope about their waists. As fast as this storm was coming on, they might lose someone in the time it took to reach their paltry shelter.

The line of men struggled forward. Finally they reached the area and clung together for warmth, silent and grim, and waited. The storm seemed to go on for an eternity. Jareth completely lost track of time. All he could focus on was drawing frigid air into his lungs, filtered through a scarf; staying close to the others as the wind and snow battered against their huddled bodies. At last, well into the night, the storm died down. The sky started to clear, revealing a black sky and a sliver of moon.

Cautiously, the men got to their feet, brushing mounds of snow from their backs, heads, and shoulders. They had no more energy for words, but they all knew that it was too late to try to make it back. They would have to spend what was left of the night here. Exhausted, shivering, soaked, they lit a pathetic fire after many failed attempts and agreed to take turns feeding it. By twos, they went out to scrounge for dry kindling deep in the forest and large branches that would somewhat block wind and snow if another storm manifested during the night. Jareth didn't think it would come. He looked up at the stars, seeing them cold pinpoints of light against a soft blackness.

Toward dawn, the gods began to play in the sky. Red, blue, green, purple, the lights chased each other, turning the night sky into a riot of dancing, shimmering colors. The headman grunted.

"A good sign," he said. "If the gods are so happy they are playing for two nights in a row, perhaps they are beginning to look kindly upon us again."

Jareth thought about a group of blue tigers, chasing one another back and forth like kittens, and hoped the headman was right. Perhaps this was a sign that things would improve. Perhaps the winter would begin to retreat.

Let me know what you want me to do, he thought silently. *I have always striven to honor this gift. Why have you taken it from me?*

Well before full light, aching and exhausted, the hunting party trudged back in silence. Their tracks had been obliterated by the storm, but they knew in which direction home lay.

It was heading toward dawn when they saw the torches that marked the path toward the village, warm and golden against the purple-blue of the retreating night. Jareth's heart gladdened slightly at the sight. The rabbits they had caught were not much, but even a little meat would help to thicken a stew. He need not feel quite so helpless when he returned to his family this morning.

A figure moved in the dim light, moving quickly toward them on snow walkers.

"Jareth!"

Words of greeting died in Jareth's throat at the stricken look on Altan's face.

"Taya—" Jareth's hand shot out and seized the boy's arm, fingers digging in tightly. He pleaded silently with Altan to say *she's fine, they're all fine, don't worry.*

Altan's mouth trembled and his eyes filled with tears. "The storm—it was so violent, I went to check on them this morning—oh, gods, Jareth, I'm so sorry—"

A moment before, Jareth had been quivering with exhaustion, cold, and lack of food. Now raw, panicked energy surged through him and he began to move as quickly as the snow walkers would let him, dropping his weapons, the food sack, anything that might hinder his speed as he raced out of town and up the twining path toward his house.

He bargained with the gods as he went. *Let them be all right, and I will give you everything I have. Let them be all right, and you can take my powers away forever, all of them. Let them be all right, and I will cut open my own wrists and feed my blood to the forest.*

Let them be all right—please let them be—

The door was open. Snow had poured into the house. Someone had dug through the drift, had left tracks all around—Altan, seeing what Jareth saw, forcing his way inside—

"Taya!" screamed Jareth, his arms digging wildly at the entrance Altan had made, tunneling through the snow that had come in so quickly and so deeply—

Altan had uncovered her face.

Jareth stared as if mesmerized by the pale features that floated up through the coating of snow as if Taya were surfacing from the lake. She was almost as pale as the snow that had been her death, save for her lips which were a dark blue. He reached and touched her, found her cheek hard and cold as if she had been sculpted from stone.

Or from ice.

Her expression was oddly peaceful. How had she not woken as the storm screamed around her? Had it covered her like a lethal blanket, chilling her so slowly she never realized what had happened? How could she not have heard the wind slamming the door open, the howl as the snow rushed inside?

And then, bizarrely, all Jareth could think about for several stunned, long moments was the trembling doe rabbit and her squealing kits.

He had to see if somehow the offspring had been heartier than the mother; if perhaps Parvan had been so well swaddled in his crib he still breathed, if Annu might be coaxed back into the realm of the living. So he dug through the snow yet again, and again the reality that someone he loved was dead slammed his spirit so hard he sank down into the white stuff himself and begged the snow to take him too.

Soon Jareth lay next to his wife, holding the tiny, frozen body of his infant son to his breast. On the other side of the room, Annu lay, as still and white as if she had been carved from stone. He watched his breath curl upward as his lungs continued to function, aware he was dancing on the edge of madness and praying to the blue tiger gods who supposedly took care of his people that he would slip over that edge. He didn't want to see his breath anymore, didn't want to be reminded of the enormous gulf that separated him from his family. So he closed his eyes and drifted.

When Altan shook him some time later, frantically rubbing his icy hands and calling his name, Jareth exploded with rage. He had been about to join them, he sensed; had been about to bridge the chasm that kept the dead from the living. But he was so cold he could not move quickly, and his fingers were too numb to choke Altan as he wanted to. He let Altan wrap him in a thick blanket, let the boy he had brought into this world walk him away from the frozen bodies of two women and a baby, sipped the hot drink Altan pressed into his hand.

And began to think.

Jareth paid little heed as the men from the village came in to take the bodies away. He knew where Taya and Annu and Parvan would rest until spring came…if it ever did. The ground was too hard for the earth to take the bodies of his wife and children; they would join the others who had died this winter in a specially built building until such time as they could be buried. And from their corpses would spring new life, he knew; flowers and trees and grasses would transform dead bodies into living things. It was sacred, it was holy, it was the natural, inevitable way of things.

He frowned and started to shiver, knowing that with that uncontrollable movement life was starting to return to his body.

But *was* it the natural way of things? Jareth had been the Spring-Bringer for several years now. No one knew the power of the earth and living things better than he; no one respected those powers more. But something was...wrong about how his family had died. The winter was unnatural to begin with; it was impossible for it to have lasted so long, yet it had. No natural storm could have swept so thoroughly through the cabin to overcome two strong women so quickly, and yet it had.

And if the way they had died was not natural, perhaps Jareth need not obey the natural laws.

He thought of blue tigers, and their powers, and that the one thing he knew for certain was that life always came after death.

Jareth heard the crunching of snow and looked up. The men were bringing out Taya now. They had tried to cover her, but the body was clearly that of a woman, and too short to be Annu's.

"Wait," he said, getting clumsily to his feet. The blanket and cup of hot tea fell to the snow.

"Jareth," said Altan in a worried voice.

Jareth ignored him, moving toward the body of his wife. He touched her cold face, and reached around her slender neck to remove the pouch she always wore. He slipped it around his own neck, tucking it carefully inside his many layers of clothing with hands that did not tremble.

Don't leave me, he had cried the night they had first loved.

Never, she had answered with a kiss.

"Now you may take her," he said. The men looked surprised at how steady his voice was. Jareth turned and went back into his house. He pawed through the piled white matter like a fox, searching single-mindedly for what he wanted.

"Jareth, please, come away from there. Come stay with me, let me take care of you."

Altan's voice was like the buzzing of a fly to Jareth; noisy, irritating, and ignorable. He grunted with satisfaction when he found it: a handful of frozen dirt, which he dropped into another, larger pouch tied to his belt. Now, he turned to Altan.

"I will come," he said. Let the boy think him agreeable, accepting, ready to mourn and then begin the tortuous process of recovering.

For a moment, he regarded Altan, blazing the image into his brain. He remembered when the boy had been born, slipping into life next to his stillborn sister Ilta, whom his parents had buried, had mourned. He had watched Altan grow from an appealing little boy to a gawky youth to a handsome young man with an extraordinary talent. Altan had a good heart, if on occasion a sharp tongue, and Jareth loved him.

To Altan's surprise and his own, Jareth stepped forward and embraced him with a warmth and ease he had not been able to express to his own family. Slender and delicate, a willow to Jareth's oak, Altan tentatively returned the embrace. His head against Jareth's shoulder, he murmured, "You are always welcome in my home, Jareth. There will always be a place for you."

Jareth let Altan take him to his house, ate the food the boy prepared for him, and in general permitted the *huskaa* to think Jareth stunned, but resigned to the inevitable. It was well past the middle of the night when, reassured by the sound of regular breathing on the pallet next to him, Jareth woke and stepped quietly out the house.

Don't leave me.

Never.

Both Taya and the earth itself had promised this; both had broken their promises.

He was not going to grieve for his dead family. He was going to make the gods bring them—and Jareth's other great love, his connection with the earth—back to him.

And if the gods would not oblige, he would kill them.

6

Kevla-sha-Tahmu sat easily atop the back of the great red Dragon who had once been a god to her people. The beat of his mighty wings created a wind that caressed her body and tousled her long black hair. She stroked his scales as they sailed over the jagged peaks of the northern mountains, savoring the smoothness against her hand, content to be exactly where she was.

She glanced down at her hands, long-fingered but strong and callused. Here and there were the lighter-hued scars from countless nicks and cuts. She smiled a little as she regarded them and thought of how profoundly her life had changed.

Not so very long ago, Kevla would have been more comfortable chopping vegetables, carrying water and tending to the kitchen fires than perched atop a beast out of legend. But after hardship, fear, and the agony of devastating loss, Kevla had accepted her destiny. For perhaps the first time in her brief life, she felt calm and tranquil. At peace. Free.

Idly, she glanced down, and realized where they were heading. She frowned.

"Dragon, why do we go this way?"

"You must find the others," came the Dragon's rumbling reply. He craned his head on his long neck to look at her. "We have sensed only one thus far, and his land lies to the north."

Kevla closed her eyes, recalling her visionary dream. Again she saw the man who awaited their arrival, though perhaps he knew it not. Tall, fair-haired, clean-shaven. So different from Kevla's people, with their black hair, dark eyes and brown skin. This man's eyes were blue, and he stood on a hill covered by a white substance that seemed to resemble sand but, the Dragon had told her, was called *snow.* The thought of meeting this man, who seemed so strong and calm, who understood what they were both working toward, was thrilling. Kevla had borne her burdens alone for so long. She would be grateful to surrender them into his capable hands. Surely he would know what to do next.

But still...

"Is there not another route?" she asked. "We are flying directly over the Emperor's land!"

"I am not unaware of that," the Dragon said. A wisp of smoky annoyance rose from his nostrils. "But this is the swiftest way, and time is precious."

So are our lives, Kevla thought. Her joy in sharing this flight with her companion ebbed, replaced by apprehension. In her heart, she knew the Dragon was right. Her dream had been tinged with urgency. Time was indeed precious. And yet...

In her two decades of life, Kevla had learned to fear many things: poverty, ridicule, the seemingly senseless laws of her people and her own potentially lethal abilities. She had learned to fear death, and killing, and the excruciating pain of losing someone she loved more than anything in the world.

And she had learned to fear the man known to her only as the Emperor.

The Emperor commanded a mighty army that would have destroyed her land, had not Kevla and the Dragon stood to help defend her people. That the Emperor possessed some kind of magic, Kevla knew; that he was bent on seeing that Kevla failed in her mission to gather the other four like her, Kevla also knew.

And that was quite enough for her to not want to fly over his country.

"Dragon," she began again, glancing down as the mountains that had once presented an impassible barrier for her land gave way to hills and then rolling plains, "perhaps under cover of night, it is less likely that we would be seen."

He chuckled. It sounded like the rumble of a volcano.

"Night or day, it matters not to those who have magic, as the Emperor does. We have a long way to go yet. You received the best education Arukan had to offer, but Arukan knows nothing of what lies beyond its borders."

"And you do?" Kevla was skeptical; the Dragon had dwelt at the bottom of a volcano for five thousand years.

"This world? No. But I have known four other worlds, and the creatures in them, and I remember how long it takes to fly from north to south. The Stone Dancer is always as far from the Flame Dancer as each world allows. Think you we can find him in a single day?"

"You're a dragon," Kevla replied. "Can't you?"

"A creature of magic I am, but even I can go no faster or farther than my wings can take me. Although I do not need rest or food, you do. I will go as swiftly as I may."

Kevla sagged a little on the Dragon's back. Somehow, she had assumed the difficult part of her journey was behind her. She had endured so much; lost so much.

As always, the Dragon sensed her mood and thoughts. "I know what you have suffered," he said softly. "I wish I could simply carry you while you rested and recovered. I wish I could fulfill your destiny for you, but I cannot. I am a part of you, but I am not you, and this duty is yours alone."

"I understand," Kevla said. The burden, it would seem, was not yet to be surrendered.

Her tongue had no yearning for speech. The Dragon respected her silence, and they said nothing more until the sun began to sink slowly to their left and the sky turned deeper shades of blue and then purple.

"We will rest for the night," the Dragon said. "I will make for as safe a place as I can, in a remote area far from the cities of this land. Before I do, I must warn you, the fact that we are in his land could well strengthen the Emperor's powers, and it is certain he will be looking for us."

Kevla tensed. "Then is it wise for us to land at all?"

"We must," he replied. "You need to rest and eat and move. I will keep watch while you sleep, never fear. But you must not use any of your Dancer abilities. Magic calls to magic. If you would protect yourself while we are in his realm, quiet your mind. He's trying to sense you, right now. I can feel it. We know he knows about you. But he may not know about the others yet. You must not be the one to inform him."

Kevla's heart sped up; the exact opposite of what the Dragon needed her to do. A strange bubble of mirth welled inside her. She bit it back, but she wondered if the Dragon appreciated how difficult it was to do as he had requested.

She was not to think about the man they were seeking. So instead, as the Dragon tucked his mammoth body with startling grace and headed for the earth, she deliberately thought about something else.

Kevla summoned an image that would do no harm to her or anyone if somehow the Emperor were to read her thoughts. She thought about her time as a servant in the House of Four Waters. Her mind was filled with the tasks that had occupied her days: massaging the feet of Yeshi, the great lord's wife, cutting vegetables, carrying water from the vast caverns that never ran dry. Everyday, ordinary things.

The earth approached quickly. They left a sky crowded with stars to descend on a grassy plain. Kevla slipped off her friend's back and her knees buckled as she hit the earth.

Her laughter surprised her. "I guess I did need to move," she admitted, rubbing life back into her numb limbs. Her bladder was full and her belly empty, and she had to acknowledge the wisdom of her friend. She might be a powerful woman, but her body was no more and no less than human, and it had its own needs.

The Dragon had set them down near a small stream. Kevla stood for a moment, marveling at the casual ease with which this land bestowed water. In Arukan, water was more precious than gold. Her clan, the Clan of Four Waters, held much of its power because it controlled a key position at the juncture of the country's two largest rivers. But here, the grass was green and the water flowed freely, unaware of how rare and special it seemed to her.

She knelt and splashed her face. It revived her, and made her think of her daily baths in the caverns at the House of Four Waters. She had left an Arukan where the clans had united against the Emperor's army instead of fighting one another, where many of the old, crippling ways were being discarded. She hoped this progress would continue.

Kevla drank deeply, and refilled the waterskins her old friend Sahlik had packed for her. Her throat closed up tightly as memories washed over her, memories of the elderly head servant who had done what she could to make Kevla's existence at the House of Four Waters bearable. Sahlik had even seen to it that Kevla and—

No. I mustn't think of him. I don't know the extent of the Emperor's powers and he might sense it.

Quickly, she got to her feet and headed back to where the Dragon lay. He had stretched out to his full length, and not for the first time, Kevla marveled at him. She had feared him once. He had haunted her dreams and terrorized her, but only because she didn't understand who and what she was. Now she did, and the Dragon seemed to her the most devoted of creatures despite his enormous bulk and powerful teeth and claws. Not to mention the sheets of flame he could breathe at a thought.

That did not frighten her, for she, too, could summon fire at will.

Kevla plopped down beside her friend and opened her pack. She reached in and pulled out a loaf of bread wrapped in cloth and inhaled the scent deeply. Her mouth watered.

"You were right," she said, "I'm famished. It was so good of Sahlik to pack some food for me. I didn't even think about it, and I'd—"

The words died in her throat. Curious, the Dragon inclined his massive head to see what had silenced her so abruptly.

"What is it, Kevla?" he asked.

Kevla held a wooden board. It had been painted with interlocking circles of white and black, with the overlapping areas painted gray. There was a large pouch still sitting in the pack. Her heart raced and she had difficulty breathing.

Shamizan. Sahlik had packed a *Shamizan* set. She had known how much Kevla and the young lord of the House of Four Waters had enjoyed playing it when they were children, and no doubt, the old woman had likely thought that a set would comfort Kevla. She was suddenly plunged back in time as she stared at the board, remembering her first encounter with the game.

"Can you play Shamizan?*" he had asked.*

"What is Shamizan?*" His eyes lit up. For the first time since she had known him, Kevla thought that he looked like a boy her own age, not a small adult. "Oh, it's so much fun! Let me go get my set—"*

He rose and ran out of the hut, returning only a few moments later, flushed and out of breath. Kevla suspected he had run the entire way. Hardly proper behavior for a future khashim, *but it was good to see him so happy.*

"It's easy to learn."

Easy to learn, hard to stop, *Kevla thought. At one point, she looked up from the board and saw the* khashimu *regarding her with an intent gaze. His face dissolved into delight as she ducked her head and smiled.*

"You like the game, then?"

"Oh, yes, very much."

"I am so glad. I hoped you would."

Kevla could no longer hold the memories at bay: the memories of what they had been to one another, how they had loved…how he had died.

Even then, even when we were too young to understand it, we loved each other.

Kevla clutched the board to her breasts for a long moment. She wanted to scream, to rage, but somehow held on to sufficient sense to deny the almost overwhelming urge. They were in danger every moment they were in this land, and shrieking and shouting her grief could attract unwanted attention.

Kevla got to her feet. She hurled the wooden board as far away from her as she could, grunting with the effort. Fumbling with the drawstring, she reached into the pouch. Her shaking fingers closed on dozens of small, round, polished pieces of glass. She threw them into the distance as well, tears pouring in stony silence down her face. Then she collapsed against the strong side of the Dragon, burying her face in her hands as her shoulders shook.

He said nothing to try to comfort her; he knew well enough that nothing would. Time stretched endlessly, the pain not subsiding, the memories raw and fresh. She did not have many of them; the time a Bai-sha servant girl and the heir of the Clan could steal together was limited. Each memory was precious. Each touch, each word, from her first startled encounter with him as their eyes locked at a feast to those ecstatic yet horrifying last moments together, from their whispered conversations and dreams of dragons and shadowed other lives—

Something soft and dark as a shadow brushed her mind. *Yes, that's right. Think of your Lorekeeper. What did he tell you?*

Kevla gasped. The bittersweet memories shattered like a glass goblet falling upon stone. The Emperor was in her thoughts, crawling and scratching like a mouse in the granaries, digging busily for what he wanted to know—

"Don't let him in, Kevla!" cried the Dragon, startling her out of her stunned horror. "Think of something useless to him! Quickly, tell me how you would treat an insect sting!"

"Rub it with garlic, and then apply a white clay poultice." The mundane information calmed her, and she felt the mental probing lessen slightly.

"Good, good. How would you prepare *eusho?*"

Kevla dutifully recited the elaborate steps that went into preparing the hot, bitter drink.

No! I have you. You're in my *land now.*

The attack changed. The Emperor was no longer burrowing into her mind, but her heart. She clawed between her own breasts, as if she could get to her heart and keep it safe before—

"Fire!" cried the Dragon.

Still pressing her hands on her chest, Kevla envisioned her heart surrounded by walls of flame. Warmth flooded back into her being. There was a harsh, searing pain in her temples. Then suddenly, unexpectedly, she was free, and she sucked air into her lungs in a great gasp.

She sighed deeply and slumped forward. She felt the sides of the Dragon heave with relief as well.

"That was close," he said. "We are lucky he did not expect to encounter you again so soon. He would have been better prepared."

Kevla's voice shook as she spoke. "I should not have thought of him." She could not bring herself to speak the name, but knew the Dragon would know whom she meant. "I could have revealed everything he had told me. He would be so disappointed in me if he—if he were still alive."

"I think not," said the Dragon, in as gentle a voice as so powerful a being could manage. "I think he would be very proud of you."

Kevla's stomach growled. She laughed shakily, wiping at her wet face. Clearly, her body didn't care about Emperors or Lorekeepers or love or duty, it just wanted food. Almost everything Sahlik had packed was dried and would travel well. Kevla would not need a fire to cook, and after what had happened, she wasn't about to light one. She thought it would be like setting up a beacon.

She chewed on a strip of dried meat and washed it down with water. It tasted like sand in her mouth, but she forced herself to choke it down. The bread was a little easier, still soft and fresh. After she had eaten, she felt better; calmer, more in control. She sighed, then stood.

"Where are you going?" asked the Dragon.

"To collect the *Shamizan* pieces," she replied.

"It's dark."

"I don't care. It's all I have left of him."

"In the morning. When there is light."

She could not argue the logic of that, although she ached

to have all the pieces once again safely in their bag. It had been foolish of her to hurl them away in a fit of anger; foolish, too, to want to keep them so badly. She leaned against the Dragon's warm, gently moving side. As the waning moon began its path across a sky crowded with stars, Kevla realized this was the first night she had spent away from her homeland. The thought was at once exciting, sorrowful, and frightening.

She had put both them and their quest in jeopardy by surrendering to her emotions. She would not make that mistake again.

She looked at the stars, her eyelids growing heavy. She would be like the stars, she thought; doing what they needed to do, shining above the world, above its cares and sorrows and trials. Kevla-sha-Tahmu flew on the back of the great red Dragon. She would do what she needed to do from that lofty perch. The earth and its pains would have no hold on her. She and the Dragon were flying north, to join with another like her, one with more experience, who could lead from now on. She knew what he looked like, had seen the blend of strength and kindness in his strong, milk-pale face.

She slept at last, and had no dreams.

7

Kevla winced as she moved stiff limbs and sat upright. Her hand came down on something wet and she jerked it back.

"What..." She looked at her hand, covered with small droplets, and realized her *rhia* was damp as well. "Dragon, there is water on the grass."

As Kevla got to her feet, the Dragon too, rose and stretched, extending one leg and then the other like a gigantic cat. He chuckled slightly and Kevla blushed, embarrassed.

"I do not laugh at your ignorance, dear one, only your endearing inexperience. That is called *dew*. At night, water collects on the ground, and in the morning, with the heat of the day, it disappears."

Kevla rubbed the little miracle between her fingers. Water,

just manifesting on the ground like that. "Is this part of the Emperor's magic?"

"No, it is simply how the world works here. You have just begun to experience how different things will seem to you. Arukan was cut off from others by the mountains, and unlike some lands, there was no trade with those from foreign places. Arukan doesn't even have tales of anywhere else."

Kevla gingerly touched her tongue to her finger. The Dragon was right—it *was* water. She felt her lips curve in a smile of delight.

The Dragon looked around, his golden eyes scanning the horizon. "I'm not sensing him, are you?"

Kevla's delight vanished, much as the Dragon predicted the dew would vanish with the arrival of the sun. Her childlike enjoyment of the water that seemed to bead on every single blade of grass was forgotten as she, too, became alert. Nervously, she opened her thoughts, trying to sense the enemy in whose realm they were trespassing.

"No," she said, aware that her voice sounded tense and heavy. "But I'm not sure what I should be trying to sense."

His mighty head turned this way and that. His nostrils flared and a thin stream of smoke issued forth. "There is no mistaking it if you had sensed him. Nonetheless, we had best not linger."

Kevla swallowed hard. "I suppose there isn't time for me to gather the pieces, then." *I deserve it for being so foolish,* she thought.

"Of course there is time," he said. "And I will help you."

Kevla reached up and hugged his neck.

Fortunately, the small glass pieces caught the early morning light and were not as difficult to find as she had feared.

Still, it took time. The Dragon's eyes were sharper than hers by far, but there was no way his mammoth claws could close over so tiny an item. He told her where to look and she picked up the pieces. Each time her fingers closed about the cool, smooth glass, she felt a pang of loss and remembered joy. It would have been sweet to abandon the pain associated with this game, but that would be to abandon the memory of the one she had loved with all her heart. And it was simply not possible for her to do that.

The sun rose higher in the sky, but at last, all of the pieces, nearly a hundred of them, were safely in the leather sack. Kevla looked longingly at the stream, wanting to step into its depths for a quick bath, but she knew they had tarried here too long as it was. Tearing off a hunk of bread to eat on the way, she climbed atop the Dragon's back.

The two companions of Fire fell into a rhythm. During the day, the Dragon would make great progress, flying with only occasional stops so Kevla could stretch and grab a quick bite of food, and at night, they would come to earth so that she might seize a few hours of sleep. With each day that passed, Kevla wrestled with a new tumult of emotions. She was happy to be embarking on a journey; she missed the life she had known. She was calm and free, soaring above it all; she grieved for the man who had called her his soul. She looked forward to surrendering the burden of the quest to this stranger from the North; she shrank from meeting someone so alien to her.

The land changed as they traveled. Though Kevla never truly felt cold, it was easy to tell that the climate of the Emperor's land was not that of the desert. The yellowed, grassy plains of the first night gave way to rich green meadows starred with flowers that looked to Kevla's eyes like scattered jewels. Two nights after that, the Dragon landed in the only clearing in the midst of an uncountable number of trees.

Kevla dismounted, noticing that her feet landed on a soft carpet of discarded leaves. "I have never seen so many trees in a single place before, not even the groves."

"The term used to describe such a large amount of trees is *forest,*" the Dragon explained.

Slightly dazed by the size and health of the trees—in Arukan, only fruit trees were cultivated and therefore flourished; all others were stunted, twisted things—she walked among them and touched their trunks. There were many different varieties, and their leaves were a riot of colors. Gold, red, orange, yellow—

"And I suppose you will tell me that this wonder, too, is not part of the Emperor's magic?" she challenged the Dragon.

"No magic. Arukan is a desert country. The changes are infrequent—a rainstorm now and then, or times when it is hotter or cooler than others. Here, and in places like this, change is much more vigorous. Most places have four seasons—spring, when growth is new, summer, when growth flourishes, autumn, when there is a harvest of summer's bounty, and winter, a time when everything lies dormant and still."

Kevla shook her head in wonderment as she plucked a golden leaf and twirled it between her fingers. "It is hard for my head to hold all this, but my eyes do not lie." She frowned as she mulled over something the Dragon had said.

"I can see how people would flourish in a place that has

so much growth," she said. "But this last season—this winter. It is not good, is it?"

"It's not necessarily bad, but it is not a fruitful time. Everything goes to sleep. No crops grow, nor does fruit ripen on the tree. The animals have a difficult time finding food, as do people. Some animals fatten themselves up and sleep away the winter in a cave rather than face its harshness."

"How does anyone survive this winter?"

"They know it is coming, and they plan for it. They harvest and store food."

"Like we do when the men go on raids," said Kevla.

"Exactly. Then, when the spring comes, they plant new crops, and the cycle begins again."

Kevla smiled a little. There was something about this cycle, this sense of rhythm and steadiness, that she found comforting. Her land knew only the desert. As the Dragon had said, there were periods of flooding, cooler and warmer times, and the occasional sandstorm, but overall there was a sameness about the days and months that she only now realized was...dull.

She walked among the trees, touching the thick, soft green growth that the Dragon told her was *moss,* trying to reach her arms around a tree only to find that it was too big and therefore very old indeed. Some of the trees did not have leaves that turned color; instead their leaves took the form of needles and their scent was intoxicating, almost overwhelming.

"If the Arukani oilcrafters could capture this scent," Kevla told the Dragon, bringing a branch to her nose and inhaling deeply, "their fortunes would be assured."

That night, she dreamed. She was at a feast, in the hall of

the Clan of Four Waters. Kevla had witnessed many such feasts in her life, but always before, she had sat behind the *khashima* she served, veiled and silent, eating only after her mistress had eaten, lifting bites of food under the veil for delicate nibbles no matter how hungry she might be.

This time, she sat in the center of the low table of dark, polished wood in a place of honor. She had no veil, and realized that this meant she was the highest-ranking female present. She reclined upon embroidered silk cushions, and knew without looking that she had her own servants sitting silently behind her. The fare was lavish—roasted meat and fowl rubbed with aromatic herbs and glazed with honey, fresh bread to sop up the juices, succulent fruits with flesh that was ripe and red, dates and olives and all manner of other delicacies.

Kevla ate and ate, laughing and talking with ease and grace, as if this was the life she had been born to live, not that of a Bai-sha child, illegitimate and unwanted. In the background she heard music, as noisy and vibrant as the feasters.

On her right was the *khashim* of the Clan, Tahmu-kha-Rakyn. Tall and strong, with aquiline features and curly black hair that still bore no touch of gray, he looked upon her with affection, and now and then reached to touch her face in a paternal gesture. There was an ease between them that had never existed in the waking world, and somehow Kevla knew that she was living the life she would have if Tahmu, her father, had claimed her as his daughter when she was a child.

She kept her eyes on Tahmu, because she sensed who was sitting to her left, and even in this dream state Kevla could not bear to look upon him. She felt his hand, tender and gentle, brush her hair back, felt sweet warm breath on her neck, and closed her eyes. It was a dream, but it was so precious. She never wanted to awaken.

I have forgotten much, Flame Dancer, her beloved whispered. His lips nuzzled the tender spot where earlobe joined neck. She trembled, but would not open her eyes. *Tell me. Tell me—*

She could deny him nothing. She never had been able to, and in this lovely dream that she yet knew was a dream, she parted her lips to tell him what he wanted to know.

Her eyes flew open in the dream as the table burst into flames. The heat and brightness caused her to cry out, to throw up her hands—

And Kevla awoke fully to feel the Dragon breathing a sheet of flame upon her. It did not hurt her, for she was flame herself. But she realized with a jolt of terror as she lowered her hands from her face what had happened.

The Emperor had violated her dreams. He had pretended to be Jashemi, her Lorekeeper, her love, and was trying to get her to reveal everything she knew.

The Dragon crouched. Kevla seized the pack and scrambled atop her friend's back, clinging to him as he sprang into the air with more speed than she had ever experienced. Her stomach lurched and she almost lost her grip.

"We will not stop again until we are clear of the Emperor's land," the Dragon cried. "This attack was stronger than the ones before. One more night and he might have you."

Kevla was furious. How dare the Emperor use her precious memories of the man she loved like that! She trembled as she clutched the Dragon, but not with fear, not this time.

Instead of trying to shield her thoughts, she gathered them together and hurled them like a weapon against the face-less, nameless enemy.

You will not break me! You will not get what you want from me! And you will never, never again use my love for him against me!

She summoned fire in her mind; called it into roiling flames and aimed it directly at her attacker. To her own surprise, she felt him recoil, stumble back, withdraw overhastily from her mind.

Another tried to touch her mind now; another whose mental touch was loving and welcome. *Well done, Flame Dancer,* came the Dragon's thoughts. *Well done indeed. He will think twice before bothering us again.*

Yet I would still rather not set foot in his lands again, Kevla thought, finding this method of communication easier with the wind whipping her hair and howling around her ears. The Emperor's realm had seemed so pleasant, so peaceful, yet now she shuddered at the thought of her bare feet on the soil, of searching for the colored stones that represented Jashemi.

As you wish, the Dragon replied in her mind. *But if you decide otherwise, I will set down.*

No, and her own vehemence shocked her. *Not if I were dying.*

Wisely, the Dragon did not reply. Kevla settled down on his back, stretching her whole body down on the space between the spinal ridges, and clasped him.

While she did not sleep, the rest of the trip took on a dreamy, timeless air. The winds died down and eventually only a gentle breeze caressed her body and played with her hair. The Dragon flew steadily, his wings beating a soothing rhythm, and Kevla permitted her mind to drift.

"Kevla," said the Dragon. "Look down."

Kevla blinked and yawned, aware that the sun was starting to clear the horizon. She obeyed the Dragon's request, glanced sleepily down—and gasped. The world beneath her was white. The white expanse stretched as far as she could see. The only relief came in the form of dark patches of forest.

"Snow!" she cried, recalling the Dragon telling her about this water that had turned so cold it had become a new substance entirely. "It must be snow!" Kevla gazed in delight as the rosy colors of dawn transformed the world beneath her.

"It's so beautiful," she breathed. "I've never seen anything like it. No, wait," she corrected herself. "This reminds me of some stones I saw once in the market. They were white and solid, but caught the light as this does when held just so. Oh, Dragon, what is that?"

She pointed at something that looked like a silver snake twining through the vast expanse of white.

"I would say it is a river, but—"

"It is," the Dragon said, "but it is frozen solid. It is now almost as hard as the stone you mentioned."

"This is a marvel," breathed Kevla. "And look, there are so many trees! But—their leaves are all gone. They look like skeletons," she said, her voice dropping on the last word.

She was silent for a minute, drinking it all in. The more she saw of the landscape unfolding beneath her, the more uneasy she became. She thought again of the man she had come here to find. What would he be like? How would she find common ground with someone so inherently different from all she had known?

"I wonder what kind of people live in such a place?" she murmured. "People who are aware of these seasons, and plan for them. People who know heat and cold and rain and snow, and not the sand and heat and sameness of the desert."

The Dragon chuckled, and folded his wings slightly. "You're about to find out," he said, and dove.

The harsh crimson glow that bathed the Emperor's face was fading, replaced by the gentle orange light from the crackling fire. The advisor to the Emperor glanced from his lord to the black-clad figure who stood behind the Emperor. Gloved hands dug into the Emperor's shoulders for a moment, then released their grasp.

The advisor shrank back as his lord emerged from his trance. After two such definitive and humiliating setbacks, he was convinced that the Emperor would be in a black mood.

Instead, he sighed heavily and reached for a goblet of wine with a hand that trembled. With the other, he grasped the hovering object that had enabled him to have such access to the Flame Dancer. At once, the scarlet object, round at its base and tapered at the tip like the drop of blood it so resembled, settled into his hand, all its magic now quiescent. At the Emperor's feet, as ever, crouched the ki-lyn. Was it the advisor's imagination, or did the beautiful, captive beast look pleased?

"That," said the Emperor heavily, running his thumb absently over the smooth red surface of the object, "was not the success I had envisioned." Carefully, he replaced the goblet on the table next to him.

"Regretful, my lord," the advisor said, his gaze flickering

from the Emperor's face to where that of the Mage should have been...if he'd had one.

"I thought I had the chance, when she was here, but..." His voice trailed off and he dangled the fingers of his free hand to stroke the ki-lyn. It tried to duck from his touch, but when the chain about its elegant neck prevented the movement, it endured the caressing.

"You are not yet as familiar with the tool you are using as you might be, Your Excellency," said the Mage in the cold voice that made the advisor's skin crawl. "Give it time."

"I am certain that my lord has other plans," lied the advisor.

"You would be correct, my old friend," said the Emperor calmly. "She has gone beyond my direct influence now, that much is true. But I am not without my servants in other lands. Servants who crave what I have to offer, whose minds are molded to my way of thinking." He looked at his advisor beneath lowered lashes and suddenly laughed. "Come, you expect me to have revealed everything?"

"If I may speak frankly—yes, my liege," replied the advisor somewhat testily. "I am after all your advisor. How may I advise you properly if you do not tell me everything?"

The look was no longer surreptitious. The Emperor stared at him boldly, and inwardly, the advisor quailed. But he stood firm. He did not dare show signs of weakness, not to this ultimate predator. The Emperor respected only strength and power.

"Those who know too much could pose a threat," the Emperor said, his voice deceptively mild. "But trust me, old friend." He dropped his gaze to the object the Mage called the Tenacru, *staring at his reflection in the glossy surface as if entranced by it.*

"I have allies you cannot imagine. Allies that are bound to

*me by the most primal of emotions—love and grief. Some al-
lies that don't even know they are allies."*

   His lips curved in a smile that chilled the advisor. For a moment, the advisor's gaze flickered to the large, sensitive eyes of
the imprisoned ki-lyn, and he read in those limpid depths a reflection of his own fear.

8

The white surface seemed to surge to meet them. Despite her trust in the mighty creature, Kevla found her fingers clutching a spiny ridge on the Dragon's back. She need not have worried; the Dragon came to earth as softly as a feather falling, his landing muffled by this white stuff called snow.

The Dragon had warned her that the snow was cold to the touch, but Kevla knew that it would not chill her, as it would others. She was always warm, no matter where she was or what she was wearing. It was something that had been granted to her with the onset of her power. Still, she was not prepared for the sensation of the snow on her skin as she slid off the Dragon's back.

It was indeed cold, and— "It's wet!" she yelped accusingly at the Dragon. He threw back his enormous head and laughed. "You did that deliberately!" She was thigh-deep in the white wetness, and the more she tried to brush it off, the wetter it—and she—became.

"No, I did not do it deliberately," the Dragon chuckled. "But I confess, it's amusing to watch you."

She eyed him, not pacified by his comment. "It's fine for you, it barely covers your toes. How am I to walk in this? I thought it was like sand, but instead it turns to water."

Water. "I know the people here suffer under this winter you speak of, but to me they seem rich. To have this much water simply lying on the fields and hillside...." Her voice trailed off as she took in the stark beauty. "A *khashim* would lead many a raid for this treasure."

"What is valuable depends on the time and place," the Dragon said. "Ten thousand gold coins mean nothing to a man starving alone in the wilderness. And water covering every surface does not mean much when everything it covers is dead. The people of this land may never thirst, Kevla, but it is likely that they are cold and hungry."

Kevla was becoming used to the heavy wetness of the snow, and now she noticed something else: the profound silence. She had been slogging through the white stuff, her *rhia* becoming increasingly soaked and heavy, but now she paused, listening. There were no bird calls. The wind did not stir the branches.

"It's so quiet," she said, her voice dropping to a whisper, reluctant to thrust the sound of speech upon this silence. She gasped. "My breath—I can see it!"

"So now you can breathe smoke, too," the Dragon joked. She smiled at him, grateful for the little jest.

The snow bowed down the still-green, needled trees and limned every branch of the skeleton trees. As she stood observing, her breath coming in small white puffs, she felt small, cool pricks on her skin. She looked up, and as the snow kissed her face, she realized that it came from the sky, like the rare rain in Arukan. Kevla bent and scooped up a handful, tasting it, feeling it dissolve on her tongue. She stood in the falling snow, taking in the bowed trees, the dim light and the shadows of the deep forest. The silence seemed to swallow her voice when she spoke.

"I don't like it here, Dragon, plentiful water or no. I want to find the other Dancer quickly and move on."

"That may be harder than you think," the Dragon said. "You were able to sense that he was in the North, but thus far, that is all we know. We are in the North, Kevla, and we are discovering that it is a large place indeed."

Her spirits sank even lower. "How *are* we to find him, then?"

"Try to remember, Kevla." He looked at her intently. "You've done this before. The strongest bonds are between a Dancer, her Lorekeeper, and her Companion animal, because they form a complete whole. But all the Dancers have a connection with one another. Jashemi would have been able to sense the Stone Dancer, to feel him more strongly because he was a Lorekeeper. Such was his duty. But you can do some of that yourself, as can I. You were quite good at it once. Keep trusting in your ability to sense him. Practice reaching out to him. Listen when a little voice says, go this way. The Dancers are unique in this world. Their abilities would be known. Someone will be able to point us in the right direction."

The Dragon's reassurance heartened her somewhat, but even so, the enormity of the task was intimidating. She leaned against a tree trunk. Absently she ran her hands over its white bark with curly, rough patches of a darker hue.

"This is not Arukan, with its open stretches of desert," she said. "This is a land with dark forests and hidden places. We will not be able to learn much from the air, Dragon, and if this forest is any indication, you are too large to walk between the trees."

He narrowed his golden eyes. "Let us fly, and see what we can see, and feel what we can feel, before you give up."

Her eyes flashed. "I'm not giving up!"

"Good. Because for a moment there, it certainly sounded as if you had."

"You know me better than that."

His scrutinizing gaze softened. "Indeed I do," he said. "Come. Climb aboard my back, and let us find the people who dwell in such a harsh place."

She was relieved to leave the ground, to be safely in the air once again, away from the wet snow and the dim forest and the eerie silence. Seated atop the Dragon, Kevla wrung out the sodden *rhia* and with a thought, dried it. They continued on, no longer flying directly north this time. The Dragon flew in a search pattern, lower to the ground, so that they had every opportunity of finding places where people might dwell. Kevla tried to extend her thoughts, to sense the Stone Dancer as the Dragon had told her she could, but all she could feel was an oncoming headache from concentrating so hard.

She abandoned the attempt and concentrated on scouring the landscape that unfurled beneath her. She realized that she didn't even know what they were looking for.

"What kind of dwellings should we be watching for?"

"What is the greatest resource here?" replied the Dragon, answering one question with another.

"Snow," she joked, then added more seriously, "trees. They probably build their shelter out of trees." Now that she thought about it, she supposed that wood would make an adequate building material, though no one in Arukan had ever done so. No one was *rich* enough to do so. Not even the Clan of Four Waters could afford to throw away gold on wooden housing when stone was more plentiful and easy to quarry.

"And if they make their homes out of trees," she continued, working it out in her mind, "we should look for clearings where it appears that trees have been harvested."

The Dragon lowered his right wing and swerved. "I think I saw such a clearing a few leagues to the east."

They were flying over open land now, away from the forests and rivers. Within a few moments, Kevla saw small dwellings. As she had surmised, they appeared to be made of wood.

"There," she cried, pointing. "Over there. To your left."

"I see them," the Dragon replied. "Let us hope they are in a mood to welcome visitors."

The houses were clustered together at the edge of the forest, but the Dragon had been right—there was a large clearing where several small lumps bulged beneath the snow. *Probably the trunks of the mighty trees, felled to create the shelters,* thought Kevla. She was both nervous and excited as she slid from the Dragon's back into the snow. But as soon as she approached the first house, she felt hope die inside her.

The houses were constructed of logs from the white,

slender, straight trees Kevla had observed earlier. The timbers had been cut and arranged atop one another so that they interlocked well, and what chinks remained had been stuffed with some kind of daubing material. But now that she was closer, she could see what she hadn't been able to see from the air—that the roofs, covered with the bark of the slender white trees and what appeared to be chunks of sod, were in great need of repair. In some areas, they had collapsed.

No one had dwelt in these houses for a long time. Apprehension building inside her, Kevla drew nearer. The doors, heavy wooden things that bore intricate carvings, had either been left open or had come off completely. Some still had metal locks attached to them. Over time, the snow had intruded inside, an unwelcome guest, to almost completely fill the space.

Kevla stepped inside and looked around. The snow had drifted deep and high, covering everything. The only light came from the open door and through the slats of the shutters that covered a single, small window. Here and there, shapes swelled, enveloped by snow. Kevla brushed snow from one such lump, her hands finding the hard curve of a small wooden stool. The walls were bare, and the entire place spoke of abandonment and desertion.

"Well?" the Dragon asked as she emerged.

"The houses are filled with snow. Perhaps people tired of the harshness of...of winter and traveled south, where it is not so bitter."

"A possibility," agreed the Dragon. "Did you find anything inside?"

Kevla inhaled swiftly. "Yes. Furniture," she said softly as

the full impact of the realization swept through her. "They left their furniture."

She and the Dragon regarded each other. The unspoken question hung between them: If these people had left of their own accord, wouldn't they have taken their furnishings with them?

Kevla knew what she had to do. Dreading what she now suspected she'd find, she reentered the house.

She concentrated on the snow piled so thickly and gave a mental command. Like water slowly receding from the bank of the Nur River, the snow obeyed her, melting and running in warmed rivulets over her feet and out the door. And slowly, inexorably, the horror was revealed to Kevla's gaze.

Some of the lumps were indeed furniture, like the stool she had touched. But the others...

"Kevla, what do you see?" asked the Dragon.

"They...they didn't leave," she said in a trembling voice. "They're still here."

Six of them sprawled on the bedding and floor. Two men, three women, and one child, bodies emerging from the blanket of snow that had mercifully hidden them. Kevla's first thought was that somehow they had frozen to death, but as the snow melted, it began to turn red. Blood once frozen began to thaw and drip from wounds that gaped like open mouths. As Kevla stared, unable to tear her gaze away, she saw that the corpse of one of the women had been hacked nearly in two.

She backed out the door quickly, almost running into the Dragon. She looked up at him, knowing her face told him more than her words would.

"Marauders found them," Kevla rasped. "They were—they were killed."

"When the land does not provide enough to eat," the Dragon said in a low voice, "some take what they need from others. By any means they can." He craned his neck and looked around. "There are other lumps in the snow out here as well. More victims, I would think."

Kevla looked where he had indicated and shuddered. "Are the men who did this still in the area?" Kevla asked. She was torn between apprehension and a furious desire to exact revenge for the brutality she had witnessed.

The Dragon sniffed the air. "No living flesh is nearby." He frowned. "I have seen no tracks, either. Not so much as a squirrel's."

Kevla was too agitated to ask what a *squirrel* might be. She tried to calm herself, pressing her hands to her temples and breathing slowly and deeply.

"If the Stone Dancer was ever here, he is not now. I think—I think I would know if any of the other Dancers were dead."

"You and I would not be here if any of the others were dead," said the Dragon. "The Shadow comes with haste, once a champion of the world has fallen."

Kevla looked at her friend. "The bodies are thawing," she said, surprised at how calm she sounded. "We need to burn them."

The Dragon shook his head. "We don't have time," he said. "We must press on."

"No," Kevla said quietly. "They deserve to have their remains respected. I would imagine there are predators in these woods, similar to the desert dogs or *simmars*. I won't have these people gnawed on like—" A wave of nausea washed over her, but she forced it back. "Will you help me or must I do this by myself?"

The Dragon sighed. "Let us be about it quickly, then."

The Dragon had been right. When Kevla melted the snow in the clearing, several more victims were revealed. She went into each house, melting the snow she found within. Every dwelling had its share of corpses. Her heart breaking for them, she gathered pieces of furniture and piled them in the center of the clearing. The Dragon removed the roofs from the little houses, gently brought forth the butchered bodies and placed them on the pyre. As she worked, Kevla realized that there was at least some comfort to be taken. She was in the right place to find the Stone Dancer, for each body that was piled atop the pyre had milky pale skin and tresses as yellow as the desert sand of Arukan.

"So many," Kevla murmured. "They must have killed everyone in the village."

She walked toward the pyre and gazed at the broken bodies with compassion. "This is probably not your rite for the dead," she said aloud, as if they could somehow hear her. "But I won't leave you for carrion. May the winds carry you to whatever gods you believe in."

She closed her eyes, extended her hands, and thought: *Burn.*

With a *whumph,* the pyre exploded into flames. For a moment, Kevla watched the crackling, curling fire, recalling how she had lit a similar pyre not so long ago for her own people, after the battle with the Emperor.

"You have done what you needed to do here. We must go."

She nodded, knowing the Dragon was right, but for a moment unable to stop staring at the conflagration. The often-pleasant scent of burning wood was becoming tainted with the stench of flesh as the bodies began to be consumed. Kevla deliberately turned away, and once again climbed atop the Dragon's back.

They found nothing else the rest of the day, and the night seemed to come on more quickly than usual. When Kevla commented on this, the Dragon said, "We are continuing to travel north, and it is winter. The sun does not shine strongly now, and night lasts many hours. In some places it lasts for months."

As he came to earth, the sun slipped below the horizon. Kevla slid off into the snow and realized that there was no place that was not piled high with the stuff.

"I cannot sleep on wet snow," she said, hearing how petulant her voice sounded in her own ears.

"The trees keep the snow from falling on the earth in the forests," the Dragon said. "You can pile up some branches and make yourself quite a comfortable bed."

Her *rhia* was again soaked. The slender straps of leather that served her for sandals were utterly insufficient to the task of walking through the drifts. She stared at him, her arms folded tightly across her breasts, knowing that she looked like a lost child. It was not altogether inappropriate; after what she had experienced, she felt like one. It was a strange feeling. She had hardly had a sheltered childhood, calling for men to come and pay to visit her mother's bed, and she had negotiated the tricky intricacies of Clan politics successfully for many years. But this—the combination of being away from everything she knew, the strange, sinister aspect of this snow-draped land, and the corpses she had seen had unnerved her, and for the first time in a long time, she felt vulnerable. The strength of will that had enabled her to build a pyre and burn the bodies had long since ebbed. She was physically exhausted, emotionally drained, and hungry. Again she wished they would find the Stone Dancer quickly, so that she could step back into the supportive role she was more comfortable with.

The Dragon trundled over to some trees, snapped off huge branches as if they were twigs, and shook them free of their blankets of snow. He then cleared an area and arranged the branches. Curling himself around the pile, he said, "Come then, little one. Sleep next to me."

The branches were hard and their needles jabbed her, but Kevla uttered no word of complaint. She would rather sleep next to her companion on a pile of stones than in a soft down bed in the ominous forest.

Now that they were out of the Emperor's demesne, Kevla felt it safe to light a fire. It sprang to cheerful life, burning brightly despite the wetness of the wood, and Kevla found comfort in its yellow-orange flames.

She could do more than summon flame; she could scry in it, or use it to transport her from her fire to that of another's. A thought occurred to her.

"I'm going to see if I can locate the Dancer." If she could see him, she could speak to him—and find him.

"Excellent idea," rumbled the Dragon, leaning his head in for a better view.

Kevla gazed into the fire, letting her gaze soften. "Show me the Stone Dancer," she said.

Nothing. The fire did not change. Disappointment knifed

through Kevla. Somehow, she had simply assumed she would be able to locate him.

"He may not have built a fire yet," the Dragon pointed out.

"It's getting dark," Kevla retorted, frustration making her words sharper than she had intended. "Surely there is a fire in his home by now."

"And he may simply not be beside it," the Dragon continued reasonably. "Your powers are great, Flame Dancer, and they will only increase as you perfect them. But even they have limits."

Kevla sighed and rubbed at eyes that had seen too much today. "You speak sense, Dragon. But still, I had hoped…"

He bent down and brushed his chin against the top of her head in as gentle a nuzzle as he could manage. "Keep hoping."

The next day, they saw more clearings. Kevla and the Dragon both tried to extend their senses, and listen for the "little voice" of which the Dragon had spoken. At first, she sensed nothing, only the stillness and emptiness of winter. But when they flew over a clearing which boasted a small cluster of houses, something inside Kevla jumped. Her heart sped up as she remembered what she had beheld the last time they had seen such a falsely pleasant image. She was not happy about the prospect of descending and investigating this village, but somehow she knew that they needed to try.

"I think we should go down."

"Do you sense the Stone Dancer?" the Dragon asked.

"I'm not sure what I'm sensing. This is all still so new to me. But something is telling me we need to land here."

"That's enough for me," the Dragon said. As the Dragon

searched for a place to land, Kevla noticed there was something else in one of the smaller clearings, on the top of a hill. Several somethings, in fact; dark and unrecognizable from this height, standing in a row and moving slightly in the wind. A faint sound reached her ears as the Dragon glided over the hill to land in another open area not far from the ones that contained the houses.

"You will have to approach on your own, Kevla," the Dragon said as he landed on the cushioning snow. "I cannot make it easily through the forest."

She nodded her understanding. "Perhaps it's just as well. You would probably terrify them. Wait until I call for you."

Kevla slid off him into knee-deep snow. At once, her *rhia* was soaked. Not for the first time, she wondered how people managed to travel at all in the substance. Resignedly she slogged through the white stuff, thinking that if she had to do this often her legs would become powerful with muscle.

The strange, but not unpleasant, noise increased as she ascended. It sounded like music, but if it was, then it was made by no instrument she had ever heard and the notes seemed to her ear completely random. She stumbled more than once, going down in the fluffy whiteness and clambering to her feet again. By the time she crested the hill, she was panting, her eyes down at her feet to make sure she didn't slip.

When she reached the top, Kevla glanced up. She uttered a startled cry and almost fell again. She was staring at corpses suspended from pikes stuck in the ground, twisting slowly in the wind.

The relief that washed through her as she realized that the "corpses" were only slaughtered animals made her legs feel weak. The blood that had dripped when the meat was still fresh had frozen into small, scarlet droplets. The flesh was gray and likely quite hard to the touch now.

Kevla was not unfamiliar with such a practice. She realized that the people here needed to rely on the wind to dry the meat, not the heat of the sun. She now also saw what had made the bright, singing sound—strips of metal hung together. When the wind blew, the metal pieces were jostled against one another, and the pleasant sound was produced. It was probably to keep animals away.

She stared a moment longer at the swinging, musical metal and frowned. Helpful to keep animals away, yes, but surely a people as hungry as these snow-people must be would not trust to that alone. They probably had someone watching—

Kevla whirled around.

9

There were at least two dozen of them, and they looked like no other people Kevla had ever seen. Tall and swaddled so thoroughly in fur that they first seemed to be part animal, every one of them carried something that was clearly intended to be used as a weapon. They wore head coverings and strange footgear—poles and wide shoes that seemed to be strapped to their feet. Like the corpses, these people all had pale faces and yellow hair. Those white faces now wore expressions of open hostility. Even as Kevla stood wondering what to do next, they closed in and formed a circle around her. Her eyes searched the crowd, hoping to find the familiar face of the Stone Dancer.

Kevla was not alarmed, although she was outnumbered

several to one. An array of torches and wood-and-metal farm tools would be no match for her powers. There were a few archers among them, arrows nocked and ready to fly, and a handful of swords. Even those were no true threat, not to her.

I could destroy them with a thought. But she was not here to fight them.

Kevla drew herself upright and looked at them calmly. "I am Kevla-sha-Tahmu," she said. "I have come from the land of Arukan in search of the man known as the Stone Dancer."

The wall of strangers continued to clutch their weapons. It was as though she had not spoken. She tried again. "I am no threat to you," she said. "But I must find this man."

Again, there was no reaction, other than a shuffling of feet and a few exchanged glances. Kevla looked around, trying to find the group's *khashim*.

"Take her," came a woman's voice. "But don't harm her."

The circle began to close in on Kevla. She tensed. She had no desire to hurt these people, but she could not permit them to take her captive. Perhaps a demonstration of what she was capable of—

"Burn!" she cried, and immediately the trees closest to her burst into flame.

The pale-skinned people recoiled and cried out. Some fell to their knees. Others turned and fled, the peculiar things on their feet enabling them to speed over the top of the snow instead of trudging through it. But one woman did not flee. Instead, she called after the others, "Would you abandon weeks of food so easily, you cowards?"

A woman stands her ground in front of such a display of power, Kevla thought. The words of the Dragon floated back to her: *The people of this land may never thirst, Kevla, but it is likely that they are cold and hungry.*

Apparently the woman's argument was a compelling one, for those who had started to run halted and turned, obeying the implied order of this fair-haired woman who clutched a scythe and trembled visibly and who yet did not flee.

Kevla thought the woman's courage deserved acknowledgement. She bowed, waved her hand, and at once, the fires scorching the trees were extinguished.

"You are very brave," Kevla said impulsively to the woman. The stranger's blue eyes narrowed.

"You make the trees burn to frighten us, *taaskal.* Are you now attempting to enchant me as well?"

Kevla stared. The woman's response made no sense at all, unless— A troubling thought struck her. Keeping her eyes on the woman with the scythe, Kevla sent a thought to the Dragon.

Dragon, what is going on?

They do not understand you, he replied.

Kevla's eyes widened. Somehow, this had not occurred to her. *But we must speak with them!*

I can speak their tongue. Although if they are frightened of you, they will be utterly terrified of me.

Still, you had better join me. How do you know their language? Kevla asked, her eyes never leaving the woman.

She felt the Dragon gather himself to fly the short distance as he answered her. *The Dancers and their Companions would have a hard time of it indeed if they were not able to communicate. You already comprehend this language. Soon, you will understand how to speak it.*

Kevla heard the familiar sound of the beating of powerful wings. Her would-be captors looked up and, if such a thing were possible, went even paler. Some of them moaned, soft and low, and fell to their knees in the snow. But they did not flee this time. Either they were terrified past action or the woman's courage inspired—or shamed—them into staying. The Dragon flattened several trees as he landed, and the earth trembled from the impact. Quickly, Kevla went to him and stroked him, letting the villagers know that he answered to her.

"So, what would you have me say to them?" The Dragon turned his piercing golden gaze on the crowd. "They do look rather distressed."

Kevla chose the words carefully. "Give them honorable greetings. Tell them I am the Flame Dancer and that you and I come as friends, seeking one who will know us."

The Dragon relayed the information, and again Kevla frowned. She understood everything the Dragon had said, yet somehow she knew he had not spoken in her native tongue.

This time, it was clear to Kevla that the villagers understood. The Dragon's greeting, however, did not seem to put them at ease.

"Monster of the sky," the woman with the scythe said in a deep voice, "we do not fear you or the *taaskal* who commands you. Leave our land and our food, or we will fight."

Kevla wondered what a *taaskal* was and continued to admire their courage.

"Monster of the sky, indeed," the Dragon muttered to Kevla. "These Northern folk are quite rude."

"They're afraid," Kevla said compassionately. "Tell them, their bravery brings them honor, and we are no threat to them. We don't want their food. We have come to this land in search of a man who might be known to them as the Stone Dancer."

Again, the Dragon spoke for both of them. The woman listened, but shook her head. "That name means nothing to us." She jerked her yellow head in Kevla's direction. "Why does she not speak to us?"

"Tell them I cannot, though I understand the conversation." Kevla hoped that the Dragon was right, that soon she would be able to speak this strange language as easily as he seemed to. This method of communication would grow tiresome quickly. "Tell them I will learn their language. They will find us helpful," she added. "As they have noticed, you are able to take to the skies. You can assist their men in the hunt."

The Dragon repeated everything she had said. For some reason, it was the wrong thing to say. The woman gripped her scythe more tightly. "We need no assistance."

It was then that Kevla realized just how few men there actually were in the crowd. Most of the adults were women, all as grim-faced as this one who apparently led them. There were two or three old men, whose weapons appeared to be as much for support as defense, and a few boys with their first growth of beard.

"The men are gone," Kevla murmured to the Dragon. "Otherwise they would be here, to fight the threat they think we pose."

"Perhaps the men from this village were the ones who attacked the other homes we saw earlier," said the Dragon.

It was an awful thing to contemplate, but Kevla knew it needed to be considered.

"It is possible," she agreed, "but it is equally possible that their men are victims of marauders as well."

Kevla hesitated. Her instinct was to aid them, but if they were responsible for the massacre she had seen earlier...

I will not condemn them without being certain of their guilt, she thought fiercely. "Can you find something for them to eat?"

"I can try," the Dragon answered. "Although I have not noticed an overabundance of animal life in this land."

"I'll stay here. I want to show them what I can do—how I can help them. Maybe if we demonstrate that we have good intentions, they will believe us."

"As you wish." The Dragon gathered himself and sprang into the sky. The villagers watched him, mouths hanging open. When he had disappeared from view, they again turned their attention to her. She shifted uncomfortably under their scrutiny, and for several long moments, no one spoke.

Suddenly a cry of fury shattered the air. Out of the corner of her eye Kevla saw a blur of movement. A boy charged at her, screaming and brandishing a torch.

"Olar, no!" cried the head woman.

Reacting instinctively, Kevla gestured. The orange-red flame at the top of the torch blazed higher and the youth, shocked, dropped it. He clutched his hands, checking to see that they were undamaged. The fire sizzled and died in the snow.

Kevla was frustrated. She didn't want to frighten these people further, she wanted to win their trust. She stepped forward and picked up the torch the youth had dropped.

"Burn," she said.

The sodden torch flickered to life and an instant later blazed as strongly as if it were good, dry wood. Slowly, smiling, Kevla stepped toward the boy who had attacked her and extended the torch.

She locked gazes with the youth. He was so very young, and his blue eyes were wide with terror. Even though she knew he couldn't understand her, she said softly, "It's all right. Take the fire."

Cautiously, the boy reached out a trembling hand and took the torch from her. Their fingers brushed and he hissed, startled. She kept the smile on her face, and as she hoped, he relaxed ever so slightly.

Kevla looked up from the boy's face to discover the head woman watching her intently, blue eyes shrewd.

They think the fire's a threat, even though I gave it to the boy, Kevla realized. What else could she do to win their trust? How could she use her skills in a positive way that would not frighten them? If only the Stone Dancer were here! He knew these people, he could...

Stone.

Kevla squatted and began to paw through the snow. The villagers murmured to themselves but made no move to stop her.

They probably think I'm mad, thought Kevla. *There are moments when I wonder that myself.*

At last, she found what she was searching for—a large stone, bigger than her head and partially buried in the frozen earth. Kevla cleared the snow away from it, so that the villagers could see it easily. She pointed at the rock and motioned them forward. Not surprisingly, no one moved.

Kevla placed her hands on the rough surface, hoping that after such an obvious display that she would be able to execute her idea. She had only recently come into her powers and she did not know their limits. With luck, this would work.

Heat, she thought.

Immediately the large rock began to grow hot. Within five heartbeats Kevla could see the waves of heat distorting the air around it. She made a sound of pleasure and held her hands out to the rock as she might to a fire. To make sure they understood and did not hurt themselves, she tossed some snow on the rock. It hissed and melted at once.

Kevla stepped away from the stone and waved them to approach. The woman was the first to do so, stepping forward hesitantly on her strange footgear and reaching her hands out to the rock. Her lips curved in a slow smile. It did something remarkable to her face, which suddenly softened and seemed to lose many hard years. She waved another, younger woman forward who repeated her gestures. They spoke in voices so soft that Kevla couldn't hear them.

The woman turned to regard Kevla. Kevla returned the gaze, although she wanted to duck her head. She had spent most of her life as a servant who had not dared to be so impertinent as to look an *uhlala* straight in the eye, but Kevla sensed that to break the gaze now would be unwise, possibly even dangerous. Kevla had never felt as *seen* as she did now.

"The sky-monster said you could understand us. Is this so, fire-woman?"

Kevla nodded.

"You have shown us you can make warmth that does not harm. Are you offering to aid us?"

Again, Kevla nodded.

"*Taaskali* are a dangerous lot, but you have skills that

we need." She glanced up at the gray sky. "When winter lasts forever, we must take aid where we may. Even from a *taaskal*. I do not know where your monster has gone, but if you wish to come to our village, you would be welcomed."

Kevla was pleased, but she pointed up at the sky.

"He is returning?"

Kevla nodded.

"Then we will wait."

And wait they did, all of them. One by one, at first, then in small groups, the villagers came forward to warm themselves by the heated stone. Their fear seemed to dissipate as they extended wrapped hands to the welcome heat Kevla had provided. Kevla regarded them, wondering if they were victims or perpetrators.

At length she heard the familiar sound of the Dragon's wings as he approached. In his forepaws, the Dragon clutched two large animals. They were covered in brown fur, dotted now with blood, and faintly resembled *liahs*, save that their horns branched into several smaller ones and their fur was thick and shaggy. More murmurings, but this time there was a definite note of appreciation in the sound. The Dragon landed and dropped the limp bodies to the earth.

"Dragon, you are wonderful!" Kevla exclaimed. He inclined his head modestly. "Tell them that these are gifts."

The Dragon obliged. The woman turned again to regard Kevla, smiling. "We will take a Fire Maiden over an Ice Maiden gladly," she said, "and rejoice to have a *taaskal* with us and not against us."

Kevla smiled in return, relieved. At least now, she had begun to win their trust. She wondered at the term "ice maiden" and had opened her mouth to have the Dragon inquire about that term and *taaskal* when the older woman spoke.

"I am Gelsan Tulari, and I am head woman of Arrun Woods. You may stay with me until you can speak our tongue."

"Thank you," Kevla said.

"The Flame Dancer is grateful for your hospitality," the Dragon translated.

The young woman Gelsan had spoken with a moment ago now stepped forward. She was an attractive girl, with wide blue eyes, ruddy cheeks, and a soft flower-bud mouth. Thick ringlets of golden hair peeped beneath her fur hat.

"I am Mylikki, Gelsan's daughter," she said. "It would be my honor to show you our village. Come with us."

The group headed back down the hill. Kevla again noticed the strange items strapped to their feet. Some of them had long, flat poles tied to their boots. Others had wide circles that looked to be made out of curved branches interlaced with animal sinew. She made her way downward carefully, stepping sideways to avoid slipping as much as possible. Mylikki slid quickly down the hill on the poles, making a wide, graceful turn to wait for Kevla.

"I hope you will forgive us, especially Olar," Mylikki said. As Mylikki spoke, Kevla realized that she was starting to grasp some of the stranger words. It was as if the learning was taking place inside her, somehow. "We were not always so unwelcoming to strangers. The killer winter has been hard on us. But ever since the *bayinba* started—"

Raids, Kevla thought, translating the word in her mind. *The word* bayinba *means "raids."*

"—we have, unfortunately, had good cause to fear strangers."

The people of Arrun Woods were victims, then, not attackers. Though sorry for their losses, Kevla was pleased to confirm that she was not aiding murderers. Mylikki had said something else, though, that confused Kevla, and she didn't think it was her not understanding the word. She tapped Mylikki's shoulder and the other girl looked at her questioningly.

Kevla repeated a word Mylikki had said, cautiously wrapping her mouth around the unfamiliar term. She had apparently gotten it right, for Mylikki said, "Killer? The killer winter? Oh…you don't know. You must be from a far land indeed."

Mylikki looked up at the gray sky. "Winter usually only lasts for a few months, even in the most northerly parts of Lamal. Then of course spring comes. But this year, something happened. Something went wrong. Winter never went away."

She looked at Kevla gravely. "We have had nothing but winter for over a year."

10

Kevla stared at Mylikki. No wonder there were so few animals left, and some of the people had begun behaving like animals themselves. If only she could talk to them! Kevla had so many questions. She put a sympathetic hand on Mylikki's shoulder as they made their way toward the houses in the clearing.

The Dragon had made room for himself, Kevla saw, by uprooting several trees and placing them in a pile. The villagers were chattering happily and pointing to the pile; clearly they appreciated not having to cut the wood. Looking rather pleased with himself, the Dragon had settled down, folding his forepaws like a granary cat, and was lowering his head to talk to the villagers.

Kevla made a small, amused noise. "The people of Lamal

are great of heart," Mylikki said. "We do not fear something for long. Here is our house."

Kevla turned where Mylikki indicated. In her mind's eye she saw the ruined house she and the Dragon had happened upon earlier. She blinked, banishing the image. Mylikki opened the door and Kevla was immediately struck by the smell of smoke.

It was dark inside, as the other house had been. Kevla stepped cautiously into a single large, long room and looked around. Hard-packed earth served as a floor. As her eyes became accustomed to the dimness, she saw the source of the smoke. In a pit in the center of the room, a fire burned. A cauldron hung on a tripod hovered over it. Smoke curled upward, escaping through a small hole in the ceiling. Oil lamps also provided some illumination, adding their smoke to that produced by the fire. Kevla's first thought was to extinguish the fire and simply heat the room with her thoughts, but she realized the flame was needed for cooking. She herself was unaffected by smoke, but Mylikki began to cough almost as soon as they entered. *This cannot be good for them,* Kevla thought. *But it is so cold, they need the fire burning all the time if they are to even survive.*

Gelsan looked up as they entered and emptied a bowl filled with chunks of meat into the water boiling in the pot. "It will not take long for the meal to cook, since the sky-monster brought us fresh meat," she told them.

"Dragon," Kevla said. She pointed outside.

Gelsan looked out the door where she pointed, smiled, and nodded. "Dragon, then. Whatever he be, we will eat well tonight." Gelsan had divested herself of her heavy outer garments and now wore a stained, oft-mended overdress in a shade of bright blue. Beneath it, she wore a long-sleeved linen underdress. Her hair, once clearly as golden as that of her daughter's but now shot through with silver, was braided and pinned to her head. In place of the long poles that had been strapped to her feet, she wore leather shoes.

Mylikki hurried over to her mother and whispered something in her ear. Gelsan's eyes brightened as her daughter spoke, but then she frowned.

"We should not ask her for such a trivial thing," Gelsan chided.

"It is *not* trivial," Mylikki retorted. "It is cleansing and healing. We know it is no great thing for her to do it."

Gelsan sighed. "Very well, Mylikki. Show the Flame Dancer the hut, and let her decide if she wants to misuse her powers for our entertainment."

Mylikki grinned and turned to Kevla. "Let me take these off first and I'll show you."

Kevla leaned against the carved wooden door as Mylikki sat on one of the raised platforms that lined the rear walls of the house. Quickly, she removed the poles from her feet and hung them on a hook, then hurried back to Kevla.

Kevla smiled at the young woman. Curious, how she thought of Mylikki as "young." The other woman was no more than a year or two younger than she, but Kevla no longer felt a mere two decades old. She felt ancient; she had seen too much. Done too much. Her innocence had died with her lover.

"Come, Kevla!" Mylikki darted out the door, her short legs churning through the snow. Kevla followed, wondering why Mylikki had removed the poles that had helped her glide so easily over the snow. Then she understood—they were heading into the forest.

Kevla had not ventured deep into any of the woods that she and the Dragon had encountered. They were too dark, too dense, to feel comfortable to a woman used to living in a spacious, bright house in a land in which trees were as rare as rain. She reluctantly followed her guide through a well-worn path that suddenly opened up to the banks of a frozen lake.

Kevla stared at the flat expanse of solid water. Most of it was covered with snow, and that part was indistinguishable from the land. But there were some places where the wind had cleared the surface, and there Kevla saw a deep, rich green.

So beautiful, she thought. *If only* he *could be seeing these marvels with me.*

"Here we are," Mylikki said. Kevla dragged her gaze away from the green ice and saw what seemed to her to be a smaller version of one of the houses in the clearing. Mylikki tugged open the door and Kevla peered inside. There were no windows, indeed, the little building seemed to be well sealed. The interior was entirely black, and for a moment, Kevla thought that the place had been burned.

She looked back at Mylikki and shook her head, trying to communicate her lack of understanding.

"This is the stonesteaming hut," Mylikki said, as if that explained everything.

Kevla shook her head, still not understanding. "Hmm," Mylikki said, chewing on her lower lip. "I thought when you heated the stone, you knew about it. How to explain...long ago, our ancestors designed the stonesteaming huts. They're made of wood and we seal them up well. We light a fire to heat up several stones, just like you did earlier. When they're hot, we bring them inside and pour water on them to create steam. It feels good—very warming, very cleansing, and very relaxing."

She pointed. Kevla could now see a cluster of rocks sitting in the fire pit.

"It takes a long time, almost all day, to get the stones hot. And with so few people left, we don't stonesteam as often as we would like. But this place means more than just comfort to us."

Mylikki spoke of a sacred place of birth and death, a place of community, where the seasonal changes were celebrated by ritual both practical and meaningful. Kevla nodded as the other girl spoke. She felt the power of the place as she stepped gingerly inside.

"Careful," said Mylikki. "The benches are safe to sit on, but don't touch the walls or ceilings, or you'll get all sooty."

Kevla, who had been just about to do precisely that, nodded and kept her hands in close. To her surprise, the wooden benches, as Mylikki had promised, yielded no soot to the touch. Their surface was a rich, shiny black, as if somehow the soot had been sealed and baked into the wood.

She looked at the stones in the center of the hut. Gathering up her *rhia* so she didn't accidentally brush any soot with it, Kevla squatted beside the stones and extended a hand. Pleasure was warm inside her. In her effort to connect with these people without speech, she had inadvertently stumbled upon something they cherished: the ability to heat stone.

Heat, she mentally instructed.

The stone obeyed. Kevla touched another, and another, until all the stones were putting out a great deal of heat.

Mylikki stood in the doorway, her hands to her mouth. Her blue eyes were wide with shock. "It is hard to believe," she whispered. "Even when I see you do this with my own eyes." She suddenly grinned. "Maybe we should have tried to befriend your people long ago."

Kevla again wondered just what they thought she was. She got to her feet, dusted off her hands, and smiled.

"Thank you, Kevla. You don't know what this means to us. It's been so long...." She blinked hard, and Kevla saw tears in the blue eyes. Quick tears of sympathy sprang to Kevla's own brown ones. Well did she know how it was to live a harsh existence with few luxuries. She recalled a girl who loved to swim in the cool caverns of the House of Four Waters, and how that simple indulgence restored her. If the stonesteaming made Mylikki and the others happy, then it was as good a use of her Dancer's abilities as any she could think of. And despite Gelsan's dismissal of Mylikki's request, the place clearly represented far more than simply a place to relax.

Mylikki cleared her throat. "Let's go get the others."

Within the next few minutes, several of the women who had not so long ago been eyeing Kevla with suspicion now clustered around the stonesteaming hut. Mylikki filled a bucket with snow, which she placed inside near the hot stones. Kevla's eyes went wide with shock as the women quickly divested themselves and stepped, quite naked, into the building. They handed their clothes to one of the younger girls, who carefully wrapped them into small bundles and put them into a large sack.

Mylikki, whose pale skin and rosy breasts looked to Kevla like something out of a storyteller's tale, noticed her discomfiture.

"If you don't want to participate, it's all right, but I think you'll enjoy it. It's thanks to you that we have this at all. It would mean much to us if you shared this with us."

Kevla looked at the dozen or so women, all fair-haired, all pale-fleshed, sitting on the benches and talking quietly. They were thin...so very thin. She could clearly see the outlines of ribs underneath their pale breasts.

Kevla swallowed, knowing that it would be a good gesture to join them, her own cheeks hot at the thought of being naked in front of so many strangers.

When she had been a handmaiden to the *khashima,* she had slept in a room with the other women. And she had often enjoyed a bath in the caverns that made the Clan of Four Waters the envy of all other clans. But she had worn a sleeping *rhia* at night, and timed her visits to the caverns when she could be alone. To disrobe in front of so many—

She forced a smile and tugged off the *rhia.* The women fell silent and Kevla's blush deepened as she realized they were scrutinizing her body, with its bronze skin and dark-tipped breasts, as she had earlier scrutinized theirs.

I suppose I ought to be grateful there isn't mixed stonesteaming, she thought. *I could be sitting naked with everyone in the village.*

Mylikki moved over so Kevla had a place to sit. Gingerly, Kevla perched on the bench. Gelsan pulled the door closed, and suddenly the only light came from the glowing stones.

Kevla relaxed as the dry heat began to penetrate her body. She was comfortable in the heat, around flames or embers, and in the darkness, she could not see the other women. But she could hear them, moving softly, speaking in quiet tones. It was a soothing sound, and Kevla closed her eyes and sank deeper into the warm, anonymous darkness.

She was walking on the snow, her feet sinking into the white stuff, and she was not alone. Beside her walked the Stone Dancer. Though she was comfortable clad only in her red rhia, *this man was wrapped warmly in layers of thick woolen clothing and a green cape. He was speaking, and she turned her head to listen to him and smile at something he said. He was tall, taller than she, and she was no small woman. He was as she remembered him: handsome, yet sad, with golden hair and eyes as blue as the sky.*

Beside them both, regarded not with fear but acceptance, even affection, walked the blue, black-and-white-striped simmar. *It was an enormous beast with thick, shaggy fur and golden, knowing eyes. It walked over the snow with fluid grace, its shoulders and hips rolling in that smooth movement granted to all cats, large or small.*

The three crested a hill. Behind her, Kevla heard the beating of powerful wings, and knew her friend the Dragon was flying behind and above them. The thought gave her comfort.

Her skin prickled. They were being watched. The thought ought to alarm her, but instead she felt warm and taken care of...loved. She reached out her thoughts and tried to—

A sudden hissing sound chased away the vision. Kevla gasped and started up. Mylikki laid a gentle hand on her arm.

"It's the *hamantu,*" she said. "Gelsan has just put some water on the stones to make steam. You'll notice that it's getting hotter now."

Indeed it was, though it would have to get much hotter

than this for Kevla, who had acknowledged her true identity in the depths of a boiling pit of molten earth, to feel any
discomfort. The moist heat felt strange to the desert dweller;
it clung to her skin like her own sweat. She closed her eyes
again, hearing another splash of water on hot stone, feeling
the heat rise in a moist wave to caress her. A wonderful las-
situde stole over her. She had never felt this relaxed, not even
when bathing in the caverns at the House of Four Waters.
Now she understood why. She was Fire. Water felt good on
her human skin, and she enjoyed the cleansing coolness. But
sitting in this place of darkness and deep heat, of smoke and
steam—this called to her soul more than the baths did. Perhaps these people were not as alien as they seemed.

She drifted, and for a while time stood still. She hoped she
would sink back into the vision, but it did not come a second time. There was only the heat and darkness, and the soft
sounds of women moving, and for now, Kevla thought, that
was enough.

11

The sun was setting by the time the women emerged from the stonesteaming hut. Before she left, Kevla placed her hands on the stones and heated them again. The men would be coming, to take their turn in the stonesteaming hut, and she wanted to make sure their experience was as pleasant as hers had been.

Kevla felt marvelous after several sessions of sitting in the hot steam, and then plunging into the refreshing coldness of the snowbanks. She had not realized how much tension she had been carrying in her body until she had been able to release it with the blessing of the vision, which comforted even as it confused and intrigued her, and the *hamantu*. Once the women began to trickle back toward the village,

Kevla heard a whistle. Not long after that, a trail of men began coming up the forest path. There were so few of them it pained Kevla to see it.

When they reached the village, Mylikki said, "My mother enjoyed the stonesteaming as much as any of us, but she won't want to delay the meal. I must go help her."

She hurried into the house, closing the door behind her. Kevla watched her go.

"You look relaxed," the Dragon said.

"I am," she replied, happy to be able to talk to someone. "It was lovely. I do not look forward to traveling across the snow after that."

"Let us hope our travels will be brief."

"I do hope that." She sighed. "I suppose I will have to learn how to walk on those poles they strap to their feet."

"They are called *skeltha,* in case you're wondering. It means, long sticks."

"Ah," said Kevla. "A simple term for a simple thing."

"These people respect words. They know they hold power. Things are named simply, and I doubt there was much idle chatter among the women in the hut."

"Now that you mention it, no, there wasn't." She looked up at the darkening sky. "Twilight. When people start fires, if they haven't already." It was time, again, to attempt to locate the Stone Dancer. Kevla gathered a few sticks and piled them together.

"Burn."

They leaped into flame, and Kevla found herself smiling as the cheery red and orange warmth chased away the blue and lavender tints of the snow and twilight. She leaned toward the dancing flames and made her vision soft. "Show me the Stone Dancer."

The fire flickered. In its depths, Kevla thought she could glimpse the outline of a face. Her heart beating faster, she leaned closer, willing the image to focus.

With shocking speed, the unclear face disappeared and Kevla found herself looking at the sole of a boot. She jerked back, feeling for an instant as if that boot was about to come crashing down on her face. Then, nothing.

A deep rumbling sound drew her attention away from the fire. The Dragon was laughing!

"Clever, clever fellow!" he gasped between peals of bone-chilling Dragon laughter. "He saw you, Kevla. He saw you trying to find him and he stamped out the fire! It seems our Stone Dancer dislikes being spied upon."

Kevla was embarrassed, but after a moment, she also began to laugh. She supposed if she didn't know what was going on, a strange face appearing in the fire would alarm her, too.

"I doubt I'll get another chance, if he's wary of my face in the fire. We'll have to try to find him some other way," she said. "I will see if I can help Gelsan. It has not been so long since I worked in the kitchens. Perhaps I can assist her."

"You must be careful, Kevla," the Dragon said, surprising her. "You want them to like you and trust you, but they must not regard you as an underling."

She smiled sadly. "A woman who calls flame with a thought is more to be feared than despised. A night chopping vegetables or seasoning a stew will not cost me respect."

"Perhaps not," said the Dragon. "But there are those who might not understand."

"These people are better than that," Kevla said with certainty. She entered Gelsan's house, easing the door open and stepping to a small table where the headwoman and her daughter were chopping what Kevla realized were dried vegetables. She pointed at the vegetables and pretended to cut them.

Gelsan seemed pleased at the offer. "Certainly. Cut them into small bits and then put them in the cauldron."

The time passed quickly, but in silence. The Dragon had been right; the people of Lamal wasted no breath in words that served only to fill the air. After a while, Gelsan tasted the stew and pronounced it ready.

"Go round up the household," she told Mylikki, who threw on a cloak and hat and hastened to obey. A few moments later, there were ten people seated cross-legged on the cold earthen floor of Gelsan's hut.

Gelsan ladled the stew into bowls and passed them around. Kevla took a spoonful with a bite of meat. Her eyes widened. It was all she could do not to spit it out. Gamey, stringy, tough, it was the most unpleasant thing she had ever eaten. She chewed determinedly and got the bite down. Sipping the broth, she found it weak and flavorless. She glanced around surreptitiously and saw that everyone else seemed to be enjoying themselves. They ate in silence, but they ate happily. If winter had indeed lasted for an entire year, then this must be a feast to them. She recalled how painfully thin the women seemed to her in the stonesteaming hut, and wondered how much longer they cold survive with no end to winter in sight.

Willing her stomach not to reject the food, Kevla took another bite. It would not do to insult her host, and she was sure she needed the nourishment regardless of how bad it tasted. Others went back for seconds, even thirds. Gelsan had prepared a generous amount, but even so, there was nothing left in the cauldron by the time the meal was over.

"Now it is time for some entertainment, to honor our guest," Gelsan said. She nodded to Mylikki, who leaped to her feet and went to a corner of the room. Gelsan indicated that Kevla should sit with the others on the benches that lined the room. Mylikki returned, carrying something that Kevla presumed was an instrument.

It appeared to be made out of the same black and white wood that the houses were constructed of. Small pegs were inserted along its length, and though it was too dark to see, she assumed there were strings of some sort running down it. Mylikki sat on a small stool and put the instrument in her lap.

With the first few brushes of Mylikki's fingers along the strings, Kevla felt a chill inside her. It was the most beautiful sound she had ever heard. Clear and sweet and haunting, bright and metallic-sounding somehow, it seemed the perfect instrument to have been created in this place.

It sounds like snow, she thought.

Mylikki played for a time, weaving a web of sound about them all. Kevla barely breathed, hanging on every note produced by the strange instrument. After a while, Mylikki began to sing. Her voice was pure and clear, like the stars Kevla had seen in the night sky, but the song was not a sweet one.

Men-at-arms turn pale,
And their hearts within them quail
As the Dark bleeds the Light from the sky.
Who of woman born

will survive to see the morn?
Will you be among them? Will I?

And still, we few stand
Upon the blasted land—
Fighting back the Shadow.

Kevla gasped, and more than one fair head turned to stare at her.

Shadow. The Shadow that was destined to come and challenge the Dancers. The Shadow that twice before had been defeated, but twice before had won. The Shadow that had erased whole worlds as if they had never been.

She dreaded what words would come from Mylikki's lips next.

Like his father before,
My son rode off to war,
With a smile and a song in his heart.
The cold Dark unnamed
Another life has claimed—
And upon my lost soul left its mark.

Again, Mylikki sang the chilling chorus. For the first time since she had been given her powers of fire, Kevla felt cold.

My daughter's grown wild,
Her belly big with child
And she sings soft and low of the dawn.
They tell me she's mad,

And perhaps I should be glad,
For her husband's dead, and still the Night goes on.

And still we few stand,
Upon the blasted land—
Fighting back the Shadow.

Something about this song was familiar to Kevla, something more than just the mention of the Shadow. Had not Jashemi mentioned a previous lifetime when he was a beggar boy, standing next to a *khashima* whose pregnant daughter had gone mad?

I once ruled as Queen,
Long ago, when all was green,
And this castle kept watch o'er the realm.
But now, nothing grows
In the icy wind that blows,
And the Darkness will soon overwhelm.

This last verse proved it. Her mind was beginning to translate for her; she somehow knew that *queen* meant *khashima,* that *castle* indicated a Great House. This could not be a coincidence.

The song unfolded, chilling in its depiction of utter despair: the food had run out, the well had gone dry. Torches were lit in a defiant, futile effort to keep the Shadow at bay.

And still, we few stand
Upon the blasted land—
Fighting back the Shadow.

Tears filled Kevla's eyes. She knew that all the characters in this song had once lived, once breathed, once loved.
Including Jashemi.

'Tis now merely hours
Till we fall to Shadow powers,
For how much can mere mortals endure?
And when we few fall—
Why then, that will be all;
The silence is the one thing that's sure.

The sound of the instrument, snowlike and bright, faded into silence itself. Kevla applauded politely with the rest, but as Mylikki launched into a lively song about a hunter and a farmer's wife, her thoughts were not on the bawdy lyrics.
One thought pounded in her head.
Someone in this land was a Lorekeeper, and she had to find out who.

12

Kevla did not pay much attention to the rest of the stories or songs that were performed. Others drifted in during the night, and Gelsan had passed around a sweet, powerful wine made from fermented honey. After the final song, Gelsan rose and offered Kevla the hospitality of her house. Kevla realized that the ten who had joined her for dinner all planned to sleep here, on the raised areas that extended from the walls. At the House of Four Waters she had slept in a single room in the company of many women, but never with men. She knew her eyes widened.

She pointed outside. "Dragon," she said, and hoped that Gelsan would understand.

The headwoman nodded her fair head. "You want to be with your friend," she said. "Do you need a fur or blanket?"

Kevla was about to refuse, but then thought that a fur between her and the wet ground would be pleasant. She nodded, and selected one. It was thick and brown, but she could not identify what kind of animal it had once belonged to.

As she left, she caught Mylikki's eye and waved her to follow. Mylikki looked puzzled, but grabbed her cloak and accompanied Kevla. They trudged out into the snow to stand before the Great Dragon. He had curled up into a ball and was breathing steadily, little puffs of smoke curling from his nostrils into the frosty air. At their approach, he uncurled and stretched like a mammoth cat.

"Dragon, Mylikki sang a song this evening about a queen standing alone, watching the Shadow come," Kevla said. Mylikki's head whipped around. "There were lines of the song that sounded familiar—like what *he* told me. I think there are Lorekeepers here."

"I understood you!" Mylikki exclaimed. "Some of what you said, anyway."

"You are beginning to open to this language," said the Dragon. "Good."

"If we can find the Lorekeepers, they might be able to help us," Kevla continued.

"Help? Help you with what?" Mylikki asked. She seemed excited that Kevla was learning to speak her language.

"Mylikki, who wrote that song that you performed? Did you compose it?"

Mylikki's pretty face furrowed in a frown. "What about the song?"

"Kevla wants to know if the song was an original composition," the Dragon said. Kevla sighed; apparently her grasp of this new language was still spotty.

"*Fighting Back the Shadow?* That's a very old song indeed," Mylikki said, dashing Kevla's hopes. "Several hundred years old, at least. I don't know who wrote it. It's rare because it's a song sung by a woman; most of the compositions told by a narrator are male. And a woman of great power, too."

"Gelsan has power," Kevla said.

This was apparently a simple enough sentence, for Mylikki replied, "Only because the men are gone." She fell abruptly silent, gathering her thick cloak more tightly about her frame and glancing up at the overcast sky. She turned to Kevla, her face a dim white smudge in the darkness. "Let us not speak of this at night," she said, almost pleading. "In the morning. We will tell you everything in the morning."

Impulsively Kevla reached to squeeze Mylikki's arm through the cloak. "We have much to tell you in the morning as well," she told her new friend. She watched as Mylikki trudged through the snow back to the smoky warmth of Gelsan's small house.

"Something haunts them," Kevla said.

The Dragon nodded. "Something is very wrong with their world. Of course they are haunted."

Kevla shivered, but not from cold. She spread the fur next to the Dragon, and when she sat on it, it sank into the snow, making a little hollow. Kevla leaned against the warm strength of her friend, her hand reaching to caress the smooth scales.

Kevla awoke to the smell of cooked grains. She opened her eyes to see a bowl beside her, along with a steaming mug.

She sat up carefully and reached for the morning meal, knowing what a gift it was to these people who were a few meals away from starvation. She sniffed gingerly at the mug. It smelled like tea of some kind. She took a cautious sip. It was strong and slightly bitter, but there was a generous dollop of something sweet in it. The cooked grains were also palatable.

As she lifted the mug to her lips, she turned her head slightly and almost spilled the hot liquid. Not ten feet away, every child in the village sat on the snow, staring at her and the Dragon. She smiled and waved a little at them. Uncertainly they waved back. When Kevla looked around, she saw that others were staring at the pair as well, although the adults were slightly more discreet in their ogling.

"How long have they been watching us?"

"For the last few hours, since dawn," the Dragon replied, clearly unperturbed. "I pretended I was asleep."

"I feel like I'm on display," Kevla murmured, turning her attention to the meal. She ate steadily, the unknown grains hot and filling and the tea easy to drink. When she had finished, a small boy rose from where he had been unabashedly watching her to take the utensils.

"Thank you," she said, smiling at him.

He ducked his head. "You're welcome," he said in a voice so soft she could barely hear him.

Kevla was not surprised to find everyone else in Gelsan's house awake. The sleeping materials had been put away and everyone was silently finishing their bowls of grains. Kevla was greeted with smiles when she entered, but no words.

"Thank you for the meal," Kevla said.

Gelsan stared. "You can speak our language!"

"It seems as though I can," Kevla said, understanding the words that rolled off her tongue although she knew it was not her native language. Perhaps this, too, was part of the gift of being a Dancer. "Gelsan, I must speak with you. In private."

Gelsan nodded, her eyes searching Kevla's. "Help us clean up and we will talk."

Kevla obliged, gathering up the bowls and taking them outside to be scrubbed with snow. The young man who had rashly attacked her when she had first arrived—Olar, she believed his name was—lugged out the heavy cauldron. His long yellow hair was tied back in a ponytail and fell to the middle of his back. His young body strained with the effort of hauling the iron pot. Kevla now saw a resemblance between the three she hadn't noticed before. When Olar went back inside, she said to Gelsan, "He's your son."

"Yes. And grateful I am that you burned only his torch, not his flesh."

"You must forgive him," Mylikki said, whispering lest her brother overhear. "He tries so hard to act like a man, but sometimes he doesn't understand how. Ever since the men—"

"Mylikki!"

Mylikki drew herself up to her full diminutive height and gave her imposing mother stare for stare. "I told Kevla we would tell her," she said. "She deserves to know."

"And I have much to share with you," Kevla said. "You don't yet know what is at stake. Why my task is so important."

"Few things are more important to me than the well-being of my village," Gelsan said.

"I understand. And I hope to help you."

Gelsan sighed. "Bring in the bowls." They returned inside. Olar knelt on the floor, trying to get the wood to catch.

"Olar, we need to be alone for a time," Gelsan said.

He nodded his head. "Yes, Mother. I will go with Ranin and get more wood from the forest." He looked shyly at Kevla. "Will...will the Flame Dancer heat up the stones for the hut again today?"

"Of course," Kevla said. Olar's young face brightened. She watched him go. "How old is he?" she asked.

"Thirteen sum—" Mylikki caught herself and smiled without humor. "We count ages by summers, but as we have not had a summer for so long it seems silly to phrase it thus. Will you help with the fire, Kevla? Olar was not able to get it going."

"I'll do better than that," Kevla said. She thought about the room being warm, and it became so. "No need for the smoke."

Gelsan shook her head. "You *taaskali* are remarkable," she said as she pulled up a stool. She reached for a large sack and withdrew two garments and a small box. Handing one dress to Mylikki, she said, "Mylikki and I've mending to do. We do not have the luxury to simply sit and talk."

Kevla nodded her understanding. The other two women fished out what looked like bone needles and sinew. For a moment Kevla watched the bone needles darting through the brightly colored fabric, and when at last she spoke, it was in a hushed voice.

"Tell me about the men," she asked.

Gelsan inhaled swiftly. A bright spot of blood appeared on the garment. She sucked her finger for a moment. "Your words first, Fire Woman."

"I have told you who I am. I am Kevla-sha-Tahmu, and I am the Flame Dancer. The Dragon is my Companion. You have seen the sort of power I possess. I do not know the term *taaskali,* nor what it means, but I do know that while I am unique in my particular abilities, there are others who have similar ones."

Mylikki's hands had stilled and she regarded Kevla with wide eyes. Gelsan kept her eyes on her work and her needle never slowed, but Kevla knew the headwoman was listening intently.

"One such is the man I seek," continued Kevla. "He is the Stone Dancer."

"What abilities does he have?" Mylikki's expression had changed slightly.

"I'm not sure. But his element is earth, as mine is fire. Whatever his abilities are, they would center around that."

Mylikki opened her flower-bud mouth to speak again, but Gelsan interrupted her. "Why do you seek him?"

Kevla suddenly realized what the older woman was thinking—that perhaps Kevla and the Dragon had come to harm this man.

"The Dragon and I need his help," she replied.

"For what?"

Instead of replying directly, Kevla seemingly changed the subject. "Your song last night," she said to Mylikki. "You said it is an old song. It's a story about standing against a Shadow, a Shadow that will wipe out everything in the world as if it had never been."

Mylikki nodded. "Yes, that's right."

"Were there any other verses? About a beggar boy, about a Dancer lying dead in the streets?"

Mylikki's blue eyes grew enormous. "Yes, there are," she whispered. "The song has many verses and is almost always shortened for performing. Where did you hear them?"

"I never heard that song until last night," Kevla told her. "But I know the story behind it. I know because—because someone I knew lived that story in a life before this one. He was the beggar boy on the parapet, and I was the Dancer lying murdered in the streets."

She had their full attention now. They stared silently at her, mouths slightly open.

"That man was called a Lorekeeper," Kevla continued. "The Lorekeepers are the only ones who remember what has happened in the past. They find the Dancers and help them remember."

"Dancers?" Gelsan's voice was sharp with disbelief, but Kevla noticed that she had stopped mending the garment.

"That's what we're called," Kevla said. "I'm not sure exactly why." She took a deep breath and decided to reveal everything she knew.

"I am the element of fire incarnate. The man I seek is earth. There are three others—water, air, and spirit. We five have lived four times before, fighting to protect the worlds into which we are born. We stand against the Shadow and somehow—I don't yet know how—we try to hold it back. If we win, that world survives. If we fail, it is engulfed by the Shadow, erased as if it had never been. Twice we have won, twice lost. This is the final time—the final Dance. The fate of more than one world rests upon what we do here."

Gelsan made a dismissive noise, but when she spoke, her voice trembled. "Kevla, forgive my disrespect, but—this sounds more like a fantastical song that a *huskaa* would perform than anything close to fact."

"I didn't believe it either, at first." Kevla swallowed hard. "Someone I loved had to die before I fully understood what was happening." It was the first time she had mentioned it to anyone since beginning her journey, and she felt the pain and guilt wash over her yet again. She fought it back.

"So that is why I need to find this man. And also any in your village who might be Lorekeepers."

"How would we know such a thing?"

"My people didn't know about the Lorekeepers and the Dancers, either," Kevla said. Her mind went back to the dreams she had had, of the Dragon repeatedly breathing sheets of flame upon her in an effort to force her to acknowledge her identity. To the dreams Jashemi had had, that he had been afraid to utter. "The truth kept trying to come through in dreams the Lorekeepers had. I think whoever wrote that song was a Lorekeeper. Has anyone here mentioned troubling dreams, or visions?"

Gelsan, who had returned to her mending, grunted. "I don't think anyone would openly speak of such things," she said. Then, more gently, "But if it is important to you, I will ask."

"I have told you how important it is," Kevla replied. "And now you know whom I seek and why."

Gelsan cleared her throat. "I do not know if this has anything to do with your—your quest. But I will tell you what has happened here. Mylikki is right—you should know."

Kevla waited, barely breathing.

"I understand that Mylikki told you that winter has been visited upon us for over a year. We had stored enough supplies to take us through a normal winter, but quickly went through most of that. We have turned to relying almost exclusively on what we can hunt. And now even the animals are starving. The meat we thought you had come to steal— that and a few sacks of grain and dried vegetables are all we have left.

"Our hunters ranged farther and farther afield in search of food, and just...didn't come back. Others seemed to go mad, leaving to terrorize other villages, to kill and take what they wanted. Strange storms come out of nowhere, do terrible damage, and then disappear. Women in Lamal are not men's servants, but there are clear divisions of duties. We have had to take on the responsibilities of the men in addition to our own. We have learned to hunt, to butcher meat, to cure hides for protection against this cold that will not depart."

Her eyes locked with Kevla's. "This can be no natural winter. The spirits that live in the forests are silent. Dead or simply too afraid to show themselves, I do not know. We do not know if this is punishment for something we have done, or an evil spell by some powerful *taaskal,* or—" and she smiled, as if embarrassed to say so "—or if the Ice Maiden of the *huskaa's* songs is real and is locking us in her winter. And into the midst of this you come, with your strange but welcome powers, and speaking of others like you and dreams and the end of worlds. We need your help, Kevla Flame Dancer. We need you to somehow bring back spring."

"I do not know if I can," Kevla said, "but I will try."

She noted that Mylikki had grown quiet. The girl sat back in the chair, her arms folded, her eyes distant. "Mylikki? What is wrong?"

"Tell me again all that you know of this Stone Dancer," the girl replied, her voice thoughtful.

"Not a great deal. I do not even know his name. He is…" Kevla closed her eyes and reached for the dream she had had. "He is tall, with yellow hair. Strong. His eyes are blue. There are laugh lines around his eyes, but now those eyes are hard with pain and anger. He…he has suffered much. At his feet is a huge cat with blue stripes. In my mind, they wait for me on a hill covered with snow."

She opened her eyes to find both Mylikki and Gelsan staring at her. Hope surged in Kevla.

"Do you know him?" she cried.

Dashing Kevla's hopes, Mylikki shook her braided head. "No, I don't," she said. Suddenly she grinned. "But I think I know someone who does."

13

"A few weeks ago, a *huskaa* came to our village," Mylikki continued. "They wander from town to town singing songs and bringing news. They are greatly honored. He taught me that song you heard, as well as many others. His name is Altan Lukkari."

Mylikki turned bright red. She cleared her throat and continued. "He comes from a village far to the north. He described a man in his village that did not look like the *taaskali*, but who had powerful magic. He changed the seasons. They called him the *Kevat-aanta*—the Spring-Bringer."

"But...I thought the seasons changed on their own."

"They did, but according to Altan," and again Mylikki's color rose as she said the name, "this man made them change at will. He enhanced them, somehow. The trees bore more fruit, the harvests were more bountiful because of him. But then his powers deserted him."

Kevla was horrified. How could a Dancer lose his power? He *was* the element, how could the abilities simply vanish? "How did this happen?"

"Our gods are as you described them," Gelsan said quietly.

Kevla turned her attention to the other woman. The comment seemed to have nothing to do with the conversation. "I don't understand."

"You mentioned this man standing with one of our gods," Gelsan continued. "That means your vision must be true. You are obviously a stranger to this land, and yet you described them perfectly. Giant cats, with blue and white stripes. We call them *tigers*. They live high in the mountains. They made the world and determined the cycles. In the old days, they would descend and walk through the world, and flowers would spring beneath their feet."

"When the Spring-Bringer began to change the seasons, everyone thought that the gift of the gods had been passed to him," Mylikki continued. "But when his powers deserted him, people said the gods were angry with him, and took his powers as punishment."

"But my vision," Kevla said. "I saw him with the *simmar*—the tiger. So he must be still blessed by the gods."

"Then why is there still winter?" Gelsan's voice was harsh. She was angry, and understandably so. If what Mylikki had said was true, and the Stone Dancer had lost his powers, everyone in this land was suffering.

Kevla passed a hand over her forehead. Jashemi would have been able to help her make sense of this information.

But he was gone, and could not offer advice, or comfort, or love anymore.

She took a deep breath. "I don't know. But it does sound as if this man is the one I seek. Where is Altan now?"

"Long gone," said Gelsan before Mylikki could speak. "And a good thing, too. Planting ideas in my daughter's head."

"I have talent," Mylikki retorted. "He said I could play almost as well as someone who had been formally apprenticed."

"Women don't become *huskaas*," Gelsan said.

"Women don't become head of their village either," Mylikki snapped, then gasped at Gelsan's expression. Clearly, Mylikki had spoken before she had thought.

Attempting to forestall the argument, Kevla said, "I fly on the back of the Dragon. I will be able to find the Stone Dancer if you tell me where to look."

Mother and daughter regarded each other intently. Mylikki swallowed hard. "I won't tell you," she said, and dragged her gaze to Kevla's. "I'll show you."

"Mylikki," Gelsan said in a warning voice.

Abruptly Mylikki leaped to her feet, her stool toppling backward. "This is the first hint of hope we have had, Mother! If Kevla is like the Spring-Bringer, then maybe she can help him get his powers back. Maybe she can bring an end to this horrible winter!" Her voice grew thick but no less angry. "We are dying slowly, one by one, and if this goes on much longer everyone and everything in this land will be dead. You know how little food is left. You did what you had to do. Let me do what I must!"

"You want to follow the boy because he had a pretty face

and spoke kindly to you!" Gelsan, too, was on her feet now, clutching her mending so tightly her knuckles were white.

"And if I did?" Mylikki was trembling with anger. "He is still the only chance we have—that Kevla has. I am weary of this winter, Mother. I am weary of the cold, and the poor food, and the fear and sorrow that hangs over our land like a snow-cloud. I want a little bit of hope. I want to think that I'm doing something, not sitting in this house mending old clothes and dying a little bit more each minute!"

Gelsan opened her mouth, then closed it again at once. When she did speak, her voice was low and soft. "Shame is on our household, to speak this in front of a stranger, daughter."

Kevla could stay silent no longer. "I intend no disrespect," she said, "but if Mylikki is willing to lead me to Altan, then I will accept her offer. I must warn you both that the Dancers have an enemy—a powerful man I know only as the Emperor. I appear to be eluding his gaze in this land, and I am grateful for it. But if Mylikki comes with me, she might very well be in danger."

Gelsan gazed at Kevla and her eyes blazed. Then, suddenly, the older woman seemed to sag a little.

"Mylikki is right," she said, her voice hollow. "We *are* dying a little bit more each day. I would keep her safe, but perhaps she will be safer with a Dragon and a fire-woman than here in this village, where madmen lurk in the woods and food grows ever scarcer."

Mylikki stood still, hardly breathing.

"Let us pack your things," Gelsan said. Both mother and daughter looked as if they wanted desperately to reach out to one another, but something held them back.

Kevla, who had gotten to her feet moments before, said quickly, "I will let the Dragon know," and slipped out the door.

His eyes narrowed when he saw her. "You have learned something. I see it in your face." Kevla told him. "Another clue on our journey, then," he said. "Another piece of this puzzle."

Kevla sighed. "I am tired of journeys and puzzles, Dragon. I would find this man quickly and be done with it."

"Of course, but that is not how things usually work," the Dragon replied, maddeningly philosophical. He rose and shook himself. "I will see if I can find them any more food as a parting gift," he said, suiting action to word.

Alone in the center of the circle of houses, Kevla looked around, again taking in the extreme poverty of the place. Though they were far apart in distance and circumstance, the little village of Arrun Woods had much in common with the place where Kevla had spent the first ten years of her life. Death lurked here, as Gelsan had said, in the form of madmen in the woods and in the slow pinch of starvation. It stank of fear, and yet the people had not given up. Kevla thought of the harsh mien of her mother, forced to sleep with men for money to feed herself and her child. She thought of the beggars on the street, already half out of this life. She found herself smiling at one of the children who shyly waved at her as he zipped past on *skelthas*, and realized she was growing fond of Gelsan and her family.

Don't do it, Kevla, she told herself. *This is not your land; these people are not your concern. They must take care of themselves. Perhaps Mylikki is right, perhaps you can bring back spring to this place; but your real task is to find the Stone Dancer. It's his land and his charge.*

Nonetheless, Kevla used the time waiting for the Dragon and Mylikki to walk up to the stonesteaming hut and heat the stones as strongly as she could.

Some time later, Mylikki and Gelsan emerged from the little house. Mylikki carried an awkwardly wrapped bundle and Gelsan had two large sacks.

Concerned, Kevla said, "I have plenty of provisions, and we have the Dragon. We will not lack for food."

Gelsan replied, "You are on your way to try to bring back spring to the land. I would not have you fail because of lack of supplies. And there is more to surviving in this land than food. Mylikki's not a fire-woman." She let the sacks drop and straightened, her hands on her lower back.

"There's a shelter, dry clothing, and cooking tools as well as dried meat, grains, and fruit," Mylikki explained. Kevla nodded. "Also snow walkers and *skelthas*."

Sahlik had been the only one with forethought enough to send Kevla off with food and, Kevla thought with a pang, the *Shamizan* set. But Mylikki did not have Kevla's ability to stay warm no matter hold cold it was, and Kevla had to admit that she would need to learn how to walk over the snow as these people did.

"The cold poses its own dangers," Gelsan continued. "If anyone in your group falls into a river or is caught in a storm, they must be warmed, but carefully. Remove the wet clothes and lie skin to skin. Too much heat too quickly can kill as surely as the cold."

Kevla listened carefully as Gelsan described other dangers of exposure to the cold and how such ills might be treated. As she finished, everyone heard the sound of the Dragon's wings. No longer afraid, the villagers gathered to watch him come to ground. In his forepaws he clutched three large animals with thick, shaggy fur. Kevla never had learned what they were called. As she watched Gelsan's eyes grow bright with unshed tears of gratitude, her own eyes stung.

"Food for some time. We are grateful to you both. Luck go with you. Kevla…I asked, as you requested. There is no one here who has been having the sort of dreams you described."

Disappointment knifed through Kevla. There were no Lorekeepers in Arrun Woods. Where were they? If there was any time she needed the wisdom and memories of a Lorekeeper, it was here and now, in this strange country where she was searching for her fellow Dancer.

"I will carry the packs," the Dragon said to Mylikki. "You can hold on to Kevla." Mylikki nodded. The three packs disappeared into the vastness of the Dragon's palm and he closed his claws gently. Mylikki turned and went to her brother.

"I want to go with you!" said Olar. He stood straight and firm, but his color was high and his lips trembled.

"Mother needs you here," Mylikki said as she went to him and hugged him. "You have to protect her and the others."

He nodded and stepped back, wiping quickly at his eyes. Mylikki turned to Gelsan. The older woman folded her in her arms and held her tightly. It was the first time Kevla had seen any of them embrace.

"Make us proud, daughter," Gelsan said.

"I will, Mother," Mylikki replied. "We will bring back spring. You'll see."

Gelsan nodded and smiled, but Kevla saw her eyes cloud with doubt. Mylikki quickly said her goodbyes to the rest of the village; to the people she had known all her life. Kevla thought her perhaps a bit overeager to depart. She, who had only recently discovered that she had family and a place among them, had been loath to leave, even though her life in Arukan had been far from the family-centered environment she saw here. She thought about how Mylikki had colored when she spoke Altan's name, of Gelsan's comment that the *huskaa* had spoken kindly to the girl, and thought she understood why Mylikki was so anxious to leave.

Reading her thoughts as he often did, the Dragon sent, *I wonder if this Altan of Mylikki's will be able to help at all, or if we are about to embark on a journey that will do nothing but squander precious time.*

We have no choice, Kevla thought back. *This is the closest we've come to the Dancer so far, and we must follow where this path leads.*

Mylikki finished her farewells and approached the Dragon. He lowered himself as much as he could, extending a forepaw to help his traveling companions clamber atop his massive back. Mylikki looked unsure of herself as she settled in.

"I once was wounded and fell from the Dragon's back," Kevla told her as Mylikki's arms went tightly around her waist. "He dove and caught me."

"That's supposed to reassure me?"

Kevla laughed. Unexpectedly, she felt warm and happy inside. She liked Mylikki, and she had never had a female friend before. She was suddenly glad that she did not have to make the rest of the journey alone.

The Dragon craned his neck to look back at them. "Where to, Mylikki?" he asked.

"He said he was going to the nearest village, Galak-by-the-Lake. Head southeast, and we should see it soon."

Part II:

The Ice Maiden

14

Mylikki's arms around Kevla's waist were so tight that Kevla had trouble drawing breath. "He won't let you fall," she told Mylikki. The girl did not loosen her grip. Trying to distract her new friend, Kevla asked, "What do you think of this?" She indicated the land that unfurled below them.

"It's so high up," Mylikki said. "But it is so very beautiful. The ice and snow look lovely from here."

As the wind whipped her hair, Kevla wondered if the other girl was cold. She wore heavy clothing and a cloak, which was, Kevla supposed, the best she could do. Travel by Dragon had advantages and disadvantages.

"You know what we are looking for, Mylikki," Kevla said.

"Stay alert and keep looking down. Let us know when we come across this village."

"It's called Galak-by-the-Lake," Mylikki said. "It's one of the largest lakes in the region. In summer, everyone..." Her voice trailed off, and Kevla did not press for summertime anecdotes.

It had been late morning when they left. Time passed, and the sun made its low, dim pass across the sky. Finally, Kevla saw something shimmering below them, catching the dying light.

"There!" she cried, pointing. "Is that the lake?"

"Yes," Mylikki replied. "The village should be right... there."

And there it was, Galak-by-the-Lake, looking even smaller than Mylikki's village. The Dragon dove, coming to earth between the large, oval lake and the collection of homes. Smoke issued from holes in the roofs of some; others seemed empty.

"No one is coming to greet us," Kevla said.

"They're afraid," Mylikki answered. "We only came out because we feared you would take our only source of food. And the Dragon isn't exactly helping matters."

"Ungrateful girl," muttered the Dragon.

Mylikki looked both chagrined and horrified. "I meant no insult," she said, "only—"

"He knows what you mean, Mylikki. Dragon, you must admit, you are quite powerful and intimidating."

The compliment placated him. Kevla slid down to the Dragon's upper arm, then dropped to the snow. She held up her arms to help Mylikki dismount.

"Are you sure this is the right place?" Kevla asked.

Mylikki nodded. The cloak hood had slipped, revealing her golden hair. She looked about with intense blue eyes; breath rose from her lips in little puffs. Kevla let her lead; in this frightened land, Mylikki would be more readily welcomed than she.

Many of the houses were roofless ruins. If it were not for the telltale smoke curling up into the sky, Kevla would have thought this village abandoned.

Mylikki strode forward. "Mylikki of the village of Arrun Woods gives greetings to the people of Galak-by-the-Lake," she called in a voice that trembled only a little. She was greeted by silence. "I come with my friends Kevla and the Great Dragon. We seek a *huskaa* by the name of Altan."

No one emerged. Kevla reached to touch the Dragon, wanting to feel his warm smooth scales beneath her fingers.

Abruptly Mylikki turned around and headed back. "The packs," she said. "I need my *kyndela.*"

Kevla was confused, but she helped Mylikki unwrap the instrument. Shrugging it over her shoulder by the leather strap, Mylikki again strode forward in the snow.

"I too am a *huskaa* and I invoke the Law!" she cried, swinging the instrument so that it hung in front of her.

For a few long moments, Kevla thought whatever ploy the girl was trying had failed. Then, one by one, the doors opened a crack.

"We give greetings to *Huskaa* Mylikki, and we honor the Law," said a thin, reedy voice. An old man, so gaunt as to be almost skeletal, stepped out of one of the houses. "Strange times are upon us when a woman is a *huskaa,* but nothing is ordinary now. You and your..." He cleared his throat and stared wide-eyed at the smoke-puffing, silent Dragon. "You and your companions are welcome."

Relief washed over Mylikki's pretty face. "I thank you, and we will not tarry long. We must find Altan. He was about so tall, curly fair hair, blue eyes. Is he here?"

"He has come and gone," the old man answered. Disappointment flooded Kevla. She couldn't help but notice that the headman still did not step out of his house, even though he had offered hospitality in the name of the Law. "Two days since. We had a bad snowstorm," he glanced up at the darkening sky, "and it looks as though another is hard on its heels. He was heading toward Riversong. A nice young man, and a beautiful voice. I hope the snow has not silenced it."

Mylikki swallowed. "Thank you," she said. "We will try to find him." She hesitated, then said, "Forgive me, but it seems to me that your village is suffering. Go to Arrun Woods. Tell them Mylikki sent you. They have food to share with friends, but not with those who would take it by force," she added, no doubt suddenly recalling the madmen in the woods.

The man chuckled, a sad, raspy sound. "We could take nothing by force if we wanted to, child," he said. "We are simply waiting for death. But I think perhaps now, Death may have to wait a bit for us. Luck go with you."

And the door closed again, softly, but firmly. Mylikki stood in the snow for a moment longer, then sighed and walked back to where Kevla and the Dragon waited for her.

"You heard," she said tiredly. "We have to head for Riversong."

"I heard," said the Dragon, lifting his huge head to the sky and sniffing. "And I think the man you spoke with is right. A storm is not too far distant."

"Neither are Altan and Riversong," Mylikki said. "We at least have shelter, food, and the Dragon, Kevla. If he hasn't made it to Riversong, he'll be out in the wilds alone. We have to go after him!"

Mylikki was right. They might not find Altan, but they needed to try. "Come, then, let us make haste," Kevla said.

But they had only been mounted and in the air for a few moments when something cold and wet dotted her cheek. A snowflake. Soon, there was another, and another. The sun had disappeared completely and the earth was barely visible.

"Dragon, can you continue in this?" Kevla asked.

He craned his great head to look back at her. "I can," he replied, "but the question is, can you?"

Kevla glanced back at Mylikki, who had pulled the hood down over her face. Kevla couldn't see her eyes, but she could feel the girl's body shivering.

"I'm f-fine," Mylikki stammered, clearly lying. "We must keep looking for Altan! He could b-be out in this!"

But Kevla knew, and surely Mylikki did as well, that if Altan were indeed out in the storm instead of taking shelter, they would likely fly right over him and never see him. Even as she hesitated, the snow began to fall more quickly. She felt the cold although it did not chill her, and the flakes clung to her lashes.

She made her decision. "Dragon—we must go to ground and wait this out," she cried.

The Dragon obediently changed course and headed for what Kevla assumed was an open space. The snow was coming down fiercely now, and she could barely see. She wiped at her face and blinked rapidly. When he landed, he told them, "Stay there for a moment. I will make a shelter for you."

Snow slid down Kevla's bare shoulders as she looked back at her companion. Mylikki's back and head were almost solid white, and the cruel wind buffeted them so hard that her cloak whipped about her. It tore the hood off and Kevla gasped to see that the girl's eyebrows were coated in ice and her lips were turning blue.

The Dragon undulated, doing something that Kevla couldn't see, and even she had to hang on tightly in order to avoid sliding off his wet, slippery back. She remembered what it was like to be cold, but this—there was no time, no place in Arukan where one would encounter something like this.

"I have hollowed out a place in the snow," the Dragon said, his rumbling voice coming to them through the falling sheets of snow. "I will stand over you until it stops. Come, hurry!"

Kevla extricated herself from Mylikki. She slid off the Dragon to a soft, albeit wet, landing in the thick snow. She could now clearly see what the Dragon had done—he had made them a safe place beneath his enormous red body.

"Come on," she cried, turning her face up to the snow's assault. The wind tore at her hair and snatched the words from her lips. A particularly harsh gust almost made her stumble and she reached for the Dragon's leg.

Normally, the Dragon crouched as low as possible so that it was fairly easy to dismount. But now he stood over their shelter, protecting it for them, so the distance from his back to the earth was much greater than usual. Kevla turned her face back up to the now-white sky. The only color she could see was the vivid red of the Dragon an arm's length away. She held up her arms as Mylikki started to climb down. At one point, though, the wind blew particularly hard and My-likki lost her grip. She yelped, startled, as she fell hard onto Kevla and they both went down into the snow.

"I'm s-sorry!" Mylikki said, her teeth chattering.

"It's all right," Kevla reassured her, helping the girl to her feet and physically turning her in the right direction. "Let's get beneath the Dragon's belly." Together they slogged through the thigh-deep snow.

The sensation of coming into even this little shelter after the ordeal of the snowstorm was one of pure relief. Mylikki fell to her knees, wiping the crusted snow from her eyebrows and hair. As soon as Kevla stumbled in, the Dragon settled his great bulk down slightly. They had formed a tunnel in the snow as they entered, and light and air still came in.

Kevla concentrated and the "room" she had made for them became warmer. She did not want it to get too warm; wetness would be worse than the snow.

Dragon, I need branches. She began to dig downward, packing the snow into the "walls" around her, until her questing fingers brushed dried grass. She tugged up a few wet, yellow blades and brought them into the center of the area.

"Burn," she said, and the pathetic blades obeyed. So did the Dragon; he moved above them, lifting one huge forepaw. They heard a ripping, cracking noise and then Kevla saw a large branch at the entrance to their makeshift shelter. Mylikki stumbled to her feet and together they hauled it inside. Kevla looked closely at the girl; the exertion seemed to be bringing color back into her face.

"This is too big," Kevla said. "We'll need to break this into smaller pieces."

"There's an axe in the pack," Mylikki said. She looked none too cheerful at the thought of going back into the snow.

"Come on," said Kevla. They didn't have to go far; the two large packs and the smaller one were waiting for them a few feet outside. The two women brought them inside and Mylikki proceeded to rummage through one.

"Won't a fire hurt the dragon?" asked Mylikki, glancing up at the living roof of yellow scales.

Kevla laughed. "The Dragon's home is a pit of rock so hot that it is liquid. This will be a little warm tickle."

Mylikki produced two tools with a flourish. One was the promised axe and the other was a small shovel. Working together, the women shoveled the snow from the center, packing it into the walls, until they uncovered a small circular spot on the earth. Then, while Kevla steadied the huge branch, Mylikki hacked it into manageable pieces and arranged them in the makeshift, snow-encircled fire pit.

"Burn," Kevla said, and at once a cheery light filled the area. Mylikki sighed with pleasure and extended her hands toward the fire, drinking in the welcome warmth.

"The Dragon is a better shelter than anything we brought," Mylikki announced.

"There will be times and places where he won't be able to accompany us," Kevla warned. "It is well you brought them. Get out of those wet things and give them to me."

Shivering, Mylikki rose and unfastened her cloak. Kevla took it and concentrated, using her Fire-gift to warm the frozen garment. The cloak was stiff with ice. As the ice melted, the cloak began to steam. Understanding now, Mylikki began to shed the rest of her clothes more quickly, removing her outer dress and stockings. Kevla handed her the now-warm and dry cloak, which she used to wrap herself in while she removed her underdress. Soon, she was comfortably clad in clothes that a few moments ago had been sodden and cold.

Kevla dried her own *rhia* on her body with a thought. She had made the clothing from fire itself, drawing forth flame in the Dragon's lair and dressing herself in it. If ever need arose, she knew she could do so again.

"Thank you," Mylikki said humbly. "I thought I was well on the way to becoming an Ice Maiden myself."

"It is a gift," Kevla said. She did not tell the other woman that the gift was like a sword that could cut both ways. It might have kept Mylikki warm today; but it had also claimed the life of the person Kevla loved more than anyone in the world.

To distract herself, she said, "Something hot to eat will help you stay warm." One of the things Gelsan had packed was a small pot. Kevla filled it with snow and put it on the fire while Mylikki added dried meat and spices, stirring the soup with a wooden spoon. Kevla knew she could have ordered Mylikki to prepare her meal for her, and that the other girl would have jumped to the task. But Kevla was no great lady, no *khashima,* no queen. She had been born illegitimate, raised on the streets, and her highest rank had been as a handmaiden. She was more comfortable tending others than being tended.

"We would have missed Altan if we had kept going," Kevla said. "You know that, don't you?"

Mylikki sighed. "Yes. We will try again tomorrow. He's not stupid, he would have found shelter somewhere." She stared at the flame, her eyes distant, her mouth curved in a frown of concern.

"What was that you said to the headman? Something about the Law?"

"What? Oh." Mylikki laughed. "I told a little lie, I fear. I passed myself off as a *huskaa*. *Huskaas* are always welcome, even in times such as these. It's an ancient code of hospitality, the *Huskaa* Law. If a *huskaa* requests food or shelter, it must be given to him. In return, he will play and tell stories and share what news he has. They might not have talked to Mylikki of Arrun Woods, but they would have to open their doors to Mylikki the *huskaa*. Women aren't supposed to become formal *huskaas,* though we are allowed to play. The headman commented on that, as you recall."

"Then we were lucky," said Kevla. She recalled something else Mylikki had said. "Who is the Ice Maiden? I've heard that name before. Is she the one who brings the snow in the winter?"

Stirring the pot, Mylikki shook her head. "No, the term 'ice' was never meant to be taken literally. At least, not originally. It's an old song cycle called 'Circle of Ice,' about a girl whose heart was broken and who decides to wreak vengeance on all men because of it. It has nothing to do with winter. But when the winter started to last so long," Mylikki continued, "people grew fearful. We knew this could not be the gods' doing—they bring spring and rebirth, not winter. Something must be preventing them from tending to us. The only story we had was the Ice Maiden, and she took on this new aspect of eternal winter."

She smiled, wistfully. "That always used to upset Altan," she said, her voice tender. "He felt this new interpretation ruined the story by trying to make it literal. 'The Ice Maiden has a *heart* of ice, not a *body* of ice,' he said."

Kevla looked at the wall of snow surrounding them. "It *is* all a story, isn't it?"

Mylikki looked up from the *kyndela*. "Something's gone wrong. It could just as likely be the Ice Maiden as anything else."

"Will you sing one of the songs for me?"

"Most of them are meant to be sung by a man. Each song tells a story, and each story is part of the whole. Let's wait until Altan is with us, and we can both perform for you."

"What about the *taaskali?* Tell me about them."

"Well, I only know what I've been told. They're supposed to look more like you than like us," said Mylikki. She reached for a ladle and spooned up some hot stew for herself and Kevla. "They have dark skin, eyes, and hair, and are believed to have all kinds of magical talents. They are believed to be closer to the gods than we are. They follow and tend the herds of the white *selva,* whose milk can bestow long life. A cloak woven from their fur can turn arrows." She ate a bite of stew. "I've never met anyone who's actually met a *taaskal,* or even seen a *selva.* But when we saw you standing on the hill, with your dark skin and hair and wearing only this light little garment—well, you can understand why we thought you a *taaskal.*"

Kevla nodded and ate hungrily. She listened to the howling wind outside, and for the thousandth time, it seemed, was grateful for the Dragon's presence. She hoped that Altan had found shelter and that they would locate him soon. They finished the meal in silence, washed the bowls, utensils, and cauldrons in the snow and packed them back in the sacks. Mylikki pulled out several blankets and prepared to make a bed. Kevla rose and went to help her.

"That should be big enough for both of us," Mylikki declared, lying down.

Kevla was taken aback. She knew nothing of Lamali customs. She had thought Mylikki was pining for Altan, but then again, there were some who appreciated the beauty of both sexes.

"I am fond of you, Mylikki," Kevla began, "and it's not that I don't think you are attractive, but…"

Mylikki stared at her for a moment, then threw her head back and laughed. "And you are attractive as well, Kevla, but I have no desire for your body. I am used to sleeping close beside others, and I will be honest—though you do not need the warmth, I do. If that is all right with you."

Kevla felt her cheeks grow hot. "Of course."

As Kevla crawled into the blankets beside her and took the other girl into her arms, snuggling so that Mylikki's thin body curved into hers, Mylikki said, "Thank you, Kevla. I'm sorry if I made you feel uncomfortable."

"I'm sorry I didn't volunteer my warmth," Kevla said. Impulsively, she squeezed Mylikki gently and the other girl nestled closer.

"You should be happy we're clothed," Mylikki said, and Kevla could hear the mirth in her voice. "When someone has gotten too cold, the best way to warm him is skin to skin."

"I'll be sure to remember that," Kevla said wryly.

They lay in comfortable silence for a time, then Mylikki said into the darkness, "Kevla…do you know much about men?"

Kevla tensed. "Why do you ask?"

"I was wondering…well, I think it's pretty obvious that I care about Altan."

"There's nothing wrong with that."

"Sometimes...sometimes he makes me think there is."

"What do you mean?"

Mylikki was silent for a moment, then said, "When he came to Arrun Woods...I'd never felt anything like that before, not with other boys. He made me feel like I was a queen."

Kevla thought about how Jashemi made her feel. *I belong to you completely, Kevla. I always have, and I always will.* She tried not to remember anything more.

"But then, one evening he performed the Ice Maiden cycle, and on the second song—one in which a young man seduces a woman he doesn't love because his heart is bound to the Ice Maiden—he stared right at me and he looked... disgusted with me."

Kevla felt her draw breath, and softly sing a verse.

Don't fall in love with me, my girl;
Don't fall in love with me.
For I shall take thy body
And then I'll let thee be;
By afternoon tomorrow,
I'll have forgotten thee.

She was trying to keep the pain out of her voice, but failing. Kevla hugged her tighter, feeling her move to wipe her face. "Why would he do such a thing?" Kevla asked.

"I don't know. But the next day he was as sweet as ever, as if nothing had happened. It's very confusing. Have you ever been in love, Kevla?"

Quietly, Kevla answered, "Yes."

"What happened? Did he—did he abandon you?"

If only that had happened. I would have a broken heart, but he would be alive. "No. He died."

"Oh, Kevla, I'm sorry, I didn't mean to pry."

Kevla shushed her with a gentle pat. "It's all right. It's just—I don't know much about how men treat women here, so I can't really advise you."

"When we find him, will you tell me what you think of him?"

"Yes, of course."

"I love him, Kevla." The words were a hushed whisper, issuing forth in the anonymous darkness. "I love him with all my heart, even though I've only known him a short time. I'd do anything for him. Anything. But I don't know if he wants me. I don't—I don't want to end up like the Ice Maiden, alone and angry and hurt...."

"You're a wonderful girl, Mylikki. Let's see what the future holds before we fear it. Now, go to sleep. And no dreams of Ice Maidens and snow."

15

Kevla poked her head out to a dim morning. Despite her admonition to Mylikki, she herself had slept fitfully, haunted by dreams of a beautiful woman made of ice. She stretched and crawled outside. The Dragon's head hung above her, his nostrils flaring. He exhaled two small puffs of smoke.

"It is overcast, but not snowing," the Dragon said, lowering his head for her caress. "We can fly for some time."

"That is well," said Kevla. "Perhaps it is just that this land seems so alien to me, but I am anxious to find Altan and the Stone Dancer and leave this place."

"It is not your unfamiliarity with this place that makes you feel so," the Dragon assured her. "We need to be on our guard." He eyed her. "We are not alone."

She looked in the direction he had indicated. The air was thick and gray and it was hard to see, but she could have sworn she saw a movement in the forests. On the soft, powdery surface of the fresh snow, Kevla noticed a cold glitter that caught what little light there was. It was a thin ribbon of ice that curled in on itself in a sort of ring.

"What is it?" Her voice had dropped to a whisper.

"Men," the Dragon said. "They've been here all night."

"The wild men?"

The Dragon cocked his head in a gesture that Kevla knew meant he was puzzled by something. "Perhaps. There's something awry with them, Kevla. They smell…wrong."

"Why didn't they attack?"

Slowly, the Dragon looked down at her with a faintly amused expression and she burst out laughing. Even if the men in the forest had seen her and Mylikki last night, two apparently defenseless women, they had been completely sheltered by a huge dragon. An army would think twice about attacking.

Mylikki crawled out from underneath the Dragon and smiled. "Hearing you laugh, Kevla, makes me think the day is off to a wonderful start."

Kevla's mirth faded, but she kept the smile in place for Mylikki's sake. She did not want to alarm the girl. Besides, soon they would be many leagues from here.

"The day seems clear," Mylikki said, gazing up at the blue sky. "I am sure we will find Altan today!"

Kevla and the Dragon exchanged glances. Kevla desperately hoped so, too; hoped they would find the youth alive. The storm last night had been severe. If he had not been able to find shelter…

Kevla and Mylikki ate a quick meal of tea and dried fruit, then gathered their belongings and climbed aboard the Dragon. The day was bright and clear and they could see for leagues. Mylikki had sketched a simple map in the snow, showing them where they would be headed. Riversong was not too far away.

There were no tracks to follow from Galak-by-the-Lake, of course; the storm had seen to that. Kevla had hoped to see telltale *skeltha* trails leading to the village of Riversong, but there was nothing.

A small cluster of houses appeared below them, dotted along the gentle curve of a bright, frozen river.

"Riversong," Mylikki said dully.

"He could have weathered the storm in the village," Kevla said.

Mylikki shook her head. "He couldn't get there in just two days." Her voice was thick and laced with fear. "And not with another storm earlier."

At once, the Dragon lowered a wing and made a smooth circle, turning back to retrace their path. "We will find him," he assured the two women. "I will fly closer to the ground, to see if I can catch his scent."

Even as he spoke, Kevla felt her friend's thoughts brush hers. *See if you can sense him, Kevla. He might not be the Stone Dancer, but he is important in our quest.*

I'll try, Kevla thought back. She closed her eyes and calmed her mind, extending her thoughts. She felt Mylikki's arms around her tremble, felt the Dragon fly lower and lower until he was almost skimming the snow.

She was able to communicate with the Dragon by thinking words. Perhaps reaching Altan would be similar to that.

Altan. Singer of songs. Friend to the Stone Dancer. Let me know where you are....

Nothing. She opened her eyes, disappointment and apprehension surging through her. If only there were someone who could explain how this worked. How was she supposed to—

And then the knowledge came. Swift, sure, precise—as if she'd known it all along. She was so surprised by the revelation that it took her a moment to tell the others.

"The woods on the left," she said. "He's down there. I—I feel it."

The Dragon headed for the forest she had indicated. He came to ground in a clear area at the edge of the woods and the two women dismounted.

"You sensed him?" Mylikki asked.

"I think so," Kevla said.

"How?"

"I have no idea. My powers—even I don't know their full extent. But I think he's in here somewhere."

She had been pleased, excited, but now realized that the forest was enormous. Mylikki was starting to breathe too quickly, fear for Altan consuming her.

Kevla grabbed her hands. "Mylikki, I know you're worried, but I need you to be calm." Mylikki turned her blue eyes to Kevla and nodded. Kevla entwined her fingers with those of her friend. "I want you to think of Altan. See him in your mind. Try to capture what it is about him that makes him special."

Her eyes were bright with unshed tears, but her mouth curved in a smile. "That will be easy."

Kevla closed her eyes and concentrated. She had thought that perhaps she might see Altan in her own mind, but no image came. But one thing did come: a very clear sense of direction.

Squeezing Mylikki's hands, she dropped them. "Dragon, wait here. I will call you when we've found him. Come on, Mylikki!"

They turned as one and stepped into the dark shade of the forest, leaving the Dragon behind. The trees grew thick and dark. Humans had not come here, and any small animal trails they might have followed were lost beneath the snow. The going was difficult, and more than once Kevla lost her footing in her thin sandals. She was grateful beyond words for the little sensations and thoughts that came to her; *turn left here, go a little farther there.* Mylikki was hard on her heels as they stumbled through the woods.

Without warning the forest opened into a small clearing. Large, snow-covered boulders jutted upward. Kevla knew they were close now. Her heart was racing.

"Call him," she told Mylikki.

Mylikki cupped her hands around her mouth and cried Altan's name. Her clear voice carried on the crisp air, but there was no answering call.

He's hurt, Kevla thought, not knowing how she knew. She closed her eyes and willed herself to find the boy. He was nearby, she was sure of it. She turned, her body being pulled by something she couldn't control.

She opened her eyes and found herself staring directly at a small entrance into the jumble of boulders—a sliver of darkness she had missed before. The entrance had been almost completely covered by last night's snowfall.

"There," she said. "He's in there." She hurried to the boulder. Mylikki quickly joined her and both women pulled armloads of snow away from the entrance.

"Altan?" Mylikki called as they dug. "Altan, we're coming, hang on!"

Finally, they had dug out enough snow so that Kevla could edge forward. Before she entered the darkness, she cupped her hand and called a small flame. She wriggled into the narrow opening, feeling her body heat melt the ice, and extended the hand that cupped the little fire.

The faint light illuminated a small cavern. She saw something in the darkness, a motionless shape lying beyond the reach of the small fire's light.

Please be all right, she thought, digging in with her left elbow and stretching out her right hand as far as she could. Suddenly she gasped and her body strained. There was a sudden, sharp drop-off and she almost tumbled forward.

As Altan had before her.

She could see him now, a huddled lump on the floor of the cavern. His cloak covered most of him, but she saw a white hand clutching a pack and a hint of golden curls.

She pulled back, closing her hand over the flame in her palm and extinguishing its insufficient light. "He's here," she told Mylikki, "but he's hurt. Get me some branches, I need more light."

Mylikki went pale, but did as she was told, returning a moment later with two sturdy branches. Kevla gave one to her and lit them both.

"Follow me," she said. "Be careful. There's a drop-off that comes up quite suddenly."

The two women crawled forward. Kevla held the burning branch in her right hand and felt for the ledge with the other. Once she could see it, it was not tricky to negotiate. But Altan, crawling in blindly, half-frozen from the storm, had been at its mercy.

She turned over, swung her legs underneath her and lowered herself carefully. Her feet touched sturdy stone. She reached up to help Mylikki descend. Once Mylikki's legs hit the earth she hastened to Altan, pulling the cloak from his pale face and grasping his hand in hers.

"Altan?" she said, her voice cracking.

He was so still…. Kevla reached in between them, feeling for a pulse on his throat. It was there—thready and faint, but there. Wedging the branch in a crack between the rocks so the light would stay steady, she saw that the boy—for he was in truth little more than a boy, perhaps even younger than Mylikki—was unnaturally pale and his lips were a dark color.

Kevla had been trained as a healer, but she had never before had cause to treat anyone who lay nearly frozen to death. Sickness from the heat, burns from the sun, yes, but not this. So instead of relying on training, she reached for instinct. She found both of Altan's hands and clasped them to her heart. At the same time she leaned forward and slipped her hand down Altan's throat, past the collar of his cloak and shirt, and onto his bare skin.

"What are you doing?" Mylikki asked.

Kevla ignored her. She closed her eyes and called the power that dwelt inside her.

No rushing surge of heat, not this time; she needed the gentle, steady warmth of the ember, not the licking, consuming conflagration of flame. She felt her body grow warmer, felt that warmth penetrate into Altan's body from his hands on her heart and her hand on his. She tried to see the heat in her mind's eye, as it moved along his body, into his skin, his blood, his bones.

"He needs more," she told Mylikki, thinking even as she spoke: *Dragon! We need your help!*

"His clothes are soaked," Mylikki said, quickly divesting the young *huskaa* of his outer garments.

Something flashed through Kevla's mind. He was in a fragile state, like a wounded man.... "Cut the clothing off," she cried. "Don't move him too much."

"I don't have a knife," Mylikki began, but she was cut off by a crashing sound that made the earth tremble. Dirt and small rocks showered them. Scarcely had they recovered from this than they heard the horrifying, grinding sound of the boulders above them moving. Mylikki screamed and ducked, covering Altan's body with hers to protect him from the huge rocks that were sure to come crashing down on all three of them.

Instead, the boulder moved upward, and sunlight streamed in. Kevla looked up and saw the dear face of the Dragon. He had come when she needed him. Her heart surged with love for her friend.

"Altan's almost frozen to death," Kevla said to him. "We need the packs!"

The Dragon dropped them down and Mylikki dove on them, finding the knife and cutting at Altan's clothing. The fabric was almost frozen stiff.

While Mylikki removed Altan's garments, Kevla fumbled for the blankets. She looked again at the youth. He was moving now, and a soft groan escaped his lips. Kevla rolled him gently to one side and then the other so she could tuck the blankets around him. His skin was almost icy to the touch.

He was bare to the waist now. Where his flesh was exposed, Kevla covered it with the blanket as best she could. Mylikki was at the boy's feet, trying to tug off his boots. Kevla went to help her. Once the boots were off Mylikki started to fold the blanket up around Altan's lower body, but Kevla stayed her hand.

"The breeches," she said. "They are soaked through as well."

Mylikki nodded. She and Kevla cut away the breeches and Altan lay naked before them. Slender, almost ice-white, with golden hair catching the light at groin and crown, he looked as beautiful and as fragile as a dying *liah* to Kevla.

She thought about how Mylikki had described Altan's voice; strong, beautiful, pure. A voice that Kevla now realized she might never hear. The thought infuriated and grieved her. *No!* Kevla thought. *That voice will not be silenced!*

What was it Gelsan had said? Skin to skin contact, and a gentle steady warming was what was called for when someone was in Altan's state. Mylikki had confirmed it last night: *You should be happy we're clothed.... When someone has gotten too cold, the best way to warm him is skin to skin.* Heedless now of her own modesty or his, knowing only that she needed to warm him with the fire that burned deep inside her heart, Kevla tore off her *rhia* and lay beside him. She stretched the entire length of her body against his, twining long legs and arms about him. His chest pressed against her breasts, his limp *kurjah* brushed against her *sulim*. At another time, it might have been an intimate embrace, but for Kevla, it was devoid of eroticism. Altan hung suspended between life and death.

"Wrap us tightly!" she cried. Mylikki did so, tucking the blanket snugly around them. Kevla looked up to see the Dragon sitting on his haunches, golden eyes full of concern.

"Dragon, hold us!"

Kevla felt herself and the barely conscious Altan being lifted and pressed to the Dragon's breast. His scales were very warm, almost but not quite hot, and Kevla felt her own body heat up again. Heart to heart they lay in the Dragon's paws, Kevla-sha-Tahmu and a boy she had never before seen, bodies entangled in life-giving warmth.

Cling to me, she thought, wrapping her arms more tightly about him. *Cling to life, Altan.*

How long she held him, she did not know. At last, she felt his chilled flesh warm, his heartbeat become steadier. Kevla felt him move, felt his arms tighten around her. She did not stop him; he was past knowing what he did and the fact that he was moving at all gladdened her.

"Put us down, please," Kevla asked the Dragon. He obeyed, gently lowering them to the earth. Mylikki had not been idle. She had set up a tent, spread blankets on the ground and had started a small fire. She stirred the cauldron and Kevla smelled tea.

Good, she thought. *A hot beverage will warm him once he is able to drink.*

She moved away a little and found herself staring into a pair of large, blue-green eyes. He had a face that was at once both sweet and masculine, heartbreakingly beautiful. No wonder Mylikki had been so charmed. But to her surprise, that face shifted from puzzlement to anger. He craned his neck and peered down, uttering an exclamation of annoyance when he saw Mylikki. She smiled in relief as their eyes met, but his words stilled her expression of pleasure.

"You again! Curse it, will I never be rid of you?" he snarled.

His voice was slightly slurred but still musical and entrancing, but the ugly words chilled Kevla. He continued speaking and Kevla was relieved when she realized he was spouting nonsense: "Big hands...too crowded...."

His eyes closed and he fell unconscious again. Kevla pulled him to her as the Dragon lowered them both, not wanting to see the pain in Mylikki's blue eyes.

16

For the next few hours, Altan was almost like a drunken man. His speech was slurred and full of nonsense and he drifted in and out of sleep. When he was awake, they gave him tea and hot broth; when he slept, Mylikki held him with a fierce possessiveness.

Kevla knew her actions had saved Altan's life. She was fire incarnate; the warmth that burned within her could be directed and channeled in a way that the natural heat of Mylikki's simple human skin could not. Mylikki knew this as well, but there was a wistfulness that told Kevla more strongly than any words that she wished she had been the one to hold Altan. Kevla hoped that the cruel words Altan had spoken to Mylikki were as mad as the rest of his cold-induced ravings, but wondered; after all, he had been cruel to Mylikki before.

You were the right one to hold Altan, the Dragon thought to her. *Mylikki might have wanted to, but you couldn't risk Altan's life.*

I wish she had *been the one to do it,* Kevla thought. She folded her arms across her knees and gazed at the fire. *Altan's touch was pleasant, but his is not the touch I long for.*

Her eyes suddenly blurred with tears and she placed her head on her arms. Her heart contracted with remembered pain and guilt. The touch she longed for, she knew, she ought never have experienced...and would never experience again.

I miss you so much, Jashemi. And it's all my fault. If I had been stronger, better able to resist; if everything had unfolded as it was meant to, you would be here with me now. I would give anything to have you here with me, to see your face, hear your laugh...but you are gone from me forever and I have no one but myself to blame.

Altan still slept and Mylikki held him, her face pressed to his. Her pretty blue eyes were closed and she was singing softly to the unconscious *huskaa.* It was a poignant image, a private one, and suddenly Kevla wanted to be alone.

She rose and stalked off. The Dragon said nothing, but let her go. Kevla slogged through the snow, its impersonal resistance to her passage making her angrier and more frustrated and at last she stumbled and fell into the soft white blanket.

She wept then, realizing how she had taken her feelings and placed them in a little corner because they were inconvenient. Not conducive to learning about Lamal, or finding the Stone Dancer. But the innocent press of Altan's body against hers had reminded her skin that it had once been caressed by a man she had adored; that her body had once joined in passionate lovemaking with one who knew her better than she knew herself.

She wept for him, for herself, for the life she had left behind, for everything she had lost, and when she was done pouring her grief into the snow, she felt a little better. This wave of anguish had come and gone. But she knew an endless river of agony lurked, ready for the next time she was distracted from the task at hand; ready to bite like a sandsnake and pump its venom of shame and guilt into her soul.

She washed her face with a handful of snow, feeling no stinging bite from its coldness, and took a deep, shuddering breath. There was something she had wanted to do for some time now, and finally, she gave herself permission.

Kevla gathered a few fallen branches. "Burn," she said. When the fire was crackling cheerfully, she swallowed hard. In a voice that trembled, she said, "Show me Tahmu."

Immediately, the face of her father, the *khashim* of the Clan of Four Waters, appeared in the flame. He jerked back, no doubt startled at the apparition, then smiled in recognition.

"Kevla!"

She smiled back, tremulously. "Hello, Father." The term felt so strange in her mouth still.

"It is so good to see you, my daughter." There was an awkward pause. "Are you well?"

Kevla nodded. "Well enough. How are you? And Sahlik, and Meli?"

"We are all very well. We were very busy after you left, though."

"What's happening? Tell me." She leaned forward, knowing that all she needed to do to physically be with him was step into the fire, too afraid that if she did so she would not have the strength of will to return. Though she had once been treated badly there, Arukan was and always would be her home.

"Most of the Clans agreed to form a council. We are trying to arrange when to meet and determine how much control it should have." He smiled again, somewhat wistfully. "I wish you were here to share your wisdom. We still do not agree on everything, and it is much easier to obey the Great Dragon when he is present to make his wishes known."

The lump in her throat made it hard to speak. "I am glad to hear that you are making progress, however slow it might be. How are the *kulis?*"

"It is a sweet thing, my daughter. You would be moved to see how welcomed they have been," he said. "It was as if we as a people were waiting for this for years."

You were, Kevla thought. *So much was waiting to be changed.* She wiped at her face.

"We speak of you often. Have you found what you sought?"

"Not yet. This is such a strange land, Father. There are wonders and beauty and darkness here. I cannot even begin to speak of it."

"I hope one day your travels bring you home," her father said softly, his dark eyes sad and yet hopeful. "We—we miss you."

"I miss you too," she said, and found to her surprise that it was true. Here in this alien land, she longed for the familiar—the smell and bustle of the kitchens, Sahlik's brusque kindness....

Her eyes filled with tears. "Perhaps one day I will return," she said. "Give my love to Meli."

"I will. I once would have said, 'Dragon go with you,' but in your case, he did."

The comment made Kevla laugh a little. She wiped again at her wet eyes. She still did not truly regard Tahmu-kha-Rakyn as her father; she wondered if she ever would, even though she had taken his name. In a way, she fiercely envied Meli, her little sister. Meli's first ten years had been difficult beyond Kevla's imagining, but now the child was in a home where she was welcomed and honored; where their father was free to express his love for her. There was so much Kevla yearned for that could never be hers.

Kevla wondered how things would have been different had Meli been permitted to spend her first years safely in the House of Four Waters, not only for the girl's sake, but for her mother's. Yeshi had been devastated when Meli was taken from her. Would Yeshi have become such a bitter, murderous woman if she had been able to keep her daughter? Somehow, Kevla didn't think so. Before that awful incident, Yeshi had been vain and shallow, but not evil. Not then.

"I need to go," she said thickly.

"Will we hear from you again?" Tahmu asked.

"I don't know. I'll try to stay in contact. Goodbye, Father."

"Goodbye, Kevla. I am so very proud of you."

With a wave of her hand, Kevla extinguished the little fire. She sat and stared at the black, burned wood for a long time.

* * *

When at last she returned, Mylikki was alone with Altan. The Dragon was gone. As Kevla slogged up to their campsite, Mylikki regarded her with relief. "I wasn't sure where you'd gone," she said.

There was a rustling in the blankets and Altan Lukkari sat up. He looked nothing like the still, cold figure they had found a few hours ago. His color had returned, and he was alert and smiling. He pulled the blankets around his still-naked frame self-consciously.

"You must be Kevla," he said in that lovely voice. "Mylikki has told me all about you. I understand I owe you my life. 'Thank you' seems inadequate."

"You're welcome," Kevla said. "I am glad to see you looking well." This polite, earnest youth was a world away from the cruel boy who had snarled such unkind words. Kevla set about preparing something hot for them to eat. "How are you feeling now?"

"Exhausted," Altan admitted. "And weak."

"Sounds like the Ice Maiden nearly got you," said Kevla, somewhat mischievously.

As she had hoped, Altan looked annoyed. "I see Mylikki has been talking to you about the legend," he said. "I keep trying to explain to her that the Ice Maiden got the term because she was unfeeling, not because she—"

Kevla caught Mylikki's eye and saw an impish smile spread on the other girl's face. Both of them started laughing. Altan looked confused, then he joined in.

"All right, all right," he said, his voice warm with mirth. "You two have saved my life. I suppose I should let you tease me all you like."

"I'd rather ask you some questions, if you feel up to it."

Altan shifted in his blanket. "I know why you needed to cut off my wet clothes, and I don't want you to think me ungrateful," he said, "but could I trouble you to give me my pack so I can find something to wear?"

Mylikki sprang to hand him his pack. Both women politely turned their backs while he dressed.

"Much better," he said. A sudden, worried expression crossed his face and he clutched at the pack. "My *kyndela!*" he cried, sounding like he had lost a child.

"I've been keeping it out of the weather for you," Mylikki said. "Here." She drew it out of her own pack, where she had wrapped it carefully.

"Thank you," he said fervently, reaching for it eagerly. He frowned a little as he examined it. "I could trust you to understand how important it is." He gave her a radiant smile, and Mylikki seemed to blossom in front of Kevla's eyes. Mindful of her promise to Mylikki, Kevla watched Altan closely, but the words and the warmth behind them struck her as genuine. Flexing his fingers, Altan plucked at the strings and winced at the sound. "You can hear it protesting," he joked.

Kevla stirred the thin soup. Gelsan had been generous in giving them supplies. Still, it was only their second night of traveling, and who knew how long this would last them. She glanced up at the darkening sky. "I assume the Dragon went hunting?"

"Yes," Mylikki said. "I'm surprised he hasn't returned yet."

Kevla was, too, but she said nothing. Neither she nor the Dragon had told Mylikki about the strange men that had been lurking in the woods last night, and Kevla was slightly worried for her friends. She told herself that they had flown many leagues and that the Dragon would not have left if he did not feel it was safe to do so.

Altan shook his golden head. "Dragon," he said, in a voice of awe. "Never had I thought to see such a marvel. He was gone when I awoke. I am anxious to meet him." His lips curved in a smile. "What a song I shall make for him."

Altan cocked his head and leaned down to hear every note as he continued to tune the instrument. Even these sounds, one note at a time, made Kevla's skin prickle. She had heard tales of magical instruments; if any instrument was enchanted, then surely it had to be a *kyndela*.

"You have seen marvels, though," Kevla said. "Mylikki tells me you have told her about a man from your village who could do amazing things."

He looked up from tuning the instrument. "She told you about Jareth Vasalen?"

Jareth. Kevla was inordinately pleased. At last, she had a name to put to the Stone Dancer. She nodded.

"I know him better than any man, I think," Altan continued. "He helped bring me into this world. He was like a big brother to me."

His voice was warm with affection, and Kevla's own heart warmed hearing it. This, indeed, was a worthy Dancer.

"He was quite famous, of course, because of his gifts. He called the seasons. He also called animals for food during lean times. He refused to do it during the softer months. He said that wasn't fair, that we should work for what we needed. But he would never let anyone go hungry."

Kevla felt her mouth curling in a smile. She liked Jareth

better and better the more she learned about him. He sounded kind and compassionate.

"Once, when a little girl from another village got lost, he asked the trees and the stones to tell him where she had passed. Her family found her before nightfall."

He saves life with his powers—with Earth magic, Kevla thought. Her pleasure abated somewhat, as she recalled what she had done in Arukan with her powers. *He saves lives...I take them.*

"But then the winter came, and would not leave," said Kevla.

"Yes," said Altan heavily. "I am ashamed to say how Skalka Valley treated him after that. Many whispered that he was cursed." Anger flared in those blue-green eyes. He was silent for a time, his hands softly caressing the *kyndela* as he stared into the flames. "When his family died, I'm sure he *did* believe he was cursed."

Kevla felt a rush of sympathy for a man she had never met. "What happened?"

"The snow," Altan said, simply. "He was off with a group of hunters, trying to call some animals for food. The storm came so quickly, so unexpectedly.... It looked as though the wind had broken down the door and the snow had come in too fast for them to get out. It seems impossible—but then again, once I would have said a winter that lasted a year was impossible, too."

He swallowed hard. "I was the one who found them," he said. "I was worried about them...they lived too near the mountains for safety, I always told him that...."

Mylikki squeezed his arm. Altan gave her a sweet smile, but his eyes were still sad. "I wanted him to come live with me, but he left that night," he said. "Not a word to anyone, not even to me." He shrugged. "So I decided to try to find him myself. I'm worried about him."

So am I, thought Kevla. "He's not dead," she said aloud to reassure Altan. "I'd know it if he was. We...we all would." She told him about the Dancers, about their task, and again asked hopefully if he knew any Lorekeepers. He shook his head.

"This is all new to me," he said. "Wonderful and fascinating, but new. I have never heard of anyone having the dreams you speak of, Kevla, or any visions. There must not be many Lorekeepers in Lamal. But as you know, we are a scattered people. We used to trade with other villages, but since the snow and the madmen came...well. I have been to some villages where they did not even honor the *Huskaa* Law. I was shocked."

So, apparently, was Mylikki. "Really? They would not open their doors to you?"

"No. Some just kept their doors closed until I went away. At one village I even sat on the snow and played for them, to prove I was a *huskaa.*"

Mylikki seemed stunned. She sat back, pulling her cloak around her, confusion on her face. Even more than an endless winter and killers in the forest, this seemed to shock her to the very core.

Kevla felt a prickling. "The Dragon comes." She could see him now, a small but growing speck against the darkening sky.

Altan looked up and his eyes widened. His mouth opened slightly. He, too, got to his feet, still holding his *kyndela* in one hand. Kevla watched for the look of fear, but saw only wonder. As the Dragon grew closer and finally landed, folding his massive wings against his side, Altan's lips curved in a faint smile.

"I begin to think I have died after all," he said quietly, "to behold such things."

The Dragon cocked his head. "Rather not dead, I think— you are looking much better than the last time I saw you," he rumbled. "You are a fortunate man, Altan. I hope you are properly grateful to Kevla."

Still gazing rapturously at the mighty creature, Altan said, "Indeed I am, Great Dragon. Indeed I am."

The Dragon sighed and opened his forepaws. "Poor hunting today, I fear. A few birds I snatched out of the air. I saw nothing on the ground."

"This will be a wonderful meal," Kevla reassured him, her mouth watering at the sight of the three large birds with gray-white plumage and long, slender necks.

The Dragon again dug a shelter into the snow while the meal was prepared. Mylikki and Kevla plucked the birds, then cut the flesh into small chunks and added them to the soup. Altan, still not fully recovered from his ordeal, drowsed again, reviving some time later. He sniffed appreciatively.

"Since I have begun traveling," he said, "the only meals I have had when I was not in a village have been cold dried meat and water. This is a feast!"

Sheltered beneath the protective covering of the Dragon's huge, warm body, they ate their fill of the scrawny birds that Mylikki called *gahalgeese*. It truly was a feast. Kevla hoped they would continue to be lucky enough to obtain fresh meat. Both Altan and Mylikki still seemed so thin to her. When they were done, Mylikki cleaned out the pot and Altan reached for his *kyndela*.

"I assume you have heard Mylikki play and sing?" he asked Kevla. "She is quite accomplished."

Mylikki blushed, her eyes glowing with pleasure from the compliment. "I had a good teacher," she said.

He grinned at her affectionately. "If you were a man, I'd have taken you as a *huskaa-lal,* you know."

Mylikki's delight seemed to abate. "I know," she said, softly, returning her attention to scrubbing the cauldron.

"Mylikki performed the song that made me think there might be Lorekeepers here," Kevla said, "the one called *Fighting Back the Shadow.*"

"Ah. No one sings that better than Mylikki. We spoke earlier of the Ice Maiden. Have you heard any of the songs?"

"She asked me about them," Mylikki said, "but I told her to wait until we had found you." She did not mention she had sung one of the crueler verses to Kevla last night.

His face softened. "If you had not come for me, Mylikki, no one would have ever found me," he said. "Thank you." Turning his attention back to his instrument, he added, "Even my fingers are still whole, so that I can play. Truly a miracle."

Kevla scooped up some snow into the freshly cleaned cauldron and increased the fire's heat. She dropped some dried herbs into the pot for tea.

Altan began to play.

A stranger came a-riding,
And thus he me did greet:
"I seek the cold Ice Maiden,
A challenge for to meet.
I've sought the maid no man can move

For ten months and a year,
And now my search has reached an end—
They tell me she dwells here."

I gazed upon the rider,
A noble lad in truth;
But overbold and reckless,
As I was in my youth.
Though strong, he'd not be strong enough,
I knew he must not stay,
And so for tender pity's sake,
This I to him did say:

"She is called the Ice Maiden,
And she's perilous fair;
There are stars in her eyes,
And the sun's in her hair.
Though her lips be wine-red,
You may take it from me—
There is ice in her breast where
A warm heart should be.

Kevla was captivated by the silvery sound of the instrument and the clear purity of Altan's youthful male voice. He was a wonderful performer; it was no surprise he was a full *huskaa* even at his tender age. The song, though, was disturbing to her in a way she could not articulate, and the melody haunting.

"You see me as I stand here,
An old man now I be.

But not so long ago, lad,
I was as young as thee.
'Twas then the Maiden claimed my soul,
And sod beneath the snow
Is warmer than her icy touch.
Believe me, lad, I know.

"There's some that call her spirit,
Claim deep woods are her home.
Some say she's but a lassie
Whose lad left her to roam.
But me, I say, she's nightmare born,
And others think so, too—
All those of us who've felt her gaze,
And know what it can do."

As he repeated the chilling chorus, Kevla felt her skin prickle, but not from the beauty of the melody, not this time. There was something very real about this song, folktale though it was. Perhaps it was just how the human heart could turn so dark and cold after a bitter disappointment. She herself had never wandered down that particular path of revenge and hatred. For who could she blame for her pain but herself? No, her pain had been and was still hot and fiery, not icy.

The song continued to a conclusion that Kevla dreaded.

"For twenty years and longer,
No village girl has wed.
Marry some sweet maiden,
Take her to your bed.

Raise you a family, love them well,
And lay this quest aside.
Seek not to woo this Maiden.
She'll never be your bride."

He laughed then, long and hearty:
"Old man, you've made me smile."
He tossed a coin and left me,
The Maiden to beguile.
And I have not seen that poor lad since,
And this was long ago;
But of his fate, I'm certain,
What happened, ah! I know!

He has seen the Ice Maiden,
And she's perilous fair;
He has seen her eyes shine,
He has seen her gold hair.
Now he thirsts for wine lips—
He's become just like me,
And there's dust in his breast where
A heart used to be.

The last silvery note floated into the icy night air and hung there for a moment. No one spoke.

Finally, Kevla broke the silence. "That was beautiful, Altan. But now I am very sad."

"I think I have had enough of ice maidens and snow songs," the Dragon said. Mylikki and Altan jumped, startled to hear his deep voice, and Kevla chuckled good-naturedly. Apparently the two Lamali natives had forgotten that their "shelter" was the Dragon, and he had heard everything, in-cluding the song.

"Perhaps something more cheerful, to send us to sleep with peaceful dreams," Kevla suggested as she served the tea. Both Altan and Mylikki closed grateful fingers around the warm ceramic mugs. As she sipped the hot beverage, Kevla tried to put a name to what she felt. It was with some surprise that she realized she was cold. Not physically; but her heart was cold. The song had chilled her emotionally, and no amount of hot tea could take away the sensation.

Where are you, Jareth? she implored silently, as if some-how he could sense her thoughts over the unknown dis-tance that separated them. *I don't know this land. I don't know these people, these songs. This is your place, not mine. I need you. This world needs you.*

Altan and Mylikki sang a sprightly, silly little duet, their voices blending perfectly, their faces smiling and happy as they gazed into one another's eyes. Kevla relaxed against the wall of hard-packed snow, but she couldn't shake the image of the Ice Maiden and what she did to young men's hearts. *Was* the song literal, as Mylikki seemed to think? Did the Maiden replace warm, beating, human hearts with a chunk of ice? Or was it figurative, as Altan maintained—rendered them incapable of loving anyone ever again?

Either way, she thought, *it is a terrible fate.*

17

While they waited another day so that Altan could continue to recover, Kevla revealed more to her companions about the Dancers and the Lorekeepers. They were both enthralled, and as she spoke, Altan actually reached for his *kyndela* and began to accompany her. Kevla was embarrassed at first and asked him to stop, but both he and Mylikki encouraged her to continue.

"This is how we honor the great stories," Altan said. "This is why the *Huskaa* Law was established, so that we can learn the songs and stories, and they can continue to be told."

Kevla shyly relaxed into the camaraderie, speaking of Arukan's desert landscape and harsh environment. She told them about the splintered Clans, about growing up haunted by dreams of the Dragon, about how her Lore-keeper—she did not name him—and others like him had also had dreams. She felt again a pang of disappointment that she had not yet encountered any Lorekeepers here in Lamal.

"Memories," breathed Mylikki. "Memories disguised as dreams. Memories that could cost you your life."

Kevla nodded. "Our people feared two things—the Great Dragon, the keeper of our laws, and the demon *kulis*." She was lying against the Dragon's side as she spoke, her hands clasped behind her head, and turned to smile at him. "Neither was what we thought they were," she said.

"Still, I would not want to be your enemy, Dragon," Altan said, inclining his head respectfully.

The Dragon harrumphed, sending twin spirals of smoke from his nostrils to the sky. "You are wise as well as talented, Altan. I am a part of Kevla, and she of me. You would be unhappy indeed to be the enemy of either of us."

"I'll do my best to be a good traveling companion," Altan said lightly.

The words reminded Kevla of the reason they were here. It was pleasant to sit and talk, but she hoped Altan would be sufficiently recovered to move on tomorrow. She knew that while she was not physically in the lands the Emperor commanded, there was a possibility they were all still at risk.

"The Dancers do have an enemy," she said. "I warned Mylikki about him and I must tell you as well, Altan. He is called the Emperor, and he rules the land that lies between Arukan and Lamal. He is bent on destroying the Dancers, making sure we cannot complete our task of saving this world. It was he who sent the army over the mountains to attack the Clans, and while I was traveling here, he tried to...to get inside my head, to command my thoughts."

Altan had stopped playing and Mylikki said, "But you said he hasn't been able to find you since you entered our land."

"True. Nor has he interfered with my powers. I think we are safe from him, or else I would not have involved you in this journey. But I cannot guarantee it. If you wish the Dragon to return you to your homes, he will."

Altan returned to playing, a soft, subtle tune he improvised as he went. He shook his fair head.

"You and I share a quest, Kevla," Altan said. "I set out to find Jareth, too. If he has indeed lost his abilities, he will be as vulnerable as anyone in the wilds. I have been searching for him for many months. We'll find him together."

"I will stay, too," Mylikki said. "You said that the Emperor sent his troops over the mountains to fight the Clans?"

"Yes," Kevla said. "He attacked the Clans one by one, conscripting them to serve in his army."

"Then it sounds like if he decides to attack, we wouldn't be safe anywhere," Mylikki said bluntly, surprising Kevla with her logic. "I'd rather be with you and the Dragon than in Arrun Woods. Although," she said, "I am worried about my family."

Altan looked at her with compassion. "We have been worrying about our families and homes for almost a year now, Mylikki," he said. "Our villages are enduring an endless winter and attacks from marauders already. Possibly we can help Kevla put a stop to all of that."

The night was cold and clear, and they huddled around the fire looking at the stars for a time instead of immediately moving to the shelter the Dragon so obligingly provided. The two *huskaas* huddled close to the fire, eating the boiled *gahalgoose* with their fingers. Kevla leaned back and looked at the stars, permitting herself to relax and notice the night sky for the first time since she had embarked on her travels. It took her a few minutes to find what she was looking for; apparently being so far north changed the night skies.

She pointed. "In my land," she told her friends, "that collection of stars is the First Clan Leader, and he is bowing before the Great Dragon, right there."

The Dragon craned his neck. "I don't see the resemblance myself."

"I see it," Altan said. "We know that collection of stars too, and to us it is the *Huskaa* and his *kyndela*. See the strings right there? That chain of stars?"

Kevla laughed in surprised delight as her vision shifted. What had seemed to her firmly to be a kneeling *khashim* and the Dragon become a player holding an instrument.

"Yes," she said, "I can see it now. Over there, we have the Sand Maiden, who—"

Suddenly she gasped and rubbed at her eyes. Did she really see that strange wave of color that washed over the night sky? A heartbeat later, she had no doubt. The sky was on fire! Brilliant hues of red, green and blue chased one another around the night sky. They shimmered and pulsed.

"It's the lights of the gods," Mylikki explained. "They are playing with one another, and this light sparks off their fur. It is an omen."

Kevla gazed at the shimmering, magical lights, drinking it in. She had seen the occasional shooting star, while she wandered the deserts of Arukan searching for the Dragon, but had never beheld anything like this.

Altan said nothing, transfixed by the celestial display. He was a singer, a teller of tales. He, more than most others, could appreciate the startling beauty of the god-lights, Kevla thought. The colors danced across his pale, upturned features, making him look magical too.

"They are beautiful," Mylikki said. "But somehow they frighten me now." She shivered and leaned more closely in to Altan for warmth. "They're different. The colors are different—there's so much red now—and we're seeing them much more often now. I wonder if it has to do with the winter."

Altan gave her a glance, and contempt curled his lip. "Stop being such a coward," he said, and shifted so that she was no longer touching him. He said nothing further, gazing in rapt silence at the shifting colors.

Mylikki pulled her cloak more closely around her and lowered her head, pretending not to be stung by the rebuke. Kevla said nothing more, but wondered why at some times Altan seemed so sweet and amiable, and at others, a callous churl.

He was gliding smoothly on a pair of skeltha. *She had a name for him now—Jareth. As he sped away, Kevla tried to follow, but her bare feet slipped in the snow and she fell. When she struggled to her feet, he was nowhere to be seen.*

"Jareth!" she cried, hearing the name echo in the stillness of the dark trees and white snow. There was no response. Suddenly the light dimmed and bright colors began to dance in the sky. Kevla watched for a moment, and then she realized that

Altan was right: the heavenly display of color was the gods dancing and playing with one another.

Except there weren't several blue tigers, chasing one another around like cubs. There was only one, but it moved so quickly that it seemed it must be more. She screamed as it suddenly gathered itself and leaped from its place in the firmament to land in the snow before her.

Her hands were at her mouth, and she realized she was alone. No Altan, no Mylikki, not even the Dragon. It was just her and the blue tiger god of Lamal, standing silently regarding one another in the snow.

Its tail flicked and it gazed at her with deep, knowing golden eyes. Then it turned and bounded off in the same direction Jareth had gone, but left no mark in the snow.

Kevla awoke with a gasp. Sweat dotted her forehead, made her *rhia* cling to her in dark, wet patches. She could see light outside, but Altan and Mylikki were asleep. They had begun the night sleeping apart, but had ended up huddled in one another's arms. Briefly Kevla wondered if it was by accident or design. But she had no time to waste pondering the relationship between the two. She hurried over to Altan and shook him.

Sleepily he rolled over and peered at her with tired eyes. "What is it, Kevla? Is something wrong?" Beside him, Mylikki blinked drowsily.

"Do you know why Jareth left your village?"

"No, I told you, he left without a word to anyone."

"I had a dream," Kevla said. "I think I know why he left." His hand shot out and closed on her wrist. "Tell me."

"You said, everyone, including Jareth, thought his ability to bring spring was a gift from the gods—the blue tigers," Kevla said. "Then suddenly the gift went away. I think Jareth has gone to find the gods, to bring back spring to the land."

Olar knew his mother was torn. On the one hand, she expressed pleasure that her daughter displayed both wit and compassion by pretending to be a *huskaa* and telling the people from Galak-by-the-Lake to go to Arrun Woods. On the other hand, Olar was aware that even the few people who had made the trip to his village made a difference in the amount of food stockpiled. The Dragon's hunting had helped, but could not stave off the inevitable. Gelsan could not find it in her heart to turn anyone away. Still, the food would not last for weeks, as they had anticipated, but now merely days.

It was time to go hunting, and Olar was excited.

"I'm old enough now," he wheedled. "Any other winter I'd be with the hunting party already."

His mother regarded him. "Any other winter," she said harshly, "and you would have your father with you to teach you."

Olar bit his lower lip, uncertain how to reply. His father, Veslar, had been among the first to disappear in a violent snowstorm back when everyone thought this a normal season. He missed his father still, and knew that his mother did too. With Mylikki gone, Olar knew he was all Gelsan had.

"I want to help, Mother." Gelsan's shoulders sagged and she sighed. She finished putting on her boots and opened the door. She peered at the sky.

"It seems clear," she said. She turned and looked at him

almost hungrily. Olar stood up a little straighter, accepting her scrutiny, praying to the gods that she would not find him wanting. "Very well. But you stay with me. You do not go farther than my eyes can see you. And if a storm descends, we turn around and come back home immediately. I don't care if a *kirvi* is prancing right in front of you, do you understand?"

Olar fought to keep the delight from his face, but he couldn't suppress a smile. "Yes, Mother," he said. He hurried to dress properly, finding his snow walkers and strapping them on. The group assembled in the center of the small village. There were eight of them. Most were women, who were the only ones of the right age and physically fit enough to spend the day trudging in the wilds, but there were two old men from Galak-by-the-Lake as well as Olar. He regarded them with compassionate, slightly contemptuous eyes. They wanted to help, but they were too old. They would need to turn around soon. He only hoped it wouldn't ruin the party's chances of finding fresh meat.

Increasingly, Arrun Woods and, he supposed, other villages like it, had had to rely on other means of obtaining food—fishing through holes in the ice, constructing traps of various sorts. It helped, but only a little. For the bigger prey, one had to go to them. He was thrilled that finally he was permitted to embark on his first true hunt.

Much later, chilled to the bone and so exhausted his legs were trembling, Olar wished he was home by the smoky fire. They had seen nothing; had not even come across tracks in the snow. Once or twice Olar had thought he had seen a small hare, but it was just his eyes playing tricks on him. Worse, the sky was starting to cloud over. He was grateful when Gelsan called a halt and sank down on a fallen tree. He scooped some snow into his mouth, thankful for the moisture, and listened with half an ear as his mother and the others discussed their options.

One of the old men sat next to him and offered him a piece of dried meat. Olar gnawed on it gratefully. The old man, most of his teeth gone, sucked on his.

"There is still plenty of time before the storm comes," one woman from Galak-by-the-Lake was saying. "We could at least check all the traps before turning back."

Cold as he was, heat filled Olar's cheeks as his mother glanced over her shoulder at him. She was turning back because of him! As if he was a child still. He wanted to tell her that he was fine, that they should keep going if the others wanted to, she should do anything but return home empty-handed because of him....

He looked up at the sky. It was almost completely gray now. When had that happened? They came so swiftly, the storms. Some said the Ice Maiden sent them, to weaken the hunting parties. It did seem as though a party would leave on a cloudless morning to stumble back in the afternoon in an unexpected storm...often missing a few of its number.

There was a soft noise behind him. Idly, Olar turned—and gazed right into the large, soft eyes of a *kirvi* doe. They stared at one another for a moment, predator and prey, and then the doe turned and bounded into the shadows of the forest.

Wondering if his eyes were playing tricks on him again, Olar glanced over at his companion. The old man had seen it too, and his eyes gleamed with excitement. Unspoken words passed between them as the snow began to drift lazily down.

The old man, skinny and white-haired and nearly tooth-less, had been told time and again that he was past his prime. Olar knew this to be true, although he had never witnessed such words being exchanged; he could see it in how the man held himself. He was thought largely worthless, but now, he and Olar had a chance to prove something to the others.

The snow began to fall more heavily, and the wind picked up. Olar didn't care. They would be in the forest in a few heartbeats, he and the old man whose name he didn't even know; killing and bringing home a *kirvi* while the women and the other old man stood and quarreled about whether they should turn around now or detour to check yester-day's traps.

No one noticed them slip silently into the shadows of the forest. The scent of the trees wafted to their nostrils as they moved carefully over a carpet of leaves and needles and moss, the ancient trees providing a canopy that caught the snow. Olar knelt, and pointed silently to a fresh hoof print. The old man nodded excitedly, and they continued.

At one point, Olar did feel a pang of worry at how long they had been gone. He glanced behind him, reassuring himself that he could easily find their way back; back with food for two hungry villages.

He turned around, stepping over a curious streak of ice, and cried out.

The old man had already fallen to his knees, trembling arms lifted as if in supplication. Olar felt awe and wonder sweep over him and he too dropped heavily to his knees in front of the vision that had somehow appeared before him.

She was tall and slender and clad in white. She seemed to glow, and in the light that emanated from her it seemed to

Olar that her skin was as white as the snow. Golden tresses tumbled down her back, and lips that were red as wine pulled back from teeth that were as white, as perfect, as the rest of her.

Perilous fair she was indeed, but it was already too late. Olar forgot about his mother and sister; forgot about his father, lost in these same woods months ago; forgot about his friends and his village and everything he had never known in this life except for the exquisite beauty who stood smiling before him. Even as he knew her smile was cruel, he yearned to kiss those lips; even as she laughed with triumph and hatred, he thought it the most beautiful sound in the world.

"Now, you will serve me," said the Ice Maiden in a voice that sounded as clean and as musical as the snow-songs of a *kyndela*. "Now, you are mine."

And they were.

18

"That sounds exactly like the sort of thing Jareth would do," Altan admitted, frowning and shaking his head. "I *knew* I was right to worry about him. The fool will likely die trying to find the gods, and if he actually does manage to do so...I fear they will kill him for his impudence."

Kevla closed her eyes and summoned the image of the Stone Dancer in her head. Every time she had seen him with the beast...the *tiger,* she amended...they had seemed to be comfortable with one another. One thing seemed certain to her—if Jareth did find the tigers, they would not harm him.

"Where do they live? Your gods?" Kevla asked.

"Go north as far as one can go," Altan said. "Where the world ends, there live the gods. They dwell close to the sky so that they can leap off the mountains into the stars. That's why we can see them playing sometimes."

Light flooded in as the Dragon sat up, removing the "roof" from their shelter. Kevla looked up at her friend. "I have never been to the end of the world," the Dragon said, "but I will take you as far as my wings can bear you."

"Jareth is the Stone Dancer, but he is also only human," said Kevla. "Wherever he can go, we can go. At least we have a direction now. And I don't think you need to worry, Altan. In my dream, while Jareth was trying to find the tiger...it was also trying to find him."

Altan gave her a wry look. "That does not altogether comfort me, Kevla. Our gods are not always beneficent."

Altan needed a little help to climb atop the Dragon, as he was not yet up to full strength. He seemed pleased to have an excuse to hold on to Mylikki as they flew that day, though, continuing to puzzle Kevla. She couldn't figure out what Altan's feelings toward Mylikki really were. And judging by the cautious, surprised pleasure on Mylikki's face, the girl wasn't sure either.

That evening, Kevla again attempted to scry into the fire, but she had no success. Jareth had been alerted to her presence, and if her assumption was correct, was not overeager to be found.

She tried to open herself to his presence. The next day, she kept getting little tugs: *Bear left here. Go right there. Keep heading north; to the end of the world, where the gods play on their mountains and leap into the skies.*

Her eyes closed, she silently implored, *Where are you, Jareth? We need you. This world needs you.*

Two nights later, the Dragon landed in a clearing. They slid off his back, stretching tight muscles.

"I wish I could say that we were about to find him," Kevla said. "I do sense that we're closer."

"Closer than what?" said Mylikki, grimacing as she arched her back. "What do we do if we *don't* find him?"

"Don't talk like that, Mylikki!" Altan chided. Kevla glanced at him sharply, wondering if this was another one of his cutting remarks to Mylikki that seemed to come out of nowhere. But he only seemed to want to hearten the girl.

"We'll find him. We've got to. I have faith in Kevla and the Dragon." He gifted Kevla with one of his openhearted smiles, and Kevla felt her spirits sink. She felt more like Mylikki. This was a big land, and a man was a small thing compared to the vastness of the wastelands and forests. But she did know they were on the right track. If only she could talk to him through the fire! Or even *find* his fire; she could then step into the flames and appear at his camp.

While Altan and Mylikki set up the camp for the night and the Dragon left to find them something to eat, Kevla went to the edge of the forest to gather firewood. She did not want to admit it to the others, but she was as weary as they. The constant traveling was taking its toll, and she had been forced to start rationing their food.

She frowned, scuffing the snow with her feet and searching for fallen branches. There did not seem to be much to be had, and she did not want to break limbs off of living trees. For living they still were, Altan and Mylikki had assured her, though to Kevla they seemed fragile and dead.

Her dislike of the forests, the dark, enclosed, shadowy spaces, rose in her again. Fiercely, she told herself to stop being foolish. "They're just trees, Kevla," she said aloud. "There's nothing to be worried about."

She stepped past where the snow lapped up against the trees' roots and into the shaded forest. She stepped gently here, and the deeper she went, the more tinder she found. At last, her arms full, she turned and headed back.

The arm went around her waist so hard her breath was forced from her lungs. She dropped the branches in shock. The cold edge of a knife blade pressed to her throat.

Kevla had been in this position before; at the mercy of a man who was larger and stronger than she, with a knife at her throat. She knew what to do.

Heat, she thought, knowing the knife would in an instant become unbearably hot to the touch. The man would have to drop it and then she could—

"Stop that," the man behind her hissed, "or I'll cut your throat."

She could smell burning cloth, and smoke began to float from her throat into her field of vision. How could he continue to hold the knife? Sheer will? Insanity? Something had happened to the men of these small villages. Something that turned hardworking farmers, fathers and sons and husbands, into madmen to be feared as much as the winter itself. Kevla's stomach clenched as she realized she must have stumbled upon one of them. At least she hoped it was only one....

He pressed the knife closer and she closed her eyes as a quick, startling pain told her the blade had broken the skin. At once, she ceased her attack.

Dragon!

"That's better." He moved the knife slightly away from

her soft flesh, but did not drop it. His arm around her waist remained strong, holding her like an iron band. He pressed her into his body, the better to control any movement she might make. She had yet to see his face, but already she knew he was tall, powerfully made and shockingly strong. He was breathing quickly, from exertion or excitement, she could not tell.

"Who are you?" he demanded. He spoke without whispering this time, and his voice was both cold and rough.

"My friends and I are merely passing through. We have no quarrel with—with the men of the forests."

"Men of the forests?" He sounded startled. In his surprise, his voice went from hard and angry to almost pleasant sounding. "You think I—"

Two things happened simultaneously. A clear, youthful voice cried out a single word, and next to Kevla, half a dozen trees were ripped from the ground. The man's grip disappeared and Kevla, abruptly unsupported, fell forward. It took her an instant to make sense of what had happened.

The Dragon had come, tearing up the trees to find her, and Altan had cried out the name of—

"Jareth!"

"And now, all the players have appeared on the stage," the Emperor said gleefully to his advisor, the Mage and the creature who crouched at his feet. "The Dancers, their allies, their enemies, the one who will ultimately betray them. I had thought to take them out of play one by one, but if I can eliminate two Dancers by the same treacherous hand, then I shall be well content."

The advisor drew back pale lips from white teeth in a rictus that only the Emperor would interpret as a smile. He knew this was but one game of many the Emperor was playing, and he also knew that he was being fed bits and pieces of information as the Emperor deemed fit.

In front of them, the bloodred, tapered Tenacru *hovered.*

He thought of the north, and a never-ending winter, and suddenly shivered.

19

Kneeling in the snow where she had fallen, Kevla looked back to see the man who had held the knife to her throat running as fast as he could for the safety of the forest, fleeing from the huge shape of the Dragon which must seem like the embodiment of a nightmare to him.

But he would not make his escape so easily. The Dragon slammed a forepaw down in front of him. The earth trembled and the man fell backward. But instead of cowering or crying out for mercy, he bared his teeth like an animal and bellowed wordlessly, brandishing his knife against a creature ten times his size. His other hand fumbled for and hurled a rock, which bounced harmlessly off the Dragon's scales.

Shocked almost beyond comprehension, Kevla stared at

the bloodshot, wild blue eyes darting about for escape, the scraggly beard, the dirt that seemed permanently embedded in hard wrinkles around his eyes. Another rock sang through the air and the Dragon actually rolled his eyes.

This was the Stone Dancer?

"Jareth?" she said in a quavering voice, hoping desperately that Altan had confused his friend with one of the crazy men lurking in the forest's shadows.

The man's fair head whipped around for an instant to stare at her, then he turned back to the Dragon. The Dragon sat back on his haunches, trees cracking beneath his bulk. Cautiously, Jareth got to his feet, staggering like a drunken man. When the Dragon did not move to attack again, he turned to Kevla.

"I saw your face in the fire," he accused.

Kevla's heart contracted with despair. This was indeed the man she had seen in her vision. This was the man who had seemed to her so proud and strong and capable, the man to whom she had hoped to surrender all her burdens. Instead, he was running wild in the woods, bedraggled and looking both lost and angry. How could he possibly help to save their world?

Jareth's eyes narrowed as he regarded her. He opened his mouth and was about to speak again when Altan flung himself at him.

"You're safe! Thank the gods!" Altan cried. Clinging to his friend, Altan looked even more slender and delicate.

Looking both furious and, strangely, almost frightened, Jareth made an angry noise and shoved Altan off of him. They stared at one another for a long moment.

"Altan?" Jareth's voice was soft, confused. He reached

out a trembling hand and placed it on Altan's shoulders. The boy swiftly covered the hand with his own.

"Yes, it's me, Jareth," Altan said, his voice thick. He squeezed Jareth's hand. "It's really me."

Abruptly, Jareth's demeanor changed. "You idiot!" he bellowed, releasing his grip on Altan's shoulder. "What are you doing? Why are you here? With her and this...this..." He glared defiantly up at the Dragon, who regarded him calmly.

"It's called a dragon," Mylikki said helpfully. She was making her way toward them, no doubt drawn by the commotion. Kevla got unsteadily to her feet and looked up at the Dragon. Their eyes met.

Not quite what we expected, is he? came the Dragon's dry voice in her mind. The comment was so understated that Kevla almost laughed out loud. She didn't dare, though; she felt hysteria bubbling up inside her and knew that if she gave in to the dark humor and the bitter stab of disappointment, she would end up sobbing. She brushed snow and dirt off her *rhia* and tried to collect herself.

"Who are you?" demanded Jareth of Mylikki.

Something inside Kevla snapped. Jareth had every right to wonder about her—she looked completely different from anyone he had ever known, she could scry in the fire and she came on the back of a dragon—and he could be angry with Altan if he liked; Altan could take care of himself. But to yell at Mylikki—

"You will not speak so to her!" Kevla cried. Jareth turned the full force of his gaze upon her and she stood arrow-straight, full now not of fear but of righteous indignation. "You seize me from behind, you put a knife to my throat—" Her fingers went to her neck and came away red.

"You gave as good as you got." Jareth held up his hand and she saw that the wrappings had been completely burned off.

"Jareth, what did you do to her?" asked Altan. "Oh, my friend, what's happened to you?"

Again he reached for Jareth, and again the other man shied from any kind of touch. He turned his face away and Kevla saw a terrible grief etched on those features. She suddenly felt she was intruding upon something deeply private.

We should leave them, Kevla thought to the Dragon.

Agreed. The Dragon leaped into the sky. Broken limbs and leaves fell to the earth in his wake.

Kevla suddenly felt weak and sick. To have come so far, to have endured what she had, only to find that the eagerly sought Stone Dancer was in such straits was too much.

"Kevla?" It was Mylikki, slipping gently beside her. "How badly did he hurt you?"

"It's nothing, just a little nick," Kevla said. "Come. I feel the need for some hot food." She headed back toward the clearing, leaning in to Mylikki and whispering, "The only one he'll listen to is Altan—if he'll listen to anyone in the state he's in now. Let's leave them to it."

The Dragon awaited them, curled up in his favorite position like a granary cat, while the two women busied themselves preparing food from the rapidly dwindling stores and something hot to drink. The Dragon's head was turned toward the woods, his ears pricked forward and his gold eyes missing nothing. Even if Jareth somehow tried to flee, he would not get far.

Altan wanted to weep.

Jareth had sunk to the ground. Whatever had fueled him

sufficiently to attack Kevla, to brandish a knife at the Dragon, and to shove Altan away with so much strength that the younger man feared his chest would sport bruises had been burned up. Jareth now sat with his arms on his knees and his head in his hands, taking great, gulping breaths.

Miserably, Altan squatted beside him. "Jareth," he said for perhaps the dozent time. "I'm so sorry. I'm so sorry."

Tentatively, he reached again to touch Jareth, sickly realizing as he did so that most of the bulk on what had once been powerful shoulders was now merely layers of clothing. "Please talk to me," Altan begged. "Tell me what has happened to you."

For a long moment, he feared Jareth wouldn't—or couldn't—speak. At last, he lifted his head. His face was hollow, haggard...old.

"I went to find the gods," Jareth muttered, still not looking at Altan. "Something wasn't...wasn't right about the storm that night..." His voice broke and for a moment he was silent. He continued in a flat voice. "I went to the mountains, but they weren't there."

He dragged his reddened gaze to Altan's and said almost petulantly, *"They weren't there!"*

Altan stroked Jareth's shoulders like he might a cat, soothingly, rhythmically. His mind raced and he felt a chill. Had Jareth believed the gods could bring his family back? Did he still think that? What could he say to get Jareth to join them, to abandon this disturbing quest, to sit at their circle and listen to the information Kevla had for him? He couldn't think of anything, just kept staring at the emaciated figure who seemed to have only his mission to keep him alive.

"So I'm going to find the *taaskali*," Jareth said, nodding to himself. "The *taaskali* would know." His gaze darted to Altan's face, lit there like a butterfly, then flitted away again. "She a *taaskali?*"

"No," said Altan, grateful for the excuse to talk about Kevla. "But she does have magic. She is from a land called Arukan. She's called the Flame Dancer."

Jareth's grimy brow furrowed. "Arukan," he said, slowly, as if dredging up a distant memory. "It's warm there."

"You know it?" Altan felt a surge of hope. If Jareth knew about Arukan, perhaps he knew about the Dancers and their task as well. It would make everything easier.

"The earth whispers to me of other places, sometimes," Jareth said. "At least, it used to. Now, it is silent." He looked up, his eyes roaming the tall skeletons of trees that surrounded them. "Everything is silent."

Altan sighed. "You need food and warmth, my friend. Come sit by the fire and eat something."

"You didn't scare me, Father," said Jareth in a whisper, his gaze unfocused. "Come eat. Please, come eat something."

Chills ran down Altan's spine, and not from the cold. "What?" he said, praying he hadn't heard what he thought he had.

Jareth shook himself, blinking suddenly as if waking up. "Nothing." He looked at Altan with eyes that really seemed to see him for the first time.

Altan fought back tears. He reached his hands to Jareth's face and took it in his hands, one on each hollow, bearded cheek. Jareth sighed, a long, quavering sound, pressed the hands that cupped his face, then gently removed them.

"Please come to the fire with me, Jareth. Will you come?"

The bigger man nodded, slowly. Altan slipped his right arm around Jareth's waist, pulling the other man's left arm across the back of his neck. Gently, he helped his friend to his feet. Jareth had once been powerfully built. Now, he barely outweighed the little *huskaa* who guided his unsteady steps toward the fire that crackled, warm orange-yellow life against the blue-purple cold of the beautiful, deadly snow.

20

When the two men approached the fire, the bigger one leaning heavily on the smaller, Kevla felt again a jolt of shock. Jareth kept his eyes on the ground as Altan gently directed him to a blanket next to the fire. Altan placed a hand on Jareth's back, touching his friend with a tenderness similar to what Kevla had seen him display toward Mylikki. She wondered if the reason for Altan's ambivalent attitude toward Mylikki was because Altan preferred men to women.

The Stone Dancer gazed at the fire for a long moment. He reached his hands out to the blaze at first tentatively, then eagerly. Kevla again noted that the fingers on his right hand, which had held the knife to her throat, were bare; the rags with which he had wrapped them had been burned off. His hand seemed to be unharmed. His fingers were filthy. Dirt was caked under the nails, embedded in the creases. Kevla thought of how meticulously groomed the people of the House of Four Waters were, down to the lowest servant—herself. Jareth looked—and smelled—worse than the basest beggar on the streets of Arukan.

She tried to soften her initial revulsion by rationalization. He had left his village to wander in the woods for months—she didn't know how long, exactly. There were no stone-steaming huts in the forests to sweat out the dirt, and to try to bathe with the snow or water from the icy lakes would be to court death. Of course he was dirty.

But she sensed it was more than that. If such things had mattered to Jareth, he would have found a way to stay at least somewhat clean. She was looking at him out of the corner of her eye, and at that moment, he sensed her gaze and gave her stare for stare.

Kevla could not hold that blue gaze and quickly turned her attention to ladling out stew. It was a meal she had grown weary of days ago, but it was easy to prepare, nourishing, hot, and made good use of their rations. She handed a bowl to Jareth, who took it wordlessly with his grimy fingers.

He sniffed it and something in him seemed to come to life. He ate ravenously, spilling on his beard and the front of his shirt. Kevla felt her lip curl in involuntary disgust. She and the others were only halfway through when he stuck out the bowl and demanded, "More."

Silently she refilled the bowl and once again Jareth swiftly downed the stew. Kevla wondered how long it had been since he had eaten. When he extended the bowl for a third helping, she said, "No."

Jareth's eyes widened in anger. Altan said quickly, "Kevla, he probably hasn't eaten for days."

"We don't have that much food left, Altan. Besides, if he eats too much too quickly it will come back up again, doing none of us any good. If everyone else has had their fill, you may have some more in a while, Jareth."

"You speak to me like I'm a child," he growled.

You're behaving like one, Kevla thought, but did not say it. She wondered how she would begin the conversation she needed to have with him; how she would manage to convey to this dirty, half-mad man that he had a destiny that would demand more of him than she suspected he was willing to give.

One thing was certain—it would not happen tonight. A few minutes after he had eaten the second bowl of soup, Jareth's eyes started to close. He struggled against sleep, but after a while Altan urged him to lie down. The mighty Stone Dancer, the Spring-Bringer, nodded in agreement, sighed deeply, and stretched out on the blanket. Gently, as if he were tucking a child in for a nap, Altan wrapped Jareth in the furs. Within a few moments, Jareth's breathing became deep and regular.

"He's asleep," Altan said quietly. "Thank the gods." He rested his hand on his friend's shoulder for a moment.

"I can't believe this," said Mylikki. "I thought..." She seemed unable to even complete the sentence. Her *kyndela* rested on her lap, but she didn't touch the strings.

"He wasn't always like this," Altan said softly. He reached for his own *kyndela* and began to play quietly. "He was powerful...amazing...strong. I can't imagine what he's been through." He looked at Kevla. "You were right. He did leave to find the gods. He was trying to get them to bring his family back to life."

Kevla looked at the Dragon, knowing he sensed her feelings. *I am disappointed too, Flame Dancer. But at least he is alive. At least he has not become one of the raving madmen in the woods.*

That's a matter of opinion, if he really did try to do what Altan said. You told me he was ready, she accused.

The Dragon shrugged. *You sensed him as well as I. As did Jashemi. He was the one we were supposed to find first. Perhaps it was not because he was ready, but because he needs our help to* become *ready.*

I am not a nursemaid!

Nor is he an infant. He is a man grown, Kevla, who has had terrible things happen to him.

"I've had terrible things happen to me too, and I am here!" Kevla cried aloud. Altan and Mylikki stared at her, startled at her outburst, and she felt heat rise in her cheeks. Jareth, however, continued to sleep, for which Kevla was grateful.

After a long, awkward moment, Altan said haltingly, "Kevla...he's been wandering alone for many months. He's climbed the mountain range by himself, in the depths of this awful winter. He's lost so much weight, who knows what he's been eating or even *if* he's been eating. Give him a little time to recover before you judge him."

Kevla's embarrassment was suddenly replaced by a wave of grief and rage.

"You have no idea what I have been through," she said, her voice thick. "You have no idea what my life was like. I feel for Jareth, but from everything you told me he has led a charmed life until the last year. I was born the low-est of the low among my people. I have been beaten, locked up, and had my death ordered by my own father who thought me a demon. I was tied to a stake and fire was lit at my feet. If I hadn't been the Flame Dancer I'd have been burned alive. I have been loved by and loved only one person in my life—*one person,* Altan!—and I killed him when I tried to express that love. And here I am, ready to do what I must do, and I have no time to coddle this Spring-Bringer. You know what is at stake here. He doesn't have the luxury of indulging his grief right now. None of us does."

Tears welled in her eyes, threatening to give the lie to her angry words. Kevla did not want them to see her cry. She rose and stalked off, sitting at the edge of the clearing. The Dragon followed, lowering his head all the way to the snow as he spoke, so that the words would be for her alone.

"Dear heart, I grieve with you," he said, his deep voice gentle. "I am part of this trinity as well, and I too long for Jashemi. But not as keenly as you do."

Kevla buried her face in her hands, her slim shoulders shaking with violent paroxysms of grief. She couldn't speak.

I miss him so much, Dragon! It rips at my heart every single day. I try to force this awful sense of loss down, but it comes back up, sometimes at the worst possible moment. Like tonight. I feel as though my insides have been torn out. He was my Lore-keeper, he was my great love. There was no one who knew me better than he. And I killed him! He would be alive today if not for me and my selfish desires!

You don't know that for certain, Flame Dancer. We all have our destinies. Perhaps this was Jashemi's.

That's not true and you know it, Dragon. Jashemi said as much to me in the vision. This wasn't how it was supposed to be. He was not born to be my lover, he was born to be something else entirely. And we corrupted that.

Your culture rendered that relationship impossible, if you were to truly fulfill your destiny, Kevla. Try to be more compassionate with yourself and with Jareth.

I don't know that I have any compassion left, Dragon. I don't know that I have anything left at all.

After a long time, Kevla returned to the fire. She sat back down in silence. Above them, the sky was clear and crowded with stars.

"I apologize," Kevla said formally. "My outburst was inappropriate and served no purpose."

Altan glared at her, his arm around the sleeping Jareth. "You're right about that. You almost woke him up and he needs sleep." Altan turned to his friend and stroked his shoulder.

"Yes it did," Mylikki said quickly, to take the sting out of Altan's harsh words. "It let us know a little bit more about you, Kevla. It made you seem a lot more human to us. I'm sure Jareth will be better by tomorrow. He just needs some food and rest. You'll see."

Kevla did not answer. Altan's outburst had surprised her, though it shouldn't have. Jareth was important to him—perhaps as more than a friend. And certainly they were all exhausted and hungry.

She looked up at the stars. A faint pulse of color told her that once again, the gods would be playing in the skies tonight.

* * *

The Lorekeeper gazed upward, her eyes transfixed on the dancing lights. He spoke to her through them, and she wondered what she would learn tonight.

"You have done well, Lorekeeper," *the Emperor said, his language a pulsing pattern in the sky.* "I am very pleased. Soon, he will be yours. You do not need to fear losing him to this Flame Dancer."

The Lorekeeper dragged her eyes from the dancing lights to look at Kevla. She lay on the blanket, looking at the sky, seeing nothing more than pretty lights. The Lorekeeper struggled between liking Kevla and hating what the Flame Dancer symbolized. The Lorekeeper permitted herself to look at the man she loved, and her heart swelled. He couldn't truly see her yet, couldn't appreciate the depth of her love for him. But soon. The Emperor promised, soon.

"They trust you. They can't see who you really are. Listen, and I will tell you what you must do next."

The Lorekeeper listened, her face turned up to the sky, her fingers absently caressing her kyndela *and her eyes wide with rapture.*

21

Kevla awoke feeling as if she hadn't slept at all. For a moment she wondered why she was so tired, then recalled her outburst. The horrible emptiness of loss stabbed her again, and she rubbed her face and sighed as she sat up. Jareth would—

He was gone.

"Jareth!" she cried, waking the others. They had all fallen asleep beside the fire, and the Dragon had settled over them to provide shelter, as he had most nights during this arduous journey. Now there was an empty hollow in the snow where Jareth had lain.

"Do not distress yourself," came the Dragon's familiar rumbling voice. "The Stone Dancer and I are having an interesting conversation." He sat back, rearing above them, and Kevla saw Jareth securely held in one massive forepaw. He didn't look at all afraid of being clutched by a giant monster; he looked angry. The Dragon lowered him to the ground and released him.

Kevla didn't need to be told what had happened; Jareth had tried to slip away in the night, and the ever-watchful Dragon, who enjoyed sleep but did not require it, had prevented him from doing so. Smothering a smile, Kevla quickly lit the fire while Mylikki rummaged in a sack to prepare something hot to eat. Altan scrambled to his feet and went to his friend.

"Jareth, Kevla has lit a fire for us and Mylikki is making us some hot tea," he said, reaching for Jareth's elbow to guide him back to the fireside.

Jareth glared up at the Dragon. The Dragon glared down at Jareth. Kevla wondered what they had been discussing. When Altan touched him, Jareth jerked away.

"You should not have followed me," Jareth said in a low voice as he walked back to the fire.

"So you have said," Altan said, still stubbornly cheerful. "But if I had not, we would not be together at the fire."

Mylikki threw some herbs into the heating pot of water. Kevla felt for the girl. She was brave, cheerful, and clever, but Jareth's appearance on the scene had utterly distracted Altan from whatever Mylikki might have hoped would happen.

"Last night," Kevla said to Jareth, "you held a knife to my throat and demanded to know who we are."

Jareth frowned and wouldn't look at her. She thought he seemed slightly more in control than he had last night, but wanted to be certain.

"We do owe you an explanation. But you owe us the same, Spring-Bringer."

She used the term only as a way to convey to Jareth that she knew about his abilities, but he reacted as if she had struck him. What she could see of his face above the beard went first white, then flushed red. His nostrils flared and Kevla actually quailed from the expression in his eyes.

"Do not call me that," he said in a low, warning voice.

Mylikki flinched as she ladled tea into ceramic mugs and passed them around.

Kevla continued. "We have had a difficult time with three of us and the Dragon, trying to stay alive in this winter. How is it you have managed to survive alone?"

Jareth sipped at the hot tea, taking his time before replying. "The gods don't want me dead yet, I suppose," he said. He turned to Altan and asked quietly, "Skalka Valley?"

"I have no news. I left right after you did," Altan said. "I tried to follow you. But I had no idea where you had gone."

Jareth made a face and poked at the fire with a stick.

Kevla had had enough of the man's surliness. "You wanted to know who we are, Jareth," she said, turning squarely to face him. He didn't look at her. "You saw my face in the fire, and you stamped it out. I've been looking for you for some time now."

"What do you want? In case you haven't heard, my legendary ability to bring spring appears to have deserted me," Jareth said, his voice bitter and angry.

"I have abilities with fire," Kevla said. "You've seen them. I can create fire from anything, I can extinguish it at will. I can scry in the flames and step through them to any other fire I wish. I am the Flame Dancer, and I'm not alone. There are four others like me, scattered throughout this world. Jareth—you are one of them. You are the very element of earth made into human flesh. You, I, and the three others I've yet to find were born with a very important purpose. We have to save this world from being wiped out by the coming Shadow."

Jareth listened in silence, and then a corner of his mouth curled up. He took another sip of tea.

"Well told," he said mockingly. "Altan, what's the song version of this story? Surely you've made something up about it by now. Five Dancers, the elements incarnate, born to save the world. Much more interesting than an Ice Maiden or—"

"Stop it!" Mylikki's sweet voice was dark with fury. "We've risked our lives to find you, all of us! We've slogged through snow, and storms, and Altan nearly *died* and I don't know what Kevla's been through, but I have a feeling it was horrible, and...and..."

Altan's eyes were downcast, but he reached out an arm and pulled Mylikki into a half embrace, letting her weep angrily on his chest.

"Altan, is this true?" Jareth asked quietly. "Were you almost killed?"

Altan didn't look at him. "I fell into a hidden cave beneath some boulders while seeking shelter from one of the storms," he said as quietly as Jareth. "Somehow Kevla and the Dragon knew where to look. They saved my life, Jareth. And I think we've probably saved yours."

Jareth sighed and leaned forward, running dirty fingers through dirty hair. The hood of his forest-green cloak fell back at the gesture.

"Altan, you know I never meant—"

"It's all right. I just think you owe it to Kevla and the

Dragon to hear them out. I've seen so much in the last few weeks, Jareth. I believe them, and I think you should too."

Jareth lifted his head and turned a surprisingly calm, steady gaze to Kevla. "I have seen a great deal myself. For the love I bear this boy, Kevla-sha-Tahmu, I will listen to what you have to say."

Altan had spoken glowingly of his friend Jareth, who had helped the *huskaa* come into the world and had been like a brother to him ever since. And Kevla had sensed the power and deep feeling of responsibility that Jareth had once possessed. She desperately hoped she would reach him.

So she spoke quietly, the Dragon chiming in from time to time, of the destiny of the Dancers. How they had twice won, twice failed, and how the fate of this world and others hinged upon what they did here and now. She told him about the Lorekeepers and their animal Companions, how these three aspects formed one harmonious whole, though the Dancer could and did sometimes have to move forward without one or the other of the precious trio.

"I lost my own Lorekeeper," she said, blushing to remember how she had revealed this at the fire last night. At least Jareth had been asleep. "It has been—" *Agonizing. Unbearable, unthinkable, excruciating...*

"—difficult to go on without him." She swallowed hard, trying to keep her expression neutral, seeing by Mylikki's and Altan's sympathetic expressions that she failed. "But I have found my dear Companion the Dragon, and having him with me has enabled me to find you. You must come with us, Jareth. You are the Stone Dancer. We need you, or all will be lost."

Jareth didn't answer. Finally, he said, "I said I would listen to you. Listen I have. I can do nothing to help you."

His flat refusal surprised Kevla. She had thought when she finally explained it—he was a Dancer, he *had* to know this was the truth, *had* to come with her—-

"You would so carelessly doom a world?" The Dragon's voice was deceptively calm.

Jareth looked at the great creature. "What Kevla has said means nothing to me. I've never heard of Lorekeepers, nor have I found some magical animal to cleave to me. I've had no strange, troubling dreams of lives I've lived in the past. I have no reason to believe that what she says is true."

"So the Flame Dancer is a liar?" Smooth as polished glass was his deep voice, but Kevla tensed. The Dragon was one step away from outrage.

Jareth sighed. "I don't know any of you, except for Altan. And forgive me, my friend, but one thing I do know is how well you love a good tale. I know what I'm here for, and it's not to fight some Shadow. It's to take care of my people by changing the seasons in a way they can count on. To make sure that the trees give fruit. To make sure the harvest is good, the animals are fat and healthy, and the winter is as mild as it can be."

He laughed harshly, and Kevla winced at the sound. "And you can see how well I am doing on that task. I can't help you with yours."

"Can't, or won't?" challenged Kevla.

Jareth threw up his hands in exasperation. "It doesn't matter! I left to find the gods and force them to bring spring again. Nothing you can say will dissuade me from that quest."

Altan began talking, his voice tense and earnest. Jareth continued to argue with him. But Kevla suddenly paid no attention to their words.

In her mind's eye, she saw again Jareth standing with the blue tiger. It was so simple, so obvious...how could she not have realized it before?

Dragon—you are not a Lorekeeper, but you have knowledge of what has gone before. These gods Jareth seeks—you know Jashemi and I had visions of one of them standing with Jareth. They're not gods at all, are they? No more than you were to my people. There's only one tiger, and it's Jareth's Companion. Isn't it?

I knew you'd figure that out sooner or later, came the Dragon's pleased reply in her mind.

Suddenly angry, Kevla thought, *Why didn't you tell me?*

The Dragon shrugged his massive shoulders in a very human gesture. *It would have served no purpose. And lest you be too angry with me, know this—I will not keep anything from you that might put you in danger, but it is always, always best if you learn things in their own time. Like the seasons, there is a rhythm and ripeness to such things. Trust that, and trust me.*

Her anger abated quickly. *I do trust you, Dragon. I know you would never put me in harm's way.*

"Kevla?" Jareth, sounding irritated.

"I'm sorry, what did you say?"

"I said, I am not going with you to find the other Dancers. I am going to find the gods."

Kevla caught the Dragon's eye, and he nodded subtly. "I understand. And we will come with you."

22

Jareth stared at the beautiful fire-woman. *"What?"*

"I said, we will come with you."

"Yes!" cried Altan delightedly. "Yes, of course we will. And when you have brought spring to the land again, then you will be free to accompany Kevla!"

Guilt sat heavily in Jareth's chest. It was an old companion, and he had grown used to its weight. He knew what he was supposed to do, and he wanted to do it alone. For one thing, to drag Altan and these two women into what he was now beginning to think was a death quest was unthinkable, and for another, he had a feeling they would slow him down. His gaze flickered over to the enormous red creature that was the fire-woman's Companion. *And I'm sure the gods or the* taaskali *will see* him *coming leagues away.*

"No," he said, firmly. "Altan, you and this young woman will return to safety. It will be a hard enough journey without me having to worry about you. Kevla, you and your friend will have to be about saving the world without my help."

The Dragon, a beast unlike anything Jareth had seen or even heard tales of, stiffened. It lifted its head and regarded him balefully.

"I don't think you quite understand," it said in a deep, ominous rumble. "Kevla was not asking your permission to accompany you. She was *telling* you."

Jareth felt his face flush and his breathing quicken. He wanted to yell. He wanted to hurt something, someone. The Dragon continued to regard him, narrowing its golden eyes.

"I hope you remember our little chat this morning."

"Little chat" indeed. Jareth made a sound of contempt. He had woken before dawn and attempted to steal quietly away when the monster's gigantic claws had closed about him, lifting him high off the earth. The Dragon had said in no uncertain terms that wherever Jareth attempted to go, the Dragon would follow. *I've got your scent, Dancer,* it had rumbled. *There is nowhere you can go now that I cannot find you.*

Jareth remained silent, analyzing each of them in turn. The Dragon, a creature that had shocked him to his very core when it manifested above him, yanking trees from the earth with casual ease. Kevla, her dark skin and hair making her look more like a *taaskali* than a proper Lamali woman...but of course she wasn't Lamali at all, was she? She hailed from a land far south. For a moment, Jareth thought the word *Arukan,* and a hint of heat, of dry sand and parched earth and the footfalls of animals completely alien to him brushed his mind. He almost fancied he could feel a warm wind stir his hair, smell spicy, exotic scents. Then it was gone.

She was beautiful, of course. Anyone with eyes could see that. She reminded him strongly of the woman in his dreams, who had seemed as unmoved by the cold as Kevla and who had transformed into the blue tiger god. He would have admired her capable, calm demeanor at any other time, any other place. Here, now, she was a problem. He had been quite awake when she had broken down at the fire last night; he had thought he would learn more from this odd group if he feigned sleep, and he had been right. She had clearly suffered, though he did not quite understand everything she had said. But Jareth Vasalen had no pity to spare for anyone, not even himself.

He dragged his gaze from the exotic Kevla to the familiar, eager face of Altan. The boy was so very excited to have found Jareth safe; no less pleased was Jareth to learn that Altan had been found whole and alive after hearing about his brush with death. But still, what was the boy thinking? He was no expert in forest craft; he was a musician, a singer of songs, teller of tales. Those slender fingers could coax forth a melody to make the hardest heart ache or the most sullen lips curve in a smile. That was Altan's gift—an honored and important one, but one not conducive to the brutal necessities of survival. It was a wonder he had survived long enough to be found and rescued by the Flame Dancer and her Companion.

And this other girl—for girl she still was—what was her story? He could read part of it in her face. She was enamored of Altan, as most young women and more than a few young men were at one time or another once they'd heard him sing. Even Annu, who had grown up with Altan, had once confided—

No!

He jerked his head, as if he could shake the thought from his mind. His body tensed, twitched.

"Jareth?" said Kevla, tentatively.

Pale and cold, like the Ice Maiden was believed to be, they lay where they had somehow fallen asleep. Waiting for him to soften the hearts of the gods, to talk the great blue cats into bringing life to the land, life to those he loved so much—

Hands on either side of his face, trusted hands that yet caused a shiver of fear—

Kevla, it was Kevla, walking in the snow in that revealing red garment that showed every curve, smiling, transforming into the god, flowers blooming beneath her feet—

He found and held her gaze. He saw her swallow, but he did not look away. Maybe she was part of this. Maybe he had seen her in these dreams because she had been supposed to lead him to the gods. To bringing spring again.

To bringing back those he loved.

"All right," he said, surprising them all. He took a deep breath. He realized he was shaking and had spilled some of his tea. It was as if all the energy had rushed from him. "I could use some food," he said.

"Of course," Altan said quickly. He fished in one of the packs and gave Jareth a hunk of dried meat. The smell made Jareth's mouth water and he gnawed at the chewy, tough flesh.

"We will have some hot grains here in a moment," Kevla said. "Jareth, you must tell us what has happened to you over the last few months."

"To what end?"

"We need to know how much strength you have left," Kevla said quietly. "And what kind of challenges await us if we return to the mountain ranges."

Images flashed through his mind. Snow. Ice that cut the hands until they bled. Storms. Attacks from madmen lurking, spying upon him. Kevla's face in the fire and his subsequent determination not to light fires again. The coppery smell of bloody, raw animal flesh that had been his only source of food since then. The dreams that he banished from his waking moments but that always made him awaken screaming.

"I'd rather not talk about it," he said.

A look passed between Kevla and Altan. Jareth caught another look, one that no one else saw, from Mylikki. The girl's heart was on her face as she regarded Altan. He felt a faint twinge of sympathy, and the lyrics of one of the Ice Maiden songs returned to him: *Remember what drove me to be what I am; all that I wanted was love from one man.*

The grains were soon ready and Jareth ate hungrily. It had been weeks since his body had ingested anything hot, liquid or solid, and even as the nourishment hit his stomach he felt warmth start to creep through his body. Perhaps it was not all bad, traveling with this little group; there would be warmth, shelter and food, three things he had been able to find only sparingly. Still, he knew that if he had the chance to elude them, he'd take it.

"Our purpose until now has been to find you," Kevla told him as she gave him another ladleful of the hot, filling grains. "Now, we will go where you dictate. Altan and Mylikki say the gods live on a mountain range at the end of the world, as far north as one can go. But Altan tells me you couldn't find them. How shall we proceed?"

His respect for her went up another notch. She had accepted the situation and was asking logical questions about what to do next. He realized with some embarrassment that his own thoughts were not nearly as well formed.

Swallowing, Jareth said, "I climbed the mountains and they were not there." That had been some time ago, and the rage and bitterness still made him feel sick. Why did they deliberately elude him so? "I think the next thing to do is to find the *taaskali.* Our myths and tales have always linked them with magical powers and the ability to go between the worlds; to visit the realm of both gods and mortals."

"But the *taaskali* follow the *selva,*" said Mylikki. "You never find one without the other. And the *selva* do not stay in any place for very long. How do you think you'll find them?"

For answer, Jareth reached into one of the sacks and withdrew a handful of grain. Cupping the food gently, he closed his eyes and reached out with his mind. The sky was clear today; he always seemed to have better luck when it wasn't snowing. This was something he had thought about doing for some time, but had never before had any food with which to tempt them.

Little brothers and sisters, he thought, *I will share this with you in exchange for your aid.*

For a long moment, nothing happened. Then, he heard a soft gasp and opened his eyes.

Perched on his knee was a small songbird barely the size of his palm, so tiny he had not even felt it land. Its feathers, normally bright gold in hue, were dingy. It had fluffed them against the cold and peered at him with bright black eyes. Jareth extended his hand and the bird hopped on his fingers and began to peck eagerly at the proffered grain.

"That's our—" began Mylikki, but both Altan and Kevla hushed her. Jareth watched the little bird feed and felt a smile start to curve his lips. It was good, to give life instead of take it. Usually when the animals he summoned came, they came to die.

Others came, too; little sparrows, more songbirds in jeweled tones of blue and purple and green, and one brown, tufted-ear squirrel. Jareth let them all have some of the precious grain. When they had finished, he quietly asked:

I search for the people of dark skin, hair, and eyes. They wander the land, following the four-legged ones with white fur and golden horns. Be my eyes and ears, and let me know where they might be.

The yellow bird cocked its head. *Many wingbeats to the place where the mountains brush the sky.*

Moving steadily in this direction, so it seems, another one thought.

Isn't there anything else to eat? The squirrel looked at him hopefully, brown eyes pleading, and Jareth's smile grew.

I will travel in the direction you have suggested. Return with more news tomorrow, and I will have more food.

As quickly as they had come, the creatures scattered, fluttering into the cloudless sky or the shelter of piney green boughs. He felt an absurd surge of hope. At least not all of his abilities had deserted him.

"The birds say that the *taaskali* are currently in the north, but that they are heading our way," he informed his traveling companions.

"How do you know that's true? Wouldn't they just say what you wanted to hear in exchange for food?" Mylikki asked.

He felt a rush of anger, but tamped it down. In a heartbeat, the offense had subsided to a sort of sorrow.

"Nothing of the earth can lie," he said, "except us."

They packed camp and the tentative harmony that had been established was quickly shattered when Jareth stated, "I am not getting on the back of the Dragon."

"What?" cried Kevla.

"You heard me. And he's not to fly overhead as we go, either. Or scout out in advance." He threw the Dragon a look. Kevla expected the Dragon to reprimand the Stone Dancer, but the great beast remained silent.

"The *taaskali* are shy at best," Jareth continued. He closed the straps on his pack and shouldered it. "I'm not going to frighten them or the *selva* by having *that* hovering over them."

"The Dragon can cover many leagues in a short time," Mylikki said. "It is foolish to refuse such a gift."

"I didn't ask for the gift," Jareth retorted. "You want to travel with me? Then these are my terms. I think the Dragon understands." He shot the giant beast a look. "Don't you."

The Dragon had cocked his head and regarded Jareth intently. "Actually, I do," he said, surprising Kevla. She whirled on her friend.

"What?"

"I am not for him, Kevla," the Dragon said, and Kevla suddenly took his meaning. "And he is right. I do tend to frighten people who don't know me." A thin stream of smoke trickled from his nostrils as he added, "And I even frighten those who *do* know me. When they need it. If what the birds said was right, and I have no reason to believe the information incorrect, then our paths will cross soon enough. In the meantime," and he grinned wickedly, "you will have to learn how to use snow walkers and *skelthas* after all."

Altan laughed.

23

Olar wondered how it could be that the Maiden looked as beautiful on her throne, cold and white, as she did when she moved among the men. Then, her hair was gold as the sun, her lips as red as wine, and now, there was no color to her at all.

She had chosen him to sleep at her feet while she dreamed. Two others had protested. She had ordered them to fight one another as punishment for their audacity—how dare they question, even out of love for her! Olar, thrilled with her choice, had watched as the men went at one another with spears until they both lay bleeding on the floor of her palace. He did not give them another thought.

He looked up at her, felt an unspeakable wave of love rush through him, and longed to share her dreams.

The fire's light flickered and danced, casting leaping shadows. Smoke curled upward, filling the air with its unmistakable rich scent. The only sound was the pure, sweet voice of the hus-kaa and his instrument, as he sang heartbreaking songs of love found, then lost.

The girl was in love. With the song, with the performer's looks, with the night that seemed to her made for opening hearts and whispered intimacies. His long fingers caressed the kyndela's strings; she shuddered as he imagined them touching her. His lips curved around the words, kissing them; she touched her lips and pretended it was his kiss. His body was slender and well made, his locks fair and curling, his face like that of a hero out of legend.

The fire's crackle and glow kept darkness at bay, and served as a gathering place in the evening. The red-gold flames had drawn the stranger here, to sing in exchange for a place to sleep and some food. He would bring them news from other villages, make them laugh and weep, and then move on.

But he would not leave alone.

His eyes opened and fastened on hers, and her mouth went dry even as moisture blossomed in other, more intimate parts of her body. At last he finished. It seemed an age. She thrilled to the melodious sound of his voice, but now she wanted him all to herself. He bowed, graciously accepting the applause, slung his kyndela over his back, and yielded his place to a local youth who launched into a bawdy drinking song.

He came directly to her and clasped her hands. He kissed them, one at a time, then turned them over and pressed kisses into her palms. She trembled at his touch, his lips like a brand on her skin. She curled her fingers closed over the kiss, claiming it, keeping it.

"Your songs are so sad," she said. "Do you not have any happy songs? Any songs of true love?"

"Perhaps you could teach me some new songs, sweet lady," he murmured.

"Songs of true love," she whispered. It wasn't proper, to be alone with a man she had only known a few days. But he had claimed her heart the moment he strode into the village. He was drawn to her as well, she knew it. And why not? She was one of the prettiest maidens in the village, with her long blond hair, large blue eyes, full breasts, and trim waist. Youths had come from leagues distant to court her, but she had wanted none of their callow attentions.

She wanted to be loved by a man, not a boy; a man who would claim her and take her away to a grand and glorious destiny. And now, he had come; no warrior with a spear or arrows to pierce her body, but songs aplenty to pierce her heart.

He released her only to shrug off the kyndela across his back, then his arms slipped around her once more and pulled her to him. She felt the strength of his chest and the bulge in his breeches. When he bent his head to kiss her, she was lost.

She clung to him, willingly opening her mouth to his. She'd never had such a kiss from the local youths, a kiss that made her feel weak and dizzy. His hand crept to the back of her head, taking control. She gave it to him gladly.

"Come with me," he said, his voice deep and his breathing rapid. She went, her hand clutched in his, almost running to keep up with his long-legged, swift strides. He led her into the forest, well away from the fire and the sound of laughter and music.

Again he took her in his arms, bringing her to the soft, mossy soil which he had covered with his cloak. She reached up to him, helping his long, clever fingers undo the few ties on her dress. She felt as if she were on fire, consumed with passion, with a need to feel this man's fingers and tongue and body on her, in her—

The pain was sharp, sharper than she had anticipated, and she gasped. He paused.

"I know it hurts. But it will pass, sweetness." He kissed her lips, her throat, her breasts, until she again began to crave him. He moved, slowly and then more quickly, thrusting inside her. The sting between her legs had passed, as he had promised, and now there was only pleasure, hot and wild and liberating. She clutched at him, her fingernails drawing blood as she raked them across his broad back. His breath was hot and ragged in her ear. And then, before she could claim the burst of pleasure that she sensed she was building toward, he stiffened and cried out.

She held him through his moment of ecstasy, smiling against his cheek, and then he sighed and collapsed on her.

She kissed his ear, putting away her disappointment. No doubt that pinnacle of delight would be achieved next time. She looked forward to the striving.

Startled, the girl felt a sudden brush of cold across her naked body as he rolled off her and reached for his clothes. Of course; he would want to return before she was missed. She smiled at his thoughtfulness but said, "There is no need to worry, love."

He paused. "What do you mean?"

"We will tell them tomorrow. They will have to know that I am leaving with you."

He laughed, reaching and patting her cheek. "Oh, sweeting, that's rich. I'm leaving, that much is certain, but only with my instrument."

Her stomach clenched. "Wh-what?"

"Naught's wrong with your ears. What, did you think I would marry you? That you were the first I've ever cast a lusty eye on? You were good for one thing, sweeting, and I've had it. Here, something to remember this night by."

Fully dressed now, he tossed down his scarf. By the light of the moon filtering in through the trees, she could see that there were dark, wet marks upon it.

Her virgin's blood.

The world swirled about her as she stared at the blood, black in the moonlight. She heard the crunch of his boots as he strode back toward the village.

She tried to stand, and couldn't. She tried to cover her nudity, and couldn't. All she could do was stare at the bloody scarf and slowly, numbly, begin to comprehend what he had done.

The blessed numbness shattered before the agony. She buried her face in the scarf and sobbed wildly. How could he have done this to her? She curled up into a tight ball, weeping as the pain swept over her. She loved him! She loved him!

So slowly she did not know when it happened, the pain turned to fury. It swept her along as an avalanche would anything unfortunate enough to be caught in its path. It made her blue eyes gleam, it stiffened her spine, it filled the ashy, empty place in her with purpose and resolve and hatred.

She would have her revenge. There were powers, dark and brooding, that could help her. She would grow strong in her hatred, and her vengeance would be terrible.

The heat and fury inside her turned to ice.

* * *

The travelers had eaten heartily at breakfast despite the dwindling supply of food because they had known they would need the energy. It was less difficult physically to travel on the broad back of the Dragon than it would be to move through the heavy snow step by step. Not for the first time, Kevla marveled at Jareth's determination and physical endurance. He had been doing this alone for months.

Altan suggested that she try the snow walkers first. "It's a more natural movement than the *skeltha*," he explained as he and Mylikki tightened the sinew straps, securing the apparatus to her feet. "It's still going to feel strange, but it's much more like walking. You'll get used to it quickly."

It was indeed like walking—if one normally walked with enormous flat circles strapped to one's feet, and took large, careful steps. But it was far better than sinking thigh-deep into the huge drifts.

She was surprised at how keenly she missed the Dragon. Since the day she had rediscovered him and learned her own identity, she had not been separated from him for more than a brief time. He had agreed to wait the day out where he was and rejoin them at night. Jareth had started to protest, but then apparently thought better of it at the look on the Dragon's scaly face. He nodded his blond head once, and then strode off toward the north.

The day quickly assumed a pattern that Kevla felt certain would be repeated in the days to come. Jareth would move swiftly ahead of them, leaving a clear path in the curving drifts of snow, and they would follow, Kevla trundling awkwardly on the snow-feet. She bit back her resentment, her urge to scream out, *We could have traveled ten times this far on the Dragon's back!,* her desire to beg, *Wait, don't go so far ahead.*

She knew that she was slowing all of them down. If it had not been for her—

If it were not for you, Mylikki would still be in her village, Altan would be dead, and Jareth would be an angry madman blundering about in the snow.

She smothered a smile at the Dragon's voice in her mind, and felt a little bit better.

By the end of the day, Kevla wondered if she would be able to smile about anything again. Her legs ached, burning from toe to thigh. She rubbed them as they sat by the fire, too exhausted from the day's efforts to prepare dinner as she usually did. Mylikki and Altan stepped in; the geese the Dragon brought them were not difficult to cook. Jareth ate twice as much as any of them, but she did not begrudge him a bite, now that she fully understood the level of his exertion over the past several months. He was a big man and once had clearly been wreathed in muscle, though now he was gaunt.

Kevla forced herself to eat, although she was so tired she had no appetite. She leaned against the Dragon while Altan sang and played something that almost lulled her to sleep. She jerked back awake, though, when Mylikki said, "I don't think Kevla has heard the last song in the Ice Maiden cycle."

Uneasily, she glanced over at Jareth. She was not in the mood for songs about snow and ice, and she didn't think he was either. He was sharpening his knife; the same knife he

had pressed to her throat. He seemed completely uncon-
cerned about songs, *huskaas,* or Ice Maidens.

"You remember the first two, Kevla?" Mylikki asked,
her fingers moving gently over the instrument as she
tuned it.

"Yes," said Kevla. "One was a warning from an old man
to a younger, the second was sung by that young man who
did find the Ice Maiden."

Mylikki nodded. The sky was clear and had been all day,
for which Kevla was grateful. Soon enough, they would
have to deal with more storms, but she was happy for the
calm times when they came.

"That's right. The third one is sung by the Ice Maiden."
Her blue eyes met Kevla's. "It's a very sad song, even though
it's sung by the Maiden herself."

She began, in a soft, urgent voice.

On nights by the fire, when shadows grow long,
A huskaa may sing you a slow, haunting song;
He'll sing of a Maiden with ice in her breast
Whose beauty kills some men, enslaves all the rest.

The Maiden is evil, the Maiden is cold.
The Maiden is heartless—or so you've been told.
The Maiden's a spirit—but oh, 'tis a lie;
The Maiden was mortal; the Maiden is I.

Hark all ye lads who know nothing of pain!
Desire and longing shall be your refrain.
Take care ere ye love me—can you pay the price?
Come forfeit your soul to the Maiden of Ice.

Altan studiously looked at his own instrument, his long fingers still on the strings. Jareth seemed engrossed in sharpening his knife, but Kevla sensed he was listening. She herself was barely breathing, hoping this song would not unfold the way she feared it would.

> *My story's an old one; a poor country maid,*
> *I loved a young man, and that love was betrayed.*
> *"Ah, sweetheart," he told me, "I took ye to bed,*
> *But you're far too simple and plain to be wed.*

> *"For I've loved a Maiden with eyes like the stars,*
> *With pale, creamy skin that no blemish mars;*
> *With lips that are wine-red, and hair like the sun.*
> *That's who I love, lass, and you're not that one."*

Again, Mylikki launched into the bitter, harsh words of the chorus. Her pretty face was flushed with the passion of the words, her eyes closed. It was as if it was her own pain she was pouring out, not that of some mythical woman. And Kevla wondered, as she looked from one singer to the other, if that was not indeed the case.

> *Love, then, means nothing, for beauty is all.*
> *In anguish and rage, on dark things I did call—*
> *I called on the spirits, I called on the Dead,*
> *Too full of hatred to feel any dread.*

> *My softness, for vengeance I bargained away.*
> *My laughter, for beauty as cold as the clay;*
> *My soul, for the power to catch men like flies,*
> *And watch as their manly pride withers and dies.*

Kevla knew that by law, all formal *huskaas* were men. But clearly the Law did not forbid women from learning how to play and sing, merely denied them the title. She wondered, listening to the angry, heartbreaking song, if it had been a woman who had penned these words, long ago. She couldn't imagine a man, even someone as sensitive as Jashemi, fully grasping the ache of a woman's heart.

Even as the thought of her beloved came, she wished it away. His face rose up in her mind and, as always, guilt and pain raked her with merciless claws. Suddenly the song seemed slightly less tragic. Both this Ice Maiden and the pretty young maiden who was currently performing the song knew the shame and pain of rejection. She'd seen Altan by turns flirt with and scorn Mylikki, and knew how badly it had hurt. But the Lamali girl knew nothing of the agony of forever losing her beloved by her own actions—someone who had loved her with all his heart.

Kevla wiped at her eyes, grateful for the pain in the song, hoping that it might hide her own deeply personal grief.

Instead of one lover, I've legions of slaves.
My name's on their lips as they go to their graves.
Some of them die for me, some linger on,
Bereft of emotion, wills utterly gone.

So when you hear ballads of Ice Maiden cold,
With lips that are wine-red and hair sunshine-gold,
Remember what drove me to be what I am—
All that I wanted was love from one man.

Softly, Mylikki repeated the chorus. The crystalline sound of the *kyndela* faded into the clear iciness of the snowy night.

Altan was the first to speak. "That was beautiful, Mylikki," he said quietly. "The student has surpassed the teacher."

Their gazes locked. Suddenly Kevla couldn't bear it anymore. She was physically weary, mentally and emotionally wrung out from the song and the feelings it had roused.

"I have been spoiled by flying on the Dragon's back," she said. "Perhaps tomorrow my legs will be cleverer with the snow walkers. Sleep well, I will see you in the morning."

Kevla awoke fully alert. She must have heard something.

It is all right, came the Dragon's voice in her thoughts.

Jareth?

Do not worry. I can see him from here. He's not attempting to leave.

Curious, Kevla emerged from the shelter of the Dragon's body as quietly as she could. Her legs were stiff and sore, but they obeyed. The moon was bright and she had no trouble seeing the huddled shape of the Stone Dancer at the edge of the clearing. He was bent over something, but she could not tell what.

What is he doing?

Listening, and the Dragon's mental voice was very tender.

Kevla could hear it now; a soft, odd-toned voice, but she could not distinguish words.

Why does this not wake the others?

They are not Dancers, Kevla. Jareth thinks no one but he can understand the voices of the things that speak to him. But every Dancer can hear what he hears, though only he can speak to them.

Kevla nodded her understanding and slipped back into the shelter. As long as the Dragon kept an eye on Jareth and the Stone Dancer made no attempt to flee, he could listen to whatever he wanted.

She feigned sleep when he crept back a short time later. She heard the soft crunch of snow and felt him standing over her. Kevla kept her breathing soft and steady, and he moved away. She heard a deep, long sigh as he lay back down on the blankets, then silence.

As they walked the next day, her legs shrieking in protest, Kevla thought about the strange incident that had happened last night. What was Jareth listening to? And why? She sensed that the Dragon understood, but respected Jareth's privacy sufficiently not to share his secret, not even with the Flame Dancer.

Kevla did not want to pry either, but she was not sure she trusted Jareth fully. He had not committed to his duty as a Dancer, not yet. She couldn't help but wonder if he ever truly would. He was linked to the land in a way that not even she could fully appreciate. Her skill, her affinity, her nature was fire. His was earth. And unlike Kevla, Jareth's powers had been honored and celebrated—even craved—by his community since he was thirteen years old. Fire was transitory. Any fire, anywhere, was as good as another to her. It was, she suspected, why she could scry and even transport herself via their crackling flames.

But earth...land was a deeply personal thing. She saw this even in Arukan, a place where many clans were nomadic and had no real roots. But they shared the same sun, the same sand, the same heat. They were bound together despite their many differences by this shared experience. How much more intimate a union might there be between the people of Lamal, deeply and powerfully connected to the earth through its seasons and its bounty, and the ground upon which they trod? Jareth probably knew each tree, each river in his little village. Even if his people weren't suffering, might he not be reluctant to join Kevla and leave them—leave the land in which he was born, of which he had been caretaker for most of his life—possibly forever?

It worried her. And because it worried her, she overcame her reluctance to invade his privacy and waited for when he slipped quietly into the night, after he thought everyone else was asleep.

The second night, she realized with a shock that she was able to comprehend words. She moved closer to the entrance and strained her ears. Sure enough, just as she had experienced when she first arrived in Lamal, she was starting to understand a language with which she had initially been utterly unfamiliar. She tried to slow her racing heart and quiet her breathing, so she could hear better. The "voice," if voice it could truly be called, sounded like nothing she had ever heard. It was deep, and rich, and as she listened, Kevla could almost smell the moist, earthy scent of soil.

Earth am I, soil and sand, ever-changing and ever the same. I am the flesh that was once living things, and the anchor to the roots of the trees and grass and all growing things. Earth am I, and I shall speak.

He trod with gentle feet, the boy, and sensed the stirring within. Kneeling, he placed his hands on me, young hands, wise hands, digging deep into the rich loam hidden beneath its white blanket of snow. I knew him to be kin to me, though I un-

derstood not how, and when he asked, "Let the spring come forth," we all answered.

The snow melted at his word, surrendering its icy grip. Roots, huddled and dormant, awoke and their tender green grasses emerged. Soft blew the winds, bright shone the sun. And all who beheld this marveled at the youth, barely past thirteen summers, who had summoned spring by asking in a gentle voice, and who seemed more stunned than all the others at what he had wrought.

And when spring had waxed to its burgeoning fullness, came the youth to me again. Again he sank his human fingers into me, merging with soil and sand, and called summer. And summer came, obedient to his asking, bright and warm and welcome. Autumn and winter followed, and spring, and summer again.

So passed the years, and the seasons always came when he called.

There was more; flowing words and images that thrilled Kevla to her very core to hear.

The earth itself was speaking.

Kevla inhaled swiftly. She couldn't see what was happening, but she could guess. Jareth had gathered a handful of dirt from the site where he had first called spring. And now that his powers were gone, he was reliving that moment.

How often had he done this, over the months that he had spent wandering alone? Remembering, listening to what he had once been and now was no longer. Two emotions washed over her: pity and a sense of horror that he was so obsessed with this that he listened every night to a reminder of his past glory.

She heard the crunching of snow and hurried back to her

blanket, hoping he didn't come and listen to her breathing, because she was certain it was rapid and shallow with the revelation she had just experienced.

24

Night after night, Kevla stayed awake until Jareth quietly moved from his blanket out into the crisp, open air. Night after night, she listened to his memories, captured forever by a stone, a leaf, a clump of dirt. During the day, Jareth was taciturn, saying little about anything and nothing at all about himself, although Altan always tried to draw him out while they sat beside the fire in the evening.

Jareth was the first person Kevla had ever met who was truly like her. While Jashemi, her Lorekeeper, and the Dragon, her Companion, were an intrinsic part of her, Jareth was complete unto himself. And yet, he was a Dancer. He was an element made flesh. She burned to ask him questions, to share her own experiences, but he kept them all at arm's length.

These illicit moments, deep in the quiet of an icy night, were the only times Jareth revealed any part of himself to her. And though she was ashamed of herself, Kevla was willing to live with that shame in order to glean knowledge about this withdrawn, bitter man.

She heard him rise, heard the squeak of snow as he walked away from the Dragon and the clearing. She crawled to the entrance and listened.

The voice this time was sweet and lyrical; exactly the way the voice of such a speaker ought to be, she thought as she strained her ears to catch the soft sound.

Wildflower am I, stem and petal and leaf still here though torn from my roots, brief lived but beautiful. Petals red as blood, center blue as sky, I follow the sun on its path from dawn to dusk. Wildflower am I, and I shall speak.

With fingers soft as water he tore me from my roots; he felt me bleeding and sorrowed for me, but nonetheless took my long green stem and pressed it between the fingers of a woman. She brought me to her face and inhaled my scent, and for the tenderness the man showed me I blessed her with my fragrance. Held in her tender grasp I was then, and later I adorned her hair, and my petals were trailed over lips and breasts and body.

Cherished I was, my death an offering of love.

Kevla made a small sound and then clapped her hand over her mouth. The song of the wildflower, dying so that Jareth might give it to his wife, clearly used in their loveplay, nearly broke her heart. Fearing she had given herself away, she hurried back to her blankets, closed her eyes, and tried to steady her breathing.

Sure enough, she heard the quick sound of Jareth's footsteps, then silence as, she assumed, he peered beneath the

Dragon's belly to see if anyone had heard him. After a long, tense moment, she heard him moving off again and relaxed.

Does he weep, Dragon?

I do not watch him closely, Flame Dancer, but no, I believe he does not weep.

And yet he forces himself to listen to...this...every night.

Sometimes, our pain is our comfort. It is the only thing that makes us feel alive.

Too tired to stay awake, Kevla drifted into an uneasy slumber wondering if the Dragon's words were not entirely about the Stone Dancer.

Kevla was determined to learn to use the *skeltha*. Altan and Mylikki strapped the long, awkward poles onto her feet and did their best not to laugh at Kevla as she flailed, fell and struggled. If she had thought herself sore after a few days with the snow walkers, she had not understood the proper definition of the word. By the end of her first day, she could barely hobble to the fireside. Mylikki started to prepare supper, but Kevla saw her pause as she went through the packs.

"We're down to the last of the provisions," Mylikki said in a somber voice.

"What's left?" Kevla asked. She eased herself down on a blanket beside the fire, arranging her *rhia* so Altan could massage her legs.

"A few more days' worth of grains, about a handful of dried vegetables, eight strips of dried meat and another potful or two of tea," Mylikki replied.

"We'll need to start rationing," Kevla said. "Make the soup with half the usual ingredients."

Mylikki nodded and started the meal. Kevla hissed as Altan massaged her legs, but gritted her teeth and accepted the pain, knowing from experience that her muscles would be the looser for the attention the next day.

"What I wouldn't give for one of your stonesteaming huts right now," Kevla said as Altan worked on her calf.

Altan sighed. "What *I* wouldn't give," he said. "Don't suppose we could construct a makeshift version?"

Jareth had been sitting silently by the fire, but now he spoke. "Kevla might be able to heat the stones sufficiently, but building even a basic one would be a waste of energy and time. We can't afford to do that. We need to save all our strength for the journey."

Altan sighed. "I suppose you're right. Though it would be awfully pleasant. How about you, Mylikki? You and Kevla had one only a few weeks ago. Missing it yet?"

Mylikki muttered something, but clearly was in no mood for conversation. Kevla caught Altan's eye, and in that fleeting instant saw confusion in their blue-green depths. Was it possible that Altan didn't realize how his cutting comments hurt Mylikki? The youth quickly looked away and intensified his efforts on Kevla's calf.

"Forgive my inexperience, I'm not skilled in such things," Altan said as he watched her wince.

"Too bad it's not one of you who's sore," Kevla said, forcing a smile. "I *am* skilled in such things."

"How convenient of you not to have mentioned before," Altan said in arch voice, the corners of his mouth lifting a little to make sure Kevla knew he was teasing. "Now that I know, I'll make sure to remember that. Jareth, Mylikki, you heard her."

He patted her thigh to indicate he was finished and she extended the other leg. "We know so little about you, Flame Dancer," Altan continued. "Yet it seems you know all about us."

Kevla glanced at Jareth. She knew more about him, at least, than he fully realized. Jareth had put up all sorts of barriers between himself and his traveling companions. Spying on him—for she was spying, no amount of calling it anything else would change the fact—had brought her closer to him than she would have been otherwise. She thought about the flower, and her heart ached as if the experience had been her own.

She felt it was time to balance things out. "I will tell you, then," she said quietly. Something in her voice made Jareth look up and regard her with narrowed eyes.

While Mylikki quietly stirred the watery soup, Jareth worked on repairing a damaged leather boot, and Altan massaged her legs, Kevla spoke of her life. She spoke of how, as a child, she used to solicit customers for her mother. Of the day when Tahmi-kha-Rakyn, *khashim* of the Clan of Four Waters, had whisked her away to what appeared to be a comparatively glamorous life in the great House.

"He was my father," Kevla said, "but I did not know that until much later." She lay on her back now, protected from the wetness of the snow only by a thin blanket, not in the least bit cold. The night was again clear, and she wondered if they would see the dancing lights that indicated frolicking tiger-gods. Altan rubbed her feet with hands that were both strong and gentle if not experienced.

Kevla continued, speaking with only a slight hitch in her voice of her half brother Jashemi, who had befriended her and stood fast beside all that followed. She told of her powers, and how terrified she had been.

"But I was most frightened of all of the Great Dragon, who was the Lawgiver and protector of our people. He came in dreams every night, breathing fire on me, demanding if I knew who I was. You utterly terrified me!"

The Dragon shrugged his massive shoulders. "It was what was required," he said matter-of-factly.

Kevla's smile faded. It was one thing to speak of playing *Shamizan* with a half brother, and bad dreams, and taking care of the *khashima*. But what followed took a much darker, much more tragic path.

She gently placed a hand on Altan's shoulder, stilling the movements of his strong fingers on her legs. "Thank you, Altan. That was lovely." Kevla sat up. "I think that is enough for tonight." Altan nodded, knowing that she referred both to her story and to the massage.

He sat up. "Where's Mylikki?" he asked. Indeed, the girl was nowhere to be seen.

Jareth shrugged. The Dragon said, "She went to be by herself for a while."

Altan tried and failed to hide a smile. "Looks like we're almost ready to eat. I'll go find her."

It was easy enough to tell in which direction Mylikki had gone. The tracks betrayed her, and Altan followed them quickly, seemingly eager to have a moment alone with the girl.

Now, it was only Kevla, the Dragon, and Jareth. She went and stirred the soup, surprised despite Mylikki's warning to see how thin it was. "Dragon, I hope you'll be able to catch us something for tomorrow," she said.

"I will do my best, but I cannot call the animals as Jareth can. I must hunt as the hawk and the bear do and I am not always successful."

Kevla eyed Jareth. "Why is it you do not summon something for our meals, Jareth?"

He frowned. "I have lived on nothing but snow and animal flesh for almost a year," he said. "The last few weeks, I've eaten it raw. We have some provisions left. It was...good not to have them come to me only to die." Then, as if remembering something, he added, "I won't let any of you starve, Kevla, if that's what you're implying."

"Of course I wasn't implying that!" She stared at him, exasperated. In his own way, he was just as moody as Altan, and she wondered if all Lamali men were so contradictory. It was as if he were two people—the sullen, moody, angry man who seemed perpetually irritated by everything and everyone, and the man who roused each night to listen to inanimate objects sing in haunting voices of past joys and sorrows. Her annoyance fled as she recalled the voice of the earth, singing of the Spring-Bringer, and the flower, singing of Jareth's beloved, and all the other voices who had spoken of the births of children, of the terror of losing one's powers, of the agony of finding one's beloved cold and lifeless, and all the other pieces of a shattered life.

Impulsively, she went and sat down beside him. He shied away, almost imperceptibly, but she didn't miss the gesture.

"You said for the last few weeks, you've been eating raw flesh. Jareth, did you never light a fire?"

He looked down at his hands. "After I saw your face in the flame, I couldn't risk it."

She was silent for a moment, wondering if she would have had the strength to endure what he had.

"I know this wasn't how you imagined things turning out," she said at last, very gently. "My life certainly hasn't turned out the way I thought it would, either. I know you wanted—"

He whirled on her so suddenly she gasped out loud. His lips were drawn back from his white teeth in a feral snarl, and his blue eyes were like chips of ice. For an instant, she thought he would strike her.

"I don't want you here!" he growled. "I don't want you, or Mylikki, or the Dragon, and certainly not Altan here. I don't want you coming from your house of—of olives and dates and scented oils and soft pillows into *my* land, *my* life, and telling me what you 'know' I think or feel or want or imagine. The only reason I'm even here right now is because your big red bully of a Dragon physically won't let me leave. Do you understand that? You're not my friend, you're not my ally, you're nothing to me. What you want me to do is *nothing* to me. You don't know anything about me, Kevla. You don't know one cursed thing!"

But I do, she wanted to tell him. *I know everything that matters.* Kevla tried to imagine this big, gruff, broken man making love to a petite woman on a harvested wheat field; tried to see him holding a baby daughter and kissing her forehead as he wept tears of joy. It was almost impossible, and yet she had heard such things with her own ears.

Jareth's nostrils flared with each angry breath. He was daring her to respond as he would, daring her to grow angry and hurl cold words at him. Instead, she reached and squeezed his arm, and returned to the fire.

* * *

"Leave me alone."

Altan stopped, surprised. "I thought when you left, you wanted me to follow. So we could have a few moments together, away from the others."

Mylikki made a contemptuous sound. She faced away from him, huddled in her cloak.

"Mylikki, sweeting, what's wrong?" he asked. "Are you angry with me? Have I done something wrong?"

She laughed shortly, a harsh bark. "You know."

"Truly, I don't. Is there anything I could do to make you feel better?"

"No." The anger had faded, leaving only a deep sorrow in her voice. "There isn't, so please, just go away."

Altan sighed. "Look at me." He reached for her hands. She tried to pull away, but not very forcefully. Reluctantly, she turned to face him. He held her hands between his, caressing them, noting their coldness and the delicacy of the fingers.

"You've got calluses on your fingertips," he said. Not knowing how she would react, he brought her fingers to his lips and gently kissed the rough flesh. She trembled.

"That tells me you've spent hours and hours practicing. You have done an amazing job of learning to play, especially with no one to really teach you. I've been instructed by a *huskaa* since I was thirteen, and I think you'll surpass me soon if you keep this up. You certainly surpassed me the other evening. I've never heard such a passionate rendition of that song in my life." He squeezed her hands. "Was it just talent I was hearing, or was it something else?"

She looked at him fully then. Her cheeks and lips were flushed and her eyes swollen from crying.

"What do you think?"

"Mylikki, my lovely, dear girl, what have I done wrong?"

"Do you not hear yourself speak sometimes?"

Now it was Altan's turn to look away. *Not Mylikki. Please let me not have said anything to hurt Mylikki.*

He wondered, worried, what he had said to upset her so. Carefully, he felt his way.

"If I...said anything to you that hurt you, I didn't mean it. There's so much happening. This strange winter, Jareth losing his powers, meeting Kevla...."

"Yes, Kevla and Jareth," she said, a hint of heat in her words. "They're so very important."

"They *are* important and you know it," he said a touch more harshly than he intended. Maybe this was what she was talking about. Maybe if he explained it to her so that she understood— "You know what's going on here. And I've known Jareth all my life—literally. He was at my *birth,* Mylikki—saw me and my sister coming into the world, helped my mother accept my sister's death. What he went through—he needs me right now. He needs me and I want to be there for him. Can you understand that?"

"I understood that song," she said quietly.

"You're not being fair. I never did that to you!" Altan said indignantly. "I've never even kissed you, not that I haven't wanted—"

Before he quite knew what was happening, her lips were on his, cold but full, soft and moist. Altan's eyes closed as if of their own accord and relief surged through him as he kissed her back, his arms going around her to pull her tightly to him, his body responding to her softness by becoming hard and firm.

Cold, her flesh was so cold where his hands, warm and limber from the massage, touched her. But the inside of her mouth was hot and sweet. Her fingers reached to tangle themselves in his curly blond hair as she opened to him. Altan's lips traveled to her cold ear, her cold throat where the vein beat, wanting to take away this chill he found in her, wanting to give her his heat. His arms moved under her cloak, around her waist, along her thigh, snaking upward beneath the fabric to press with a trembling hand flesh that was round and apple-firm yet so, so soft, and at last, warm to his touch—

What are you doing?

It was as if the voice had come from somewhere else, as if it was not part of his own hazy, desire-clotted thoughts at all. It seared through him and jolted him backward almost as if he had been struck.

Mylikki gazed at him through half-closed lids, still tasting his kiss on lips that curved in a smile. Then, slowly, her eyes widened and the smile faded.

"Altan?"

"You should pay better attention to the songs you sing," Altan said, his voice dripping contempt. "Your heart wouldn't get broken if you didn't keep throwing yourself at men like this."

He rose, dusted off his pants, and strode back to the circle. Mylikki felt as though he'd kicked her in the stomach. What was *wrong* with him? Why was he doing this to her? Was this a test? Was he pretending to scorn her so she would prove her love?

"I don't understand," she whispered, though he was

gone. Tears again filled her eyes, spilled down her cheeks. "I love you, Altan. I'd do anything to make you love me. Anything."

25

It was a grim and silent group that set forth the next day, and the weather mirrored their mood. They pressed onward, heading due north, following the advice of the birds that came to Jareth's summons. Despite Altan's best efforts at massage, Kevla ached all day as she tried to negotiate the *skelthas* with a body that was tight and stiff. She bit her lip when she wanted to hiss in pain, and said not a word of complaint.

Mylikki and Altan studiously avoided one another. Altan was hunched and miserable as they went, and Mylikki looked raw and broken. Jareth, of course, was as unreachable as ever. Kevla would not try again to engage him in intimate conversation. She knew what he had undergone, but she could not tell him that she knew. She wondered if he would ever be able to lower the walls he had built around himself like a fortress.

Around midmorning, the snow that had been threatening finally started to fall. They kept going. It did not lessen until after sunset, and it did nothing to brighten anyone's mood.

Dinner—three small hares cut up and boiled in the pot—was eaten quickly and in silence. Neither player seemed to want to perform, and the *kyndelas* stayed carefully wrapped in their packs. At one point, the night cleared and the gods appeared in the skies. Everyone watched them without speaking. Kevla suspected they all found it so entertaining merely because it was something to do that did not emphasize the tension and unhappiness running rampant in the group.

Days passed in such a fashion. After a few days of heading steadily north, to where Jareth predicted they would find the *taaskali,* they finally ran out of supplies. From this point on, they would be forced to rely upon what the Dragon could provide and any creatures Jareth could summon. There was more than one day that passed with nothing to eat and only weak tea to warm bodies that grew increasingly vulnerable to the bite of the ceaseless cold. Mylikki frightened Kevla badly one morning when it took several minutes for the Flame Dancer to rouse her. Kevla could no longer bear to continue to listen to Jareth's pain, spoken through the things of the earth. She wondered how he could. Neither did she have any patience left for the two younger ones and their might-be, might-not-be romance.

At one point, they had removed their *skelthas* and were moving single file through a tight tangle of trees. A sharp wind was blowing, and Kevla was glad for what little shelter the trees provided. Jareth had taken the lead and Kevla was behind him. She was looking down at her feet, negotiating the tricky roots, and ran right into him.

A retort was on her lips but it died there as she saw his face. For the first time since she had met him, there was a pleasure on his features. Beneath the bushy beard, his mouth curved in a smile. In his fabric-wrapped hands he held a piece of cloth and as she watched, he brought it to his face and inhaled deeply.

"I thought it was just a myth," breathed Mylikki as she and Altan stepped forward.

"What is it?" Kevla asked.

In the gentlest voice Kevla had ever heard him use, Jareth said, "It is a *taaskali* blessing cloth. It's woven from the fur of the *selva*."

He held it out to its full length, and Kevla saw that it was about the size of a kerchief. The fabric seemed to glow as if lit from within, and she was unable to resist caressing it.

She murmured in pleasure. It was the softest thing she had ever touched. Not even the *khashima's* bedsheets were this soft, this smooth between her fingers. And this was woven from the fur of a beast? It seemed almost impossible to contemplate.

"Smell it," Jareth said. She looked at him sharply. He gestured. "Go on."

She lifted the soft cloth to her nose and obeyed, thinking to smell a typical animal scent like wool or fur. Instead, her eyes widened. She inhaled no musky scent, but something sweet and clean and fresh, like grass, or fruit, or blossoms, or...

"It smells...it smells like spring," she managed in a faint voice.

He nodded, then took the scrap of cloth and handed it to Mylikki and Altan. Kevla was shocked into silence, wondering how such a thing could be.

When Mylikki handed the cloth back to Jareth, he held it up so that the wind caught it. It snapped and danced.

"Listen."

Silently they strained their ears, and then as a particularly brisk gust made the white, nearly radiant cloth flutter, she heard the sound. Like a *kyndela,* but not quite; like a sweet human voice, but more profound. Like nothing Kevla had ever heard, the song of the cloth filled her ears and made her skin prickle. Then, to her shock, Jareth let the cloth go. The wind caught it and bore it aloft to the blue sky.

"No!" she cried, startled by how painful the thought of never again touching this marvel was to her.

"It is not meant for keeping," Jareth said. "The *taaskali* weave the blessing cloths during each season of the year, when the *selva* decide to stop moving for a time. They weave into its strands their songs and prayers and hopes, for themselves, the *selva* they protect, and all the peoples of Lamal. Then they release these cloths to the wind, to carry the blessings throughout the land."

"I've never seen one before," Mylikki whispered. Kevla looked at her, and for the first time in many days, Mylikki looked like the sweet, bright girl who had first chosen to accompany Kevla.

"Nor have I," Altan said, his voice hushed with awe.

"I have," Jareth said. "When I first discovered my abilities. I wanted so badly to keep it, but I knew what I was supposed to do. I had to let it go, so that it could continue to sing its blessings."

"What happens to them?" Kevla asked.

Jareth shrugged, and at the gesture Kevla realized all over again just how broad his shoulders were. "It may get caught in a tree branch, and a bird might make a nest of it. Or it may fly until the wind rips it to tatters and the final song is sung. Whatever betide, it's not for humans to keep."

"You are wise indeed," came a voice. "Had you kept it, you would never have found us."

Kevla whirled.

They had materialized from nowhere, it seemed; now every tree she beheld seemed to have an archer behind it.

It was the *taaskali;* it could be no one else. They were smaller than the Lamali people, and Kevla now saw why everyone had first mistaken her for one of them. Their skin was as dark as hers, their hair, worn in various lengths and styles, a blue-black hue. Some of the men had long beards; others were clean-shaven. More than a few of those pointing the weapons at the little band were women. All of them looked deadly serious.

They wore garments that seemed to her to be made of the same shiny material as the cloth. Kevla wondered how they withstood the cold in such seemingly flimsy garb.

"I am Hanru. You are looking for us." The voice, which sounded more like the wind in the trees than that of a human, belonged to a slender man who stepped forward, lowering his bow. "Which is a good thing, because we have been looking for you."

They offered no further explanation. Hanru pointed wordlessly in the direction in which they had been traveling. Kevla and her companions exchanged glances. Jareth was the first to move; this was, after all, what he had been seeking. In stunned and slightly anxious silence, Kevla and her companions followed the *taaskali* out of the forest.

The *taaskali's* feet never seemed to stumble as they touched lightly, then lifted off roots or earth. Kevla noted the boots on those clever feet, supple and smooth, apparently seamless; the clothing, the cloaks, all in that incredible shade of white that seemed to glow. Against their dark skins, the material seemed almost blindingly white. At one point, she stumbled and one of them was there to catch her before she fell.

The hand on her arm, warm and strong, was almost the same color as her own flesh, and she looked up into the first pair of brown eyes she had seen since arriving in this land. Even as this was familiar, it was strange; the *taaskali's* face was rounder than the aquiline features of the Arukani, and her eyes were larger and seemed more deep-set. The woman who had caught her smiled slightly, in acknowledgment of their similarity, then moved on in lithe silence.

Finally, they emerged from the woods onto a flat plain that seemed to stretch as far as the eye could see. The snow, which Kevla had always thought so white, seemed dull and gray compared to the clothing of the *taaskali*. Kevla looked around, puffs of steam rising from her lips.

She had thought to be greeted by the sight of the *taaskali* camp, perhaps even catch a glimpse of the *selva*. But nothing met her gaze other than the wide expanse.

Kevla glanced at the others, who seemed as puzzled as she. She looked at the woman who had kept her from stumbling earlier and asked quietly, "Are we...here?"

The woman's face slowly stretched into a grin. In a tongue that Kevla did not understand but that made her long to hear it spoken again, she called out to her companions. They all chuckled.

"Look again," Hanru said, his strange accent caressing the words. "Look with soft eyes."

Kevla understood what he meant. She looked out again at the white stretch of snow before her with the same slightly out of focus gaze she adopted when she scried into the fire.

She gasped at what she now beheld. What had at first seemed like snow clear to the horizon now resolved itself into various forms. She could make out tents and cloak-clad figures and—

"The *selva*," she breathed.

How could she not have seen them earlier? They were enormous, striding calmly across the snow, pausing to dig at the white stuff with long, slender legs. They resembled *kirvi* deer, but only in the way a child's sketch resembles the object he is attempting to capture.

They were much bigger than deer, and their coats were pure white and looked incredibly soft to the touch. Strong yet slender necks supported delicate heads crowned with branching golden antlers that gleamed as they caught the sunlight. Long, slim tails with tufts at the end swished lazily. She could not see what color their eyes were, but she knew they watched her carefully. The hooves with which the graceful creatures dug in the snow were as golden as their horns. Kevla felt a soft sigh escape her as she regarded them. She felt she could stand so and watch them until the end of time. No wonder these people were content to do nothing but tend to the creatures.

Beside her, Jareth stood as still as if he had turned to

stone. His eyes were wide and he gazed at the *selva* as if stunned. Mylikki let out a soft, "Oh."

"For nearly a thousand years, our people have tended them," said Hanru. "They grace us with their milk and their soft wool, from which we weave our clothing and the blessing cloths. We follow them as they graze, keeping them safe from predators—of all kinds."

"May...may we approach them?" Jareth's voice, soft, awe-filled.

"If they permit you," Hanru replied. "If they will not, leave them be."

"Of course," Kevla breathed. She walked slowly toward one of the beasts. She could not tell at once if it was male or female. While they resembled *kirvi* deer, the *selva* seemed to have at least one thing in common with the *liahs* of Kevla's homeland in that both sexes had horns.

Step by step, feeling ungainly and graceless in the presence of such wondrous creatures, Kevla continued to approach. It lifted its great head from where it had been nibbling beneath the snow and regarded her calmly.

She almost forgot to breathe. Only a few steps away from the being, Kevla now saw that its eyes were gray, almost silver. Her heart was racing as she and the *selva* locked gazes.

Kevla felt—there was no other word to describe it—its willingness to let her approach and touch it. There was nothing so complex as words or even thought in the exchange, but Kevla understood it in her bones. Licking dry lips, she closed the short distance between them until she stood beside it. With a hand that trembled, Kevla reached out and touched thick, smooth fur.

And when the *selva* lowered its great head and nuzzled

her cheek with its soft muzzle, Kevla felt something inside her shatter. She felt understood, accepted, welcomed... loved. She threw her arms around the slender neck and wept fiercely, her hot tears taken and absorbed by the soft, warm fur that smelled of spring blossoms and sunlight.

26

How long Kevla stood clasping the *selva's* neck, she did not know; nor did she understand why she wept. She only knew that when she finally drew back, dragging an arm across her wet face, she felt better.

"Thank you," she whispered to the creature, and it flicked its large, creamy white ears as if it understood her.

A hand touched her shoulder and she turned to see the woman who had helped her before. The woman gestured, and Kevla saw that someone had started a fire, large and crackling. She followed the woman and sat on a blanket as she was bade.

Hanru was waiting for her. "There are always a few among my people who keep the knowledge of your people's language. We do not often have dealings with you, but when we must, we wish to be able to communicate. I know you have been looking for us, and as I told you, we have been looking for you as well."

"Took you long enough to find us," Jareth muttered. Kevla shot him an angry look, but fortunately, Hanru appeared to be unperturbed.

"We go as fast as the *selva* and no faster," the *taaskal* said mildly.

"I need to find the gods," Jareth said bluntly. "I need—"

"We know what you need," Hanru said, his voice sharp. "Do you not think we have watched you try and fail?"

Jareth gaped. "You—you watched me climb the mountains? You did nothing?"

"We did a great deal," Hanru replied. "We protected the herd. That is what we always do. We have not moved from here for several weeks—this seems to be where the *selva* wish to stay, and we always obey the *selva*."

Jareth rubbed at his eyes. "How is it I didn't see you?"

"How is it you didn't see us when you first emerged from the woods?" was Hanru's answer. "We can shield ourselves if we have need."

"You know that the land has not had spring for too long," Jareth said. Kevla, who was starting to get to know Jareth better than he knew, realized that he was keeping his anger in check with difficulty. "Surely even you, even the *selva*, suffer when the land is dead. If you can help me find the gods, I can bring the spring back to the land."

"How do you know this?" challenged Hanru.

"I have done so many times before."

"Then why do you not do so now?"

Color flowed and ebbed in Jareth's face. Altan looked down. Mylikki seemed to be watching everything, focused and alert.

"I have...lost my powers. But I know that the gods can return them to me, if they so choose."

Hanru regarded him impassively. "You want more than spring."

"That does not concern you," Jareth answered harshly.

"You did not come with love in your heart," Hanru said. "You came to demand, to force."

Jareth didn't back down. "I did, and do," he replied. Inwardly, Kevla winced. She knew that this was not what the *taaskal* wanted to hear, but she also knew that it was not in Jareth's nature to lie. "So many have died, humans and animals alike. I cannot understand why the gods withhold this from me, when no one benefits and the land and its creatures are suffering!"

"She has her reasons," Hanru replied. "She did not wish to see you before. Hence, you were not able to find her. Now, she is willing to appear before you. And here we are, to take you to her."

"Her?" Now Jareth did notice it. "Is there only one god willing to meet with me? But what about the others, why are they—?"

Hanru held up a hand. "You will understand everything soon. In the meantime, you are in our care."

Kevla heard a familiar sound and looked up. The Dragon seemed like a small dot in the sky at first, growing larger and larger as he descended. Kevla glanced at Hanru, ready to speak, to let him know that the Dragon was a friend, something not to be feared, but welcomed, as they had welcomed Kevla and her traveling companions.

She need not have worried. Hanru looked up with an expression of mild curiosity. No one among the *taaskali,* and indeed not even the *selva,* seemed distressed as a giant red reptilian creature circled and landed. Kevla felt another wave of astonishment wash over her. Did nothing rattle these people and their herd?

Kevla rose and ran toward her friend, pleased to see that he clutched two *kirvi* deer, skinny and sad-looking things, in his foreclaws.

"We accept your hospitality," she cried over her shoulder to Hanru, "and we would be honored to contribute to tonight's meal."

The two deer the Dragon had brought to share were tough and stringy, but the meat was complemented by *selva* milk and cheese, creamy and as white as the beasts themselves. Perhaps it was because she was so hungry and had eaten so little over the last few days, but Kevla thought she had never tasted anything as delicious as the tangy, soft cheese and the rich milk. As night fell and everyone ate before the fire, slicing meat from the spit as he or she chose, Kevla could hear the beautiful creatures moving quietly just beyond the ring of firelight.

The Dragon had been welcomed in such a casual fashion that Kevla wondered if the *taaskali* had been told of his coming. She knew that the huge blue Tiger who awaited Jareth in the morning was no god, but Jareth's Companion. Perhaps the tiger had told the *taaskali* that the Dragon was a being like herself. Kevla pressed the Dragon with mental questions, all of which he declined to answer.

"At sunrise, I will take you to the tiger, Jareth," said Hanru.

Something about how the words were spoken alerted Kevla. Clearly, Altan had perceived it as well, for he said immediately, "I'm going with him."

"He goes before the tiger alone," Hanru stated.

"Perhaps," said Kevla. "But he will not make that journey without his companions."

Jareth looked at her. She couldn't quite decipher his expression. Surprise, certainly; she herself hadn't planned to speak. Pleasure? Annoyance?

"I'm coming too," said Mylikki.

"I am staying," said the Dragon.

Kevla turned to him, shocked. *Why?*

I have...a task to complete. You know who awaits Jareth, Kevla. It will be an ordeal for him, but a necessary one. No one, no thing, in this world loves the Stone Dancer as much as the tiger does, although Jareth doesn't understand that yet.

You could save us much time and trouble.

That's not what I'm here for. I have something else to do.

There was no swaying him, and Kevla wondered what sort of task was so important to the Dragon that he would let them climb the mountain on their own.

"There is no need for anyone else to come," Jareth said.

"I am Fire, Jareth," Kevla said. "You cannot argue that I can be of use if you run into trouble."

She had him there and he glared. Altan said, "And unless you want Mylikki and I to go to our deaths following you, you had best agree to let us come."

Jareth swore under his breath. "You are fools, to leave the comfort of the camp when you don't need to," he said. "But it appears I cannot escape any of you. Hanru, it seems as though you will take Kevla, Altan, Mylikki *and* me to the god."

"And you will go before her alone," Hanru repeated.

"I agree," Jareth replied, and Kevla thought that this would be how he would have wanted it to unfold anyway. She could not know, of course, what he would face when he encountered the tiger. But she did know that once he had undergone this meeting, he would emerge the better for it.

After night had fallen and the meal was eaten, Kevla snuggled against her friend and regarded the lights in the sky. What were they, then, if not the gods playing? She supposed she would never know.

"Will you be our shelter again, Dragon?" she asked.

"Not tonight. The *taaskali* have prepared a place for each of you to sleep. Pay attention to your dreams."

The Lorekeeper stared up at the sky. He was speaking to her again.

Time is growing short, the Emperor urged her. *The inter-ference of the* taaskali *has complicated things. You must act quickly. Tomorrow. If you do not act, then it will be too late, and he will never be yours. And you know what will happen if he chooses to leave Lamal, to stay a part of this group.*

Licking dry lips, her eyes open and unblinking, the Lorekeeper nodded ever so slightly. She didn't want anyone to notice the gesture and ask about it.

It will be difficult, but I know you can do it. I have faith in you. Will you do it? Tomorrow?

And again, she nodded. For love of one man, she would betray all the others who trusted her.

* * *

Kevla felt odd about not sleeping next to the Dragon. This entire part of the journey felt odd to her. She knew things were transpiring that she was not privy to, and the *taaskali,* despite their hospitality and apparent willingness to help, still unsettled her. Hanru beckoned them forward to stand in the center of the gathering. Kevla found herself wanting to clasp hands with the other three, but knew that Jareth would reject the gesture. So she stood, straight and tall, trying not to be nervous as the *taaskali* regarded her with dark, expressionless faces.

After a moment, she saw movement just beyond the ring of firelight. A graceful head rose; golden antlers gleamed, catching the fire's orange light. Three *selvas* stepped forward.

One moved to stand beside Altan. It lowered its head, and the boy reached to pet its soft neck. Altan followed the creature as it moved gracefully into the darkness. Another claimed Jareth, who, after glancing at Kevla and Mylikki, accompanied it. The third moved to Kevla, and she was fairly certain it was the same one who had let her weep on its soft white coat earlier.

As she stepped out into the snow, her hand on the creature's neck, she looked back. Her heart sank as she saw Mylikki standing alone by the fire. She had never seen a more stricken, unhappy look on anyone's face, and she knew that the rejection of the *selva* must feel like a physical blow to the girl. Why hadn't they come for her? Only they, and perhaps the *taaskali,* knew. They must have their reasons, but she couldn't imagine what they would be. She wondered if it were a bad omen and suddenly, irrationally, feared for Mylikki.

She forced herself to look away. She felt a quick pang of comfort as she heard the Dragon say, "Kevla is not sleeping with me tonight, and I need some company. I have some wonderful tales to tell, if you would like to listen, Mylikki."

She did not hear Mylikki's reply, but hoped the girl would accept the offer. Better to sleep next to a Dragon than alone, rejected by the *selva*.

Kevla walked with the creature for a ways, until she came to an area that had been cleared of snow. Someone had gathered pine boughs and had draped several blankets over them, creating what was a fairly comfortable space. As she settled down, the *selva* gracefully folded its long legs and lay beside her. She snuggled up to its furry warmth and inhaled the fresh, clean scent. Within moments, she was fast asleep.

For the second time, Kevla found herself standing on a mountainside that was now familiar to her. This was where her visions originated; this was where she had learned what it meant to be a Dancer, where so much had been revealed before.

Once again, the wide expanse of still water spread before her. The wind blew gently, running invisible fingers through long, thick black hair and making her red rhia cling to her body. She stepped forward, bare feet on soft green grass, and gazed at her reflection in the mirrorlike surface, both wondering and fearing what she would see this time.

An image seemed to float up from the dark depths, and as it came into focus, Kevla gasped. Her knees buckled and she fell to the grass.

"Jashemi," she whispered, her heart aching.

Something else floated up through the water, and she realized, confused, that it, too, was Jashemi.

"We are here," came two voices in perfect unison. "And you must choose between us."

What? How—

Suddenly, the images in the water disappeared. Kevla felt a presence on either side of her and she looked to her right and left, seeing Jashemi standing on each side of her. As one, they reached down to her and helped her to her feet. She drew her hands back quickly.

"What's happening?" she cried, wanting to embrace each of them and terrified of what would happen if she did.

"It is time to make a decision, Kevla," said the Jashemi on her left.

"It is slowly killing you, to hold us both in your heart," put in the Jashemi on her right.

"I don't understand," Kevla said. She put a hand to her temple as dizziness began to descend.

"I am Jashemi, the khashimu, the secret friend of your youth and the man who loved you with every beat of his heart and every drop of blood in his veins," said the Jashemi on her left. His voice trembled and his brown eyes fairly glowed with desire. He wore only a damp pair of breeches, his hair wet and curly; he looked exactly as she remembered him when they had made love for the first and only time.

Her eyes roamed over him and she felt desire rise inside her, felt her physical body respond, as it had that moment that seemed so long ago to her now. Heat flowed through her. Every place on her body ached to be touched. Trembling, she took his hands and placed them on either side of her face. Jashemi's long fingers slid across her cheeks, her throat, to gently cup her breasts and caress the hardening peaks. She closed her eyes at the emotions that rushed through her at the contact, the loving *touch she had thought never to feel again. Moving closer, he lowered his lips to hers. His arms pulled her tight against his strong, lean warrior's body, and she tangled her fingers in his hair. She loved him so very much; had loved him almost since they had first met as children.*

"At its heart, we knew this love was true and good," he whispered in her ear, and she shivered as he flicked the lobe with his tongue. She inhaled deeply, savoring his familiar, beloved scent of spicy oils and warm skin. "Born of a need to be close, of turning to one another because we were all we had. I do not regret anything that happened."

Then the memory, the scalding, brutal, devastating memory returned. Kevla pulled back and stared at Jashemi, agony stabbing her. "I regret it!" she sobbed. "I killed you!"

"I died in your arms, yes." He ran a finger over her cheek, then her lips, and she tasted the saltiness of her tears. "And we violated a great taboo. But the memory—you will always have this." She trembled as his hands trailed lightly down over her suddenly naked back and buttocks. "Stay on this path, make this your only truth, and the memory of our coupling will never fade. It will always fill your heart with love and desire."

How could she not cherish the memory? Eyes closed, Kevla savored the touch of the only man she had ever loved. Even now, when she did not have the excuse of ignorance of their blood bond, she wanted him. To abandon that feeling would mean Jashemi had been nothing to her; that he had died to no purpose.

"That's not quite true," he replied, reading her thoughts.

Her eyes snapped open. She was again sitting on the earth, fully clothed, her passion quelled.

"I am Jashemi, your brother and Lorekeeper," said the Ja-

shemi on her right. He was dressed in the traditional men's rhia, a kerchief on his head. As Kevla looked upon him, she remembered the games of Shamizan, the stolen moments of laughter in the caverns, of holding him when he wept and the moment when he came to her in her room after the dreams had come and she had realized that she loved him; could not love him more if he were her own blood.

He grinned, and there was an ease and comfort between them that Kevla remembered from years past, before they became adults and the confusions of repressed memories of long-ago lives and physical desires had swept over them like a storm from the desert's heart.

She gazed deeply into the brown eyes that had always seen her, seen who and what she was, even when the rest of the world spat upon the Bai-sha girl. And in those eyes, she saw the other Lorekeepers Jashemi had once been: a boy in tattered clothes; a woman with golden hair; an old man with a grizzled beard, a woman with short brown hair and green eyes.

"Take my hand," he said. "Come walk with me, Flame Dancer."

Slowly, Kevla closed her hand around Jashemi's, feeling the strong, reassuring warmth. He helped her to her feet and with dizzying speed, the world around her changed.

Memories that were not real suddenly flooded her. Her first meeting with Yeshi, Tahmu's wife, Jashemi's mother, who welcomed her coolly as Tahmu's blood daughter, but whose affection gradually blossomed. Her growing friendship with Jashemi, arguing with him at the table, studying with him, riding sa'abahs together. Bonding in the way sisters and brothers did, with teasing, spats, and a deep, abiding devotion. The dreams of the Great Dragon and strange other lives that she and her brother felt comfortable sharing with their father.

Knowledge flooded her. "This is what our lives could have been like had all unfolded as it should," she whispered to the Jashemi who still held her hand.

He nodded. "Raised as true sister and brother. Our visions respected. Listened to." He squeezed her hand. "Our love stronger than ever, my sister, all the richer for the knowing that we shared a bond that extended over five lifetimes."

She turned to face him, puzzled as to why she felt no desire for him when a few moments before she had been shaking with passion. He caressed her face, and the touch was infinitely dear, but no more.

"This is how we felt toward one another," he said gently, pulling her into an embrace. She closed her eyes and breathed in his scent, clasped his strong, straight body to her, and felt completely and utterly safe.

Tears stung her eyes. He folded her closer. "No weeping, Kevla. There is no need for tears."

"You would be with me even now, had we walked this path," she said, her voice thick. "I killed you. I killed *this.*"

Suddenly, she was atop the Dragon. She was again in the battle against the Emperor's forces, except this time Jashemi was alive, was down there fighting with her. And when the arrow pierced his throat, she felt the agony of it in her own heart.

"No!" she screamed. No...

"Had we walked this path," Jashemi said gently, as if he had never left her side in this strange, confusing vision, "I would not have died in the cave, that much is true. We would never have been in that cave; would never have become lovers. But who can say if I would have lived? Many died in that battle, Kevla. I could very well have been among them, and this is one path." He smiled mischievously. "I could have taken a tumble from a sa'abah, *or choked on an olive pit, or met some other entirely ordinary end. Or I could have lived to old age surrounded by grandchildren. There's no way for us to know."*

Her legs buckled and he eased her to the ground.

"But this is the path that unfolded," she cried, "the path that led to your death. Whether I hold you in my heart as a lover or a brother, you are still lost to me!"

"But the Lorekeeper won't be," Jashemi said. "Do you remember what I said to you, when I first left for battle?"

The memory of this boy holding her hands, palms moist, gazing into her eyes and whispering fiercely, "We are not done with each other yet," returned to Kevla. They had been alone in the night, with no one to witness this urgent pledge but the stars. It had been a rare, poignant, precious moment in her life, one that she cherished. One in which she and Jashemi connected as children, not as adults.

"Of course I remember," she said.

"Then know this—those words are as true as when I first spoke them," he told her, holding her face between his hands. "We are not done with each other yet. But you must choose, Kevla. You must choose how you will hold me. Keep me in your heart as Jashemi, the man you love, whose touch you crave and for whose arms you hunger, and I will stay there. The memory of the bliss we shared will not fade. This, I swear to you. But you will have lost Jashemi the brother, the Lorekeeper, and you will keep your own sense of guilt as close to your heart as my memory."

He stepped back, and split into two images. "Choose," they said as one.

Kevla collapsed in a heap. How could she possibly choose between the lover she had adored with every fiber of her being and the man who was brother and Lorekeeper? How could they ask such a thing of her? Either way, she would lose something precious. If she chose to remember her lover, she would lose a life she ought to have lived, but never had. She would lose a source of wisdom, comfort, and strength.

But if she chose to remember her Lorekeeper, she would be turning her back on the single experience in her short life that had brought her the most joy and pain she had ever known.

"I can't," she cried, her voice raw. "Do not make me do this, if ever you loved me. Do not make me choose!"

"It is because we love you that we are asking this of you," said the Lorekeeper.

"We cannot bear to see you in such torment," her lover replied. "Choose, and there will be peace."

For a long time, Kevla huddled on the earth, wishing that she would awaken from this vision that she knew to be a vision, longing for a way to escape the impossible choice they had foisted upon her. But there was no merciful awakening to be had, only a pain that grew more and more unbearable.

Finally, Kevla stumbled to her feet, looking at each version of Jashemi-kha-Tahmu in turn. Tears poured unheeded down her face.

She made her choice.

Stepping forward, she placed her head on the bare chest of the man she had loved more than life itself. She listened to his heartbeat, strong and fast against her ear, then kissed him there, feeling the skin smooth and supple against her lips, tasting the saltiness of his sweat. He cupped her face in his hands, tilted back his head, and kissed her. Kevla opened fully to the joy rushing through her, and when Jashemi broke the kiss, she gazed into his eyes and said, "I love you with all my heart, Jashemi-kha-Tahmu. Please for-give me."

She stepped back. It was the hardest thing she had ever done in her life.

He forced a smile. "I did and do, beloved."

And then he was gone.

The pain was devastating. Dizziness washed over her and she would have fallen had not a pair of strong arms caught her. She looked up into the face of her brother—a perfect replica of the man she had loved, but so different-seeming to her now.

"He said I was his soul," Kevla said brokenly to this man who was both strange and profoundly familiar to her.

Her brother smiled through his own tears of sympathy. Pressing a comforting kiss on her forehead, he said, "He was almost right. I am your soul, Flame Dancer. And by embrac-ing this aspect of me, you will have me with you always."

She stared at him, uncomprehending, shaking, heartsick, overwhelmed by what she had just done. Gently he lowered her to the earth and pulled her close to him. She snuggled into his embrace, and then the wonder happened.

Kevla felt the guilt and shame detach themselves from her and float away, as if they were something physical. The arms that held her were strong and comforting, even though she knew none of this could be real. Her heart was suddenly full of love for Jashemi again, but this time, it was a love that she knew to be pure and sacred; a love that she could fully embrace. The terrible, ripping ache inside her was gone. Only warmth and acceptance lingered there now. She let out her breath in a long, quavering sigh, and surrendered to this sensation.

"Do you remember what I said to you, the first time we met in this world that is not the world?" he whispered in her ear.

"*You told me that I needed to let go of the form you took when you were flesh,*" Kevla said. "*I understand that now. I didn't— I couldn't—then.*"

"*Our love is beyond the physical, Flame Dancer,*" Jashemi whispered, as he had done before. "*Death cannot stop it. It hasn't before and it won't now. I ever existed to love and serve you. And even though I am no longer flesh...I still do.*"

The Flame Dancer held her Lorekeeper, her soul, and wept with joy.

27

"Kevla?"

The voice was familiar, but Kevla somehow didn't want to hear it. She frowned and snuggled back down against the warm, soft blanket that cradled her body.

"Kevla, wake up. We need to get going soon."

She blinked sleepily and looked up. Standing against the sky and sun was the shape of a man. His position prevented her from seeing his features, but she saw that he was tall, with broad shoulders. The sun caught his hair and made it glow in a circlet of gold about his shadowed face.

"Come, now, you'll sleep the day away. Perhaps I should have gone on without you."

Kevla became fully awake. The mysterious man wreathed

in shadow ceased to be a mystery; it was only Jareth, come to waken her so that they could climb a mountain and he could confront his god. She sighed, missing the comfort of her Lorekeeper, who would now come only to her in dreams and visions.

Jareth extended a hand to help her up. She was a little unsteady; she had slept quite deeply and one foot was slightly numb from lack of blood. Quickly, Jareth caught her, slipping a hand around her waist.

"Thank you," she said, gently disengaging herself.

He smothered a smile as his eyes took in her face. "Looks like you had a very restful night." He tapped his right cheek, and for a moment Kevla didn't understand what he meant. Then her hand went to her face and she found the deep creases there. She had slept so soundly, a blanket fold had left its mark on her face. She laughed, surprised and amused and embarrassed all at once. Jareth let his own face ease into a smile.

Kevla didn't miss it. He looked well rested also, as if some of the burden that had been laid upon him had lifted, ever so slightly.

"How about you?" asked Kevla. "The Dragon told me to pay attention to my dreams. Did you dream anything interesting?"

She couldn't decipher his look. "Let's get going."

He strode off, his body tall and straight and defiant, daring the world to take a swing at him. Kevla sighed and followed him back to the encampment.

The *taaskali,* the Dragon, Mylikki and Altan were all sitting around a crackling fire. A pleasant aroma rose from the cauldron. She watched with amusement as

Altan ran a finger around the bowl, making sure he got every last bite.

The cauldron contained cooked, sweetened milk, and there was something else in it as well. Kevla took a taste and could not suppress a soft sound of delight. Rich with spices that teased the nostrils, it slipped down the throat easily. Best of all, there appeared to be plenty of it.

"It's some sort of concoction of eggs and milk and dried fruit," Mylikki said.

"It's certainly better than grains," said Altan.

Kevla ate every bite, and handed out her bowl for more when Jareth went to get seconds.

I haven't seen you eat like that since I held you in the heart of the mountain, came the Dragon's affectionate thoughts.

Kevla smiled as she spooned up another mouthful of the creamy concoction. *I remember. You wanted to know if I wanted an entire sandcow for dinner.*

Eat your fill of anything the taaskali *give you. It is wholesome and nourishing.*

Magical? She turned to look at him.

He hesitated. *Say rather...blessed.* Kevla nodded her understanding. *Kevla...*

Yes?

I know what you dreamed last night. I am proud of you.

Even though the food still tasted wonderful, Kevla suddenly found it hard to swallow. *It was the most difficult decision I have ever had to make. I know I made the right choice. I can sense him in my being now, somehow. And that is a sweet thing. But to lose one aspect of him in order to keep another... Oh, Dragon, I don't even remember what his touch felt like. And I will never know that kind of touch from anyone ever again.*

A very definitive statement from one so young, thought the Dragon.

She looked at him, angry and hurt. *You know what happened when we—I can't be with anyone like that, ever. My pleasure is lethal to others. I am condemned to a life without that, and now even my memory of what that felt like has been changed so that it seems like it happened to someone else.*

The world is wide and you are young, dear heart.

Has...has the Flame Dancer ever before taken a lover without...

She sensed his sorrow as he sent, *You were the first incarnation of the Flame Dancer who was intimate with another.*

Kevla resisted the urge to surrender to self-pity. She had a task ahead of her. What did it matter if she never felt the tender touch of a lover again? At least she had reached peace with Jashemi, whom she would hold forever as a brother, Lorekeeper, and friend. In the end, she knew she had gained more than she had lost.

"Are you all right?" It was Jareth, looking at her with concern in his blue eyes. She nodded quickly and finished eating her meal.

The *selva* seemed to ignore them today, ambling about like ordinary creatures and digging in the snow with their large hooves.

"What are they finding to eat?" Kevla asked Hanru as she watched them. He was busy assembling sacks for them to take on their journey.

"A type of plant grows on the stones," Hanru told her. "The *selva* feed on this during the winter, even this strange winter. They are very determined to locate it on their own. If you were to scrape some into your hand and offer it to them, they would not eat it." He looked up from his now-completed task. "Is everyone finished?"

Jareth looked down at his fourth bowl of food. "Almost," he said, devouring what was left. When he was done, he, Mylikki, Altan and Kevla went over to Hanru's side.

He looked at them keenly. "You have the least experience with snow and ice," he said to Kevla. She nodded. "This will not be an easy undertaking. I again say to you, Jareth will confront the tiger alone. If any of you wish to stay behind, we will make you welcome."

No one moved. Altan folded his arms across his chest, and Mylikki looked down at her feet. Hanru sighed.

"Very well. Let me give you a few lessons in how to use these tools. They could save your life."

Kevla paid close attention as Hanru described how to strap small metal hooks to their boots, to get a better grip on the ice. She hefted the small pick, and practiced with it to get a feel for how to use it. Thus far, the day was clear, but if bad weather were to strike, they would tie themselves together with rope and huddle close. The more she learned, the more apprehensive she grew. At one point, she stole a glance at Jareth. He had already climbed this path once before, alone, with no tools such as these. She wasn't sure if she should admire him or think him a fool. *Probably a bit of both.*

At last they were ready to depart. Hanru assured them it would not be far, at least not as the *selva* traveled. Even as he spoke, two *selva,* pulling a strange cart behind them, approached.

"It has *skeltha* on it!" Kevla said, then wondered why she should be so surprised. It made perfect sense. With two animals to pull the cart, it should speed along the snow.

The five of them got in. Kevla looked back at the Dragon, who sat up on his haunches and inclined his head in farewell.

The sun made its feeble ascent into the sky, hugging the horizon. The *skeltha*-cart moved with amazing speed, almost flying over the snow, and the world moved past swiftly. Part of Jareth wanted to be amazed at the *selva,* at the *taaskali,* at the dream which had come to him last night like a healing draft. But already the dream's soft tendrils had disengaged themselves from his thoughts. He was close to the goal now, and he would focus on this and this alone.

He had made this trek before, alone, struggling through storms that seemed calculated to thwart his progress. But now the sun was shining, such as it was, and by the time it set, he would have confronted the god.

He wondered why only one had consented to see him, but reasoned that one was sufficient. Unobtrusively, he slid his hand beneath his cloak to touch the large, freshly sharpened knife secure in its hilt. If the god refused him, he would attack. Jareth knew that if it came to this, it would be a foolish gesture; he would die in the attempt.

But at least he would have made that attempt. He had clung fast to the hope the remembrances of his family, whispered to him at night by flower and soil and stone, had kept alive. Something was very wrong with this world, something so out of harmony with the natural order of things that his land would soon die if things were not put right. And if he could not restore the natural cycles to the land—could not undo what the strange storm had done and bring back the people he loved most in the world—what point *was* there in living? Without that...

He shuddered involuntarily. Altan was seated next to him and looked at his friend with concern. "Cold?" he asked.

Jareth shook his head, but made no further reply. Altan sighed and sank back further into the seat, his face troubled. In front of him sat Kevla and Mylikki. Jareth had not gotten to know the female *kyndela* player well at all; he had no interest in getting to know anyone. But even he noticed how she huddled in the seat, silent and miserable. And he'd noticed too that the *selva* had not chosen her last night to offer their warmth and, apparently, dreams. He'd known Altan all the boy's life, and was used to the strange, sudden mood shifts that came upon him. Apparently, Mylikki wasn't, and was hurting from them.

Kevla often wore her hair long and loose, but today, she had braided it and it fell in a long rope down the back of the seat. It looked soft and silky, and gleamed with red highlights. For some reason, the shiny black-red length fascinated Jareth and he wanted to touch it. He reached forward, grasped the thick braid, and tossed it back over Kevla's shoulder. He didn't want the distraction. She glanced back and smiled, and suddenly heat surged through him. *By the gods, she is beautiful.* He nodded briefly, then turned his attention again to the mountains and away from the unexpected brush of physical desire.

Sooner than even Jareth had dared hope, they arrived at the foot of the mountains. He looked up at the chain as it stretched as far he could see, and realized that there was a trail that he had not noticed before. It made sense. The *taaskali* were closer to the gods than mere humans. They would know the hidden paths to reach the divine beings that played among the stars.

Jareth helped Hanru unload the equipment. The *taaskal* unfastened the two gleaming *selva,* stroked their necks affectionately, and whispered in their ears. Snorting, they trotted away and began to forage for the moss.

"They will not stray, and will come when I ask them to," Hanru assured them. "Now. Let us be about this." He turned around and pointed upward. "*That* is where we need to be."

Everyone craned their necks to see a tall peak, far in the distance, jagged and white against the sky. It seemed to be a thousand leagues distant, and Jareth felt a pang of panic.

"If we move at a good pace," Hanru continued, "we should be able to reach the peak and descend before nightfall. I am certain none of you wishes to be climbing in the dark."

"Couldn't we make camp if we don't get back in time?" It was Kevla, looking with concern at Mylikki. "I can create sufficient heat to keep us warm through the night."

"Perhaps. But even the brightest blaze cannot protect us from wind and snow and lack of food."

"We'll get there and back in time," Altan said firmly. Mylikki looked nervous. Jareth gazed at the peak a moment longer, envisioning a blue Tiger standing atop it.

Hanru handed them their equipment, showed them how to strap the packs to their backs, and demonstrated how to maneuver themselves in the boots, kicking them firmly into the snow and ice for better purchase. Jareth gave the lesson his full attention. He did not want to be slowed or stopped for a lack of education in how to maneuver up the icy path. He had to curb his impatience with the others, especially Kevla, to whom all this was completely alien, as they practiced and Hanru pronounced them ready to ascend. He wished again that he had gone only with Hanru.

But Kevla was somehow part of this; more and more, he was convinced she was the woman in his dreams, who had changed into a tiger. Altan was stubborn enough to make good his promise of following by himself, and Mylikki went where Altan went. It was unfortunate, but he could see no way around it.

"I will lead," Hanru announced. "Mylikki, you follow me, then Altan and Kevla. Jareth, you bring up the rear. Is everyone ready?"

Jareth knew why Hanru wanted him last—so that he could not move ahead faster than the group. He looked up at the top of the peak. Even as he regarded it, he saw the wind catch and lazily swirl snow.

You had better be waiting for me, he thought.

Gelsan sat silently by the fire. These days she ate little, said less, and when another had quietly assumed the duties of headwoman, she had been glad.

Her husband had been lost to the winter months ago. Then Mylikki had departed atop a dragon's back, in the company of a Fire Woman. Gelsan didn't know if she'd ever return. Olar had been all she had left, and now he, too, was gone. Gelsan was not overfond of this life anymore, and if she moved closer to escaping it by the day, well, that was not altogether a bad thing.

A cry went up, and despite her sunken misery, something in Gelsan roused. Her hair, more silver than gold now, came up and she listened.

More screams. Now she could smell smoke. Slowly, her body remembering how it used to leap into action when needed, she put on a cloak and reached for a scythe.

She opened the door to chaos.

Gelsan saw and heard as well as smelled the fire now, crackling as it consumed a house across the clearing, orange red flame leaping into the sky. Not twenty feet away, a cluster of women were fighting for their lives against adversaries much larger than they. She heard the howls of madmen and something inside her sparked to life.

You will not take them.

Gelsan let out her own loud cry and charged into the melee. She swung the scythe, feeling it move like an old friend, cutting deep into the bodies of men who didn't even look like people to her anymore. They were the men of the woods, lost during hunts, screaming insanely "For the Maiden! For the Maiden!", driven mad by the winter as she was about to be driven mad, as all of them would eventually be—

She whirled, swinging the scythe, and nearly wrenched her arms out of their sockets as she tried to deflect the blow.

Standing in front of her was Olar. He was covered with blood, his hair thick and stringy and matted with filth. He bared his teeth at her like a fox, and she lifted the scythe with aching arms to parry her son's attack. Grunting, he strained against her, the scythe's shaft grating against a wooden staff, and leaned in so she could smell his stale breath and the reek of old and new blood.

"The Maiden will have it so," he snarled. Tears blurred her vision and suddenly Gelsan stopped fighting. She would rather die by her son's hand than keep living, knowing that this was what had happened to him.

The sudden lack of resistance made him stumble as she went down. He lifted the staff over his head, about to bring it crashing down on his mother's skull.

Do it, she pleaded.

But he stood as if suddenly frozen, cocking his head like a dog trying to listen to a distant sound.

"I hear and obey, my lady," Olar said, his voice trembling with love. Gelsan heard the words repeated all around her, a rippling sound of tenderness incongruous amid the slaughter. Abruptly, every man turned and ran into the woods. It was over—for the moment.

For a long time Gelsan lay in the snow, trying to comprehend what had just happened. She got to her feet clumsily and went to aid the wounded. She went through the motions of cleaning and stitching wounds efficiently, but her mind was not on the task. Hammering in her head were the words her son had spoken: *For the Maiden! I hear and obey, my lady.*

Dear gods, Gelsan half thought, half prayed, *is it true? Is the Ice Maiden real?*

28

It was a gradual ascent at first. The iron spikes on their boots made the going safer but slower, as they had to stamp firmly with each step so that the spikes dug in well. From time to time they used their ice axes. True to his word, Hanru set a good pace. Because Mylikki was immediately behind him, the *taaskali* guide was able to assist her directly.

The sun kept traveling along the horizon. They took brief, frequent breaks for quick bites of food and handfuls of snow. The only one among them who was not panting and sweating was Hanru, who would stand and gaze from peak to sun, no doubt estimating how much time they had.

The two musicians had the hardest time. Mylikki had been in trouble practically since the outset, and Altan was clearly tiring as well. Slender as she was, Kevla had endurance, and although Jareth's body had been punished for months, he had a sinewy strength and a stubborn purpose that kept him going. The *selva*-fur cloak was becoming hot and Jareth's clothes were damp with sweat. He knew he would be exhausted and wrung out by the end of the day. If, he mused grimly, he was still alive.

After a few hours, the route's difficulty increased dramatically. They edged past a cliff wall to discover what seemed like a vertical white surface.

"We're climbing up that?" Mylikki bit her lip, but the words were said. Even Jareth had his doubts.

"It's easier than it looks," said Hanru, "but you must be careful and give it your full concentration. We'll tie ourselves together. I'll go up first and set footholds."

They tied the rope around them, leaving some room for slack, and Hanru began to climb. He moved like a squirrel, Jareth thought. Quickly, with the experience of who-knew-how-many years—the *taaskali* seemed ageless to him—he pounded in metal stakes and scrambled up them until he reached the top. As he watched, Jareth saw that it probably would be easier than it looked; it was not quite as vertical as it first appeared, and the snow seemed hard-packed.

Mylikki was next. She looked terrified, but swallowed hard and began to climb. One small hand here, one small foot there. Jareth relaxed as she neared the top and Hanru pulled her the rest of the way. Next was Altan, and then Kevla. Instinctively, Jareth held out his hands, ready to catch her should she slip. In a distant part of his brain, he appreciated the workings of her legs and buttocks, clearly visible beneath the red garment she wore, as she climbed. Kevla-sha-Tahmu might have been the worst thorn in Jareth's side, but she was also an exquisitely beautiful woman.

Once she had made it to the top, Jareth followed, forcing himself to ignore the slight trembling in his arms, shoulders, thighs, and calves that signaled weariness. He hit the snow hard and lay where he fell, breathing heavily. Everyone else except for Hanru was doing the same.

Hanru waited a few moments, untying them and coiling the rope, but the look on his face told Jareth there was no time to waste. Fortunately, the next segment looked comparatively easy—a slope of hard-packed white snow at an incline that was challenging but not as steep as the previous one.

It was broad enough so that they were able to climb simultaneously. Jareth and the others used the ice ax and the iron spikes on their boots to good advantage. Hanru reached the top first, and turned to watch as the others made their way up. He hauled Jareth the last few steps as if the much larger man weighed nothing at all. Jareth sat, catching his breath, and watched the others. Unencumbered by a heavy cloak Kevla made good time. Altan was about halfway up, and Mylikki—

Even as he watched, her feet slipped out from underneath her and with a startled little cry she began to slide quickly toward the edge of the cliff they had just clambered over.

"Use the ax!" Altan shouted.

Mylikki was clearly trying to do exactly that, but the ax was not light and Jareth knew she probably had very little strength left in her arms. She struggled to swing the ax, to secure a hold and stop herself from hurtling to her death.

With relief, Jareth watched as the ax found purchase and Mylikki slowed, stopped.

Hanru was already halfway there, but it was Altan who was closest. The *huskaa* was backing quickly down. With a grunt, he swung his own ax and embedded it solidly into the ice below the hard-packed snow.

"I can't—" Mylikki's voice was shrill. Jareth watched, wanting to move to her, knowing that Hanru and Altan were closer and he would merely add to the danger. His eyes were fixed on Mylikki's little hand, and he saw the fingers slide slowly, slowly down the handle.

She screamed as her fingers, numb from hours in the cold, lost their grip. A strap around her wrist halted her fall for an instant, but also dislodged the ax from its purchase. She slipped toward the edge.

Altan's hand shot out and closed on her wrist. Mylikki jerked to a halt. Both were now being supported solely by the weight of Altan's ice ax. Mylikki's legs dangled off the cliff into the air. Below her was a lethal drop.

Let the ax hold, Jareth thought, his heart slamming against his chest.

Then Hanru was there. He grasped Mylikki by the other arm and began hauling her upward. Now finally able to do something to help, Jareth reached to assist him. Altan now clung to the ax with both hands. Once Mylikki had been brought to safety, Jareth went back for his friend. Altan gave him a grateful smile as Jareth's arm went around his waist and he assisted the younger man in climbing. When Altan flopped down beside Mylikki, she threw her arms around him.

"You saved my life," she sobbed.

Obviously close to crying himself, Altan hugged her fiercely and buried his face in her shoulder. "You're safe now," he murmured, his voice muffled. "Thank the gods. You're safe."

"This has gone far enough," said Kevla. There was a hardness to her voice that Jareth had never heard before. When he looked at her, surprised by the tone, he saw her lovely face drawn in anger. "Altan, I know you love Jareth, and you want to be there for him. And you have. Mylikki, you are beyond exhaustion. If you keep pushing yourself you will end up dead."

She looked up at Jareth. "Go on," she said quietly. "We're slowing you down. I can keep them warm while we wait for you. Hanru will take care of us."

"Are you sure?" It was exactly what he had wanted from the first, of course; not to have to worry about the safety of the others. But to hear it from Kevla's lips—

"Yes. This is your experience and yours alone. None of us needs to be there while...we will be there afterward, I promise."

"Hanru?"

The *taaskali* guide nodded. "They are not called as you are. And the day is passing. It will be dark sooner than I would like. The path is easy enough to follow and you know what you are doing. She wants to see you. She will not let anything happen to you until she has done so. Go."

Jareth looked back at Altan, who nodded resignedly. Mylikki still clutched him and shook with sobs. For the first time since Altan had found Jareth, he looked more interested in being with Mylikki rather than with his old friend. Finally, Jareth looked again at Kevla.

"Thank you," he said, but he wasn't sure why. She nodded. He turned and again set out on the path, moving forward, alone, to meet his god.

Jareth settled into a rhythm. He was aware of what he was doing, where he put his hands and feet and ice ax, but this was not his primary focus. He kept imagining himself in front of the great beast, standing straight and tall, commanding respect from his god.

She must listen to me. She can bring them back. She can bring spring back to the land. Everything will die if she doesn't give me my powers back. I must convince her.

Jareth lost track of how long he had been climbing. He felt his muscles quivering with the strain as the time passed, felt his body growing more and more weary, but he denied it rest. He was so close to his goal. He couldn't stop now for mere physical needs.

The weather remained clear, but the wind was not his friend at this altitude. It seemed to grow in strength with each step, whipping the protective hood from his head, catching the cloak and making it billow, and swirling snow so that he soon lost sensation in his face and ears. He felt ice coating his beard and eyebrows and eyelashes. He blinked rapidly to clear his vision, and that was when he saw it.

An opening in the cliff face, barely visible from this distance. A dark blue smudge against the myriad shades of blue and green and white of the ice. Hope surged through Jareth, lending him fresh strength. He pressed onward, and before he fully realized what was happening, he had pulled himself up onto a ledge and stood at the entrance to the lair of the gods.

He swayed in the wind, trying to collect his thoughts. This

was the moment he had struggled toward for the better part of a year. Now he stood on the threshold as if rooted to the spot, and Jareth realized that he was terrified.

There could be no turning back now. There could be no more rage or self-pity beyond this point. He would either accomplish what he had set out to do or he would die. The certainty of either outcome was almost overwhelming, and he stumbled.

This is the moment, Jareth, he told himself. *This moment is your destiny. Go forward and embrace it.*

With the wind whipping his long, golden hair and tugging on his cloak, shaking in his very boots, his heart bursting with emotions he couldn't even name, Jareth Vasalen, Spring-Bringer, Kevat-aanta, Stone Dancer, slowly stumbled toward his fate.

Part III:

Stone Dancer

Part III

29

The cave of the god was formed entirely of ice. Only the stone beneath Jareth's feet was of earth, and even that was slick with a clear, shiny coat of frozen water. Above and to each side, thick, green-blue ice enclosed the area. The ceiling arched high over his head, and the cave stretched on for some distance. It was surprisingly bright inside, but there was no source of illumination. Jareth wasn't sure what to expect, but it was certainly not entering the cave and finding himself alone.

"I am Jareth Vasalen," he cried, his voice strong and clear. It echoed in the icy chamber. "I have come to speak with you."

When the sound of his voice died away, Jareth was met

with a profound silence. He could hear his own breathing, raspy in his ears; the pounding of his heart was almost deafening. Slowly, carefully, he stepped forward, moving deeper and deeper into the ice cave.

The shadow came and went so quickly he wasn't certain he had seen it. His fair head whipped around, but even as he moved, he saw another shadow, a reflection perhaps, out of the corner of his eye. Again, when he turned, it had disappeared. Blue, black, white, gray, green—colors appeared and vanished like flickering flames.

Suddenly Jareth was furious. He had come all this way, endured so much, and now the god was toying with him?

"Show yourself!" he demanded.

He heard the low, rumbling growl before he saw the creature. The sound made his skin prickle. The shadows stilled, solidified, and all at once, Jareth saw it at the far end. It lay on a block of ice that looked like a crystal pedestal. It was bigger than Jareth had imagined, the size of a small horse, its head easily as broad as Jareth's shoulders. Its sinuous curves were indeed that of a large cat, but no purring rat-catcher Jareth had ever petted had fixed him with such a piercing gaze. Its coat was as blue as the heart of the ice, chased by black stripes on its body and limbs and creamy white on the underbelly. The unnerving eyes were large and golden, and the mighty tiger lay as still as if she had been carved out of stone save for the lashing blue-and-black striped tail.

Jareth's mouth was suddenly dry. In order to reach this moment, he had focused on his outrage and loss, his sense of injustice, the pain of the dying land, the starving people and emaciated animals. But now as he stood before his god, all of that scattered like wheat chaff in a gust of wind.

The tiger made no sound. One blue ear flicked.

He had planned to make his petition from a place of strength, of logic, of selfless need for the land. Instead the words that escaped his lips were, "Give me my family back."

Slowly, the huge cat got to its feet. Its golden eyes narrowed.

"Do you know why you are here?" it asked. The voice was a soft, feminine, dangerous rumble.

Jareth blinked. His old friend anger came back in a hot rush. "I'm here to demand that you stop this land from dying!" he cried.

The tiger leaped from its perch so quickly that it was a blue blur. Pain blossomed across Jareth's chest and he fell back hard onto the cold, ice-slicked rock.

He looked down at himself in shock. Four lines oozed red blood.

"Wh—why did you—"

"Do you know why you are here?"

Jareth didn't answer immediately. He touched the wounds and hissed in pain. "Because you can give it all back to me," he said through gritted teeth. "Give *them* back…"

Again the massive creature sprang. Jareth raised his arms, trying to block the attack, and the tiger's claws raked his forearms. Blood dripped onto his face and oozed onto the stone.

"DO YOU KNOW WHY YOU ARE HERE?"

Still angry, still defiant, Jareth struggled to his feet. The hot blood on the ice was slippery. He snarled, "I am the Spring-Bringer!"

This time the tiger snarled its displeasure before the blue paw shot out and laid open Jareth's cheek. The strike narrowly missed his eye. He fell hard, and fear skittered through him. He refused to yield to it. It was not in him to beg or plead. If this being wanted his life, it could have it.

"I am here to help my people," Jareth rasped, trying to get to his feet and only managing to kneel. Blood dripped into his eye and stung. He waited for another attack, but it didn't come. He looked up and beheld the tiger standing directly in front of him. Blue eyes locked with gold.

"Do you know why you are here?"

It was the same query, but something was different. Jareth knew it. Something he had said before had been part of what the beast wanted to hear, otherwise, he knew, it would have attacked him again. His breath came in ragged gasps. He wanted to tear his gaze away from the tiger, to stand like a man in front of it, but he was too weak to move.

"I am here to...to help my people by persuading you to release your grip on the land. To give me back my powers."

Faster than Jareth's brain could register, the creature struck a fourth time. Jareth's belly was ripped open and he collapsed. The cold of the icy stone against the wounds was almost too much to bear and for a moment he thought he might lose consciousness. He couldn't rise, couldn't even sit, and he lay on his lacerated belly sucking in air as he watched the padded blue feet pace back and forth in front of him.

"Do you know why you are here?"

And then he did know.

Jareth closed his eyes against the onslaught of comprehension, willing it away, but it had the bitter taste of truth.

When he was thirteen years old, he had felt drawn to the land. He had summoned spring simply by asking for it to come. He was the Spring-Bringer, the Kevat-aanta, whose touch on the land ensured the rhythmic cycles of the seasons. And he had let himself become the Kevat-aanta. He had enjoyed the honors his position brought him and his family, even though he never exploited his gifts and lived with the secret fear that one day, everything would fall apart. This was who he was, and it was why, when his powers had suddenly failed him, he had been so devastated. Part of it, the greatest part, was indeed that he did not desire his people to suffer.

But part of it had also been arrogance and, to an even greater extent, that constant fear. What was he supposed to do if not be the Spring-Bringer?

Who was he?

He had come thinking to reclaim this title he had held for all his adult life. He had come thinking to cow and bully his gods into bringing the dead back to life—both his family and the dead land. And he had come thinking that somehow, in this pilgrimage, he would atone for not being able to do these things himself, for not being able to feed his people, not being able to save his family—

But that was not why he was here. He was here, standing before the blue Tiger, existing in this world, to be not the Spring-Bringer, but the Stone Dancer. He was, as Kevla had tried to tell him, the element of Earth made into human flesh. She had been part of his dreams since his youth, the dark-skinned woman who changed into a god, and now he understood. She wasn't taking him to the gods—she was leading him to his Companion.

And suddenly, as if making this connection had opened a door, memories flooded him.

The Tiger, the secret friend, found as a cub by a little boy who bonded with her and placed her on his standard. The Legion of the blue Tiger fought well for their king and country, even stood...and fell...against the Shadow when it came for them....

A scholarly girl, terrified of the mighty beast until her father, her Lorekeeper, explained the powerful connection of these three separate beings....

The only time he had preferred to feel a horse between his thighs rather than the warm, supple strength of the Tiger, when he had been part of a tribe that worshipped the animals....

A slender woman of eighteen, with dark skin and hair, gazing out at an ocean that was suddenly, unnaturally still, feeling the trusted hands of her Lorekeeper on her face before they tightened....

Before him stood not a god, but his Companion, also an aspect of Earth. Jareth was much more than an instigator for the changing of the seasons; more than a friend to the trees and grasses and animals and stones. Jareth's allegiance was to things greater than Lamal, for *he* was greater than Lamal.

And if the Tiger is my Companion, and not a god...she can't give Taya and Annu and Parvan back to me.

Jareth closed his eyes as blood seeped from his warm body onto the cold ice, this knowledge more painful than the blows he had endured from the Tiger. He understood now that he was here to set aside his personal wants and needs, however deep and raw they might be. He was to help his people by leaving them, possibly forever; to save them by saving the world they lived in. By accepting that his destiny lay not with the mountains and fields and deep, green forests of the place where he was born, but in places so alien to him that he knew it would make him weep.

By walking with Kevla and the Great Dragon, and searching for the rest of the Dancers.

He did not want this. But it was why he was here.

Taya, my love, you are gone, and I can't even stay in the land where you lie....

His voice cracked when he spoke.

"I am here to be the Stone Dancer—to save my people by saving *all* the people," he whispered. He squeezed his eyes shut, expecting another blow. But what happened next startled him more than anything he could have imagined.

With the gentleness of a mother with her cub, the Tiger stretched out a paw and pulled Jareth to her breast. A deep rumble sounded and Jareth felt the rasp of a warm tongue across his face, his chest, his belly. Fur softer even than that of the *selva* brushed his skin. The Tiger bathed him, and beneath the caress of that slightly rough but loving tongue Jareth felt his wounds close and heal, felt strength slowly seep into a body that had been abused and punished for almost too long.

How long the moment lasted, Jareth could not tell. He surrendered to the tender ministrations of the Tiger, and simply accepted. At last, he sighed deeply and opened his eyes, and when he gazed up at the Tiger, it was with true recognition.

"You," he whispered. "It's you!"

Healed by the powers of this being that he suddenly remembered was a part of him, Jareth reached up and threw his arms around the creature's powerful neck and buried his face in the warm fur. He felt one paw—the paw that had moments before been slicing his flesh with apparent mercilessness—go around him to pull him even closer.

Jareth closed his eyes. His fingers gripped the striped blue fur tightly, as if he clung to a lifeline. In a very real sense, he did.

"Where were you? The last time, where were you?"

"You had not found me before the Shadow came," was the loving reply. "You had found your Lorekeeper, but not me. I was a continent away."

Yes, he had found his Lorekeeper...and his Lorekeeper had murdered him.

Jareth shuddered at the memory, then let it go. He heaved a deep sigh, feeling the last strains of fear and resentment escape with the cleansing breath, and sat up. He did not pull away from this being that he now knew was a part of him, but leaned, still weary, against his newly discovered old friend and drew strength from the furry warmth.

"Where is the last of our three?" he asked. "Kevla spoke of the Lorekeepers, but I have not met anyone like them. I have certainly not met mine."

"And I have not been able to sense him or her," said the Tiger. She rolled over onto her back, lazily pulling Jareth, no small man, with her. "It is unlikely that your Lorekeeper would be in another land, but such a thing is not impossible. We might have difficulty finding this part of ourselves, considering what happened last time. To murder one's Dancer, even out of a misplaced sense of love—such a thing cannot help but do harm."

The Tiger knew what had happened, even though she had not been there. Such was the power of their bond. Jareth sat back, taking a hold of one of the forepaws and examining it absently. It was large and soft, the claws retracted so that the Tiger could hold Jareth gently. Jareth squeezed the paw, and the Tiger obligingly extended her claws. They were as long as his fingers; the paw itself, bigger than his head. The Tiger made a deep sound of amused affection, sheathed her claws, and patted Jareth's face. Jareth felt only comfort and trust. Never again would those claws be turned against him.

"So we find my Lorekeeper, and Kevla and I must travel to far distant realms to gather the other three Dancers." *And my family stays here, their bodies hard and cold....* Jareth refused to follow that train of thought. He could not bear to let them go, not yet.

"Tiger...you have not told me...why did you remove my powers? How is it that I could even lose them, if I am truly the element of Earth?"

"Your powers were never gone," the Tiger said quietly. "Were you not able to speak to the birds and animals?"

"Yes," Jareth said. "But I couldn't call spring. I couldn't sense the stones, or the trees, or the soil anymore. I couldn't influence them, make things grow." The pain of that stabbed him anew and he swallowed.

"Your powers were not taken," the Tiger said. "They were blocked."

"How? Who could have done this?"

"The snow that has fallen since the first day you tried to call Spring is nothing natural," the Tiger said. "It has awareness. Consciousness. And it has a mistress."

"Who?"

Looking deeply into Jareth's eyes, the Tiger replied, "The Ice Maiden."

Jareth laughed. "Now you're teasing me."

The Tiger shook her head. "I would not toy with you about such a thing."

Sobering, Jareth said, "But she's just a story, a character in a collection of songs."

"That might have been true once, but no longer. She is very real, and very powerful. She controls the snow and she is able to block your powers when it is present."

"And it's ever-present," Jareth finished, thinking. "This makes sense. I could only call the beasts when the sky was clear—when there was no snow falling between me and them."

She controls the snow. The snow that had somehow come in so quickly and so deeply that it had killed his family. He had known all along that they had not died natural deaths, and what the Tiger had just said proved it. He might not be able to bring them back, but at least he could avenge them.

Another thought came to him. "The men who got lost when they left to go hunting. The men who sometimes returned insane...they saw her, didn't they?"

The Tiger nodded her massive head. "They did."

It was so much to take in all at once. Jareth rubbed his temples, thinking. "We have to stop her. We have to find her and stop her." He was suddenly cold and he shivered, rubbing his arms as the chill shuddered through him. "'He has seen the Ice Maiden, and she's perilous fair....' The lyrics...can we trust what the song tells us about her?"

"I do not know, but it stands to reason," the Tiger said. "At least it is a starting point."

For the first time, Jareth was glad that Altan had decided to accompany him. They would need the input of a *huskaa* if they were to learn how to defeat a creature born of legend.

Suddenly he laughed. "Altan has always maintained that she was just an abandoned girl with a broken heart, that the term Ice Maiden was never literal. He'll be quite annoyed to hear this."

He got to his feet. Inside, he was warm. He felt strong and capable, no longer beaten and despairing. He had discovered his true purpose, had remembered who he had been, and had found, again, his dearest friend.

"Let's find them. Let's find them and tell them everything."

30

Altan had been terrified when it appeared as though Mylikki had been about to plunge to her death over the cliff
face. He had moved faster than he had thought himself capable, heedless of the danger, to come to her aid. When they
were finally pulled to safety and he felt her body pressed
against his, shaking with sobs, the relief that she was safe,
was *safe,* was overwhelming.

He had lingered in Arrun Woods for over a week, claiming the poor weather as an excuse. But the real reason he
had stayed, despite his desire to find Jareth, was to spend
time with Mylikki, to instruct her on the intricacies of the
kyndela and watch with glee as her sharp mind picked them
up at once. If she had been a man, he'd have claimed her as

his *huskaa-lal* after hearing her perform a single song. But she was female, and the Law did not permit such a thing.

When they sat and performed together, he would look at her, and feel a stirring in his heart and loins. Her golden head bent over the instrument, catching the gleam of the firelight; her smile that broadened whenever she looked at him; the soft swell beneath many layers of clothing of breasts that he now knew were even softer and fuller than he had imagined.

When Mylikki had taken that tumble today, for a moment, he thought her gone forever. He was surprised at how much he cared. So when she clung to him, he held her tightly, and made no move to disengage himself.

I love her, he realized, and said a short, heartfelt prayer to the gods that they would guard his tongue and keep the darkness that sometimes consumed him at bay, so that he would never, ever say anything hurtful to her again.

There were no branches to use as fuel for a fire, so Kevla merely heated some stones. The effect was the same—welcome warmth pouring out to the shivering travelers. She herself sat back, having no need of the heat, and took pleasure in seeing the taut, exhausted faces of Altan and Mylikki relax as the warmth began to penetrate.

Since Mylikki's accident, she had literally not let go of Altan, and the young *huskaa* seemed more than happy to hold her. Kevla hoped that Altan's days of alternately casting affectionate glances at the girl and making cutting remarks were over.

Hanru had shared cheese made from *selva* milk. Mindful of the Dragon's words, Kevla ate everything she was offered.

Sharp and yet mellow on the tongue, the cheese quieted hunger and provided energy. Kevla was grateful that they had happened upon the *taaskali* and their herds. Not for the first time, she wondered at these people who had appeared so conveniently and had to be more than what they seemed. And she wondered just how safe she, Altan, and Mylikki really were with them, but decided that if the Dragon trusted them, that was enough for her.

At one point, Hanru looked at the sky and shook his head. "Night will be coming soon," he said.

"We're not leaving without Jareth," Altan said.

"Do not worry about Jareth," Kevla said. "He is safer than we are, I assure you."

Mylikki, one bare pink hand still clutching Altan's, was munching a bite of cheese. Swallowing, she said, "You know something we don't, Kevla. What is it?"

Kevla was surprised. She had not expected Mylikki, focused on Altan and exhausted as she was, to be quite so astute. "I will tell you when he returns," she said. "But yes, I do know something. And what I know tells me that Jareth could not be in better hands."

Or paws, she thought with a slight smile.

She was looking forward to seeing him with his Companion, and wondered how changed he would be. She had been profoundly affected by her own meeting with this aspect of herself. Would it be the same for him? She hoped that at least by the time he and the Tiger descended the mountain, Jareth would be ready to join her and embark for...where? Who was the next Dancer they needed to find?

No doubt you'll determine that once Jareth joins you, came a familiar, beloved voice in her head.

"The Dragon is coming," she said to her companions. She saw relief wash over their faces. If the Dragon came for them, they would not have to make the long, cold, dangerous descent in the growing shadows of nightfall.

A few moments later, her *rhia* was stirred by the powerful wind of his wing beats. He hovered in front of them. He was too large to land anywhere near them, and Kevla realized he would have to carry them down in his foreclaws.

"Is your task complete, Dragon?" she called to him.

"My part of it, yes," he replied. Then, turning his head on his long serpentine neck, he looked up toward the peak. As one, they all turned to follow his gaze. In the gathering darkness, it was hard to see at first, but soon they realized that they were seeing movement. Kevla squinted, and then inhaled swiftly as she understood what she beheld.

The moving blur against the snow and stone of the mountainside was Jareth, and he sat proudly astride the blue Tiger.

The big cat leaped from precipice to precipice, stone to stone, with a power and an abandon that made Kevla's heart leap into her throat. At any moment she expected her to slip, to hurtle off the face of the cliff with Jareth clinging to her.

Hardly, thought the Dragon. *This is her place. I would as soon fall out of the sky as the Tiger find false purchase.*

And Jareth must have known it, for he rode the Tiger like a burr on a horse, moving as if he were a part of the mighty beast. The speed of the great cat as it came toward them was such that the hood of Jareth's cloak was ripped back and the white garment flowed behind him.

At last, the Tiger leaped onto a nearby boulder, landing

squarely and settling itself as Jareth jumped off its back. Altan and Mylikki stared in shock. They looked at one another, then both knelt in the presence of the being they thought was their god.

Jareth went to them. "She's not a god," Jareth said gently, helping the *huskaa* get to his feet. "She's my Companion, as the Dragon is to Kevla."

For the first time since his arrival, Jareth looked directly at Kevla. "I am, as you tried to tell me, the Stone Dancer."

She felt a smile spread across her face, and Jareth went to her and clasped her hands. It was the first time he had willingly touched her, save for the night so many weeks ago when he had pressed a knife to her throat. His hands were warm and strong.

"I am glad that you finally believe me. And that you have found your Companion."

"She is..." Jareth turned to look back at the blue Tiger, who half-closed her eyes in what Kevla knew to be a gesture of affection.

"I know," she said. "I know."

He squeezed her hands and let her go. "There is much that I have to tell all of you. But I would prefer the telling be done over a hot meal by a warm fire."

"Such can be arranged," said the Dragon. "But Jareth—we must make haste. Time grows short, and a task awaits you when you return to the encampment."

"Our chance is gone!" cried the advisor. He stood next to the Emperor, staring into the glowing Tenacru. *"She did not do as you instructed. Now he's found the Tiger and knows about the Ice Maiden. It's all unraveling!"*

The Emperor chuckled and the hairs on the back of the advisor's neck stood on end. He hated hearing the Emperor rage; but he disliked his lord's laughter even more. The ki-lyn too was on its cloven feet, staring into the images on the orb with fear and hope mixed on its lovely face. Behind the Emperor, silent and seemingly obedient, stood the Mage. The advisor glared at the black-clad figure. This had been his idea.

"The Lorekeeper girl did not have a chance to execute the plan," the Emperor said amiably. "Everyone was watching her. I will speak to her tonight, and we will make fresh plans. It is indeed a pity that the Dancer and the Companion have come together, though. They are stronger now, and they have a target in the Ice Maiden."

"What do you plan to do?"

"My little Lorekeeper traitor will be more than able to do what I tell her. An opportunity will come again. And do not forget— the Ice Maiden has power over men. None can stand against her. Not even the Stone Dancer."

The advisor relaxed. "That is true," he said. "But Kevla is not a man."

The Emperor drew back thin lips in a smile. The ki-lyn lowered its head, jingling the ever-present golden chain with the movement.

"Ah, and neither," said the Emperor in a cool voice, "is the Lorekeeper."

They returned to the encampment, Jareth on the Tiger and Kevla, Hanru, Altan and Mylikki aboard the Dragon. Kevla had not realized how very much she had missed this— her legs astraddle his smooth scales, her hands loosely grasping his spine ridges more for something to do than from any true fear of falling.

I think travel by Dragon is preferable to all other ways, she thought to him, reaching down to hug him.

I think you are a very discerning individual, the Dragon replied. Kevla looked down. The night was again clear and crisp, and the moon was almost full. She could see almost as well as she could in the daylight, and could easily make out the form of the running Tiger and Jareth. She smiled at the sight. Any ordinary beast such as a horse or a *sa'abah* would have fallen far behind by now.

Her smile faded as she saw the enormous black shadow dragon keeping pace with them on the snow.

Shadow.

She had been so focused on first finding Jareth, then convincing him to join her, that she had almost forgotten what they were truly facing. She shuddered, and turned her eyes forward.

They were coming up on the *taaskali* encampment now. Kevla could see at least six fire rings, dancing yellow and orange against the cool hues of the snow, and wondered why they had lit so many. The *taaskali* numbered only two dozen or so. The *selva* were all clustered together in one place, which struck her as unusual. Usually the *taaskali* let them roam as they would. Why had they gathered them together like this?

The Dragon and the Tiger reached the encampment about the same time. The Dragon landed gently and his riders dismounted into the snow. Hanru hurried up to another *taaskali* and they whispered in their musical language.

"Dragon, what's going on?" Kevla inquired. All of the

selva were regarding Jareth intently. They seemed completely unaware of the presence of the Tiger in their midst. It was a strange sight, and Jareth looked completely confused.

"I stayed behind to perform a task," the Dragon said. "Now, Jareth must complete it."

"What task?" Jareth sounded exasperated. "I don't know what you mean."

"Look again at the *selva,*" the Tiger said, speaking up for the first time since her arrival. "Behold them, and know that you look upon the Lorekeepers of Lamal."

31

"How can this be?" Kevla cried.

"A thousand years ago," said Hanru, "there was among the Lorekeepers a man of unprecedented vision and wisdom named Caldan. He was able to see into the future. He saw many things, and one thing he beheld was that the Lorekeepers of Lamal would be in danger at the time when their memories would be needed most—when the Dancers were born, and the final fight against the Shadow took place. Caldan had in his possession an object of great power, and this was how he turned all the Lorekeepers into the *selva*. Disguised as beasts, they would be safe from any who would exploit their knowledge."

He smiled slightly.

"Caldan knew the *selva* would need to be taken care of. And the spirits of the forest answered the call. We agreed to take on human form and make sure these precious beings came to no harm. Thus were born the *taaskali.*"

Kevla gasped, but she realized she was not altogether surprised. She had known that the *taaskali* were something other than human, just as the *selva* were more than simple beasts.

She recalled her confusion when she first came to Lamal and found not a single Lorekeeper. No one, indeed, had ever heard of such a thing. Yet the evidence that they had once been in this land lay in the song, "Fighting Back the Shadow."

"Paiva told me that the forest spirits were gone," Jareth said. "You weren't gone…you were just in a different form."

"Exactly," Hanru said. "For a thousand years, we have been waiting for you, Stone Dancer."

"Dragon, you knew this!" cried Kevla.

"Not until I saw them," the Dragon answered. "In Kevla's land, there were beings that the Arukani called *kulis.* They were thought to be demons, and shunned. I knew better."

"But—but the *kulis* really *weren't* demons," Mylikki said, frowning as she tried to wrap her mind around what had happened. "They were just children, abandoned by their families."

"Perception and reality are tricky things, and are often one and the same," the Tiger chimed in. "It is but a degree of difference. The Dragon could see them as they truly were, and he made them remember—"

"Who they were," breathed Kevla, tears stinging her eyes as she regarded her old friend with new appreciation. Her mind went back to when she stood before him for the first time, on a ledge overhanging a pit of fire and molten stone, and the question he asked over and over again: *DO YOU KNOW WHO YOU ARE?* He had seen at once what the *selva* were, and stayed behind when Kevla and the others went with Jareth to find the Tiger so that he could remind them of their true natures.

"I had the right question to ask them, that is all," the Dragon said.

Kevla looked at the Tiger, who gazed back at her steadily. She wondered what the Tiger's question was, and how Jareth had learned the answer.

"They now have their minds and memories restored," the Dragon continued. "But only the Dancer of this land can give them back their true forms."

Jareth stared at the *selva*. They gazed back at him, their silver eyes catching the glow of the fire, and he saw the human intelligence in those eyes.

"How do I...what do I..." He looked beseechingly at the Tiger for aid.

She half closed her eyes and rumbled, "You know what to do. Lorekeepers exist to serve the Dancers. Call them, and they will come to you."

He licked dry lips. The Tiger, the Dragon, Hanru—they were all crediting him with more ability than he suspected he possessed. He stood where he was for a long moment, unable to move. What if he tried and failed? They would be people locked in animal form for the rest of their lives. What if he—

You have lived so long in fear, Stone Dancer. The words were not spoken aloud, but inside his head. He recognized the voice as that of the Tiger. *Aren't you tired of it?*

Yes, he thought, admitting it for the first time. He remembered a night long ago, when he had cast his doubt into the harvest-fire flames and let them take it. *I don't want to be afraid of failing anymore.*

He walked steadily toward the first *selva* and placed his hands on either side of its large, white head. Gazing into its eyes, he searched for and found the human within.

I see you, he thought, and closed his eyes. *I see you as you are. Be as you were, Lorekeeper of Lamal. Find your true nature.*

He felt the fur caressing his palms shorten, become warm skin. The head grew smaller between his hands, moved closer to the ground, and when he opened his eyes he found himself staring at an older, wise-looking woman. He heard a rustle as Kevla wrapped her gently in a blanket that might have been woven from the fur of the beast the old woman once was.

"Stone Dancer," the woman said in a voice that sounded as if it had not been used for some time, "Caldan promised you'd come."

One by one, the great beasts came to him to be liberated from their assumed shapes. One by one, Jareth touched them, found the man or woman or child within, and shifted their shape from beast to human. By the time the last calf had trotted up to him, to be turned into a beautiful little boy, Jareth was almost overwhelmed by emotion.

He turned and looked at the Tiger. *It's...humbling, Tiger. And empowering at the same time.*

That, thought the Tiger, and Jareth felt bathed in the warmth of her pride, *is what it is to be a Dancer.*

This is why you wouldn't let me find you the first time I

*tried. You knew this task was waiting for me, and that I would
need the aid of Kevla's Companion to complete it.*

Abruptly Jareth's strength fled. His knees buckled and he
dropped to the snow. Immediately Kevla and Altan were
there, wrapping him in blankets and pressing hot tea and
food into his hands.

"Thank you, Stone Dancer," Hanru said. "You have released us from our charge."

Chewing on dried meat, Jareth said, "But you haven't
changed," said Jareth. "You're still *taaskali.* Do you need me
to help you change back to your true form as well?"

Hanru chuckled. "You can help the Lorekeepers because
in a way all of them are linked to you. We are linked to the
earth, and until you have defeated she who holds this land
in thrall, we cannot again become what we once were."

"The Ice Maiden," Jareth said. He looked at his companions. "That's what I was going to tell you. The Ice Maiden
is no myth. She's very real."

"What?" gasped Altan.

"She's real," Jareth repeated. "It's she who holds the land
in this unnatural winter. My powers aren't gone—she's
blocking them, preventing me from using them." He opened
his mouth to continue, looked at their stunned expressions,
and said, "Perhaps we should start from the beginning."

"A tale is usually told best that way," Altan said. To Jareth's amusement, he had found his *kyndela* and was already
setting about tuning it.

In a steady voice that carried in the clear, still night, Jareth spoke of how he had first learned of his own abilities.
He was surprised at how easy it was to speak of something
that had always been so fraught with fear and pain to him.

He told them how he had thought he was the Spring-Bringer, and how devastated he had been when the powers seemed to have vanished.

"But I have learned today that I am something...someone...quite different from who I always thought I was," he said, still feeling pain and sorrow as well as joy in the discovery. "I have a greater responsibility, and I will not shirk it. Every day, people are dying because of the Ice Maiden's winter. We have to stop her. Now."

"How do we do that?" asked Mylikki.

"You and Altan may know more about that than Kevla and I," Jareth said. "For years, *huskaas* have been performing a set of three songs called the Circle of Ice. It's the only information we have about the Ice Maiden. What do the songs tell us?"

"Well, she starts off as just a young woman whose heart was broken by a man careless of her love," said Mylikki. "She called on dark powers so that she might capture men's souls and bend them to her will, in order to have vengeance upon all men for the wrongs one had done.

"She turns men's hearts to ice, so they can love only her," Altan continued. "The first song is about a young man going in search of the maiden, thinking he can make her fall in love with him. An old man warns him about the folly of such a venture and tells his own story. The second song in the Circle is sung by the young man in the first song, who's now been enchanted. He's doing the same thing to another girl that the Ice Maiden's lover did to her—seducing her and breaking her heart."

"And the third song is sung by the Maiden herself, explaining how she came to be," finished Mylikki.

"That's not a lot of solid information," said Kevla. "Is there anything about a weakness she might have? Where she lives?"

Mylikki and Altan exchanged glances. "There are a few verses that get left out," Mylikki said. "We can analyze them. See if there's anything useful there."

"Good," said Kevla. "Examine the songs and tell us anything you can think of. Jareth and I will listen to the Lorekeepers. They may have something to say that will help us."

The hours passed well into the night. Jareth and Kevla sat side by side on a *selva*-wool blanket in front of the fire, and one by one, the Lorekeepers of Lamal came to them. The stories they told were beautiful, humorous, heartbreaking, tragic, and inspiring. Some remembered only personal anecdotes, such as when a young woman looked shyly at Kevla and said, "You gave me some coins from your purse, that day when you went to the market."

"That was the day that I was...was murdered," Kevla said softly. While the memories came back to her, they were always strangely distant, as if they had happened to someone else. Kevla looked into the girlish face and saw the old woman to whom she, as a wealthy youth, had given a handful of coppers to. "I remember," Kevla said, softly.

Other stories, other lives. Kevla was sorry that Mylikki and Altan were not here to hear these stories. There was a song in every one of them, she was certain. But the two musicians had a more important task than gathering songs for future generations. If the Ice Maiden was not stopped and Jareth's powers regained, if this world was not saved by the Dancers standing together against the Shadow,

then there would be no future generations to sing songs
or tell tales.

The Dragon returned from his hunt with two *kirvi* deer
clutched in his forepaws. Kevla's mouth watered as she anticipated the meal, and she glanced at Jareth. For a moment,
she wondered how it was that Jareth was able to eat animal flesh at all, if he could mentally speak with the creatures
that he summoned. Then she realized that the Stone Dancer
had the same connection with everything that was of the
earth—grass, trees, even rocks. Everything was sentient to
him; therefore he would need to feed on the death of something, regardless if it were animal or plant.

The thought was unbearably sad. Without thinking, she
placed a hand on his arm. Jareth gazed into her eyes, frowning a little, not understanding what she meant by the gesture. She shook her head and smiled, and let him go.

At last, all the Lorekeepers had had a chance to meet
with the Dancers. Jareth sighed heavily and said to the Tiger,
"He is not here."

"No," the Tiger said.

Kevla knew who they were talking about. The Stone
Dancer had found his Companion, but not his Lorekeeper.
Not the fellow human who would be closer to him than anyone in the world. Clearly, Jareth had hoped to find this one
unique Lorekeeper in the company of the others.

"Hanru, you are certain these are all the Lorekeepers of
Lamal?" Jareth asked.

"I am," Hanru replied. "We have tended them for generations. They are all here."

"Remember," put in the Tiger, "the Dancer's Lorekeeper
is different from the others. He or she is the Dancer's soul."

Kevla's eyes widened. She remembered Jashemi speaking to her as they had made love: *There is destiny here. I feel it...I know it. We were meant to be together. I belong to you completely, Kevla. I always have, and I always will. No matter what happens—no matter who or what we are—know that I am yours. You are my soul.* And then again, in the dream the *selva* had granted Kevla, Jashemi the Lorekeeper had said of those words—*"He was almost right. I am your soul, Flame Dancer."*

She felt him again, warm in her heart. He was her soul. Kevla knew she could have had no brighter or better one, and barely aware that she did so, she pressed her hand over her heart, sealing Jashemi in.

"He could have died," Kevla said softly. Jareth jerked his head to stare at her, and she wished she hadn't spoken.

"That is possible," agreed the Tiger. "But if he were alive here, among this group, we would know it."

Jareth sat quietly for a moment, absorbing the information. Kevla thought he was adjusting remarkably well. She remembered how much of a shock this had all been to her.

"What happened to Caldan?" Jareth asked.

Hanru replied, "He was planning to leave Lamal, after he changed the other Lorekeepers and us. That much I know. Where he went, I know not."

Jareth shook his head, as if chasing away thoughts. "It doesn't matter right now. What does matter is finding the Ice Maiden. Altan! Did you and Mylikki figure anything out?"

They looked at each other, rose, and approached. Kevla thought she had never seen them look so dejected.

"We went over the lyrics," Mylikki said, rubbing at her tired eyes.

"And over, and *over*," said Altan.

"We even went through the various regional modifications Altan had learned in his travels," Mylikki said. "Nothing. The closest clue we found is in the first song, in which the young rider says, 'They tell me she dwells here.' But of course the song never tells you where 'here' *is*."

"Although apparently the Ice Maiden is real," said Altan, "I think she doesn't really dwell anywhere, at least in the songs. She...she lives where there is cruelty and meanness."

"Not through the forest and up the hill," sighed Jareth. "I understand your meaning."

"What's the first song called again?" Kevla asked. Perhaps she and Jareth could discover something the two performers hadn't.

"Logically enough, just 'The Ice Maiden,'" Altan replied.

"All right. The second?"

"'Circle of Ice,' and the last, 'Circle Completed.' The idea is, it's like a circle. Someone gets hurt, she hurts someone else, and that person hurts a third person because he's been hurt, and we're back to the beginning."

"A circle of heartbreak," said Kevla. "A circle of ice. What a sad thing."

Hanru had been listening. "What did you say, Kevla?"

"We were discussing a song cycle about the Ice Maiden," Kevla said. "It's called 'Circle of Ice.' We were hoping to find clues to—"

A memory raced back to Kevla. She recalled awakening the morning after the storm she and Mylikki had weathered together, looking out to where the Dragon had indicated the men of the woods were lurking. She had seen such a circle, a ring of ice glittering atop the snow.

Hope surged within her. "I think I've seen one," she said. "A circle of ice. A real one."

Hanru said, "We have seen many of them. They began appearing on the ground about nine, ten moons ago. The *selva* won't—wouldn't—go near them, and neither will we. There is...something bad there. Something evil."

"Has anyone ever stepped inside the circles?" Jareth asked.

Hanru shook his head. "Not that I know of. I have not even seen them disturbed by animal tracks."

The four companions who had undergone so much on their journey together looked at one another.

"This has to mean something," Jareth said. "There's got to be a connection. They started manifesting at the same time as her snow began to fall."

"We won't know anything until we can see them ourselves," said Kevla.

"When do we go?" asked Altan.

"You and Mylikki are not going anywhere," said Jareth. "Kevla and I and our Companions will handle this."

Altan shook his head. "We've come this far, we're not going to sit and—"

"I think," said the Tiger, her rumbling voice carrying, "that these things would be best decided in the morning. You all need to rest and recover from today, even the Dancers."

"But we might be able to stop her!" cried Jareth, whirling on his new friend. "Don't you understand what that means? People are dying, Tiger. This land can't take much more of this. If we don't act now, even if spring does come, it will come too late to do any good!"

The Tiger sat up. She had been lying stretched out on the

snow, apparently oblivious to the cold, and had resembled a cat beside a fire. Now, Kevla was reminded of how large she really was, and, if she was anything like the Dragon, profoundly powerful in ways Jareth was only beginning to grasp.

"You can't stop her if you are weak and exhausted," the Tiger said in a voice that brooked no disagreement. "I cannot think that she will be an easy foe to defeat. You will need all your strength and wits about you, Stone Dancer, and at the moment, you appear to be lacking in both."

Jareth's eyes narrowed at the barb. Gently, Kevla said, "We may be stronger than ordinary humans, Jareth, but even we have our limits. The Tiger speaks wisdom. It will serve nothing to find the Ice Maiden and be too weary to fight her."

His nostrils flared and for a moment she feared he would lash out at her. But then he took a deep breath.

"Very well. In the morning, then. Hanru, you said you can take us to one of these circles?"

"Indeed I can," the *taaskal* said, "though I will do so with great reluctance."

Jareth nodded, but Kevla could tell he burned to see the mysterious circles. He would have to wait, but not for much longer.

She rose, stretched, and went to the Dragon to curl up beside him. She stayed awake only long enough to notice through heavy-lidded eyes that Altan and Mylikki lay down close to the fire, wrapped in one another's arms, and that Jareth stretched out next to the mighty blue Tiger. The Tiger butted her head against Jareth's, then curled in around the Dancer.

Things seem right, she thought driftingly as sleep claimed her. *Things are finally starting to seem right.*

32

Kevla awoke and went to the cooking fire more lighthearted than she could remember being in a long time. The Lore-keepers had been returned to the land. Altan no longer made cutting remarks and was finally making his affection for Mylikki clear, and the girl was blossoming under the new attention like a flower under the sun. Jareth had accepted his destiny and found his Companion, if not his own Lore-keeper yet, and they now understood why his powers were blocked and who had plunged this land into a devastating winter. And today, they would investigate this clue they had discovered last night.

"I've been thinking," Kevla said as she sipped hot tea. "One thing that stands clear in my mind is that in the last song, the Maiden speaks directly to the audience. She seems to want us to know that she was once human. And the last line—it's almost as if she's trying to ask forgiveness."

"'Remember what drove me to be what I am, all that I wanted was love from one man,'" quoted Mylikki, looking upon Altan with adoration in her eyes.

"It doesn't excuse what she did," said Jareth.

"Of course not," Kevla says. "But it's interesting that she seems to want us to understand why she did it."

"That's supposing that the songs really offer any clues at all," Jareth said.

Altan glared at him. "It's the only information we have."

"No it's not. We have this," and Jareth gestured at the white expanse of snow. "The Tiger told me she controls the snow. We know that the madmen are real. And there have been strange circles of ice appearing at the same time that winter refused to leave. I'd rather stick to what I know to be true than look for hints in songs *huskaas* made up centuries ago."

"There's nothing that says we can't do both," Kevla countered.

"Kevla's right," said Mylikki around a mouthful of cheese. "We should look at everything we have."

"We don't know how to fight her," Jareth said. "We don't even know if we can. How do you fight a Maiden of Ice?"

"If it's literal—if she really is ice, then I can destroy her," Kevla said. Her powers were very good at destruction. "If she is human, then she can be killed. One thing is certain— she can block your powers. Let's hope she can't block mine."

Jareth drew his knife and examined the blade in the weak morning light. "She might be able to block my ability to speak with the earth," he said, regarding the weapon. "But I will still be able to plunge this into her heart if I have to."

Altan and Mylikki exchanged uneasy glances. Kevla had noticed that, aside from the madmen of the woods, Lamal was a very peaceful culture. All the weapons she had seen had been designed for hunting animals, not people. The horror with which the Lamali regarded the *bayinba* told her that it was rare, almost unprecedented. To see Jareth speak so calmly of murdering someone, even an enemy, disturbed her.

"We had best go see these circles of ice," said Kevla. "Perhaps we can glean more information from them."

Jareth nodded and sheathed his knife. "Let's go."

Mylikki and Altan rose as well. When Jareth scowled at them, they looked at one another and smiled a little. Then Altan said, "We talked to the Tiger and the Dragon earlier this morning, before you awoke. They said we could come."

Jareth transferred the glare to his new Companion. The Tiger flicked a blue ear.

"They promised to behave and do exactly as you said," the Dragon said. "We thought it a reasonable request. Besides, they have the knowledge of the songs, even the seldom-sung verses. They may see something that might be of help."

Jareth threw his hands up in the air. "It appears I will never shake you, Altan."

Altan's grin lit up his face. The adoration he felt for his friend was obvious even as he held Mylikki's hand. "And I hope you never do."

According to Hanru, the circle was not far by foot. By Dragon and Tiger, it was mere moments' distant. Kevla could see it from the air—a ring of ice, jutting up from the snow. It looked exactly the same as the one she had seen before.

"No matter how much snow falls," Hanru said, "the ice always pushes through it somehow, so that it is never covered."

"Well, nothing unnatural about *that*," Altan said.

Gently, the Dragon came to earth. Even as he touched the ground, the Tiger, with Jareth on her back, arrived and Jareth leaped off lightly.

Slowly, they walked toward the circle. It seemed harmless enough, though strange. A perfect circle, it enclosed an area about three feet in circumference. While there were animal tracks nearby, as Hanru had said, the snow inside the glittering ring was undisturbed by so much as a bird print or fallen leaf. They walked around it for a while, examining it in silence.

Finally Mylikki spoke. "So here's a circle of ice," Mylikki said. "A magical circle of ice. What now?"

"A circle encloses a space," Kevla said aloud, working through the puzzle. "For what purpose?"

"To keep it safe, or sacred," Jareth offered. "To prevent anything from entering."

Kevla nodded. "That's one reason. Hanru, you said there are many such circles?"

The *taaskal* nodded. "We have traveled hundreds of leagues in our journeys, following the *selva*. And we have seen dozens of circles like this. All of them feel the same— bad."

Jareth frowned. "Why so many? What would the Ice Maiden need so many for?"

Kevla continued to regard the circle. It was so small. Only about the size of a fire ring—

And then it came to her. "I can transport myself from one fire to another by stepping inside it." She looked at Jareth. "Stepping inside the fire's ring."

"A portal," said Jareth, excitement rising in his voice. Before they could stop him, he had found a stone in the snow and tossed it into the ring.

It landed with a soft sound and disappeared into the drifts of snow. They craned their necks and saw that it was still there.

"So much for that," Jareth said.

"It's for people," said Altan, suddenly. "The madmen of the woods—maybe that's how she catches them. They step into a circle by accident, stumbling around in a storm, and end up wherever she wants them."

Kevla felt suddenly cold—an unusual sensation for her. There had been a circle of ice that one morning, when the Dragon had told her men were hiding in the woods. She knew Altan was right. She rubbed her arms, knowing the chill came from the dark thoughts, not the freezing weather.

"Kevla?"

She tore her gaze away from the circle of gleaming ice to meet Jareth's blue gaze.

"I think Altan's right. I think this is how the men come to and from the Maiden. I think it's a portal, just like fire is for you." Jareth held out his hand. "There's really only one way to find out."

She stared at him. Everything in her protested. They still knew so little. They had no plan to fight her, they didn't even know if they *could* fight her. But if not them, who? Who in Lamal had greater abilities than the Stone Dancer and the

Flame Dancer? Unprepared as they were, they had to act now. The land and the people in it were dying.

Kevla rose and took Jareth's hand, twining her fingers about his.

"We're going to step into the circle," Jareth told the others. "It's too small for the Dragon or the Tiger. Mylikki, Altan—promise that you will stay here with the Companions. Whatever happens, we need to know that you two will be safe. Do you understand?"

Mylikki said quickly, "Yes, Jareth. We can't do anything more to help you and we might get in your way."

Altan sighed and nodded. "She's right. But be careful, and remember the song lyrics!"

Kevla was glad. She was fond of the pair and they were wiser than she had thought—they had been helpful earlier, but now, she suspected they would be a hindrance.

She looked back at the Dragon and forced a smile, then turned back to Jareth. His blue eyes seemed to bore into hers and she knew that he, too, was utterly ignorant of what lay before them. But his hand was warm and strong.

She nodded. They each took a deep breath, then stepped into the circle.

The cold sliced Kevla to the bone and the snow almost blinded her.

She dropped Jareth's hand so she could wrap her arms around her shivering body clad only in the thin red *rhia*. What—how was this possible? She felt Jareth grasp her by the waist and turn her around. She blinked to clear her vision and then gasped.

Directly in front of them was a forest, but it was unlike

any forest she had ever seen. The trees were dark, dead, and shiny with ice. They were completely encased in the frozen water, and their limbs all had sharpened, deadly points. They grew tightly together, their dead boughs entwining, to present a barrier that seemed impassable. Everything was coated with a dull red tinge. She looked up at the sky, and saw that it was a dark crimson.

Towering in front of them, past the encircling, icy forest, was something both beautiful and terrifying. Barely visible through the swirling snow, it was a great House—the word "castle" from the song Mylikki had performed sprang to mind. But it was not made of stone, or wood. This castle appeared to be made entirely of ice. It glittered and gleamed, even though the snow was falling thickly.

"'They tell me she dwells here,'" Jareth quoted. He looked over at Kevla. "You're shaking—I thought you never got cold?"

"Th-this isn't ordinary c-cold," Kevla said through chattering teeth. "I don't think we're s-still in our world." Kevla took a deep breath and settled herself, reaching for the fire that was always banked inside her. With an effort, she found it, and gradually stopped shivering.

"You think we're someplace else?"

"She's some kind of magical being," Kevla said. "And that's the first time in ages since I've been cold, Jareth, and it was hard for me to find my powers and make it go away. And look at the color of the sky. So yes, I do think we're in someplace different. Someplace magical."

They heard the singing sound of arrows at the same moment and turned to meet the threat.

Dozens of men raced toward them, shouting something Kevla couldn't quite make out. Several others who had taken positions let loose a rain of arrows. Without even thinking Kevla extended a hand. The arrows suddenly burst into flame. Nothing but ash and stone arrowheads now, they fell harmlessly to the snow.

"Your cloak!" Kevla cried. "It turns arrows!"

"That's a folktale!" Jareth yelled back, but she noticed he heeded her advice. She heard the sound of the arrows striking the magical *selva*-fur cloak and falling harmlessly. She concentrated. Small fireballs hurtled from her outstretched hands and attacked the oncoming men. They fell, screaming in pain, and as always when she was forced to harm others in her own defense, Kevla felt a stab of regret.

More were coming. Kevla's fear turned to grief and horror when she recognized one of them as Olar, Mylikki's younger brother. These, then, were the servants of the Ice Maiden. Crazily, the lyrics of the third song floated into Kevla's mind: *Instead of one lover, I've legions of slaves; my name's on their lips as they go to their graves.*

And now she could make out what the madmen were shouting as they kept coming: "For the Maiden! For the Maiden!"

The Ice Maiden was still blocking Jareth's powers, and Kevla noticed that it was more difficult than usual for her to summon her own. Jareth had no weapon other than his dagger, and while the folktales were true about the cloaks stopping arrows, she doubted the white cloak would block a spear thrust. There was only one escape route—forward, into the black, jagged forest.

"Follow me!" Kevla cried. She turned and placed her hands on the first ice-slicked tree in front of her, called the Fire that blazed deep within her, and willed the ice to melt.

She felt herself grow warm. Heat radiated off of her with the heat of a fire, and then with the powerful heat of the molten stone that had been the Dragon's natural habitat. At first, the ice resisted her. Then, reluctantly, it melted and she was able to move forward. The branches of the trees were still sharp, and she needed to step carefully, but she could get through and she thought there was even room enough for Jareth.

She felt Jareth right behind her, ducking his big frame and cursing under his breath.

"Keep close to me," she warned.

"Don't worry. I'm so close my clothes are smoking."

"I don't know how long the branches will stay thawed." Kevla heard a movement behind them, a strange, crackling sound.

"Apparently, not very long."

Kevla didn't dare look herself; she needed every ounce of her strength and focus to keep moving forward.

Step by agonizing step, they made their way through the forest. Kevla was panting with the effort and she could smell the acrid odor of Jareth's burning clothes.

She wondered if she would have any strength left at all by the time they actually encountered the Maiden herself.

Mylikki was happy to be sitting and doing nothing.

The journey yesterday had exhausted her. But she was glad of it, even glad for her too-close brush with death. It was because of that harrowing moment that Altan sat beside her now, his arm around her, and while she feared for her friends, her apprehension could not erase her joy.

He had come to Arrun Woods with his crystalline songs, star-bright voice and beautiful face framed with curling golden hair, and she had fallen for him almost from the moment she saw him. There were times when she thought her feelings returned, others when she thought it spurned, and there seemed to be no logic in what prompted Altan to treat her the way he did. When she had summoned her courage and kissed him, she had expected him to thrust her away at once.

But he had kissed her back, had seemed to want more from her than a kiss—and then, abruptly, he had stopped, looked at her with contempt, and stabbed her with cruel words. And Mylikki was again baffled and hurt.

Yesterday, though, she had seen his heart in his eyes as he reached to stop her downward slide to death. She had thought it perhaps the last thing she would ever see, but had been wrong. He had held her tightly last night, though they had done nothing but sleep, and today, he seemed to want what she wanted—merely to be together.

It had been some time since Jareth and Kevla had stepped through the ice circle that had proven to be a portal. At first, everyone was tense, but as the sun rose higher in the sky, the Dragon and the Tiger had started to talk quietly to one another, tactfully avoiding staring at the young couple.

Altan leaned over and for a wild, wonderful moment, she thought he was going to kiss her. Instead, he said, "Let's go through."

"What?" she whispered back. "We promised we wouldn't!"

"I think they may be in trouble," he said, his breath soft and sweet on her face. Mylikki trembled from his nearness, but saw that, again, he was distant from her. She recognized that expression, had hoped never to see it again.

"I'm going," he said flatly. "You can stay here if you want to, but I'm going.'"

Mylikki felt a deep ache in her chest, and knew the answer before the words left her chilled lips.

"All right. Let's go."

He turned his attention from her to the Companions. Still deep in conversation, they continued to ignore the two humans. Altan's hand tightened on Mylikki's, and her heart sped up suddenly.

"Now," he growled, and they dove forward.

Mylikki landed face-first in snow that had been trampled by dozens of feet. Coughing, she looked up and her eyes widened. Before her was a dark, dead forest, gleaming from its coating of frozen water, and up ahead loomed a castle that looked to be made entirely of ice.

Kevla and Jareth were nowhere to be seen.

Suddenly Mylikki realized just what an enormous mistake they had made. She got unsteadily to her feet and brushed off the snow, quivering with anger and fear.

"Altan, this was an incredibly stupid thing to do!"

She looked up and a small cry escaped her.

Where Altan had stood was now a slender young woman his same age. Long, golden curls tumbled down her back. She wore Altan's tunic, Altan's cloak, though now the tunic strained against a pair of firm young breasts and the breeches were too short.

"Yes," said the girl who had Altan's eyes, smiling coldly at Mylikki's expression, "it was."

33

Mylikki awoke to agony.

Her head throbbed with each heartbeat, and her vision was blurry. She blinked several times and with an effort lifted her aching head, hissing with pain.

She tried to move and realized that she was tied to a tree. Her wrists and ankles were also bound, and in her numb hands she clutched a waterskin of some kind. She heard someone moving behind her and memory flooded back in a sickening rush—the shock at entering this strange place, and turning to behold the girl who had looked so much like Altan. Probably it had been she who had struck Mylikki with something hard.

"There, that should hold you," came a voice. Mylikki felt

bile rise in her throat. The girl stepped around to where My-likki could see her and gazed down at her captive.

Mylikki stared back, trying to comprehend what had just happened. "Who—who are you? Where is Altan?"

"My name is Ilta," said the woman. "And Altan's here." She tapped her chest.

Tears filled Mylikki's eyes. She tried to close the lids against them but they escaped. They felt hot against her chilled face. She was so tired, in so much pain—

"I don't understand," she whispered.

The girl squatted beside her. "Look at me," she demanded. "Can you see it?"

Mylikki obeyed the order, blinking the tears back. She swallowed. "You look like Altan. Where is he?"

"I should. I'm his sister. For almost twenty years I've been trapped inside his body, but now, here in this place, it's my turn. Mylikki. Mylikki, curse it, listen to me!"

Mylikki's eyes had closed again. She forced them open, forced herself to pay attention to the ravings of the mad-woman, terror slowly filling her.

"He loved you, you know," Ilta said, conversationally. "He kept trying to be with you. But I just couldn't let that happen. If he had something—someone—to live for, he'd fight me harder for possession of his body, and I have to have it. But I am sorry. This wasn't about you. You just had the bad luck to get in my way."

Mylikki's skin prickled. This was insanity—or was it? The girl looked so very much like Altan...and she *was* wearing his clothing. Sickly, Mylikki recalled how suddenly Altan's mood could shift from sweet to hostile. She thought of the words Altan had uttered when Kevla had warmed him, words that now made a horrible kind of sense—*Big hands, too crowded*. She thought of their kiss, how he had seemed to almost...become... another person right in front of her eyes....

Become Ilta.

Ilta gestured to the waterskin. "If you want to make it quick, drink that. It's not poison, but it will put you to sleep almost at once. You won't feel the cold that way."

Mylikki stared at the waterskin. "I'm not drinking this."

"Look, I told you, this isn't about you. But Altan is inside *my* body here, not the other way around. And he's not coming to rescue you. The Dragon and the Tiger can't get into the circle, and Jareth and Kevla are—otherwise occupied. You're going to die here, Mylikki. How you die is your choice. You can sit and freeze to death fully conscious, or you can go to sleep. I don't care which you choose."

She rose, sighed, and placed her hands on her hips. "Too bad he liked you so much," she said, and strode off into the snow, her slender body moving with Altan's gait. Mylikki stared until the slim figure disappeared into the snow, then turned her gaze again to the waterskin. She had no cloak, nothing to protect her from the aching cold and stinging snow.

"I'm not drinking this," she repeated.

Ilta Lukkari walked with a joyful step. She reveled in her woman's body, the body that ought to have been hers, the body that *would* have been hers had the birth cord not twined itself insidiously around her infant neck. She still remembered that moment, sentient in the womb, with full and complete knowledge of who she was and who she had been, sensing death coming closer by the moment. Back to back with her twin she lay, feeling his warmth, his life, secure and unthreatened.

This could not—would not—happen. She was the Stone Dancer's Lorekeeper, and she refused to let something as trivial as death keep her from physically being with the Dancer in this fifth and final incarnation.

So the Lorekeeper had foisted the essence of herself, the Dancer's very soul, into the body of the healthy twin. The one who would cry with a lusty wail that would proclaim him to be a future *huskaa*.

The one who got to live.

Altan Lukkari did not walk through life alone, though he was blissfully ignorant of that fact. Ilta watched and waited, hidden in a distant corner of Altan's being, seeing everything he did.

And sometimes, she forced her way out.

When she did so, Altan was completely unaware of it. He told no one of these strange "blackouts," these moments where time had passed and he had been utterly ignorant of what his body had been doing. Ilta was careful not to do anything too drastic to the body while she was in control of it. Altan was not stupid, and he would sense something wrong if she was not careful. If she pushed too hard, he would confide in someone, and that could ruin everything.

She felt him stir within her, felt his dawning understanding of the situation. She felt the shock, and finally, a demand that she return his body to him.

Sorry, Altan, she said. *It's my turn now.*

And even as she had the thought, Ilta paused. She did feel bad for Mylikki. The girl hadn't done anything except fall in love with Altan. And Altan wanted to be with her.

I'll tell you what, she thought to the second soul that shared one body. *We can make a deal. This is* his *place. I'll bet he can separate us. Give you your own body back. Then you can be with Mylikki, and I can be with Jareth. We'll both be happy. It can all be as it was supposed to have been, before—*

Her hand went to her throat and found no tightening cord about it, but her breathing was suddenly difficult.

Mylikki? Ilta let him see what she had done with the girl, and Altan's outrage made her stumble.

She's just an innocent girl! How could you do this to her?

Because you loved her, and if you had her, I would never have gotten your body, Ilta thought. *But you can have her if you like, Altan. She doesn't need to die. You can be with her and—*

And stay here? Altan shot back. *Stay in this unreal world, this place of fantasy and illusion? What about the Shadow, Ilta? It's coming, and Jareth needs to stand against it. You're his Lorekeeper! You're supposed to help him, share your knowledge, be his support. And instead you're tricking him with lies and deceptions!*

Ilta's fury was so powerful she stumbled. *It's not a lie! I love him! I've loved him before and I love him now! Do you think your affection for him was your own, you fool?*

Shocked silence.

Ilta was angry now. She was in the position of power. She'd tried to bargain with Altan out of affection for the boy who should have been her twin brother, but now she was tired of it.

It's over. This body belongs to me now, and it will appear the way I want it to here. And I want to be female.

Ilta, I'm sorry you died, I'm sorry you can't get to be with

Jareth, but stealing my body is not the answer! You've got to let him fulfill his destiny!

Stupid, stupid to think she could reason with him. Altan had been corrupted by Kevla, was going to let Jareth go with the fire-woman to his death, to the death of everything.

No. Jareth was going nowhere. Ilta would keep him here, with her. Forever.

She felt him probing deeper, seeing things that she did not want him to see, and for an instant felt her control over him slipping.

Ilta...oh, gods, what have you done...you're insane. You've gone mad. Ilta, you have to—

She roared in fury and dropped to all fours in the snow, forcing Altan back down into the darkest corner of her being. Locking him away. She had tried this before; tried to take over his body, claim it for her own. Before, in that other world, she had failed. But here, in *his* realm, she had greater strength. She felt Altan struggle, heard him cry out inside her in a soundless voice, and finally locked him away and slammed the door closed on him.

She was suddenly, violently sick.

Shaking, Ilta wiped her mouth with snow and got to her feet, weaving drunkenly. She mentally searched for Altan inside her. She found nothing, and a smile touched her lips. She'd either destroyed him or completely subdued him. It didn't matter which. Either way, Altan was no longer a problem.

Ilta had always been jealous of her twin's ability to be with the Stone Dancer when she couldn't; be with the handsome, fair-haired man named Jareth Vasalen in this lifetime. To speak to him, to touch him.

Jareth!

Ilta couldn't wait until this was all over. The Ice Maiden would deal with the troublesome Kevla, she was certain. Jareth thought he had to leave with Kevla, to stand against the Shadow. But he was wrong. There was a way around it. She knew it, and her ally the Emperor knew it. And then, after too many years, Jareth would finally see his Lorekeeper in her true form.

And he would love her.

He had to.

He always had before.

Kevla had never felt so weak, so drained, in her entire life. But she did not dare stop moving forward, stop forcing the trees to yield their thick coating of ice. The moment she did, she knew the coating with its sharp, icicle points would return. She also needed to watch where she stepped. The trees had roots that were also slick with ice. One slip, and she would stumble, impaling herself on the branches that were as sharp as huge thorns.

Step forward. Put feet between slick roots. Touch overhanging branches, preparing for them to spring back once the ice has gone. Hold the heat, hold it, send it out, take another step....

Jareth was never more than a handsbreadth behind her, and more than once she heard him hiss as he was not fast enough to evade an unnaturally sharp tree branch freezing behind him. The strain was getting to him as well.

"Are you all right?" she asked at one point, craning her neck for a quick backward glance.

"Just keep going, don't worry about me," he said. His eyes were on his feet, making sure his steps were secure. His hands and arms were bleeding from numerous cuts, and she could see wisps of smoke curling up from his clothes where they had gotten singed. Even the cloak was not immune to the kind of magical heat Kevla was emitting.

Step by slow, careful, tortuous step they went. At one point, Kevla's foot landed on one of the icy roots. Her feet shot out from under her and she tumbled forward. She cried out, seeing a dagger-sharp broken branch rushing toward her unprotected face. An instant before it jabbed itself into her eye, she was halted by powerful arms around her. Her breath was forced out with a *whoosh.*

Her mind went back to the last time Jareth had seized her around the waist. Then, she had been terrified at the strength of the arm that had come out of nowhere. Now, she was deeply thankful as she stared, not moving, hardly daring to blink, at the icicle jutting a bare finger's width from her right eye.

Jareth understood why she remained so still. Slowly, carefully, he pulled her upright and held her briefly against him. She squeezed his arm and then quickly stepped forward, seeing that the ice was already starting to return as punishment for her brief lapse in attention.

The Dancers were not all-powerful, despite their gifts. They were mortal flesh, and could be hurt. Could be killed. Kevla was keenly aware that, in her previous incarnation, she had been stabbed to death in an alleyway. Just a few months ago, she herself had lain at the brink of death because of a single arrow. And arrows of ice were all around them.

She spared a quick thought for the Dragon, wondering if

their link would continue here. But for the first time since she had rediscovered her old friend, she could not sense him. She and Jareth were truly on their own here.

At last, after what seemed an eternity, she thought she saw an opening ahead.

"I think we're coming to the end," she called to Jareth.

"Not a moment too soon."

"Something could be waiting for us. We should be ready for an attack or ambush."

Jareth made a noise she couldn't interpret. She kept going forward, gritting her teeth against the necessity that made her move so slowly when she longed to race toward the light that kept drawing closer and closer.

She wanted to stop, to assess what might be waiting for them when they stepped out of the dead forest and into the snow up ahead, but she did not dare.

"I can't stop and listen," she said, trying to keep her voice as low as possible. It was a shame she could not mentally communicate with Jareth as she could the Dragon, she thought.

"I understand," he said back, also speaking quietly into her ear. "When you get close to the entrance, just rush out. Not the best strategy, but the only one we have. I'll be right behind you."

She nodded. It was growing lighter now. She was sure Jareth, who was slightly taller than she, could see it as well.

"A few more steps," he said. His voice was a soft breeze in her ear. She took a deep breath, took two more steps, and then leaped forward into the snow, tense and alert.

The two rows of men who flanked the exit of the forest were still as stone. Quivering with exhaustion, tasting fear that her power might not come anymore when she asked, Kevla raised a hand to blast them.

Jareth's hand shot out to close on her wrist. Wildly she stared at him. Why was he stopping her?

"They're not attacking us," Jareth said in a low voice. "Remember, they're just men who are under her control. I don't want to kill any of them if we can help it."

Kevla blinked and nodded her understanding. He released her arm. As she lowered it, she saw that he was right. None of the men was moving to stop them. Now that she had a moment to look at them, she felt sorry for them. They were clad in poor clothes, certainly not enough to properly protect them from this bitter cold. Some had fingers and faces that were turning black from something Kevla knew was called "ice-poison." They had no scimitars, or swords, or shields like any proper clansman in Arukan would have with which to fight, only farmer's tools and arrows. They stood, vacant-eyed, one across from the other, forming a corridor that led directly into the castle.

"She knows we're here," Jareth said.

"Yes, she does," came a loud, arrogant voice that Kevla knew and shrank from. "And so do I."

"The Emperor," Kevla whispered.

34

Jareth glanced at Kevla. The color was draining from her face as she spoke and her eyes were wide. He'd never seen her display this kind of fear before and his own heart sank. She had mentioned the Emperor to him as someone they needed to regard as an enemy, of course, but he'd gotten the impression that this man, if man he was, was a distant threat. Clearly Kevla had not been expecting him here.

"Come forward," came the arrogant voice again. Jareth looked around, but could find no speaker. "She has willingly granted an audience with you today."

Jareth looked back at Kevla. She had regained some of her composure and had straightened, standing tall and doing her best not to reveal her fear. Admiration swept through him. When they had done what they had come to do, he would tell her so.

If they survived.

"I would suggest you make haste, Dancers. The Maiden does not like to be kept waiting. It makes her...testy."

A low, rumbling chuckle rolled like distant thunder, and abruptly Jareth's trepidation was replaced by irritation. He decided he did not like this Emperor. The shift in feeling heartened him.

He and Kevla moved forward, doing their best to stride boldly in the snow. The castle towered before them, and Jareth thought with a burst of grim humor that at the very least, they'd be out of the apparently ceaseless fall of snow.

The castle itself was a work of art, he thought as he and Kevla drew closer. He had never seen anything like it. There were spires and turrets, walkways and arches, all gleaming and sparkling. The windows were as clear as if they had been made of glass, although he suspected that, like everything, it was merely transparent ice. They carefully negotiated slippery ice steps and stood in the entrance. Mammoth white doors swung open as if of their own accord and a hall yawned before them.

Suddenly everything changed.

He was standing in his own home, back in Skalka Valley, and he heard the cheerful sound of a crackling fire. And he was not alone.

"Welcome home, Father," said Annu, reaching to take his cloak.

"I've kept your supper warm, love." Taya smiled at him from where she sat beside the fire, nursing their son.

A feeling of commingled horror and joy washed over

Jareth and he stumbled, suddenly dizzy. Annu was there to steady him, tall and strong and slim, concern on her pretty face.

"Father? Are you well? Come sit beside the fire."

She was alive. They were all alive.

The Tiger had been wrong. They could be brought back... they *had* been brought back....

He stared down at his daughter, then abruptly reached to fold her into his arms.

The sounds of merrymaking seemed to assault Kevla's ears after the silence of the wintry land. Colors and sounds converged on her. She closed her eyes for a moment and covered her ears, dazed and shocked, trying to determine where she was, what was going on.

She opened her eyes to stare at the low, carved table all but groaning with the weight of the glorious feast that seemed to stretch as far as the eye could see. All her favorite foods were here—olives, dates, roasted fowls and meats, pitchers of water with sliced fruit floating in them. She was suddenly ravenous. She had gone for so long eating nothing but grains and stews that she could not even imagine where to begin.

"Welcome home, daughter," said her father, seated on her right. He looked relaxed and smiling.

"My beloved, I have missed you so," came a voice on her left.

He was clad in his most formal attire, and the lavishly embroidered *rhia* molded attractively to his slim but strong frame. The kerchief that wrapped his head did not hide one or two tendrils of soft, curling black hair. His full lips were parted in a smile of delight, and while his deportment was perfect, his brown eyes glowed with love. He reached and touched her face.

"It can all be all right, now," Jashemi said tenderly. "You don't have to choose this time. Tell me you love me. Tell me you have not forgotten what we were to one another. We can have everything here."

Annu's slim frame was warm and strong as Jareth clasped her. He buried his face in her neck, kissing her soft skin as he had done when she was a baby.

But there was another he needed to see, to hold, to kiss, and with a final squeeze he released his daughter. Turning, he stumbled the few feet forward and fell to his knees in front of his wife. He buried his head in her lap.

"You're alive," he said, his voice muffled.

Taya ran her fingers through his long, tangled hair and laughed softly. "Of course I am."

He lifted his head and gazed into her blue eyes, the color of sky in summer. "I thought... But no. It must have been a dream."

She stroked his cheek, and suddenly he was clean-shaven, his skin tingling from her familiar, beloved touch. "No more bad dreams," Taya whispered, handing the infant to Annu and reaching for her husband. "Not here. Not anymore."

Kevla was confused. She had faced this before. She had made her choice, how she would hold him in her heart. He reached and snared an olive, and without thinking she opened her mouth to receive the offering. Moisture flooded her mouth as she anticipated the briny tang.

He placed it on her tongue. Kevla felt a stab of shock. Nothing. The olive tasted like...nothing. There wasn't even a pit.

Instinctively, she spat out the tasteless morsel. Something was wrong. Something was very wrong.

"You're not him," she told Jashemi flatly.

His beautiful face furrowed in puzzlement. "But I am. Let me kiss you, my love. It will come back to you."

He leaned forward as if to kiss her, but as he moved toward her, she drew back with a gasp.

She couldn't scent him.

All of her memories of Jashemi were tactile, sensual. The feel of his smooth skin; the taste of his lips; the musical sound of his voice and, most powerfully, his own unique scent. He rubbed fragrant oils into his skin every day to keep it moist and supple in the dry heat, as was the practice among the leaders of a great House. She had come to associate the warm, spicy smell with the man she had loved on so many different levels. A moment before, the olive had had no taste; and now, Jashemi had no scent.

But oh, it looked like him.

She pulled away, furious. She recognized this scenario. The Emperor had tried to deceive her with it once before, in a dream-state, and if it had not been for the Dragon awakening her with fire, she would have succumbed. But he would not succeed this time. Kevla realized that even if she had been fooled by the illusion, it would not—could not—have lasted. She had made her peace with Jashemi-kha-Tahmu, her brother and Lorekeeper and soul and dearest friend. She had chosen to love him in this way, not in a physical, erotic way, and she knew the passion that the master of this illusion wanted to draw from her would not have blossomed. He could have succeeded in tricking her a few weeks ago, when she was lonely and broken and vulnerable.

But not anymore.

She bit back her rage, for it was not directed at the subject of the illusion. She touched Jashemi one last time, indulging herself in a final, bittersweet brush of the lie. He looked puzzled and hurt. She couldn't bear to see him like that, even if he wasn't real, so she rose to her feet, planted her hands on her hips and cried loudly, "I see through this, Emperor! You do not fool me!"

I see through this, Emperor. You do not fool me.

Jareth blinked. The words, spoken by a voice he somehow knew, seemed to float toward him.

His wife's face was only inches away. Her lips parted, inviting him to kiss her again.

"Taya," he whispered. "Oh, gods. Taya, it wasn't a dream. You're dead. I saw you...I touched you. You were cold and hard under my fingers. You can't possibly be here."

"Of course I can," his wife insisted, and he wanted so much to believe her. But there was something wrong, something...off balance. He couldn't smell her, couldn't taste her when he kissed her. He would have given anything to ignore the awareness that now flooded him, but Kevla's words pulled him back from the pleasant illusion into his reality of winter, ice, lost powers and lost love.

Her hands reached for him, and now they seemed too eager, too cloying, and he recoiled.

"She's dead," Jareth cried, getting to his feet and looking

wildly around for the callous being that had perpetrated the awful deception. "She's not here. She's *dead!*"

Kevla heard Jareth's voice, raw with grief, and her own heart ached in sympathy. She, at least, knew that Jashemi would be with her forever; he was her soul. But Jareth had yet to acknowledge his loss fully, and she was furious at the Emperor for toying with him so.

Ignoring the pleas from the illusory Jashemi who was still trying to coax her back into a realm of falsehood, Kevla cried, "I warned you once before, you will never use my love for him against me. You can't give him back to me because he's never really left me and he never will. Stop this foolishness and show yourself!"

The illusion faded. Kevla found herself standing next to Jareth in an enormous formal hall of ice. There was, of course, no fire to light it, but light was coming in from some source. Kevla suspected that the hall alone was half as large as the entire House of Four Waters. It cried out for decoration, for feasting, for *huskaas* and songs and a crowd of people, but it was completely empty save for a raised area at the far end.

On the dais was a throne, carved from ice. And upon the throne was a woman as white as that throne. White hair, white skin, white lips, closed white eyes. She didn't look real; she looked like one of the stone statues Kevla had seen in her father's gardens. Was this the Ice Maiden of song and story? A carved image made of ice, nothing more?

"Approach," the Emperor ordered.

Kevla looked over at Jareth. His eyes were bloodshot, his skin was pale, and he was shaking. He looked again like the wild man who had accosted her in the woods, not like the man she was coming to trust and respect. Impulsively, Kevla reached for his hand. He started to jerk it back, but then he met her gaze and squeezed her hand.

Her mind went back to the discussion they had had earlier. *If she really is ice, then I can destroy her.*

"Now," she whispered, hoping he understood her. Slowly, he nodded.

And Kevla attacked.

35

Kevla summoned every ounce of strength she possessed, and fire exploded from her fingers to hurtle toward the Ice Maiden.

The Maiden never moved. Instead, a wall of ice suddenly materialized in front of her. The two balls of fire Kevla had hurled struck the walls and while the ice was vaporized instantly, the Maiden remained unharmed.

Beside Kevla, Jareth cried out. She spared him a quick glance and saw that the ice around his feet was churning as if it was water. Before she could do anything, it had splashed over Jareth's feet, chaining him to the floor, and was beginning to climb slowly up his legs. He bent and chipped at it with his dagger, and Kevla saw the blade snap. The ice remained solid.

She started to dive toward him, to put her hands on his ice-encased boots and free him. With no warning, she slammed into a sudden wall of ice that erupted between her and Jareth. Clear as glass, the ice was as hard as stone, and Kevla grunted in pain as she cracked her cheek against it. She staggered back, bumping into a second wall of ice...and a third, and a fourth, all as thick as her hand. She realized she was now completely enclosed. Kevla reached out a hand, summoned her waning strength. The ice melted slightly. As she attempted to free herself, Jareth roared in anger, and she saw the ice had crept upward to midcalf.

"Jareth!" she screamed. He glanced wildly at her. Again she pressed a hand to the ice, and again it melted somewhat. But this time, she saw the ice jump upward along Jareth's legs to his knees. Every time she tried to free herself from her cage, the ice moved farther up Jareth's legs. She could liberate herself—but she would doom Jareth.

"You could have made this pleasant for yourselves," the voice of the Emperor declared. "I tried to give you a place you would enjoy. People you loved. But you rejected that."

"It was all a lie!" Jareth cried, his voice breaking with his rage.

"Would it not have been a more pleasant way to pass your days than standing here, enclosed by the Maiden's ice?" the Emperor countered.

"What do you want from us?" Kevla screamed, pounding impotently against the wall of ice.

"I would think it would be obvious—to stop you, in any way I can. However you spend the rest of your lives, it matters not to me. My earlier offering would have been much easier on you."

Kevla blinked back tears of rage. Weeping, even with anger, would not serve her now. She looked at Jareth, still struggling to free himself; at the Ice Maiden, seated as if carved of ice herself, upon her throne.

Was the Maiden even real, or was this just the Emperor playing with them again? And if she was real, was she his ally, or his puppet? Was there a way to reach her? Again she recalled the last lines of the third song in the cycle: *Remember what drove me to be what I am, all that I wanted was love from one man.*

"Maiden!" Kevla called. "Maiden, I would speak with you!"

The Emperor laughed, and Kevla's skin erupted in gooseflesh as the sound echoed in the vast chamber.

"She can't hear you," he said in that chilling, disembodied voice that came from everywhere and nowhere. "She is lost in her dreaming, reliving the pain of her tragic life."

The words should have been spoken with compassion, but they were mocking. He felt no sympathy for the Ice Maiden's story of heartbreak and vengeance. Kevla ignored him.

"Maiden!" Kevla cried again. "Sister, you suffer. I know this. I know the stories. Tell me of your pain!"

Nothing. Then, Kevla saw it: the Maiden blinked. She was alive...at least, as alive as she could be, made of ice as she was....

"Maiden!" Kevla called again, heartened by the movement. "Speak to me. I would hear your story from your own lips."

"You waste breath, Flame Dancer," said the Emperor, but Kevla thought she detected a faint note of worry in the arrogant voice. She waited, barely breathing. She was stalling for time, time in which to think of something, anything, to save herself and Jareth.

The Maiden's lips turned a deep wine-red. She began to speak.

"My story's an old one—a poor country maid, I loved a young man, and that love was betrayed—"

Her voice was like bells, like a *kyndela,* silvery and pure, but frighteningly devoid of emotion.

Out of the corner of her eye, Kevla saw Jareth stop struggling. He stood, swaying a little because he could not move his feet to adjust his balance, and stared at the awakening Maiden as she began to speak. Kevla's heart sank. Of course; Jareth was a man. And men were "caught like flies" by the Ice Maiden's charms. Kevla could count on no more aid from that quarter.

"Stop!" Kevla cried, and the Ice Maiden halted in midrecitation. Her eyes narrowed, and Kevla saw them taking on hue, becoming blue. And was her hair more golden now than white?

"That's a song made up by the *huskaas,*" Kevla continued, speaking urgently. "I've heard it. That's not what I want to hear. I want to hear *your* story from *you.* Speak to me, my sister. Tell me your pain."

Slowly, the beautiful, white hands twitched, and the Maiden got stiffly to her feet. Yes, her hair was definitely yellow now, starting to take on a sunlight-gold color.

"Sister," the Maiden said, as if tasting the word in her mouth. "Sister. Yes. You are a woman, as I am a woman. And we suffer. Yes, we suffer."

Hope surged in Kevla's heart. "Tell me," she urged. "Tell me everything."

The Maiden slowly stepped down from her throne as she spoke. With each step she took toward Kevla, she seemed to become more alive. Color began to fill her cheeks, her face, her hands, and her movements became more fluid.

"He was a *huskaa*, from another village," the Maiden said. "He played so beautifully, and he was so beautiful himself. I fell in love with him, and we stole away together on that warm midsummer's evening. He lay with me; he took my maidenhead, and then he laughed. He *laughed!*"

Her expression changed. The red mouth twisted, and tears filled the blue eyes. Rage and pain warred on a face that was suddenly a battleground of emotions. Kevla noticed that the Emperor, so talkative before, was now conspicuously silent. Why?

Kevla returned her attention to the image of the beautiful young woman approaching them. She was lovely, Kevla had to admit. Tall, slender, pale, except for those red, red lips and golden hair. Tears slipped down her face. They froze as they traveled, dropping off the edges of her cheeks to fall to the floor as perfect little crystals.

"I am sorry," Kevla said sincerely. Whatever the Maiden had done, she had been wronged first. She had been seduced and abandoned. "What was his name?"

The Maiden stopped dead in her tracks. Puzzlement filled her blue eyes. "His name?"

"Yes, of course," Kevla continued. "His name."

"I—I don't—"

"Do not answer her!"

The Emperor's voice was both commanding and alarmed, and Kevla froze, barely breathing.

"Who dares speak so to me?" cried the Maiden. She raised an imperious hand and the men who had stood so rigidly at attention outside her fortress now rushed inside. "There is

someone in the castle," she told them. "Find him. Kill him."
They scattered to obey, ducking into doors that opened at
the end of the hall.

Kevla couldn't believe her luck. She had thought the Ice
Maiden an ally of the Emperor, or perhaps a tool. Perhaps she
still was, but if so, she was ignorant of the alliance. She seemed
genuinely offended that anyone would trespass in her hall.

"I am not here in flesh, but in spirit only," the Emperor
said. He was still a disembodied voice. And this time, the
voice was soothing. "The fire-woman is your enemy. She
tried to attack you! I am a friend, Maiden, who—"

"A friend?" She laughed harshly. "No man is my friend."

"But I am not a man." The voice had shifted, had become
soft, feminine. But the Ice Maiden, as animated and passionate now as she had been immobile when they had first entered her hall, was not so easily fooled.

"You are a man indeed," she snapped, "for you fall into
deception at once. I will hear you no more, spirit. And I will
answer the fire-maiden's question!" The Maiden again
turned her attention on Kevla, and again, looked confused.

"I don't remember his name," she said, stunned by the
admission.

"But you must," said Kevla. "Every woman remembers
her first love. And since he devastated you with his abandonment, his name must be forever written in your heart."

"You have no heart," said the Emperor, his voice again
masculine. "You have only ice in your breast."

"I have only ice in my…" repeated the Maiden, then shook
her head angrily. "No! I will not listen to you!"

"You *will* listen to me! I *made* you and you will do what
I say!"

And suddenly Kevla realized what was going on. The Emperor had magics the like of which she had never heard of. He had the skill to create realistic images of Jashemi and her father, images so accurate that if he hadn't slipped up on the subtle details of scents and tastes, Kevla would have believed them utterly. Judging from Jareth's stricken cries and haggard expression, he, too, had been deceived by the illusions the Emperor had wrought.

Now Kevla was certain that the Ice Maiden was something similar, except the Emperor had gone even farther with her. He had created her based on the old legends and songs, right down to the details of wine-red lips and hair like the sun. The Maiden knew the songs, but she couldn't remember the name of the man who had so devastated her. And apparently, she had no memory of the Emperor, either. Before the Emperor could again attempt to stop the conversation, Kevla hurled more questions at the Maiden.

"What was *your* name?" Kevla demanded, leaning up against the clear ice wall that separated her from the Maiden. "What town were you from? Who were your parents? What did your beloved look like? Smell like, taste like? If you loved him so much that he broke your heart, you would know these things!"

The Maiden's eyes were enormous. "Remember what drove me to be what I am—all that I wanted was love from one man...."

"What man?" Kevla insisted.

"Silence!" roared the Emperor. "You will not listen to this woman any—"

But it was the Emperor no one was listening to now. Jareth continued with his fixed stare fastened upon the Maiden.

The Maiden had eyes only for Kevla, and Kevla did not dare look away from that hurt, puzzled gaze. She felt sorry for the Maiden, not because of her sad story, but because of how she had been created and used by the Emperor.

"All the songs about you come from a land called Lamal. There, it is women who ask for a man's hand in marriage," Kevla said, her voice soft, intense. "And in Lamal a woman who is not a maiden does not lose worth in the eyes of her people. Indeed, coming to the marriage bed already great with child but proves her fertility."

"But…but he…"

Kevla pressed her advantage. "The song says you called on dark powers. What powers, Maiden? Who did you bargain with?"

Tears filled her eyes and froze before they were halfway down her completely human-looking face. *"I don't know,"* she whispered, her voice raw.

"You will not—" And suddenly the Emperor's voice fell silent.

"Take down this wall, Maiden," Kevla urged. "Let me come to you. You are not what you think you are. You have been cruelly deceived, my sister."

The Maiden was now on the other side of the ice. She placed her hand on her side of the wall. Kevla placed hers on the other side, so that if the wall had not been between them, their hands would be touching.

"Why can't I remember his name?" the Maiden whispered.

"Because," Kevla whispered back, very gently, "I believe this memory you have never happened. The Emperor—the man whose voice tried to tell you not to talk to me, who invaded your hall—made you to serve his own ends, and gave you these memories. You heard him say so yourself. Because of him, you have done things I don't think you fully understand. You have taken the minds of dozens, perhaps hundreds of men, left them to die in the woods—"

It was the wrong thing to say. The Maiden's blue eyes narrowed and she snatched her hand back.

"Men!" she spat. "Nothing is too cruel to do to them! You know that, sister. I can see the pain in your own heart. You have been hurt by loving someone."

"Not the way you think," Kevla said. "These men did nothing to you. They were not the ones who wronged you."

"How is it you can be a woman and not understand this?" the Maiden raged. "They are all the same! If he had not died, this man you loved would have left you one day. He would have broken your heart, devastated you."

Kevla felt Jashemi again in her heart, and answered with absolute certainty, "Never."

"I am a *friend* to women, do you not see that?" Her eyes were wide, her voice impassioned. "I am a friend to you! When I take the men away, I am giving women a gift, a life without the pain of heartbreak now or ever to come."

Kevla stared at her. "Do you really not see?" she asked aloud, hardly able to believe it. "When you came with your winter, you made it all but impossible for people to find food. For animals to survive. The men left their homes to get their families something to eat so they would not starve to death. When they stumbled into your circles of ice, they were *protecting* their wives and children, not abandoning them!"

The Maiden blinked. Doubt crept into her face.

Kevla continued, speaking quickly. "When you took them as slaves—when you sent them back to their villages as madmen—they turned on people they loved. For every man that you hold here as a slave, there are women who are slowly dying of cold and hunger directly because of your actions. You are an enslaver of men and a killer of women and children!"

The Maiden recoiled as though Kevla had struck her. Even her hands went up in a protective posture. "No," she whispered. "This cannot be. I protect women and children. I would never harm them!"

"You lie!"

Jareth's voice cracked in the hall like a tree bough snapping under the weight of ice and snow. Kevla was startled. She had thought him enraptured by the Maiden, as all men were, but now she realized that his stare had not been hopeless desire, but hatred.

"You murdered my family!" he cried.

The Maiden turned, her eyes flashing. *"I did not!"* Her voice was deeper now, filled with outrage. Nothing Jareth could have said could have offended her more. "You are a man, and as a man, your words are lies!"

"Not these words," Jareth hissed. "Think back, Maiden, if you're even capable of doing so. Think back to a snowstorm that swept through a little town called Skalka Valley nine months ago. Think of a storm so violent that it filled a house with snow and ice in a matter of a few heartbeats, smothering a woman, an infant, and a *twelve-year-old girl.*"

Kevla held her breath as silence fell. The Maiden turned from Kevla and walked slowly toward Jareth. Kevla saw that the ice was now up to Jareth's waist. But the cold that was wrapped around his lower body had done nothing to cool his fury. Standing in front of him, just out of his reach, the Maiden searched his eyes with her own.

"You speak truly," the Maiden said, her voice hushed with sympathy and wonder. "You did behold this. And you have not fallen under my spell. I am...sorry for you. For your family. But I swear to you, I did not do this thing. I would never send my snow and ice to kill a woman and children."

Jareth's eyes held hers. Finally, his voice hoarse, he said, "I believe you."

The Maiden looked at Jareth for a moment longer, a variety of emotions flittering across her beautiful face. Then, turning to Kevla, she said, "Do you, too, speak truly, Fire-Woman? For your power is my deadliest enemy. Why should I believe you?"

"I am your enemy," admitted Kevla, "for you are killing this land and the people—men, women and children— who live here. But I don't think that's what you intended to do."

The Maiden shook her head. "No," she whispered. "Women suffer enough. To think I have added to that...."

She wiped at a tear, sending the frozen droplet falling to the floor. For a long, long moment, she stared vacantly. Kevla didn't dare avert her gaze. Out of the corner of her eye, she saw Jareth start to shiver. She couldn't imagine what he was feeling, encased in ice to his waist.

Finally, the Maiden looked up at Kevla. Resolution was in her gaze.

"I do not wish to cause harm anymore," she said, her voice quivering. "But I do not know how to stop."

She stepped forward and placed her hand on the ice cage that surrounded Kevla, and it shattered into dozens of pieces.

The Maiden extended her hands to Kevla.

"Help me."

36

Slowly, Kevla stepped forward and took the outstretched hands in hers. The Maiden gasped in pain and snatched them back, staring at them in horror. Kevla saw that from her mere touch, the hands made of ice had begun to melt and the fingers had fused together.

Kevla looked at Jareth. "Let him go," she asked the Maiden. With a wave of her hand, the ice that had encased Jareth turned to water and he stepped free, shivering. "What do you need us to do, Maiden?" Kevla asked quietly.

She wondered where the Emperor was, why he was not doing everything he could to intervene. Perhaps he couldn't. Perhaps when the Ice Maiden realized that she was her own person, he could no longer control her. Whatever the reason, Kevla was grateful.

The Maiden stared at her disfigured hands. "I do not know," she said.

"You command the snow," Jareth said, anger and hardness still in his voice.

She looked at him. "I do," she said, "but I can only tell it when to snow and when not to. I can tell it where to fall. I cannot make it disappear or even stop falling for very long."

Kevla and Jareth looked at each other, and she thought she saw a hint of regret in his face when he said, "It could be that you *are* the snow. And as long as you…live…it will never go away."

The Maiden gasped, catching his meaning. "I do not wish to die!" she cried.

Kevla's heart was heavy. She understood now that the Maiden was as much a victim of the Emperor's whim as any of the men she had enslaved or any of the women who had suffered under her unnatural winter. And now that the Maiden knew what she was, what she had done, she wanted to stop it. But like any sentient being, she cherished her life.

The Maiden buried her head in her hands. Kevla stepped toward her, careful not to touch her.

"I believe you were made for a single purpose," Kevla said gently. "To stop this man," and she indicated Jareth, "from bringing spring to the land. To block his powers so that the man who created you would defeat us. Not only Lamal, but the entire world is in danger. We are the only ones who might be able to save it. The Emperor knows this. To try to stop us, he filled your mind with a story cobbled from fireside songs, and that was your only reality. All you knew was pain. No one could have expected you to behave any differently."

The Maiden shook her head in fierce denial. "Why should I believe you?"

"Because you have no memories other than what the songs say. Because you can't tell me the name of your lover. Because," Kevla said gently, "when you search your heart, you will find nothing there except for what I have said. I think you know my words are true."

"It hurts," the Maiden said softly, her voice muffled by her deformed hands. "The memory of my betrayal…of that night… still hurts so badly. Even though you tell me that it was all false."

"I'm sorry for your pain," Kevla said sincerely. "I understand that for you, it's as real as anything I've experienced. But because of that pain, you have made innocent people suffer. You have even killed. Maiden, I've seen the bodies." She swallowed hard, remembering the frozen corpse she had uncovered when she melted the snow—the woman hacked nearly in half.

The Maiden gasped. "I—I can see what you see. But a man did this—"

"A man directly under *your* control. A man who would never have done such a thing had you not claimed his mind."

"No!"

"You have to atone for that," Kevla continued ruthlessly. "You have to do what is necessary. Even if you believe that everything else I've said is a lie, you can't run away from the fact that if this winter continues, everyone in this land will die."

"Perhaps if I do not make it snow so much," the Maiden

said. She was clutching at anything to save her life, and Kevla couldn't blame her. "Perhaps if I send the men back. Although they do not deserve it...."

"Talk to them," Jareth said suddenly.

The Maiden removed her hands from her face and looked at him. "What?"

"Talk to them. You still don't truly believe that we're anything but monsters. Call them in and ask them. Ask them what they think about the women in their lives."

"They will doom themselves," the Maiden said. "With their own words, they will doom themselves, for they cannot lie to me while under my spell."

Kevla felt a brief stab of worry. She had never suffered as the Maiden had, from rejected love; but she knew that such a thing was not uncommon. Mylikki and Altan had played out a version of that story in front of her eyes. But Jareth looked completely confident.

"Then they doom themselves," he said. "But ask them. You owe them that much. I think you will find that there is not a one among them that does not cherish the love of a woman in some way."

She rose shakily. "Very well," the Maiden said. The doors swung open and the Maiden's slaves entered to stand before her. She looked them up and down and walked down the line, contempt in her gaze.

"This man here," she said, stabbing a partially melted finger at Jareth, "would have me believe that you care for the women in your lives. You...tell me of the women you have violated."

The man, short and stocky, said in a dull voice, "I have a wife of seventeen years and two daughters."

"Have you lain with another? Broken your vows?"

"Never."

The Maiden frowned, slightly. Kevla saw that Olar stood next to the first man, and the Maiden now turned to him.

"You...you're a pretty boy. How many hearts have you broken?"

"None that I know of, for I have never even kissed a girl," Olar intoned. "But I love my mother and my sister. I think they are very brave."

The Maiden turned to a third man, and asked him similar questions. He had similar answers. She kept going, kept hearing stories of affection and love, until she reached one man.

"Have you lain with a woman and felt no love for her?"

"Yes," the man answered.

The Maiden shot Jareth a triumphant look. "Did she feel love for you?"

"Yes."

"And does she suffer from your cruelty?"

"I do not believe so. She is married to my cousin, and is suckling her second child," the man replied. "No man could love a woman more."

The Maiden's face fell. Even here, even when she had found a man who admitted to intimacy with no love, the woman in question had not suffered forever.

Still she persisted. "Tell me," she said to one man with a handsome face and cold eyes. "Tell me of the women you have seduced and abandoned."

"There are many," the man replied.

"So then, there is no woman you love?"

"My sister and her daughters are precious to me. I would protect them with my life."

Down the line she went. Nowhere did she find a man who did not have a wife, a mother, a sister, a daughter he loved.

"Enough of this, Maiden," said Jareth, but his voice was gentler than the words he spoke. "You see what you have done. There is no one here who deserves your vengeance. Each man has a woman who needs and loves him. Let them go home to their families. Give them fruit, and crops, and a good harvest."

"My life depends upon the ice and the snow," she said dully. "And you tell me that the life of everyone else in this land depends on that going away. Tell me then, what kind of choice do I have?"

Again, Kevla and Jareth exchanged glances. She was prepared to destroy the Maiden, if such a thing was even possible, if she decided to choose life instead of sacrificing herself.

"You weren't ever meant to be," Kevla said. "Your life was bought at the cost of so many others. We have come to do whatever is necessary, but I hope you will choose what is right of your own will."

"I have nothing," the Maiden said. "No reality. You are right, Fire-Woman. I have no memories that are my own. My desire to have vengeance upon men has resulted in harming innocent women. The only things that I have truly done have been to enslave and cause suffering." She looked up at Kevla. "I don't think I can continue to live with that."

Kevla smiled sadly. "You are brave," she said. She stepped closer and opened her arms. "I am the Flame Dancer. Come into my arms, my sister, and I will hold you. It will be quick, I promise."

"I'm afraid," said the Maiden, and then, "I wish...I wish I had something good to remember."

"You're about to do something very courageous," Kevla assured her. "Something that very few people are willing to do. To die for the good of others. When people speak of you, I will make sure they know that. There will be new songs of the Ice Maiden—songs about her courage and sacrifice."

The Maiden wiped her face, looked Kevla in the eye, and stepped forward.

"No," said Jareth, startling both women.

Fearing that he wanted to exact his own revenge on the Maiden, to make her suffer before she died, Kevla said quickly, "Jareth, it's all right."

"You don't understand." He turned and faced the Maiden squarely. "You've done nothing but hurt people your entire existence. You were led to believe that this was justified, that men deserved everything and anything you did to them. But you don't know anything about love, or heartbreak, or even men at all. You heard the truth from their own lips. Most of us aren't at all like the memories that the Emperor gave you. We *want* to find someone to spend our lives with. We *want* to fall in love. Have children. Go to sleep at night in the arms of the woman who means the world to us."

His voice broke. The Ice Maiden gazed at him raptly.

"You've never known love, or even kindness. Not from a man, not from anybody. You said you wanted to have something good to remember. I will try to give you that, if you'll let me. I will do what I can to dispel this lie that is the only truth you've ever known."

"What are you offering?" asked the Maiden, quietly.

"I will hold you," Jareth said simply. "It will not be as quick a...a passing as it would be with Kevla. But I am warm flesh and blood, and you are ice. The result would be the same."

Kevla looked at Jareth. He was soaked through, and was shivering. The Ice Maiden in her true form, as they had first beheld her, was solid ice, and colder than anything Kevla had ever encountered. Still, Kevla knew that she could melt her in an instant, if she summoned her powers. Against simple human flesh—and she had no reason to believe Jareth was anything other for this purpose—it would take hours and would chill him to the bone. She had learned enough about the dangers of the cold to know that prolonged exposure could permanently damage his skin, or even cause his death.

"Jareth—" Kevla began.

"I want to offer her this, Kevla." His voice was calm, quiet. "She needs to know that we're not monsters."

Kevla bit her lip. But she knew it was not her decision to make. Jareth had made the offer; to accept or decline was a choice that belonged only to the Ice Maiden.

"Will this...harm you?" the Maiden asked.

"I don't know," Jareth said, and Kevla knew he spoke the truth. Not even he knew how his Dancer's body would react. "But I want to do it."

She rose and went to him. "Then...I would like you to hold me...until I am gone."

Jareth unfastened his white cloak and placed it on the floor. It would be the only thing between him and the solid ice. He sat on the cloak and held out his hand.

Slowly, the Ice Maiden's partially melted hand closed over Jareth's. Both of them inhaled swiftly from the shock—he of her cold, she of his warmth. Gently, Jareth eased her down into his lap. Kevla saw him swallow and stiffen slightly as the Maiden settled into his arms. She draped her arms around his neck and rested her head on his chest. Jareth took a deep breath, closed his eyes, and folded her close.

Hushed and reverent, Kevla sank down beside the two, pressing her hands to her own warm heart, aware that she was bearing witness to something almost sacred. The Maiden's color began to fade almost at once, and a smile curved her white lips.

"I feel...safe," she whispered.

Jareth laid his cheek upon her white hair. "You are safe," he murmured. "You are your own self now. No puppet of the Emperor. And I will hold you."

Tears filled Kevla's eyes, spilled hotly down her cheeks. For so long, Jareth had battled the winter. He had raged at it, had cursed it, had challenged it. Had stalked the gods of his land and even threatened them so they might destroy it. Now he sat still and oddly serene, holding the being at least nominally responsible for the dreadful winter as close as he might a child or lover. An awesome humility in the face of this compassion flooded her.

How long it took for the Ice Maiden to pass, Kevla would never be able to tell. Jareth told the Maiden stories of his family; happy, funny stories, the sort a husband and father would enjoy relating. Sometimes he sang to her, his voice not as perfect and pure as Altan's or Mylikki's, but sweet and clear nonetheless. It seemed to Kevla, silently watching, that the Maiden melted from the inside. She became more and more translucent as the time passed, growing hollow and terribly delicate.

Jareth never expressed discomfort or pain the entire time. And the Maiden did so only once, when she shifted and cried out.

"It...hurts," she whispered. By now, she was almost transparent. There was no hint of white about her, only glistening, fragile ice.

"I'm sorry," Jareth murmured.

"Is this how it is with men and women?" the Maiden whispered. Despite the tragedy and pain the Maiden had caused, Kevla wept as she beheld her. "This...tenderness, this care?"

"It can be," said Jareth, and then more fiercely, "it should be."

She took a deep breath, and Kevla feared the mere gesture would shatter her, but somehow the Maiden remained whole.

"This is sweet," the Maiden said. "I wish I had been a mortal girl, and tasted this." Then, "Now."

Jareth closed his eyes and pulled her to him, pressing her hard against his torso.

The Ice Maiden shattered into a dozen thin pieces, each of which itself crumbled as Jareth moved.

She was gone.

Jareth's blue eyes flew opened and he gasped. His clothing was soaked, and Kevla, startled from her place of deep reflection and reverence, realized that there were areas on his tunic and breeches that were coated with ice. Jareth's eyes rolled back into his head and he began to slump forward.

Kevla was galvanized into action. She called on the fire within her and it flared so quickly and so powerfully she was startled by the intensity. It seemed as though the Maiden's presence in this land had been dampening her powers, although they were not as completely blocked as Jareth's had been. Kevla banked the deep heat and hastened to Jareth, catching him as he fell. He felt nearly as cold to her touch as the Ice Maiden herself, and had stopped shivering—something she recognized as a bad sign.

Kevla tore off his shirt, so thick with ice that it was stiff in her hands, then tugged off her *rhia* so there was no barrier between his nearly frozen flesh and her inner fire. She pressed herself into him, her breasts on his chest, her arms entwining him. His hair was thick with ice and she placed one hand at the back of his head. His skin, white and cold, pressed against her, and she closed her eyes and directed heat into his body.

He's a Dancer. This would have killed an ordinary man. He can handle more heat than Altan could, she thought, and with that thought, she increased her body's warmth.

With a gasp and a deep shudder, Jareth moved. His arms closed about her slowly, awkwardly, and he pressed his face into her neck. Kevla's eyes closed in relief. He was alive.

"M-Maiden?" he stammered.

"She's gone," Kevla whispered softly. She wondered if she would be able to enlist his aid in his recovery. "But she almost took you with her. Open to my warmth, Jareth. Take it inside you."

She felt him nod against her, and Kevla again increased the heat. Slowly, she felt life coming back into his limbs and powerful torso. The cheek pressed against hers grew warm, and the trembling first increased, then subsided.

He was all right. She had brought him back. She should disentangle herself from him, put on her *rhia*, have him don his cloak. But she found she didn't want to move.

Safe, the Maiden had said, while clasped in Jareth's arms. *I feel…safe.* Kevla understood what she had meant. She, too, felt almost unspeakably safe in Jareth's strong, warm embrace. It had been a long, long time since Kevla had last felt safe. Not even with the Dragon had she been able to stop, to really rest, to put down her burdens even for a moment.

His arms slid slowly up her bare back, pressing her more securely into him, and she felt his body heave with an enormous sigh. While that trusting gesture made her want to stay within the circle of his arms even more, it also broke Kevla's reverie.

They were far from done with their tasks. Gently, Kevla moved away from Jareth. He kept his eyes averted while she slipped quickly into her *rhia*. There was a warmth in Kevla's cheeks that was not due to the inner fire which had burned so brightly a moment ago.

"Thank you," Jareth said quietly.

Unable to help herself, she reached and touched his cheek, turning his face to look at her. "You did a great and kind thing, Jareth Vasalen. It was an honor to bear witness to it."

He nodded, looking uncomfortable. A sudden wetness splashed on Kevla's head and she looked up.

"It's melting," she said. "The castle is melting. We've got to get out of here—fast."

37

Jareth stumbled to his feet and almost immediately fell hard on the ice. Kevla, too, fell, and he heard a crack and a grunt of pain as her elbow struck hard. There was about a finger's breadth of water over the floor now, and the droplets were falling like rain. He heard a deep groan, and realized it was the blocks of ice that comprised the castle.

The sounds were joined by the exclamations of the men, who appeared to have been freed from the Ice Maiden's spell by her death. They jabbered frantically and looked panicked.

"Come on!" cried Jareth. "This way! You've got to get out before the whole place comes down"

The men turned and one cried out, "Kevla!"

"Olar, follow us!" Kevla cried, and the men did so. They

were all forced to move forward on their hands and knees; the ice coated with water was simply too slippery for anyone to stand. Kevla looked up nervously.

"The ceiling's buckling," she said.

"Keep going!"

The groaning noises increased and Jareth began to wonder if they'd get out before the ceiling and walls collapsed in on them.

He was not sorry for what he had done. The Maiden had at first represented everything that was evil to him about the winter that had strangled his land and killed his family. But he believed her when she said she would not deliberately kill women and children, and had actually felt a stab of pity as he saw her begin to comprehend the depth of the wrongs she had unknowingly perpetrated. When the impulse to make his offer had struck, he had honored it. He had not anticipated how risky the task would be, however; he doubted he would have survived had not Kevla immediately folded herself into his arms to take the cold into herself.

He shook away that memory; it was a distraction now. Scrambling and sliding, crawling as fast as they could in the rapidly melting ice palace, they were almost to the doors. Jareth looked up and saw that they were closed and had started to melt together. It would be almost impossible to force them open.

Kevla reached them before he did, and placed a hand on the doors. She closed her eyes to aid her concentration. Heat radiated from her, and Jareth saw that she was melting an opening just large enough for them to slide through. Anything larger, and the doors might have collapsed on top of them.

"Hurry!" Kevla cried over her shoulder. Jareth needed no urging. He followed her through the oval she had made, slipping on the wet surface, and then they were both outside. The other men followed, sliding down what was left of the stairs until they were on good, solid ground. All of them were soaked and shivering.

Behind them, the palace that had housed a maiden made of ice had fallen in on itself and was melting before their eyes. A pool of water started to seep outward. Kevla watched, unable to tear her gaze away.

"Kevla, turn around," Jareth said.

She did. "The forest," Kevla said, puzzled. "It's gone."

Jareth nodded. The landscape now looked nothing like the somber, black, icy realm they had fought their way through to reach the castle. It was gentle and rolling. The sky was clear and its normal shade of blue, no longer the strange red color. The trees, growing in clumps here and there rather than close together, looked completely different. Kevla glanced back to where the palace had been and saw only a stretch of white snow.

"Where's the circle?" Jareth asked.

"The circle of ice we stepped through?" Kevla looked around. "I don't see it anywhere."

Their eyes met. "I think we're back in Lamal," Jareth said. "Look at the sky. And doesn't it...feel different to you now?"

Kevla narrowed her brown eyes, thinking, and then nodded slowly. "You're right. The ice circles take people into the Maiden's realm. Or the Emperor's realm I suppose I should say, since he created her. And now that she's gone, we're out of that place. Wherever, whatever it was."

The young man who had called Kevla's name now rushed up to her. She hugged him.

"Olar! I'm glad you're all right."

"What happened? Where are we? How is my sister?" the boy asked.

"Mylikki's fine," she reassured him. Jareth raised an eyebrow, realizing the connection. "She's waiting for us."

"Where?"

Kevla looked up at Jareth. "An excellent question," she said. "Shouldn't we be back with the Dragon and the others?" Kevla asked.

Jareth shook his head. "I have no idea how this all works, Kevla," he said tiredly. "I just know that I'm glad we're alive and the Maiden is gone."

He started. How could he have forgotten...?

"And if she's gone, then her grasp on the land is gone," he said. Kevla looked deeply into his eyes and a slow smile spread across her beautiful face.

"Then call spring, Jareth," she said softly.

He swallowed hard. To try this again, after so many failed attempts—but everything was different now. Everything was right. Still, he hesitated.

Kevla looked at him searchingly, then said something quietly to the boy, who nodded. Olar strode off through the snow to where the others were and they began to talk amongst themselves.

"Come on," Kevla said. Jareth followed her until they had walked away from the group of men and the rolling hills and trees hid them from their eyes. He felt a wave of appreciation toward Kevla; she did not want him to feel as if he were on display.

Alone with the Flame Dancer, Jareth knelt on the snow and scraped it away until he could reach the frozen soil.

I'm afraid, he thought. *I'm afraid it won't work.*

But there was no time to indulge his fear. Far too many people had suffered from this winter. It was time to end it.

He took a deep breath, feeling Kevla's eyes upon him, and dug his fingers deeply into the soil.

The pent-up needs of the wounded, weary earth surged through his fingers, sang along his veins. He gasped with the sensation that rushed to flood him. While this moment, calling the season, had always been exhilarating, it had never felt like this. This time, the feelings were tenfold more powerful, more pleasurable, with a sharp delight that was almost pain. He felt the life stirring deep within the earth, felt the roots of countless flowers and trees and grasses stir to wakefulness and begin to take succor from the fertile soil. Whereas a few heartbeats before he had been kneeling in snow, now he knelt in mud that grew warmer by the moment. Grasses shot through the soil, tender and green and waving. Trees exploded into flower.

As if from a great distance away, he heard Kevla gasp. "Flooding!" he heard her say, and although he knew the word, it meant nothing to him.

Suddenly a warm hand clamped down on his. His eyes opened and he stared into Kevla's wide, brown orbs. Her lips were parted slightly in a small circle of amazement.

Jareth's concentration was utter, and Kevla was loath to disturb it. She watched in delight as the snow melted rapidly away and grasses began to cover the muddy expanse. Almost immediately, though, she realized something they should have thought about—probably would have thought about, had they not been exhausted and at the end of their strength.

Winter usually lasted three months. The Ice Maiden's winter had lasted for a year. The beleaguered earth had received four times as much snow as usual, and now it was all melting at once. There would be massive flooding, and the damage the out of control waters would cause would be as disastrous as the winter itself had been.

Kevla recalled the Dragon telling her about dew, how it turned from water into mist with the warmth of the sun, and realized that she had to at least attempt to aid Jareth, to add her Fire powers to his Earth powers. So she reached and placed her hand over his.

She was completely unprepared for the wave of sensations that crashed over her.

She had never felt so...*alive*. The life force of the returning spring, delayed for so long and now being released by the Stone Dancer, was overwhelming. Her body tingled. Every sense was heightened. The sight of the blossoming growth was so clear to her it was almost sharp. Scents, rich and beautiful, combined into a heady elixir of fragrance so potent that she swayed as she filled her lungs in wild gasps. She could have sworn she *heard* the stretching, crackling sound of the buds opening, the grasses shooting forth their roots. And where her hand closed over Jareth's, she sensed the tiny, down-soft hairs that finely coated the back, the very texture of his skin folds.

Her heart raced, slamming against her chest so hard that her body shook with each beat. How did he bear this exquisite joy? How did he bear to *not* experience it every moment?

Her gaze locked with his. She saw the very earth invigorate the Stone Dancer right before her eyes. His bare torso, thin, almost skeletal with nearly a year of malnourishment, was filling out. Wasted muscles grew strong again, the skin that covered them becoming supple and smooth. His face lost its familiar haggard appearance, becoming chiseled instead of angular and sharp.

His eyes seemed to see deeper into her than they ever had before; here, in this moment, caught up in the powerful bond with his element, Jareth was unguarded and completely open. He turned his hand in hers, so that they were palm to palm. Kevla entwined her fingers with his, gripping tightly. And when he suddenly pulled her to him with that strong hand and wrapped his other arm about her, she had already swayed toward him.

She turned her face up for his kiss, craving him as the growing things bursting through the soil craved sunlight and water. His lips on hers were warm and strong, almost bruising her, but she responded with an equal intensity. Kevla pressed into his body as she had earlier, but this time, the need was entirely her own. His arm tightened around her waist and her arms snaked around his neck.

It had caught him off guard. Weakened as he was, heartsore, emotions running rampant, Jareth was unprepared to handle the onslaught the awakening land thrust upon him. And when Kevla had touched him and he saw her eyes widen, he knew that she was feeling the same overpowering sensations as he.

He had been so empty, but now he felt like a chalice filled to overflowing. He saw the rush of need, of *life,* in Kevla's soft brown eyes, and in a moment beyond thought he had pulled her to him.

She smelled of smoke and tasted of honey, and Jareth kissed her with a hunger that was knife-sharp. She was hot and supple in his arms, and he wanted to feel that long, lithe body against his. She tangled her fingers in his hair and tugged, and the slight twinge of pain only aroused him further.

The world had gone away for Kevla. Her senses were filled with this man, his taste, his touch, his scent of pine and loam, and all she wanted was to bring him closer, closer. At this moment she was so filled with desire that she knew it would not take much to—

She started and broke the kiss, pulling away slightly as memory and knowledge penetrated the red haze of passion roused by the life-filled earth.

She could not permit him to touch her like this, to give her body such pleasure. Could not permit *any* man to do so, for it would mean his death—

"I'm sorry," he said.

She blinked at him, breathing heavily, still dazed from the kiss. "I—" she began.

"I'm so sorry, Kevla. That should never have happened." The strong arms that had clasped her so close were now firmly pushing her away. Jareth swallowed hard. He didn't meet her eyes. She saw that he was shaking and a thin sheen of sweat covered his chest. "I didn't expect—I've done this before—felt something similar to this before—but it's never been like this."

"It's all right," said Kevla, quickly moving to sit away from him and compose herself. "I felt it too, when I put my hand on yours."

"What I did was completely inappropriate and I hope you'll forgive me." He still did not look at her, and his face was pink.

"Of course. It was just the power of the earth coming through you, and then me, when I touched you."

"Exactly." He seemed relieved. "It won't happen again."

To her surprise, Kevla felt regret at the words. She knew that the feeling she had experienced was powerful, but she also knew that it had exposed a truth she had not seen before—that she cared for Jareth beyond what might be expected from their shared nature as Dancers. But of course, he didn't. She had never met a man who exuded less desire for companionship than Jareth. He was still grieving for his wife, and besides, it would probably be a very bad idea for them to form any deeper attachment.

"It's over and forgotten," she said.

Jareth was mortified by what had happened. Kevla had only tried to help him by joining their powers, which had been an excellent idea. The snow that would have meant flooding all over the land was now evaporating around them as harmless mist, thanks to the union of Earth and Fire magics. He had taken advantage of her, pulling her to him like that.

And why in the world had he done it? He was quick to blame the flood of feeling that had swept over him for his actions, and truthfully, it had been staggering. But Jareth knew in his heart that he would not have felt compelled to pull another woman, say, Mylikki, into his arms in such a crude, lustful fashion. No, he was attracted to Kevla, and had been from the moment they had met. He had grown to admire her courage, her compassion and steadfastness; her soft strength that was steel—or blazing fire—when needed. And of course, the fact that she had an exquisite face and a supple, strong body didn't help his restraint.

He cleared his throat, and looked around. His embarrassment shifted into a deep contentment as he beheld what he—no, he amended, what *they*—had wrought.

As if reading his thoughts, Kevla said softly, "Spring. It's finally spring."

They were both silent for a moment, taking in the change. Where before there had been an unrelieved blanket of white, now there was a riot of color. Green grasses, trees dotted with whispering leaves or bright white, pink or yellow blossoms, flowers of every color dancing in the newly formed meadows. He closed his eyes and inhaled as a soft, balmy breeze, redolent with scent, stirred his hair. In the distance, they heard the joyful whoops of delight from the Ice Maiden's former slaves.

His pleasure faded somewhat. "Oh, Kevla," he sighed. "It is spring, and that's a blessing to this poor land. But there's so much more I need to do. There's no grain for seeding the crops this year—people ate what stores they had just to survive. A whole generation of animals has died. Many, many trees simply couldn't hang on long enough to reach this moment. I can feel their deaths, throughout the entire land."

She didn't answer, and he got up the courage to turn to look at her. Her expression was guarded, wary. She had heard his words: *There's so much more I need to do.*

He had no doubt but that if he stayed, he could do a great deal to help the battered land recover. He could make sure that what trees still survived were strong. That the creatures made it through this madness of the Ice Maiden— no, put the blame where it truly lay, of the Emperor—grew healthy and bore many young. That come autumn, there would be a harvest almost as bountiful as there was in years before.

But he could do none of these things, because he had made his choice.

"Do not worry, Kevla," he said softly. "Though my heart breaks to say this, I will not stay in Lamal. I will come with you. We will find the other Dancers, somehow defeat this Emperor, and stand together against the Shadow."

It was like watching the sun come out from behind a cloud, he thought, as the apprehension vanished from her face. She rewarded him with a radiant smile that he suddenly realized he wanted to see much more often.

"We have much to do," Kevla said, getting to her feet. "We need to explain what has happened to the men, find the Dragon and the Tiger, and say goodbye to Mylikki and Altan." Jareth smothered a smile. She was absolutely filthy, as, he supposed, was he. Her *rhia* was torn and caked with mud, and there was a large brown patch on her back.

Where I clasped her to me, he thought, his mirth fading. He would have given a great deal to recover that moment, to have not yielded to desire. Now the memory would hang between them, no matter what she said about understanding the reason.

"There's something you should try," Kevla said. "Close your eyes and reach out to the Tiger. I can talk to the Dragon in my mind, and you can probably do the same with your Companion."

"We have already done so, but not at a distance," Jareth said. Obediently, he closed his eyes.

Tiger?

The Dragon and I are here.

Where is here?

Where is there? replied the Tiger. Jareth laughed aloud. *Do not worry,* the Tiger continued, *we will find you. Stay where you are and the Dragon and I will be there soon.*

The taaskali... *Did they...*

They have returned to their true forms. They once again bless and hold the land as the earth's spirits.

Jareth was relieved and almost giddily happy. Perhaps too, that was why his calling spring had been so powerful. Never before had he worked with the aid of the forest and waters spirits, for not for a thousand years had they been part of the land.

Are Mylikki and Altan with you? asked the Tiger.

Jareth felt a spark of worry. *No. Did they enter the circle after all?*

Indeed they did. But you have defeated the Maiden, for we see that spring has returned to the land. We will find them, I am certain.

Jareth opened his eyes. "Altan and Mylikki—"

"Entered the circle, even though they promised they wouldn't," Kevla finished. "The Dragon told me. He seems to think they reappeared back in Lamal, as we did. They will be safe enough, I think." She hesitated. "Would you like to ask them to come with us? It might be pleasant for you to travel with such a good friend."

"I'm not sure. Let me think about it. It's a dangerous quest we're undertaking. But you're right—I would miss them, were they not with us."

He hesitated. "The Tiger told me to wait for them, and frankly, that's just fine with me. I am in no hurry to rush anywhere."

"Nor am I. A good meal and some sleep would suit me well." She brushed at the drying mud on her *rhia*. "Nor would a bath go amiss, I think."

For some reason, Jareth was reluctant to let the moment go. Soon, they would have to explain what had happened to strangers, to assess what they needed to do to complete their journey. He was comfortable here with Kevla, just the two of them on the living earth.

And there was something else the Ice Maiden had said that he needed to investigate. He did not wish to venture into that dark place alone. He wiped his muddy hands on his breeches, cleaning them as best he could, reached into his pouch, and took a deep breath. It was time to reveal his secrets to her.

"In this pouch, I have several items that have special significance to me. I can—I can talk to things of the earth, Kevla. And they can talk to me. They can tell me what has happened to and around them."

Kevla looked down, and he saw she was blushing. "I know," she said, quietly. "I have heard you, at night."

Commingled anger and embarrassment rushed through him. "You spied on me?"

"I didn't mean to," she said. "I just—at first, I couldn't understand them. But after a few nights, I was able to comprehend their...language, I suppose. I guess it's because I'm a Dancer. I can't make them talk to me, but when they talk to you, I understand it. Like when I first arrived in Lamal. I understood the language right away, but it was some time before I could speak it."

His face was hot. "So you know...?"

She took a breath and faced him. "Everything, I'm afraid."

"I see. So, when were you planning on telling me this?"

A smile tugged at her full lips. "When you decided to tell me about them. Like right now."

Jareth sighed. First the unintended kiss, and now this. He felt exposed and vulnerable to this woman. "This was not how I would have had you learn these things about me."

"I know, and I'm sorry. But I'm glad I knew."

And suddenly, oddly, he was glad she knew, too. "One of the items is some earth from the floor of...of my house." He withdrew the precious soil and cupped it in his hands. "The Ice Maiden swore that she had no hand in the deaths of my family. The earth will be able to tell me what really happened that night."

She looked at him, worried. "You have never asked it this before?"

He shook his head. "I thought I knew what had happened. I saw no need to ask. And when I spoke with the earth...I wanted to recall happier moments in my home."

"Are you sure you would not rather wait for the Tiger?"

"No. I want to know now."

Kevla nodded, but she still looked apprehensive. Jareth dropped his gaze to the cupped soil in his palm, running his thumb over it.

Aware that his voice trembled, he voiced the request. "Tell me what happened to my wife and children, on the night of their deaths."

And the earth responded.

Earth am I, soil and sand, ever-changing and ever the same. I am the flesh that was once living things, and the anchor to the roots of the trees and grass and all growing things. Earth am I, and I shall speak.

It was a bitter night, with winds and snow swirling about the timbers and stones that arched over me. But inside, it was warm and the steps that trod upon me were at peace. The door opened on that cold night, and the musical one entered, bearing sweet drink to warm the bodies and chase away the fears of the frozen night outside.

He was welcomed and the honey drink was sipped. Quickly, quickly asleep they fell, the woman and the girl, more quickly than the honey drink could have acted. Opened the door and window then did the singing one, fair of hair and smile, and quickly came the wind and snow inside. The sleepers never woke, but dreamed dreams of soft snow and warm darkness. Peaceful was their passing. He found them thus, Spring-Bringer, Stone Dancer, their skins as hard and white as if carved of ice, and he—

Blood thundered in Jareth's ears. He fell forward to his hands and knees, gasping, trying not to vomit the bile that threatened to choke him.

Altan had done this? Altan, whom he had brought into this world, had drugged his wife and daughter, and then opened the doors so they would freeze to death?

Why?

"Jareth, I am so sorry." Kevla's voice, warm and concerned, floated to him. But he did not hear it, did not want to hear it. He slammed his hands hard into the earth, digging deep with fingers that were stiff with a burning need for vengeance.

"I demand of the earth beneath Altan's feet—*tell me where he is!*"

He felt the earth recoil from the violence of his onslaught upon it. He knew he was not meant to use his powers so, but he did not care. He gritted his teeth and forced his fingers deeper, assaulting the land, ripping from it the information he wanted, needed to know.

He runs upon me now, came the distant, floating voice of the earth a few miles away. *His feet fall in terror.*

Show me. Again, the earth quailed from his attack.

"Jareth, what are you doing?"

He ignored her. *Show me!* Jareth demanded. He was hurting the earth now. Finally, it gave him an image. His eyes opened and his head whipped around.

There. Altan was there.

Earth, trip him. Open beneath his feet. Trees, hold him in your branches. Hold him until I come.

Jareth leaped up. Again, Kevla cried for him to stop. He heard her get to her feet, start to run after him. But he would outpace her. With each footfall, he called more power, more speed, from the earth, twisting it to serve him.

If the words had come from human lips, he would have given them no credence. But as he had told Mylikki, nothing of the earth can lie.

Altan, not the Ice Maiden or the Emperor, had murdered Jareth's family.

38

Ilta ran.

It was all going so well. She had taken care of the troublesome Mylikki, the one person in the world that Altan would fight for. She had manifested in the realm of the Emperor, nominally that of the Ice Maiden, in the body of the woman she had been born to be. The Maiden was going to hold Fire forever captive in her icy realm. And then something had gone horribly wrong.

Warm inside despite the falling snow, Ilta had walked to within sight of the Ice Maiden's castle. Here, the Emperor had told her via the twinkling, dancing lights in the sky, Ilta would find Jareth. He would be hers, as he had been before. And then, with that goal in sight, Ilta had felt the very earth tremble beneath her. The snow had begun to melt with a shocking suddenness, and she felt her body start to change.

"No!" she screamed, struggling to hang on to this exciting new, lush female form, with its graceful curves, its softness, its fullness.

"No!" To her horror, her voice had dropped and was once again the pleasant tenor of her twin. She looked at her hands, the slim fingers growing larger, watched with sick helplessness as her chest broadened and grew flat and hard.

But Altan was still trapped somewhere inside her, and Ilta retained her sense of self.

It had all been ruined. She could guess at what had happened. Jareth and the Flame Dancer had managed to destroy the Ice Maiden and with her, her realm. Now Ilta, trapped in her twin's masculine body, was back in Lamal.

She breathed shallow, rapid breaths as the panic set in. Ilta knew she couldn't continue masquerading as Altan. She had endured it for years, but now having tasted what it was like to finally walk in a woman's body, she could no longer live in this stolen one. She had to escape Lamal, had to contact the Emperor. He would take care of her, change her back somehow. And then they could try again to find Jareth.

In the meantime, she needed to flee.

She didn't know where to go. She just set off running.

She hadn't gone far at all before the trees reached out and grabbed her.

Dragon!

Kevla didn't have time to form words about what had just transpired. She simply squeezed her eyes shut and the Dragon heard her thoughts.

The Tiger sensed it at once, the Dragon reassured her. *She is trying to intercept Jareth. I am coming to you as quickly as my wings will take me, and you know that is swift indeed.*

Kevla nodded, although the Dragon could not see the gesture. She was shivering, although the weather was now warm and she had never felt cold to begin with. She was shivering because of what she had just learned, and the terrifying manner in which Jareth had reacted to it. She still couldn't believe that Altan was a murderer. He seemed so sweet, so gentle. Not the sort of person one could easily visualize walking into a house, offering drugged alcohol to people who were all but family, and then callously opening the doors onto a deadly winter's night.

But she knew that the earth had not lied. It had been an awful revelation, and the violence of Jareth's response had alarmed her. She did not know the intricacies of his talents as the Stone Dancer, but she did know that what he had done had caused pain to the earth. He had forced it to do something that hurt it, and she knew that was wrong.

What troubles me the most is the hatred that is in Jareth's heart, came the Dragon's thoughts, echoing Kevla's own. *He has captured Altan and plans to exact revenge upon him. He will kill the boy if we do not stop him, and that will destroy everything. It will render Jareth incapable of carrying out his duties as the Stone Dancer, and he will fall to the Shadow.*

I don't understand, thought Kevla. *I have certainly taken lives.*

It is what is in the heart that matters, said the Dragon. *You fought only to protect your country, to save the lives of innocent people. And never did you feel any joy in doing so.*

No, Kevla agreed. *I hated having to use my powers to kill. But Jareth won't. He is filled with rage and grief, and he will exult in torturing and killing Altan. It will be as sweet as honey to him, and that delight in murder will change him forever. Jareth will be lost if he takes Altan's life. Dancers must face the Shadow with a good and open heart, or the Shadow will triumph. Once before, a world fell because of a Dancer's darkness. We cannot let that happen again, not this time.*

Kevla buried her face in her hands. She had tried chasing after Jareth for a few steps, but it became obvious that he was running with more than human speed and he outdistanced her quickly. Their only hope was if the Tiger reached Jareth in time to prevent him from becoming as ruthless a murderer as the man he longed to kill.

Jareth knew his feet ought to be sliding on the wet grass, or getting sucked down in the mud. But the earth did not hamper his flight, and his heart and lungs pumped more steadily than ever before in his life.

Images filled his mind: Altan sitting and playing beside the fire. Annu looking up at the boy with shy admiration. Parvan gurgling happily at the silvery sounds of the *kyndela.* Taya humming as she mended clothes or wove new ones. Jareth had given Altan a place in his home, in his heart, and his family had died because of that terribly misplaced affection.

He realized with a sinking sense of helpless horror that there had been signs: Altan's cutting remarks that seemingly came out of nowhere, his strange, black moods. But Jareth had loved the boy, and had paid no attention to Altan's odd behavior, and the people he loved most in the world had paid the price for it.

The trees had captured Altan. He sensed it. They had obeyed his commands like faithful dogs, and were now holding the deceiver, the betrayer, the *murderer* with a strength no human could hope to defeat.

The miles fell beneath his running feet, each step bringing him closer to his revenge. He knew exactly where he was headed. At last, he slowed, catching his breath, and walked the last few steps into a clearing.

The trees had not been kind in their capture. Their branches looked like deformed hands and they grasped Altan's arms tightly. One of the boy's arms was jerked backward at a painful-looking angle and he wept quietly. He had lost his footing and hung suspended by his arms, his knees bent and toes scrabbling for purchase. Hatred washed over Jareth, hot and vital and pure.

"You killed my family," Jareth spat, stepping into Altan's view.

Altan gasped and started up, crying out as the movement made him twist his arm.

"Jareth!"

Jareth raised a hand, curled it into a fist, and slammed it into Altan's face. With visceral satisfaction, he felt the boy's nose crunch beneath the blow.

Altan shrieked. Blood and mucous flowed down his face as he sobbed.

"I brought you into the world," Jareth snarled, pacing up and down in front of the bound youth. "I wish I'd drowned you in the lake instead, you son of a—"

He turned and was about to strike Altan again when something strange happened. Altan's face…*shimmered*. His features blurred and reformed for just an instant. The mouth coated in blood was smaller, fuller; the eyes, larger and more widely spaced.

Slowly, Jareth drew his fist back.

"Stone Dancer, can you see me?" Jareth stared. The voice was female! "Stone Dancer, I've waited so long for this moment—"

"Altan, what are you—"

"Don't call me that!" It was an anguished shriek, and it was definitely feminine. "I'm not Altan, I'm Ilta, Jareth—Ilta! *I'm your Lorekeeper!*"

Jareth staggered back, hardly able to breathe. Ilta? Altan's stillborn twin sister? The boy was going mad. And how dare he claim to be Jareth's—

But the face kept shifting back and forth from male to female, and now it seemed as though the body was trying to follow suit. Altan's slim boy's build filled out for just a brief instant, with a tiny waist and full breasts—

"Don't you remember, my love?" Altan's—Ilta's—voice was raw and pleading. She—he—writhed in the implacable grip of the tree branches. "Through four lifetimes we were together. We were everything to each other. Not always in love, no, but loving, devoted to one another. Try to remember, please, please try!"

Was *this* his Lorekeeper? The missing third of the trinity? It couldn't be!

Even as he rejected the idea Jareth realized he had to know. Had to know if this mad babbling was the truth. He took a deep breath and turned his thoughts inward.

There was no breeze; the water's surface was as smooth as glass. Somehow, Jareth knew that it shouldn't be; that there should always be waves coming to the shore. The Shadow. The Shadow was coming. Somewhere, a Dancer had died, and with his or her death would come the death of everything.

"What will it feel like?" she whispered. For in this life, Jareth was a woman; a girl in her late teens, with long black hair and dark skin.

"I don't know," her Lorekeeper admitted. A man, older than the Stone Dancer, with graying hair and somber eyes. "I do not remember. The Lorekeepers remember much, but not that; not even what form the Shadow has taken each time."

"Will it hurt?" the Stone Dancer continued. "To be...erased... or will we feel nothing?"

She felt the kiss on her shoulder. "It won't hurt. You won't feel a thing." A pause, then, "I love you."

The Stone Dancer felt his hands on either side of her face and just before the Lorekeeper did the deed, the Stone Dancer felt those fingers tighten. Her eyes flew wide, she opened her mouth to scream no, no, don't kill me, *and then—*

Jareth had ceased breathing and now pulled air into his lungs in a choking gasp. This was the recurring dream he had started having in his youth, and now he knew it was no dream, but a memory. A memory of his past life—and death—as a young woman whose lover, whose trusted Lorekeeper—

"You...you killed me," he whispered.

Altan's face was now again that of a young man. It shone with joy. "You remember!" he cried, in Altan's voice.

"You killed me!" Jareth repeated, more strongly. "You killed me, you killed my family—how many deaths are on your head?"

Tears filled Altan's eyes. "You don't understand! We were supposed to be together! Taya, Annu, Parvan—they were keeping you from me. Keeping you from your destiny. I died—the cord was around my neck—but I refused to give up. So I merged with Altan. Two souls in one body. But I've won. Altan's gone and this body is now mine, and I'm not giving it up. All we need to do is get to the Emperor and I'm sure he can—"

"The Emperor? Does your treachery know no bounds?" A sudden thought struck him. "Where's Mylikki?"

Altan made a dismissive face. "I tied her to a tree in the Ice Maiden's realm. I don't know where she is or if she's alive and don't you see, *none of that matters!*"

The face and body shifted again, back to those of a female. "I love you, Stone Dancer! I am your Lorekeeper. Whatever I've done has been because of you, to keep you safe, to keep you with me. Surely you can see that. There's nothing now that stands in our way!"

"You broke your Dancer's neck," Jareth grated. There was no sanity in the Lorekeeper's words. The memory of that deed, combined with the horror of having to live trapped inside a body that was not her own, had clearly driven Ilta mad.

"You drugged and murdered three innocent people. More, if Mylikki isn't still alive. I could never love you, Lorekeeper or no. The Ice Maiden, false construct that she was, had a warmer heart than you. At least she acted out of ignorance."

He stepped forward and placed his hands on either side of Altan/Ilta's face. A wave of pain swept over him.

"Altan? Are you—can you hear me?" The Altan Jareth had loved as a brother was the greatest victim of Ilta's madness. It had been Altan's body that had done the deed, but Ilta was the murderer. If he could still be reached somehow—

"Stop calling me that!" shrieked the Lorekeeper. "He's gone, he's gone forever. I've taken care of that. There's only us now, Jareth. You and I, Lorekeeper and Dancer. We can finally be together as we were meant to be!"

"You're insane," he whispered. "It drove you mad, didn't it? Killing me?"

"That's what the *selva* told me, too," cried Ilta, "last night. When they took us away to give us the dreams, she said I wasn't well, that guilt had stolen my mind. That I needed to turn from my path before it was too late, or something like that. But she was wrong. I'm not crazy. I don't feel guilty. It was what I had to do, you should understand, you should understand everything—"

His Lorekeeper, his soul, looked up at Jareth, pleading. It was time. He didn't need to learn anything more from this demented monster masquerading as a boy.

Goodbye, Altan. I'm sorry. I know you'd want me to stop her before she harms anyone else. And she will. She will.

"No, my love, don't, please don't—"

Jareth leaned close and whispered in his Lorekeeper's ear. "You thought I didn't feel anything when you snapped my neck," he whispered, almost as if imparting endearments. "You were wrong."

His fingers tightened.

STONE DANCER!

The unheard voice shuddered along Jareth's bones and hurled him backward. He landed hard, the wind knocked out of him for an instant. Seemingly out of nowhere, a giant blue form sprang upon him.

Jareth growled and buried his hands in the ruff of blue and white fur, muscles quivering with the effort to force the blue Tiger off of him.

She killed my family! She has perverted everything about being a Lorekeeper! She's betrayed us both, Tiger!

You will not harm her!

Jareth began to scream incoherently. He fought against the Tiger, but he was mentally and physically exhausted and the enormous beast was far too strong for him. Jareth's back was flat against the earth. He felt it, almost like a heart beating against his skin. He tried to send a command to the trees who held Altan prisoner, to tell them to rip him apart, but the Tiger's blows distracted him and he was unable to concentrate.

Suddenly there was an eruption of fire. The trees holding Altan prisoner shuddered in pain, and Jareth felt it. He cried out, first with the pain of the fire, and then with the anguish of knowing that Ilta had escaped, that she would not have to pay for the evils she had done.

Suddenly the pressure that held him down was gone. Jareth struggled to get to hands and knees and tried to dig his fingers into the soil. A mighty cuff from the Tiger's paw sent him reeling. Again he tried, and again the Tiger slapped him down.

Jareth lay in the mud, gasping for breath, the rage bleeding out of him leaving only ashy emptiness in its stead. He could feel Ilta's footfalls growing fainter. She was making good her escape.

A shadow fell over him. "Jareth?" Kevla's voice was filled with concern.

Blinking the mud out of his eyes, Jareth looked up. "Mylikki," he muttered. "Altan...Ilta...took Mylikki."

"I will find her," the Dragon said quickly. "Stay with him, Kevla."

Jareth let his head fall back into the mud and closed his eyes.

Kevla and the Tiger regarded Jareth. He was filthy. His body, now strong and healthy thanks to the rejuvenating power of the earth surging into him, was covered with mud. Seeing him sprawled in the mud, broken and gasping for air, was like seeing a mighty *simmar* brought low.

The Tiger spoke in a soft voice. "I blame myself. I did not know—I could not sense it...."

"Sense what?"

The Tiger sighed. "The body of Altan housed two souls— Altan's, and that of the sister who died in the womb. The sister, Ilta, was Jareth's Lorekeeper. His soul. It was she who killed Jareth's family, using Altan's body."

The words horrified Kevla. "His own Lorekeeper did this?" she whispered.

The Tiger nodded her blue head. "She was in league with the Emperor, who had promised her Jareth. Poor Altan knew nothing of any of this."

"It all makes sense now," Kevla said quietly. "Altan's dark moods and unkind words to Mylikki... It wasn't Altan doing or saying those things at all, was it? It was Ilta."

"His Lorekeeper. His soul. I should have known something was wrong when neither Jareth nor I could sense her. In the same way the Emperor was able to use the Maiden to block Jareth's powers, he hid Ilta from our sensing. The *selva* knew, when they were in their animal form."

"Why didn't they tell us when Jareth restored them?"

"When the Lorekeepers were *selva*, they were under an enchantment. When Jareth freed them from that enchantment, they remembered nothing of what transpired while they were under the spell. The Emperor is a very clever and dangerous enemy."

Kevla's shock at beholding Jareth brought so low was fading, replaced by a deep compassion. She had been the death of her own Lorekeeper, and while the pain had been mitigated, it would never go away entirely. She would bear that scar forever. But Jashemi had never, would never, have betrayed her in this manner. And she had to wonder—if Jareth's soul was so dark, so twisted...what would that eventually mean for the Stone Dancer?

Slowly, Jareth tried to sit up. The Tiger, who had been sitting quietly beside him, got to her feet expectantly. Jareth shot her a hostile look, and the Tiger flicked an ear.

"Kevla, stay with him if you would." The Tiger's voice was tinged with sorrow. "I doubt if he would appreciate my company now."

I doubt he'll appreciate mine, Kevla thought, but she nodded. The Tiger walked away, moving with the graceful, undulating gait common to all cats, small, large, or Companions.

Jareth buried his face in his hands. Kevla sat quietly beside him.

Finally, Jareth spoke. "You heard," he said dully.

Kevla nodded, gnawing her lower lip. "Yes. I heard."

He fell silent again. "All this time, I thought it was my fault," he said after a long pause. "That if I had been able to bring spring, they would be alive. Taya, my Taya, my beautiful girl Annu. And my little boy, just a few weeks old."

His eyes started to glisten as they stared into the distance, seeing something that wasn't there. Kevla tensed.

"I adored that woman," he said in a thick voice. "She was...great-hearted. And wise. Taya knew exactly how to handle me. And the last time I saw her, I—*gods!*"

The word was ripped from him, raw and broken and bleeding with pain. "I said things to her that I never—I didn't mean them, I didn't mean them at all, I was just hurt and frustrated and angry and so helpless...but that was the last thing I said to her. I never got to tell her I was sorry. I never got to hold her one last time, to tell her how very much I—"

The tears welled up in his eyes, spilled forth. To Kevla's horror, she saw that they did not trickle steadily down his cheeks, but got lost in the wrinkles around his eyes. *He has never wept for his family...and it has been so long, the tears don't even know where to go—*

For the third time, Kevla folded Jareth into her arms. His physical survival was not at stake, nor was she carried away by the passion a wildly awakening earth had sent racing through her. She was filled with soft, quiet, deep compassion, and a strong need to do what she could to ease the hurt.

She had a brief flash of memory—she and Jashemi stealing precious time alone in the caverns at the House of Four Waters. He was home from his first battle, sick with the poison of the horrors of war and the painful loss of his own innocence. She had gone to him then, despite her fear of impropriety, taking all the hurt and shock and angry grief into her soft, healing flesh, and now she went to Jareth with the same wide-open heart.

She eased his head down against her breast and enfolded his large frame as best she could. He clutched her desperately, and he shook with sobs.

"Taya, Taya, my sweet Annu, Parvan, Altan... Forgive me. I'm so sorry. I'm so sorry."

Jareth's hot, healing tears were wet against her skin. Kevla ran her fingers gently through his muddy, tangled hair and murmured soft words that had no meaning, yet meant everything.

Weep, she urged him in her mind, her own eyes filling with empathetic tears. *Weep, and be healed.*

And when at last Jareth's grief had run its course, Kevla held him to her as they eased onto the soft, welcoming earth, and he fell asleep in the warm circle of her arms.

39

Kevla awoke to the sound of a bird's song. It was sweet, musical, merry, and she felt a smile stretch her face. *It is almost as sweet as Altan's and Mylikki's voices*, she thought sleepily. The smile faded as memory came back to her.

She sat up and discovered she was leaning against the warm strength of the slumbering Dragon. The trees rustled in a soft breeze. Spring had come again to the land, but the pleasure she felt in its coming had been tempered by the revelations about Altan and Ilta.

Kevla got to her feet, wincing. She had slipped on the ice many times yesterday and her body had not forgotten. She stepped around the Dragon's large, red side, to where his head rested. There, she smiled, relieved. Snuggled tightly against the Dragon's cheek, sound asleep, was Mylikki.

Kevla moved carefully so as not to awaken the slumbering girl. There was plenty of time to ask her what had happened later, and to give her some good, solid food.

But where was Jareth? Sudden panic flowed through her. She had held him while he wept for the deaths of his family, something he had not done since the tragedy, and she had a dim memory of falling asleep, their limbs tangled together. But now he was nowhere to be found, nor was the Tiger.

She wanted to call for him, but dreaded waking Mylikki. Even awakening the Dragon might disturb the girl, nestled against his cheek as she was.

Kevla decided she would scout around. The earth was still soft from the melting snows, and it was not difficult for her to pick up tracks of both man and giant cat. She followed them as they led her out of the meadow and into the fringes of the forest. She heard a strange sound, a sort of soft roaring, and quickened her pace as she moved toward the noise.

She came upon the little spring so suddenly she almost fell into it. This, then, was the sound—water rushing from a higher point over stones and into a small pool. Quickly, Kevla stepped back into the shadows of the tree.

Jareth was bathing in the icy coldness of the spring. He had rinsed his clothes, stiff with the mud and blood and sweat from months of wear, and they were drying on a broad, flat rock. His back was to her, and she saw that he was using his knife to trim his long, wild hair.

She was intruding on a private moment. She knew she should draw back, and yet she lingered, watching the play of muscle in his back and arms, his skin so pale in the dappled sunlight. Kevla had always admired the many statues that decorated the lavish garden of the House of Four Waters. Jareth could have posed for such statues, and Kevla simply found herself unable to look away from such a combination of beauty and strength.

A low rumble greeted her ears and she dragged her eyes away from Jareth to see the Tiger regarding her steadily. She was lounging on a rock, a cat enjoying the sun, and she looked at Kevla with a knowing gaze. Kevla blushed, and as she turned to hasten away, she thought she saw the great Tiger wink.

Jareth completed his ablutions and climbed atop a sun-warmed rock. The water's iciness was cleansing and refreshing, but he welcomed the warmth of the stone against his skin. He turned his face up to the sun, letting its rays caress him, and thought about Ilta. Somehow he knew it wasn't over between them. One day, they would meet again, and he had no idea how he would react upon seeing the Lorekeeper who had done such evil things. But at least that day was not today.

He reached for the pouch that lay atop his drying clothes and opened it. One by one he removed the items, laying them out in a row.

He picked up the small packet of precious soil, emptying it into his palm, and let it speak to him one last time.

Earth am I, soil and sand, ever-changing and ever the same....

He listened to it narrate how he had first become the Spring-Bringer, then, taking a deep breath, turned over his hand, opened his fingers, and let the dirt fall into the water.

Other items followed; a stone, a leaf, the handful of dirt from the floor of his home that had so recently imparted such dreadful tidings. At last, there was only one item left. As he held it gently, its withered leaves and petals undulated and danced, reviving and brimming again with life.

Wildflower am I, stem and petal and leaf still here though torn from my roots, brief lived but beautiful....

Tears spilled down his cheeks as the flower spoke to him of love. He heaved no racking sobs, not this time; the tears came as naturally as summer rain or melting snow, and the pain, though deep, was also tinged with sweetness. He suspected this was not the last time he would weep for his lost family, and realized that it was all right.

He trailed the flower across his wet face as his wife had done years before. "Taya," Jareth said, aloud, as if the flower could carry the words to the one who needed to hear them, "I don't need this flower to remember you. I didn't want to believe you were gone, but you are. I have to face that. You and Annu and Parvan...."

A sudden memory came to him of a boy holding on to a white piece of fabric that glowed like the moon and smelled of summer. He had wanted to keep the blessing cloth for himself, but even then at the young age of thirteen, he had understood.

It just wasn't meant for keeping, he had told Larr. *I can't explain it any better than that.*

Nor could he explain it now. But he knew what he had to do. Ilta, the Ice Maiden—they had clung on to something long after it was time to let go. And they had caused so much damage, not least to themselves, in that struggle to hang on.

I had to let it go.

Jareth pressed the flower to his lips, then opened his fingers and watched it fall into the swiftly moving water. He followed it with his gaze as the current took it, swirling it around the jutting tops of stones and bearing it farther and farther away until his tear-filled eyes could no longer see it.

"Goodbye, my love," he whispered softly.

Mylikki and the Dragon were awake when Kevla returned. The girl had already finished skinning the hares that either the Tiger or the Dragon had caught to break their fasts, and looked up.

"There are wild herbs growing everywhere," Mylikki said. "We will have a feast."

She smiled, but Kevla saw past the brave expression to the hurt and almost unspeakable weariness in Mylikki's blue eyes. The girl had seemed so very young to Kevla when they first set out; now, she seemed to have aged years.

Kevla went to her and hugged her. Mylikki was stiff in her embrace at first, then returned the embrace. When Kevla drew back, both women had tears in their eyes.

"You are so brave, Mylikki," Kevla said.

Mylikki shook her head. "No, I don't think so."

The hares were fresh and cooked quickly, and both women were famished. They put some aside for Jareth, and ate hungrily.

A thought occurred to Kevla. "Dragon, what of the men? And the Lorekeepers?"

"We have been busy while you and Jareth...recovered," the Dragon said, phrasing things tactfully. "The men have no memories of their months with the Ice Maiden, and they all want to go home. The Lorekeepers, of course, have no homes. All the men of the various villages have offered their own to the Lorekeepers. Soon families will be reunited, and Lamal will finally have part of its history returned to it."

Kevla thought back to the surprise the Ice Maiden had expressed at the inherent decency of the human heart, male or female. But she was not at all surprised.

When they had finished eating, Kevla said to Mylikki, "Can you tell me what happened?"

Mylikki sighed. Then she nodded. "You should know," she said quietly. She spoke in a low voice of manifesting in the Ice Maiden's realm, of how Altan appeared to her as female. How he—she—had struck Mylikki, tied her to a tree, and left her there.

"She gave me something to drink that would drug me, so I wouldn't feel the cold," Mylikki said. Meeting Kevla's eyes, she said with pride, "I didn't drink it."

Kevla thought of what the earth had said to Jareth. Ilta had drugged Taya and Annu before opening the windows and doors so they would freeze to death. A shiver ran down her spine as she realized how narrowly Mylikki had escaped.

"I'm so sorry for what you've been through," she said.

Mylikki shrugged. "There's one thing that I hold on to, through all of this madness," she said. "And that's the fact that Altan loved me. Ilta said so. That's why she had to kill me. Because Altan would have fought her to stay with me—"

Tears started in her eyes but she angrily wiped them away. "What happened to Altan? Do you know?"

Kevla shook her head. "No. We only know that Ilta is in control of his body. Whether he's dead or just...trapped somewhere inside, I do not know." She hesitated, then said, "Mylikki, would you like to come with us?"

Mylikki shook her head. "No," she said. "There's much for me to do here. I'd like to help the Lorekeepers find their new homes, help the men find their families."

Kevla now realized why the Lorekeepers in their *selva* forms had not chosen Mylikki that night that seemed so long ago now. The *selva* had selected Kevla and Jareth because they were Dancers, and Altan because his body housed Ilta, Jareth's Lorekeeper. Beautiful and special as she was, Mylikki was merely a human, and they did not need to speak with her. She wondered what they had told Ilta.

"I don't think I'm cut out for adventures, Kevla. I think I'll be happiest in my own little village, singing about adventures by a fireside instead of living them."

"I will miss you," Kevla said honestly, "but I understand. I do not think I would be on this…adventure…if I did not need to be."

"The Lorekeepers and the Maiden's former captives will appreciate your presence, Mylikki," the Dragon said. "You are kind to think of them. It will not be a long journey, as a Dragon flies. Whenever you are ready, I will bear you to them."

"Now, I think," said Mylikki, startling Kevla. Both women got to their feet.

"Do you not want to say farewell to Jareth?" Kevla asked. She realized she was not ready for Mylikki to go.

"No," Mylikki said. "All I'd do is remind him of Altan. Goodbye, Kevla. There were…there were parts of all of this that were good."

Kevla hugged her tightly. "Goodbye, Mylikki. Please give my best to your family."

"I will." Mylikki climbed aboard the Dragon with ease and familiarity. Kevla was vividly reminded of the first time Mylikki had scrambled atop that broad, red back; how fearful she had been, and how much courage it had taken to conquer that fear.

As the Dragon gathered himself, Mylikki called down with a hint of a smile, "Good luck on your journey, Kevla. Rest assured that there will be songs sung about you here in Lamal!"

Kevla waved as the Dragon rose into the air, her hair and *rhia* blowing in the wind created by the beating of his enormous, leathery wings. She watched as the Dragon hovered for a moment, then elongated his neck and tail, banked to the right, and flew off into the distance.

For a moment, Kevla simply stood, thinking about all that had happened. So much, in so short a time. It was hard to believe it was all over, and the next "adventure," as Mylikki and Altan would have put it, would soon begin. Finally, sighing, she began to pack.

A soft brush of warm fur along her legs alerted her to the Tiger's presence. Smiling, she reached to scratch the ears of the big cat. She turned to greet Jareth, for she knew he would be with his Companion, but startlement stilled the friendly words.

Jareth was almost unrecognizable. His hair, cut now to shoulder length, and body had been scrubbed clean. His face was shaven, and for the first time Kevla saw the high cheekbones and strong jaw that had been hidden by his scraggly beard. His clothes were clean, if still damp and wrinkled, but most important, his eyes were clear and focused.

"There you are," she said, and he smiled a little. He could not know what she was really saying. For here he was indeed—the Stone Dancer with the blue Tiger at his feet, as she had seen him in her visions. As Jashemi had seen him. A man with a good face, a kind face with laugh lines around the eyes and mouth, but who had clearly been through a great deal. This was the man she had imagined meeting, when she first entered this northerly realm. This was the man to whom she had thought to hand over her burdens.

Now she realized that while Jareth had accepted his destiny, there were some burdens he wasn't supposed to carry, that were still hers and always would be. But for the first time, the thought didn't distress her. Kevla knew that both she and Jareth Vasalen would be able to endure whatever they needed to. Fire and Earth, Flame and Stone. Strong and powerful; battered, both of them, but not broken.

As she gazed at him, she realized how dirty she herself was. "I think I need to clean up a bit, too," she said.

"There's a spring right over there," Jareth said, reaching for the cooling haunch of rabbit they had saved for him. "Where's Mylikki?"

"The Dragon is taking her to help the men and the Lorekeepers," Kevla said. "She didn't want to come with us."

A shadow passed over Jareth's features. "I don't suppose she would," he said. "She's been through a great deal. If I could stay, I would."

"As would I," Kevla said. "The Dragon will not be long. I am aching for a bath."

Kevla relished the feel of the water against her skin as she bathed. She had not realized she was quite so dirty. Little half-moons of grime were caked under her finger- and toenails, and she scrubbed at them diligently until her skin finally felt clean, if rubbed slightly raw in the process. She spied a cut piece of some kind of root lying on a rock, and when she picked it up, it lathered in her hand. Jareth had obviously used this for soap, and she eagerly did the same. She washed her long, thick hair, until it gleamed in the sunlight, and braided it while it was still wet. Emerging from the spring, she conjured fire in her palm, and from it wove a fresh red *rhia*.

When she returned, Jareth had finished packing for them. The Tiger was curled up, nose to tail, sleeping. Jareth's eyebrows rose in appreciation as he regarded Kevla. She smiled, suddenly a bit shy.

"Well," he said, jokingly, "you clean up nicely."

"Thank you. I could say the same."

His smile faded. "Kevla," he said, looking away, "I want to thank you. For everything. You've been...well. I can only hope you haven't been too disappointed in your Stone Dancer."

She went to him, and moved so she was looking him right in his blue eyes. "I'm not disappointed at all."

"I wanted to tell you," said Jareth, "that I don't have the...the items any more. The ones I would listen to at night. I gave them back to the earth."

Admiration flooded Kevla. "That must have been difficult," she said.

"Yes...and no. I need to make my own peace with what happened. Reliving everything every single night...it didn't help. I have the memories here," and he put his hand to his heart. "That needs to be enough."

"I'm very proud of you. That took courage, Jareth."

For a long moment, they gazed at one another. Jareth took a step closer to her, his eyes never leaving her face.

"Kevla," Jareth said, softly, "I—"

The familiar sound of the Dragon's wings interrupted him. The Tiger lifted her massive head, yawned, revealing a pink tongue and sharp white teeth, and stretched.

"How is Mylikki?" Jareth asked of the Dragon.

"She was welcomed and is in good company," the Dragon said. "Her brother was there of course—and their father as well. He, too, had fallen under the Ice Maiden's spell. Gelsan will be delighted to have her family whole again."

"That is wonderful news!" said Kevla. "If only Altan..." Her voice trailed off.

"Yes," said Jareth heavily. "If only."

"There was one thing I was curious about," Kevla said, trying to change the subject. "You were in the Ice Maiden's very hall, and yet you never succumbed to her supposedly irresistible powers. Why not?"

Jareth shrugged. "I'm not sure. Maybe because I'm a Dancer, and we have the ability to resist her. Or maybe... maybe because at that moment, there was nothing she could turn cold, because I'd already done it myself."

Kevla was surprised at the brutal honesty of Jareth's self-assessment. And she supposed it was true. The man before her was nothing like the man who had stood, coldly raging, in the Ice Maiden's hall. And she was so glad of the change.

"Where to now?" she asked the Dragon and the Tiger.

"Why don't you two find out?" the Tiger replied.

Kevla looked at Jareth, and extended her hands. Slowly, awkwardly, he took them. Kevla braced herself for the rush of sensation that she had experienced before when they had deliberately joined their powers, but now she only felt a calm clarity. She closed her eyes, and they experienced the vision together.

A girl, standing beside a body of water so vast that Kevla could not even see where it ended. It stretched toward a sun that was sinking slowly down as if to submerge itself in its depths. The girl had long red hair and a pale face with large, green eyes. There was both a sorrow and a wildness about her, and beside her pranced a horse whose mercurial features were as changeable as any human's.

"West," breathed Jareth. Kevla opened her eyes. "She's in the West. She's the element of water. She's the—the Sea Dancer."

"What is 'sea'?" Kevla asked.

"I don't know, but we'll find out," Jareth stated firmly.

"You are not as prepared as you should have been," the Dragon stated, uncharacteristically solemn. "You have found us, but neither of you has your Lorekeepers. Kevla's lives inside her, but he is no longer flesh; Jareth's is mad and an ally of the Emperor. You must proceed with care, Dancers."

"I'm ready," said Jareth. "Kevla?"

She looked at the three of them—her dearest Companion, the great blue Tiger, and the Stone Dancer who now was as steady and solid as the earth that was his element. Despite the Dragon's words of caution, Kevla felt hope stir within her.

"Yes," she said, firmly. "I'm ready."

Epilogue

The exquisite creature, powerful beyond the advisor's imagining and yet so delicate and beautiful, cowered in a corner. It had managed to yank the ever-present golden chain from the Emperor's grip, spring forward and with its single horn knock the Tenacru *to the floor where it shattered into glittering crimson pieces. But the mammoth doors had been closed, and there had been nowhere for the beast to flee.*

Now the Emperor rose and stared at it. It shivered, blinking its large, soft eyes. Slowly, the Emperor advanced, and even the advisor cringed, just a little. The Emperor's wrath could be terrible.

"What have you done?" the Emperor said in a cold, flat voice. "I had them, right inside the Tenacru. *The Maiden would*

have obeyed me if I'd just had a little more time. But you...
you..."

Swift as a snake he struck, his boot landing with a sickening thud in the ki-lyn's side. It made a soft, sad sound and trembled. The advisor winced, even though he knew that nothing the Emperor could do would truly injure the creature. The Emperor lunged for the chain, gripping it with long, strong fingers.

The simple movement exhausted him and he staggered. Quickly, the advisor was there, a supportive hand under his lord's arm. Recent events had taken their toll on the Emperor, who had neither slept nor eaten for far too long.

"I built the Maiden too well," the Emperor murmured as the advisor helped him into his luxuriously upholstered chair. The ki-lyn followed, pulled inexorably by the chain the Emperor had retrieved. "I couldn't watch her every minute, not with all the things I have to manage elsewhere. So I built her to be autonomous. She wouldn't even know about me. And that was my undoing."

He glared at the ki-lyn. "That, and this imprisoned wretch of a creature," he added. "You keep trying to stop me. Eventually I will cease showing you mercy."

The Mage had moved slowly to where the shattered fragments of the Tenacru lay on the floor. He knelt and began to pick up the pieces with his gloved hands. "Do not despair, Your Excellency. The Tenacru has been broken and remade ere now. It will take a little time, but I can do it."

The Emperor closed his eyes in relief. To the ki-lyn, he said, "That's awfully lucky for you, my little friend."

"My lord," said the advisor, feeling his way carefully, "There are easier ways to destroy the Dancers."

The Emperor, eyes still closed, rubbed his temples with be-ringed hands. "Of course there are, if I wanted them dead. But if one of them dies too soon, everything is lost, you idiot."

The advisor gaped. Then what did—

There came a knock on the door, and the Emperor seemed to perk up slightly. The advisor frowned. He and the unsettling Mage were the only ones admitted into this part of the Emperor's castle. Who dared approach?

Strangely, the Emperor did not seem offended or concerned. "Ah, good. There's someone you need to meet. You'll be working with her in the future. I'll need as much advice from all quarters as I can get to stop the Dancers."

The advisor tried not to show his shock. The Emperor had appointed another advisor? But...he was the chief advisor, choosing his own council. Who was the Emperor going to foist upon him, and why?

"Enter," the Emperor called. The massive, dark doors slowly opened to reveal the slender form of a woman. She was in her middle years but still quite the beauty. Her proper, demure robes could not hide her exotic appearance, though, with her dark skin and black hair. She bowed to the Emperor, to the Mage, still picking up red pieces of the shattered orb, and nodded at the advisor, who stared at her with thinly veiled hostility.

"This is your new colleague, my old friend. She knows a great deal about the Flame Dancer and is eager to work with us."

The woman now bowed to the advisor, but he could tell the gesture was an empty one.

"Greetings," she said in a cool voice. "My name is Yeshi."

* * * * *

Under Sea's Shadow
the next Dancer
will be found
Coming from LUNA Books
in 2006!

GLOSSARY

Arrun Woods: Mylikki's village
Arukan: the name of Kevla's country
Arukani: native to Arukan

Bai: Generic term for Bai-khas and Bai-shas
Bai-sha: "female without father," derogatory term for illegitimate girl or woman
Bayinba: Lamali term for "raids"
Blessing cloth: magic fabric woven by the *tasskali*

Clan of the Four Waters: Kevla's clan

Gahalgeese: bird of Lamal

halaan: slang for "prostitute"
hamantu: the spirit of stonesteaming, embodied by the steam rising up after water is tossed onto the hot rocks
huskaa: bard or minstrel
huskaa-lal: apprentice *huskaa*

Kevat-aanta: "Spring-Bringer," term for Jareth
kha: unit of money, gold
khashim: Lord of the clan; plural *khashims*
khashima: Lady of the clan
khashimu: the young heir, prince
kirvi: Lamali deer
kyndela: Lamali stringed instrument
kurjah: Arukani term for the male organ
kuli: demon

Lamal: Jareth's homeland, the farthest land north
liah: gazelle-like creature

Riversong: village in Lamal
rhia: a flowing garment worn in Arukan by both sexes

sa'abah: desert animals, with long, fluffy tails, long legs with
    broad feet, small "hands," long ears
Skalka Valley: Jareth's village
selva: large mythic Lamali creature similar to a deer or
caribou; tended by the *taaskali*
-sha-: "daughter of"
Shamizan: board game with colored glass "stones"
simmar: big cat of the desert
skeltha: literally "long sticks" used by the Lamali as skis
snow walkers: snowshoes
stonesteaming hut: Lamali equivalent of a sauna or sweatlodge
sulim: Arukani term for female genitalia
Summer Realm: Lamali term for the afterlife

Tahmu-kha-Rakyn: Kevla's father, *khashim* of the Clan of
    Four Waters
taaskal: a wizard or enchanter, person of powerful magic,
plural *taaskali*
Two Lakes: village where Taya is from

uhlal: term of respect, "gentleman" or "sir"
uhlala: female term, "Lady" or "Ma'am"
usk: gathered bunch of birth branches used in the
stonesteaming hut

Luna's Night Sky
© Amoreno 2005

www.DuirwaighGallery.com

Can the Queen who has once done the impossible ever be free?

After awakening the "Waiting King" in
THE WIZARD'S WARD, Maura Woodbury thought
her duty to her country completed. But, her task has
only just begun.... Once again Maura is being called
to save the kingdom. Full of self-doubt and tempted
to ignore the call of fate, Maura must decide her next
steps. But what will happen to her country
if she doesn't defend it?

On sale August.

Visit your
local bookseller.

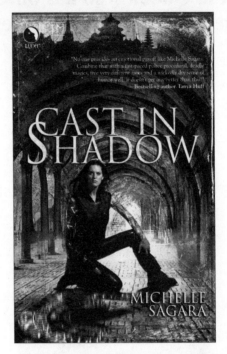